HIGHBALL RUSH

BOOTLEG SPRINGS BOOK 6

CLAIRE KINGSLEY

LUCY SCORE

Always Have LLC

Published by Always Have, LLC

Edited by Elayne Morgan of Serenity Editing Services

Cover by Cassy Roop of Pink Ink Designs

ISBN: 9781081713386

www.clairekingsleybooks.com

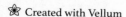 Created with Vellum

To Lucy, for being crazy enough to say yes. Thank you for this journey, this town, and these characters. And here's to all our adventures to come.
I love your guts.

ABOUT THIS BOOK

"Suddenly all those old country love songs I'd played so often made perfect sense."

Gravel-voiced Gibson Bodine takes his lone wolf image seriously. The tough guy. The bad boy. He lives alone. Works alone. His one love—besides starting a good brawl—is sitting on a rinky-dink stage in a backwoods bar playing guitar and singing about things he'll never have.

When a video of him playing goes viral, Gibson ignores the unwanted attention. He's got bigger things to worry about. Like the bomb his half-brother's mom just dropped on him. And the fallout from the memento he's been carrying around for thirteen years.

He doesn't have time for fame... or love... or meddling neighbors stopping by with casseroles and questions.

But one night in a bar, fifty miles from home, he meets her. And she changes everything.

In Bootleg Springs—home of the best moonshine and nosiest neighbors in West Virginia—secrets don't keep.

When the truth about Callie Kendall's fate brings danger home, it's up to Gibson to step up and be the hero. And maybe find what he's been missing all along.

Love.

1

GIBSON

The air in Sheriff Tucker's office was too close. Hot and stuffy. Resisting the urge to tug at my shirt collar, I sat staring at the table in front of me. Waiting.

Jayme, my family's scary-as-hell lawyer, stood behind me. Dressed in head-to-toe black with a pair of heels that looked like they could puncture a guy's nuts, she was a force in the small office. Not much intimidated me, but Jayme came close. I wouldn't have wanted to be on the business end of those heels.

At least she was on my side. Sort of. I could see her out of the corner of my eye, and by the glare she was giving me, she was none too pleased with this turn of events.

Less than twenty-four hours ago, we'd all been celebrating Bowie and Cassidy's wedding. People dancing, eating, drinking, having a good time. Then Misty Lynn had lost her shit in front of everyone. I'd publicly rejected her—not for the first time—and she'd gone and stolen my damn wallet.

Then turned it in when she found what was inside.

"One more time. You got something you need to tell me before Sheriff Tucker comes back?" Jayme asked, her voice quiet but sharp.

"No."

"Gibson—"

The door opened and the sheriff came in. His snow-white mustache twitched on his upper lip. I didn't look up. Didn't trust myself to meet his eyes. I was too fucking angry. And I knew this wasn't his fault. The problem was, I never should have kept the pictures. That was on me.

Sheriff Tucker—I couldn't think of him as Harlan right now, not under these circumstances—took his seat across from me. I flicked my eyes up for half a second. He looked uncomfortable. Maybe even apologetic.

"Gibson, I take it you know why I asked you to come in here?"

"Yeah."

He took out my wallet and pushed it toward me. "Do you recognize this?"

"It's my wallet. Misty Lynn stole it and I assume she's the one who gave it to you."

He nodded. "She found something inside that had her rightfully concerned."

It was my turn to nod.

He pulled out the strip of photos. Four of them. We'd jumped in a photo booth and made silly faces. In the last one, we were laughing. They were thirteen years old, now, and faded with age. Bent from being kept in my wallet all that time.

"Can you tell me who's in these photos?"

My eyes skimmed over them. Although I'd carried them

around with me for years, I hadn't looked at them in a long time. Hurt too much.

"They're me with Callie Kendall."

"When were these taken?"

"The day before she disappeared."

Sheriff Tucker took a deep breath, his eyes on the photos. I could practically feel Jayme holding herself back from telling me—for the millionth time—that I didn't have to answer his questions. She made a throaty noise that sounded an awful lot like a growl.

"And what was the nature of your relationship with Callie Kendall?"

There it was. The real question. Or one of them, anyway.

"We were friends."

"Just friends?" he asked. "You look awfully cozy in these pictures."

I shook my head. Of course he'd think the worst. Everyone would. "I was twenty to her sixteen. We were definitely just friends."

"But Gibson—"

I slammed my hand on the table. "I never touched her. Not once. This town might think I'm a piece of shit, but I would never have crossed that line with her. We were friends. That was all."

Sheriff Tucker crossed his arms. "Gibs, I've known you your whole life. I know you ain't a piece of shit. But you seem to have been carrying around photos of you and Callie all these years and damn it all if no one in Bootleg knew the two of you were ever together. So I need to know how it is you were friends with her without the whole town knowing. And why you never said a word about it, even after she disappeared."

I took a deep breath. "She liked music."

"What's that?" he asked.

"Callie liked music. So did I. Sometimes we'd go off and meet in the woods. I'd bring my guitar and she'd sing along while I played. We liked all the same bands, the same songs. She had a little notebook where she'd write song lyrics and I'd help her put melodies to them."

"That was all?"

"Yeah, that was all." *And she didn't look at me like everyone else did. The son of the town drunk. A piece of crap going nowhere.*

"So you're saying your relationship with her was entirely innocent."

"Yes."

"Then why hide it?" he asked. "Why didn't anyone know?"

I met his eyes. "I'm Gibson Bodine, Sheriff. How do you think her daddy would have felt about his sixteen-year-old daughter spending time with the worst of 'those Bodine boys'? Do you think he'd have believed us if we said we weren't doing anything wrong? Do you think anyone would have believed that?"

He cleared his throat. "Tell me about the photos."

"There was a band we both liked playing out in Perrinville. It was a big outdoor thing, festival style. We met in secret and I took her out there to see them play. Afterward, we saw a photo booth, so we jumped in and took these."

"And that was the day before she disappeared?" he asked.

"Yeah."

"Gibson, you need to level with me here," he said. "Did you have anything to do with her disappearance?"

I met his eyes again. "No."

"Where were you when she disappeared?"

"I was at home. I didn't even see her that day, I had to work. She was with all the high school kids down at the lake. Plus, she was worried about getting caught after leaving with me the day before, so I kept my distance."

"I'm still tryin' to wrap my head around no one knowing," Sheriff said, more to himself than me.

I shrugged. "The town doesn't know everything. Hell, an entire person disappeared and no one knew what happened. Or at least, no one who knew anything spoke up."

My damn father. I didn't know what to think about Jenny Leland's story—that my dad had helped Callie get out of town. The asshole had taken that secret to his grave. He'd let me believe all those years that she was dead. Of course, I'd kept a secret about her, too.

Jenny swore she was alive. She had postcards with her handwriting. I remembered it from her song journals. She'd even said she'd met Callie in person—a year ago, in Seattle. She swore up and down that Callie was alive.

I believed her. Maybe it was just because I wanted to believe her so badly. But I did.

"Do you have any idea what might have happened to her?" he asked. "Why she was hurt? Why she was trying to get away from home?"

Clenching my teeth, my nostrils flaring, I fought back the surge of anger. Someone—signs seemed to be pointing to her father—had hurt her. Badly. Enough that she'd begged my dad for help on the side of the road, and he'd apparently helped sneak her out of town. There was no kind of Bootleg Justice good enough for a man who'd hurt his own daughter. Made me furious.

I cleared my throat. "No. She never said anything about her parents or what things were like at home. I wish she would have."

I would have dealt with that asshole.

"Why didn't you tell anyone, Gibs? You had to have known this could come out someday. It's suspicious."

"Because I knew people would assume the worst. That I was preying on a teenage girl. That we had an inappropriate relationship." My voice rose with every word. "What did Gibson Bodine do now? Did he get her pregnant? Is he keeping her in a cabin in the woods somewhere? Did he kill her and dump her body in the lake?"

"Gibson, enough," Jayme said.

"I didn't do anything wrong, unless playing music with a girl is a crime."

"Have you had any contact with her since she disappeared?" he asked.

"No. Not a word." *I thought she was dead. All this time, I didn't think there was any hope.*

The sheriff sat back in his seat and pitched his fingers together. "All right, Gibs. You're free to go."

Without a word, I scooped up my wallet—and the strip of photos. Jayme's heels were already clicking their way out the door.

I paused in the doorway and glanced over my shoulder. "Sheriff?"

"Yeah?"

"Is this investigation aiming to find her? Or to bring down whoever hurt her?"

His gaze went steely and his voice was hard. "Both."

I nodded once. "Good."

"Let me remind you that this is a matter for law enforcement," he said, shuffling some papers on his desk. "You need to let us handle it."

"I know."

I did know. But I wasn't making any promises.

2

GIBSON

It took all of an hour before someone—Scarlett, probably—started banging on my door. I'd turned off my phone as soon as I'd left the sheriff's office. Come straight home and contemplated barricading my driveway to keep people away.

This was the part I'd been dreading since I'd realized Misty Lynn had taken my wallet. Everyone coming at me with their nosy-ass questions. I took a deep breath and got up from the couch. If I didn't let her in, she'd probably break a window. I figured it was better to avoid the broken glass.

"Gibs? I know you're in there." Scarlett's voice carried through the door and she banged a few more times. "Don't even think about trying to ignore me. Get your ass out here and—"

I pulled the door open and she stopped mid-sentence. Devlin was right behind her. Stepping aside, I motioned for them to come in.

My house—a sturdy log cabin—sat on three acres of

sweet isolation. It wasn't fancy, but I'd built it myself. It had two bedrooms—although one was just storage—a single bathroom, a living room with a wood stove, and a kitchen with cabinets I'd made custom.

I'd made some of the furniture, too. The table and chairs were mine, as was the cabinet under the flat screen TV on the wall. I wasn't much for decor, but I did have a Jameson Bodine original above the fireplace—a metal sculpture of a mountain and trees. Scarlett had added a framed photo of the five of us Bodines, taken at Clay Larkin's wedding, to the mantle. I'd gone ahead and left it there.

Scarlett stood next to the couch, arms crossed, all five-foot-nothing of her ready to fuck me up. Her red plaid sleeveless shirt was knotted at the waist and she wore a pair of old cut-offs. Devlin lowered himself into a chair and crossed an ankle over his knee. His wrinkle-free shirt and slacks were casual for him. He shrugged at me as if to say, *you're on your own.*

"Well?" she asked, tapping her foot. "Sheriff Tucker takes you in for questioning and then you turn off your damn phone? Cassidy won't tell me shit, so you better spill it. What the hell happened?"

There wasn't anything for it but to tell her. "I had a photo of me and Callie Kendall in my wallet."

Her eyebrows knit together. "What in the hell are you even talking about?"

I hated talking about this. It fucking hurt. And things that hurt pissed me off. "Look, we were friends. And before you lecture me about how she was a teenager and I was twenty, I know. It wasn't like that."

She stared at me, wide-eyed. "You were friends with Callie?"

"That's what I just said, ain't it? We both liked music, so we hung out sometimes. Kept it secret for obvious reasons."

"I have at least eight hundred questions right now. But let's start with the picture in your wallet."

"I was stupid enough to sneak her out of town to go to a concert. We got our picture taken in a photo booth." I rubbed the back of my neck. "She disappeared the next day."

"Well, that's incredibly inconvenient," Devlin muttered.

Scarlett was uncharacteristically quiet. She stared at me, her mouth half-open. "I don't know if anyone has ever rendered me speechless before, but you just did. How did we not know you two were friends?"

"I said we hid it."

"I know, but nobody hides stuff in this town. Not for thirteen years."

My back stiffened. "Dad did."

She started to reply, but stopped. Normally she defended Dad. But what could she say?

"He knew, Scar. Not only did he know, he helped her run away. And he never fucking told anyone."

"He had to have been protecting her," she said.

I threw my hands up in the air. "Here it comes."

"Why else would he keep silent? If her daddy was abusing her, and it sure sounds like he was, she was probably afraid. I bet she begged him to keep quiet. Made him promise or something."

"You really think he kept his mouth shut for her? He did it to protect himself, Scar. He helped a sixteen-year-old girl run away from home. And her dad's a judge. Can you imagine the trouble he would have been in? Don't kid yourself. He wasn't protecting *her*."

"Why can't you admit that maybe Dad actually did a

good thing? Jenny said Dad found Callie hurt on the side of the road. He didn't have to help her. He could have taken her home, or just called the police and let the sheriff deal with it. But he didn't."

I balled my hands into fists, my temper on the verge of snapping. Devlin watched us argue, eying me like he was ready to step in if he thought I was going to cross a line with Scarlett.

"Stop trying to make him into the hero," I said.

"Oh come on, Gibs, what would you have done?"

"I don't know," I barked.

I would have kept her secret if it meant keeping her safe. But I was too mad to admit that to my sister.

She let out a breath. "This is all so crazy. Callie's alive, and Dad knew, and now you were her secret friend? What else are we going to find out? That she's been living out in some shack in the woods all these years and you send Henrietta Van Sickle out to her place with supplies once in a while?"

I shook my head, some of my anger dissipating. "I don't know where she is. I always thought she was dead."

"Oh, Gibs."

Before I could stop her, she'd wrapped her arms around me in a hug. I didn't like hugs, but once in a while, I had to tolerate one from my sister.

"You know what's gonna happen now, though, don't you?" she asked, stepping away. "The whole town's gonna know about you and Callie in a hot minute."

"No shit," I grumbled.

"I assume Jayme's already told you what you can and can't say," Devlin said.

"Yeah." I plopped down on the couch and leaned my head back. "Basically, no comment."

The muffled sound of a car pulling up outside carried through the walls. I groaned. Great, who else was here?

A few seconds later, someone knocked.

"Gibs?

Jameson.

Scarlett answered. Jameson barreled in, followed closely by his fiancée, Leah Mae. Jameson looked a lot like me, with dark hair and rough stubble. He wore a faded t-shirt with a couple of burn holes on the front. Leah Mae was tall, with blond hair and a few freckles. She had on cowboy boots with her sundress.

"Gibson was secretly friends with Callie Kendall, and he had a photo of the two of them together in his wallet," Scarlett said before either of them had a chance to say a word— or ask a question. "But he didn't have anything to do with her disappearance and didn't know she was alive. He also doesn't know where she is now."

Jameson blinked a few times, like he was absorbing that information. "Well holy shit."

"Can we talk about something else?" I asked. "Or nothing, and y'all get your asses out of my house?"

"Who else knows?" Jameson asked, ignoring me.

"Only us at the moment," Scarlett said. "But that won't last."

"I'll just stay here till it blows over," I said. "I told the sheriff everything I know. People are gonna say what they say. I don't give a shit what this town thinks."

"Speaking of talking about something else," Leah Mae said. She had her phone in her hand. "There's something you might want to know."

"What?" I grumbled. I was pretty sure I didn't.

"This is amazing." She paused, excitement in her eyes. "I've never seen anything like it."

"What are you goin' on about?" Scarlett asked.

"I saw it the other day, but with the wedding and everything, I didn't want to make a fuss. And I can't even believe it, the views must have doubled in just the last twenty-four hours."

"Views of what?" Scarlett asked. "Did someone record Gibson giving Misty Lynn the verbal smack down?"

Leah Mae shook her head. "No, this is so much better. Someone filmed Gibson singing at the Lookout last week and put it on YouTube. It has over two million views."

"What in the hell are you talking about?" I stood and swiped the phone from her hand, only to have Scarlett immediately snatch it from mine. "Hey."

"Let me see." Scarlett tapped the screen and turned up the volume.

It was me. I looked over her shoulder and rubbed the back of my neck. The video was dark, but you could see me well enough. I sat on a stool, strumming my guitar, playing one of my songs. One I'd written myself.

"Oh my god," Scarlett squealed. "This is incredible."

"It really has two million views?" Jameson asked, pushing me aside to look over Scarlett's shoulder.

"I don't see why this is a big deal." I went back to the couch and sat down.

"Gibs, this thing went viral," Leah Mae said. "Look at all the comments asking who you are. People love it. They love you."

I just grunted.

"You never know what could happen with something like this," Leah Mae said. "You don't have a manager, do you? You should really consider representation. If you need an entertainment lawyer, let me know."

"Why the hell would I need an entertainment lawyer?

Between Devlin and Jayme, I'm up to my nuts in lawyers already."

Devlin rolled his eyes at me.

Leah Mae tilted her head, like she was explaining something obvious to a child. "All I'm saying is this could lead to something. There are lots of people whose careers began with a YouTube video."

"I have a career."

"Stop bein' so grumpy, Gibs," Scarlett said, handing the phone back to Leah Mae. "You know, some people would do anything for a big break like this."

I grunted again.

"He's hopeless," Scarlett said.

I liked to play, but I'd never pursued music as a career. Never would. It was what my dad had wanted for himself. What he'd blamed me for never having. An unplanned teenage pregnancy had robbed him and my mom of their dreams. That baby had been me, and my dad had never let me forget it.

Besides, some video on the internet didn't mean shit.

I had to tolerate four extra people in my space for another twenty minutes, which irritated the shit out of me —especially after everything that had happened in the last twenty-four hours. I'd already had to attend my brother's wedding. Although I was actually happy about that, and it hadn't been a bad time.

Until fucking Misty Lynn had broken a window out of my truck and stolen my wallet. And some psycho had kidnapped Jonah's girlfriend Shelby right in front of Sheriff Tucker's house. We'd found her, and she was all right, but then I had to deal with that business with the sheriff.

I was done with people in general. Just wanted my house to myself.

After snapping at everyone a few times too many for their liking—and Scarlett calling me grumpy again—they left. With my uninvited guests cleared out, I went to my back porch. Took a seat in my homemade deck chair—I only had one, to discourage company—and breathed in the silence. Birds chirped in the distance, and the August heat felt good.

Movement caught my eye near the edge of the woods. Might have been an animal, but I didn't see anything. I narrowed my eyes, watching with mild curiosity.

Henrietta Van Sickle poked her head out from around a tree. I lifted my hand in a wave. She crossed my land sometimes when she was heading into town for supplies. Once in a while I gave her a ride. Even less frequently, she wandered down here and joined me on the back porch for a spell. I liked Henrietta, in large part because she didn't speak.

"Afternoon," I said as she approached.

Her appearance put people off, and I wondered if she knew that, and did it on purpose. Her clothes were ragged, but she was always clean. Straggly hair hung from beneath her old Cock Spurs cap, and her shoes were looking worn. I made a mental note to pick her up some new ones and leave them where she'd find them.

She came onto the porch and sat cross-legged next to me. I didn't get up and offer her my seat. Knew she wouldn't take it. She never did.

We sat in silence for a good long while. Although I'd wanted to be alone, Henrietta sitting here on my porch didn't grate on my nerves. We both just stared into the distance, enjoying the quiet.

"Surprised to see you," I said finally. "After all the excitement, I figured you'd stick close to home for a while."

Henrietta had probably saved Shelby's life. The kidnapper had stuck her in the trunk of his car and drove her out to an old shack in the woods. Luckily, Henrietta had either seen or heard something, and followed them.

She'd called me—an actual phone call—and rasped out a few words. It was the only time I'd ever heard her speak. It had been enough for me to understand her meaning, and where to look for Shelby.

After we'd found Shelby and turned her over to the paramedics, I'd gone out and looked for Henrietta. She'd been watching not far from the road, keeping low behind some trees so she wouldn't be seen. I'd made sure she was all right and offered to help her get home. She hadn't taken me up on it, but that wasn't unusual.

"Hungry?" I always offered her something to eat, but not because I thought she needed it. Her brand of subsistence living seemed to suit her, and she was good at it.

She shook her head, but kept looking at me, her brown eyes clear.

"Need help with something?"

She nodded and dug in her pants pocket, then pulled out her cell phone and handed it to me.

I'd gotten her a phone several years ago, mostly for emergencies. For a hermit who lived alone in the woods, she understood technology well. She used a computer at the library, and I hadn't needed to show her how to use the phone. She didn't text me very often—usually just wandered onto my land—but occasionally she'd text asking for a ride.

The screen had a big crack right down the center.

"That ain't good. I'll get you another one."

She gave me a closed-mouth smile, deepening the wrinkles around her eyes. Holding up a finger, she dug in her pocket again. Pulled out some wadded-up cash.

"Nah," I said, waving her off. "It's on me. Consider it your saving-Shelby's-life present."

Smiling again, she pocketed the money. I didn't know where she'd gotten it, but she obviously had a supply of cash. I figured she'd brought it with her when she'd moved out to her little cabin some twenty-odd years ago.

I handed her phone back. "Keep this for now and I'll have a new one for you soon."

She took it, but kept looking at me, her eyebrows lifted.

"Wondering about Shelby?" I asked.

Another nod.

"She's fine. Jonah's taking good care of her. Cops have the guy who did it."

That seemed to satisfy her. She put the cracked phone in her pocket, brushed her hands together, and stood, using the porch railing to help herself up.

"That was a real good thing you did," I said.

She gave me a solemn nod, then walked back toward the woods. She limped a little—had ever since I'd known her. Some old injury. Like most things about Henrietta, I'd probably never know the story behind it. And that was fine by me. She was who she was, and the rest didn't really matter.

I envied Henrietta's life a little bit. She lived outside the rules. Made her own way in the world. People told stories about her, but the town gossip didn't seem to touch her.

Gossip. I let out a long breath. There was going to be plenty of that, all with my name attached. That video was one thing. Two million views. How the hell did something like that happen?

But I had a feeling even a video of me going around the internet wasn't going to hold a candle to the story of Gibson Bodine sneaking around with Callie Kendall thirteen years ago.

I'd lied before when I said I didn't care what this town thought. I'd deny it till the day I died, but a part of me did care. I knew what they thought of me. Good for nothing son of a drunk. Goin' nowhere fast.

Some of that reputation I'd earned. I was a grumpy bastard and an asshole to most people. I started bar fights to blow off steam, always spoke my mind whether or not it was what people wanted to hear, and didn't have any patience for dumbasses.

But the rest of it was down to my father. A man who'd publicly deteriorated in a town where everyone knew everything. Saw everything. Judged everything.

I didn't know if I'd ever get out from under the shadow of Jonah Bodine Sr.

3

___

MAYA

*M*y body had no idea what time it was. The clock told me nine thirteen a.m., but I was still in a haze of jet lag. I took a sip of my triple-shot latte while the elevator rose. I was used to jumping around time zones, but I'd touched down in L.A. less than twenty-four hours ago. If Oliver, my boss, wanted a fully awake and alert Maya, he should have given me another day to acclimate.

I stepped off the elevator and flashed my ID badge at the receptionist. She gave me a polite nod. I'd never met her; it had been over a year since I'd been to Attalon Records head-quarters. It looked the same as I remembered: sleek, modern furnishings. Framed awards and album covers on the walls.

Yui stepped out of her office, dressed in a black blouse, white skirt, and a pair of killer red stilettos. Her jet-black hair framed her face in a sleek bob and her lipstick matched her shoes. I glanced down at my clothes—plain white t-shirt, old jeans, and sandals—and decided I was too jet-lagged to care.

"Look who's awake," Yui said. "I didn't think I'd see your face until tomorrow."

I shrugged, cradling my coffee against my chest like it was a lifeline. "Oliver said he wanted to see me. So, here I am."

"He probably doesn't realize you basically just landed. You know how he is." She tilted her head, looking past me. "His door's still shut. I think he's on a call. You might as well come sit."

"Thanks."

I went into her office and plunked my tired self down in a cream faux-leather armchair. Yui Ito had been with Attalon Records for almost as long as I had. She'd started out as an intern and was now one of the independent record label's top publicists.

She was also the closest thing I had to a long-time friend. We saw each other about once a year, maybe less. Sometimes I crashed at her place when I was in L.A. Yui was gorgeous, no-nonsense, good at her job, had a secret love of root beer ice cream, and never dated anyone for longer than six months.

And that was the extent of my knowledge of her. It was hard to stay in touch when I traveled so much, and while most people used social media to keep up with their friends and colleagues, I had zero social media presence. I didn't even have my picture on Attalon's website. Just my name and a vague description of my job.

"Your hair is cute," she said, lowering herself into her industrial office chair. Her desk was glass and metal, her entire office impossibly cool. "I didn't notice it last night."

"Thanks. Mermaid hair." I ran a hand down my thick,

wavy hair. I'd let it grow the whole time I'd been on the road, so it was long. And multicolored.

I was a serial hair-colorer. Over the years, I'd dyed it almost every color imaginable. Platinum blond, red, brown, purple, blue, silver. I'd even had a regrettable black hair phase. Right now, my base color was my natural blond, but I had a partial rainbow of turquoise, blue, lavender, and purple mixed in.

"It works on you," she said. "How long do you think you'll be in town?"

"I'm not sure, but judging by Oliver's early summons, probably not long. I'll be out of your way in a few days at most, I'm sure."

She shrugged. "It's fine. You're easy company. I barely know you're there."

"Thanks. After all the hotels I've been in, it's nice to sleep someplace where I'm not worried about what that stain on the wall might be."

She winced. "Gross. How was the tour?"

I'd spent the better part of the last year on an international tour with Outbound Platinum. I loved those guys, but coaxing a rock band through their first completely sober tour had been exhausting. I'd been with them since they'd almost imploded while recording their last album. Oliver had sent me in to keep them from going nuclear.

My job title was producer, but around here I was known as the rock-star whisperer. I'd calmed the members of Outbound, soothed their frayed nerves and helped them redirect all that angsty energy into their music. The results had been fantastic. Their album was still topping the charts well over a year after they'd released the first single.

I didn't always tour with artists. Usually I just went into the studio—helped with songwriting or got them back on track with the recording process. But Outbound had still been too fragile, and Attalon had a lot riding on their tour. So I'd gone along, like a glorified rock-star babysitter.

"Long. Busy. Exhausting. But also awesome. Pretty much everything you'd expect when you're trying to keep five newly sober rock stars from killing each other."

"I don't know how you do it." She tipped her fingers together. "You must have the patience of a saint."

"Not really. I don't even have kids, but I definitely had to break out my mom voice regularly. But they're such good guys. They're trying really hard to keep it together. I probably could have come back a month ago, but by that point, I figured I might as well finish the tour. Plus, the last stop was Australia and I've only been there once before. I really wanted to go back."

"Please tell me you banged some hot Australian guys while you were down there," she said. "The accents alone. My god."

I laughed. My attempts at relationships never lasted. I didn't stay anywhere long enough to make it work with anyone. A quick fling was nice sometimes, but those were starting to feel pretty hollow. "Not this time. But I totally agree about the accents. Hot."

My phone rang and I set my coffee on Yui's desk so I could dig it out of my oversized purple handbag. Half my life was in this bag. I shuffled through makeup, a hairbrush, my planner, a few cords, several power adapters, headphones, two bras, a tank top I thought I'd lost, and an unopened toothbrush before I came up with my phone.

Yui stood. "I'll let you take that. I need to go talk to Tracey over in marketing."

I nodded and tapped the button to answer. "Hello?"

"Maya, it's Cole. Thank god you answered. I'm seriously screwed right now."

I leaned back in the chair. I'd worked with Cole Bryson a few years ago when he'd been suffering from a serious case of sophomore slump anxiety. His first album had been a huge hit, but he'd caved under the pressure to follow it up. When Oliver had sent me out to work with him, he'd been swimming in liquor and self-doubt. I'd helped him pull himself together, write the rest of his songs, and finish the album. And it had sold better than his first.

"Hi Cole, good to hear from you. I'm doing just fine, glad you asked."

He groaned. "I'm sorry, I'm just panicking."

"Panicking over what?"

"We're in the studio and I swear to god, nothing sounds right. I don't know if I can do this again."

"Of course you can do it again. You've done it twice. Your fans love your music."

"I know, but—"

"Cole, listen. We've been down this road. There is no *but*. Albums can flop, we both know that. It's the risk you take when you put yourself out there. But you can't worry about that when you're in the studio. All you need to do right now is put your heart into your music."

"Yeah..."

"What did we talk about before I left?"

"Turn off distractions. Get enough sleep."

"Have you been doing that?"

"Yes," he said. "I leave my phone off the whole time I'm in the studio. I've been sleeping normal hours, not going out partying. And no girls. I swear."

I rolled my eyes. Like most young men who found fame, Cole had succumbed to the allure of the countless women who were more than happy to jump into bed with him. To say they'd been a distraction was an understatement. "Okay, so what's the problem?"

"I don't know."

"You're just playing head games with yourself," I said. "Are you still recording in Seattle?"

"Yeah."

"Here's what you're going to do. Take a day off. Drive... anywhere, really. Just get out of the city. I've been there and it's gorgeous. Go to Mount Rainier or take a ferry to Whidbey Island. Find a place where you're surrounded by the natural world. A beautiful setting where you can just *be*. Let that recharge your batteries."

"Okay," he said, and I could practically hear him nodding. "Yeah, that does sound good."

"Awesome. Then get back in the studio and get the fuck back to work."

He laughed. "Yeah, I know, I know. Thanks, Maya."

"Anytime."

I hung up and dropped my phone back in my bag.

"Maya?" Oliver poked his head in Yui's office. "Good to see you."

"Hey." I stood, shouldering my big handbag, and shook his hand. "Ready for me?"

"Yeah, thanks for waiting."

"No problem."

I grabbed my coffee and followed him into his office. Unlike Yui's, which was stylishly modern, Oliver's office looked like it belonged to a hard-core music fan. He had vintage band posters in frames and several shelves displayed his collection of music memorabilia.

He sat behind his mahogany desk, dressed in a Nirvana t-shirt. His dirty blond hair was short, his face smooth. His gunmetal wedding ring stood out against his tanned skin.

I took a seat on the other side of his desk and sucked down more of my coffee.

"You kinda look like shit," he said.

I shot him a glare. "I've been in the country for less than twenty-four hours. I think. I'm actually not sure what time it is. Or what day. Who are you, again?"

He grinned. "God, I know. I'm sorry."

"It's fine. Just tell me why I'm here and not sleeping off jet lag in Yui's stupidly comfortable guest bed."

"Before I tell you, let me just say, I fully intended to give you some time off. I'm not such a dick that I don't realize you've been on tour and you just got back. So I wouldn't have asked you to come in if it wasn't important."

"It's not that big a deal," I said. "I'm used to it. Besides, you know me, I don't do time off."

"Maybe you should."

I took another sip. "Oliver, you're a great boss, but if I need someone to bug me about working too much, I'll call my parents."

"How long has it been since you've been home to see them, by the way?"

"Oh my god. You just told me you *were* going to give me time off, which means now you're not. But you're going to give me crap about how much I work and toss in a guilt trip about my parents?"

"I'm sorry, I'm probably projecting. Nat's been on my case about the holidays and how long it's been since we've seen my family. It's fucking August, and she's trying to make Thanksgiving plans."

Nat was Oliver's adorable wife. While he was managing a recording empire, she was wrangling their two little boys.

"It's fine, and tell her I said hi. But can we get to the part where you tell me where I'm going and whose ass I need to kick? Is it Saraya again? Is she having another existential crisis? Not that I mind. I love Nashville."

"No, she's fine, as far as I'm aware. I actually need you to go check out some new talent for me."

That was odd. I wasn't a talent scout. I worked with Attalon's existing artists; I didn't look at potentials. "Why?"

"Why do I want you to check him out, or why am I sending you?"

"Both."

"Because he has something," he said. "You know what I'm talking about. That X-factor we're always looking for. This guy has it oozing from his pores. I want to get to him before someone else does."

"And why me?"

"Because we can't get him to talk to us."

I laughed. "If he won't talk to you, why bother? Did you run out of wannabe rock stars who'd sell their souls for a record contract?"

"I'm telling you, he's different. I have a feeling about him."

Oliver did have amazing instincts. If he thought this guy was special, he was probably right.

"Okay, so he's good, but he won't talk to you. I still don't know why you want me to go see him."

"He's a bit... hostile," he said, leaning back in his chair. "You have the magic touch with guys like this."

"You want to send me to meet with a hostile singer who doesn't want a record deal?" I asked, my tone wry. "How could I ever say no to that?"

"I've sent you into worse situations than this. Hell, when

you went into the studio with Outbound I wondered if you'd get out alive."

I waved a hand. "They're a bunch of teddy bears."

"You're literally the only person in the world who'd say that. You handle broody rock stars like a champion bull-rider. You're a miracle worker, and I need a miracle with this guy."

He was kind of talking me into it. Not that I knew what I was doing when it came to signing new talent. But if he just needed me to get the guy to meet with us, I could handle that.

"Where is he?"

"Some small town in..." He paused, his eyes going to his monitor. He clicked the mouse a few times. "West Virginia."

My back stiffened and I kept my eyes down, smoothing my expression to keep the storm of emotions off my face. I picked up my coffee and took a sip, as if nothing was wrong. As if I didn't have a sudden surge of anxiety that made my stomach churn.

Oliver didn't seem to notice. Because of course he didn't. I was a very good actress when it came to the *everything is fine* charade.

"You know, I don't think I'm the right person to send out there," I said, still playing the part—and playing it well. I was fine. "I don't know anything about contracts or making deals. If you need someone to get an artist past a block or prevent a band from breaking up, I'm your girl. But this? Not my area. Plus, I just got back. You admitted I need some time off. Go with that instinct."

I was lying through my teeth. I didn't want time off. I never did. Oliver wasn't the reason I went straight from one project to another, never slowing down. I visited my family in upstate New York once in a while, but other than that, I was always on the road. Always ready for the next project.

Unless it was in West Virginia.

"Fine. I give. I'll send someone else. Or maybe I'll go myself. But do one thing for me."

"Sure."

He clicked his mouse a few times. "Listen to him. Someone took the video in a bar with their phone, so the sound quality could be better. But tell me what you think. Maybe I'm wrong about him. I'd like your opinion."

The screen faced away so I couldn't see—which I appreciated. Oliver was always interested in talent first and foremost, rather than looks or image. We both knew that image mattered, but a pretty face had always been a distant second when it came to recruiting new artists.

A hum of noise, like a crowd in a bar, almost drowned out the sound of an acoustic guitar strumming the first chords of a song. Someone whistled and another person hooted. The melody grew as the crowd quieted. Whoever he was, he was good.

The song was soft—almost mournful. Before the guy even started singing, it was tugging at my heartstrings. Then he sang the first line and my breath caught in my throat. That voice. It was deep and husky, with a sexy gravelly quality. I knew immediately why Oliver wanted to sign him so badly—he did indeed have that special something—but that wasn't why I suddenly felt like I couldn't breathe.

Nor was it why I found my lips parting, and words leaving my mouth. "Okay, I'll go. I'll talk to him."

4

GIBSON

*T*he Crafty Cow Tavern in Hayridge—about fifty miles outside Bootleg Springs—was crowded. Couples swayed to our songs in front of the tiny platform they called a stage. Tables were full, barstools all occupied. Not bad for a Thursday night. Tips ought to be good.

I sat on a tall stool, one foot on a rung, my guitar in my hands. It wasn't the tips that brought me to places like this. Sure, pocket money was nice. But mostly, I just liked to play. A guitar and a song. It was what I loved.

The size of the crowd didn't matter much. Two people or two hundred didn't make a difference to me. Although even I could admit there was something satisfying about an audience. But it wasn't about my ego. Music was a transaction. To really be what it was meant to be, music needed a musician to create it, and an audience to listen.

It was the kind of give and take I could appreciate. And this audience was lovin' on us tonight.

Corbin was to my left, on keyboard, and Hung behind,

our drummer. We were simple, and country, and didn't look like we made a lick of sense as a band. Hung was old enough for his hair to have gone gray, Corbin was barely old enough to be in the bar, and at thirty-three, I was somewhere in the middle. But we played damn good music.

And that was what the crowd was here for tonight. We played. They listened. Simple. I liked simple.

My fingers strummed the melody and I sang the last few lines. Applause rose in a crescendo as my voice trailed off. I gave a nod and put my guitar back on its stand.

"We'll be back after a short break."

The crowd clapped and cheered again. Seemed as if a bunch of people were holding up cell phones. Had they been recording me? Jesus. That stupid viral video bullshit needed to die a quick death. It had been over a week since I'd heard about it, and Leah Mae said it had started before that. Some jackass claiming to be from a record company kept calling me, and now this? Weren't people over it by now?

I went to the end of the bar and leaned my forearms on the smooth wood. The bartender handed me a water and I took a long drink. Felt good on my throat after singing for the better part of an hour.

A guy backed into me, spilling water down my shirt.

"Damn it. Watch where you're going, asshole."

He whipped around, crowding my space. "What'd you call me?"

The guy reeked of cheap beer and cigarette smoke. I waved my hand in front of my face. "A shower ain't a bad notion, buddy."

"The fuck you talkin' about? You want to start somethin', pretty boy?"

Pretty boy? That was a new one. I'd been called plenty of

names in my life, particularly in bars like this, but never *pretty boy*. I couldn't help but laugh.

"What'choo laughing at?" He poked me in the chest.

Instantly, I stopped laughing, my blood running hot, my mood flipping to anger like a light switch. My brothers weren't here to back me up, but I didn't care. He'd touched me. The need to hit someone—or something—made my hands twitch. I wanted to feel this fucker's nose crunch under my fist. Craved it like a drunk craved whiskey.

"Touch me again and I'll break your face," I growled.

"Is that a threat, pretty boy? You think you're famous now? You can just roll on into our town and be a dick to everybody?"

"Go ahead," I said, my voice low. "Touch me again. Please."

"Slow down there, Gibs." Hung's arm shot out in front of my chest. "Not tonight. We have a set to finish."

I held the dickhead's gaze, my eyes cold, face expressionless. *Do it, asshole. Hit me.* I loved it when the other guy took the first swing.

He looked me up and down and took a step back. "Whatever."

I didn't take my eyes off him until he'd disappeared into the crowd.

"Why you gotta do that, Gibs? We're here to play, not brawl with the locals."

I held out my wet shirt. "I didn't start shit. He spilled water on me."

Hung raised an eyebrow. "It'll dry. Let's go."

I finished my water and joined Hung and Corbin back on stage. Took my seat on the stool, slung my guitar strap over my shoulder, and adjusted the microphone.

Without any preamble, we started in on our next song.

"Take Me Home, Country Roads." It was always a crowd-pleaser. In seconds, the dance floor was packed.

I didn't bother looking for the jackass who'd almost picked a fight with the wrong guy. He wasn't important. Instead, I lost myself in the song. In the feel of my fingers strumming the strings. The harmony of our instruments. The rhythm. The way it felt to belt out the lyrics. The energy of the crowd.

The audience didn't just take. On a good night, they gave back just as much as they got. Our music made their bodies move, touched their hearts. And in turn, they filled the air with electricity. With a powerful energy. Big crowd or small, the energy was there.

It fed my soul in a way not much else did.

We rolled right into another song, keeping the energy alive. It seeped into my skin, ran through my veins. This was my high. Right here, on a little stage in a rinky-dink bar in some podunk town. I loved this shit. I didn't admit that very often, but I did.

The crowd danced, cheered, and sang along. With that song done, we paused, just long enough to murmur to each other about what to play next.

"Play the one from the video," someone called.

I glanced up. Who'd said that? I'd only played that song the one time, at the Lookout, and only because I'd lost a bet with Jameson. I'd never planned on playing it again in public. Playing covers of songs everyone loved was easy. They knew them, knew the words, enjoyed them along with us. But *my* song? One I'd written?

More people chimed in, calling for me to play the song. I looked over at Corbin, but he just shrugged. Hung nodded.

I grunted and let out a breath. Fine.

The crowd hushed as soon as my fingers hit the strings.

And there it was again—their energy. It pinged off my skin, like shocks of static electricity. I sang the first few lines and the power grew. It surrounded me, like heat from a fire on a cold night.

The lyrics poured out, my voice deep and low. I lost myself in the melody, as if nothing else in the room existed but me, my guitar, and that supernatural energy the crowd gave back to me.

Applause erupted as I strummed the last chord. I opened my eyes—hadn't quite realized I'd closed them—and stood. Gave the crowd a nod, like I always did. My heart beat a little too fast and I wanted to get out of the spotlight. Singing that song again left me with a full feeling in my chest. I needed some more water.

I started to lift the guitar strap from my shoulder when my eyes landed on a woman in the crowd.

Her hair caught my attention. It was long and blond, but in the dim light I could make out streaks of color—maybe purple and blue, it was hard to tell. She had tattoos on both arms. Dark t-shirt. Jeans. She was busy with something on her phone.

I was about to look away when she glanced up, meeting my eyes. A striking sense of familiarity swept through me, like I should know her from somewhere. She had a scar on her cheek, running down through her upper lip. That wasn't the sort of thing you'd forget. But I'd never met a woman with a scar like that, so why did it feel like I'd seen her before?

Once in a while I locked eyes with a girl in the crowd. Sometimes that ended with us in a hotel or back at my place. But this felt different. She was beautiful, no doubt about that. But that wasn't why I couldn't take my eyes off her.

She broke eye contact first, her gaze going back to her phone. I let out the breath I hadn't realized I'd been holding. That was weird.

A second later, I looked up again and she was gone.

I had an inexplicable urge to find her. But my guitar strap suddenly felt like a spiderweb, sticking to every bit of skin it touched. I tore myself free, set my guitar down, and pushed my way into the crowd.

I didn't see her in the throng of people. Not near the bar, or between me and the restrooms. Could she have made it to the ladies' room that fast? I didn't think so. Another glance told me she probably hadn't. There was a line, and she wasn't in it.

Someone bumped into me, but I ignored them. What the hell was I doing? This was ridiculous. And stupid. Why was I following some girl? I didn't chase women—literally or figuratively. But it was like I couldn't help myself.

She must have gone outside. With my heart pumping strangely fast, my veins filling with adrenaline, I pushed open the door and went out into the warm night.

The light next to the door cast a dingy glow over the quiet parking lot. The bar was right off the highway, but the road was empty this time of night. Nothing out here but the sound of frogs and crickets.

I spotted her off to the side, walking toward a car. I knew this was crazy—I knew I had to be wrong—but before I could stop myself, I said it out loud.

"Callie?"

5

MAYA

My breath hitched and I stopped in my tracks, my car keys dangling from my hand. Tension rippled down my back. I glanced over my shoulder, keeping my voice smooth and even. "Sorry, my name's Maya Davis."

"Maya?" he said.

Walk away, Maya. Just put one foot in front of the other. He didn't say more, but even without looking, I could tell he hadn't moved. I walked to my car but paused again, next to the driver's side door. "I liked your song."

"Thanks, but—"

I didn't wait to see if he was going to keep talking. Hardly aware of what I was doing, I unlocked my car, got in, and drove away without looking back.

I'm Maya. My name is Maya Davis. I gripped the steering wheel, chanting it in my head, over and over. *I'm Maya. My name is Maya Davis.*

My crappy motel wasn't far from the bar. I parked and got out, feeling dazed, like I'd just hit my head. My hands shook, making my motel key rattle against the big plastic keychain. I couldn't get it in the lock. Was this the right room? I glanced up at the number on the door. One-oh-five. This was mine; I just couldn't seem to make my hands work properly.

I never should have come here.

The door opened—finally—and I shut and locked it behind me. Touched the lock a few times to make sure it was secure. My heart raced and my limbs tingled with adrenaline. I leaned back against the door and took a deep breath. I needed to calm down.

The room was a riot of maroon and blue with carpet that made me dizzy if I looked at it too long. The light over the sink flickered, but everything smelled faintly of lemon and bleach, so at least it seemed clean.

The motel's version of a minibar was a basket of packaged snacks and some tiny bottles of Jack Daniels. I grabbed a water glass from the counter next to the sink, unscrewed the cap, and dumped in the whiskey.

It burned going down my throat, making me wince. I wasn't much of a whiskey drinker, but I took a second sip anyway.

Sip? Gulp? Semantics.

He'd called me *Callie*.

No one had called me by that name in thirteen years. I wasn't Callie Kendall anymore. I'd left her behind a long time ago.

But this was Gibson Bodine. Why had I thought he wouldn't know me?

The box in my mind—filled with old secrets—shook. It

had been the key to my survival when I was a kid. I'd put away all the bad experiences I had at home and left them there. It was what had allowed Callie to put on a smile in public. Go to school. Hang out with her friends. Act like a normal girl. And the lock I'd put on it was indestructible. It had to be. Callie's life had depended on it.

After I left Bootleg Springs, everything that had been Callie had gone into the box. Not just my home life—all of it. Who I'd been. The people I'd known. The places I'd loved. My old friends. Gibson.

And Bootleg Springs. My favorite place in the world. It hadn't just been a summer home to me. It had been *home*.

But I'd had to put it all away. Lock it up tight.

Seeing Gibson's video when I was thousands of miles away in L.A. had made the box rattle, just enough that I was reminded of its existence. But moments later, it had stilled. The lock had held. I was safe from its contents.

But being near him, breathing the same air, hearing his gravelly voice, had broken the lock and popped the lid open a crack—enough that the contents whispered their dark secrets. Memories beat at my subconscious, trying to break free.

They still threatened to come out. All those demons I'd worked so hard to hold back.

Closing my eyes, I visualized the box. It sat in an otherwise empty room. Its form had always been the same—an old-fashioned cedar chest with an enormous metal lock hanging from the latch. The lock was on the floor, open. The lid was ajar, as if something unseen was in the way, preventing it from falling closed.

In my mind, I crouched low and picked up the lock. Pressed the lid down to close it and locked it up tight.

Letting out a slow breath, I opened my eyes. Better.

Except... Gibson Bodine wasn't in the box anymore.

He'd been one of the hardest casualties to bear when I'd left. Fear had kept me from contacting him. I'd fled for good reason, and my fears for my safety had been very real. They still were. The fewer people who knew where I'd gone—that I was even alive—the better.

But god, it had hurt.

I lowered myself onto the edge of the bed, old memories flitting through my mind. Afternoons spent by a little fire, deep in the woods so no one would find us. Gibson sitting on a log, strumming his guitar. Those icy blue eyes. Stubble on his square jaw. Me singing along, finding harmony to his melody.

I'd lived for those afternoons. Just the two of us, isolated from the world. We'd talked about our favorite bands. About album covers and song lyrics. He'd taught me to play guitar and I'd filled journals with half-written songs.

When I'd left, I'd had to let that all go. Gibson and all of Bootleg Springs. I'd put it in the box and locked it. I wouldn't have survived if I hadn't.

But now that he was out, I didn't think I could put him back in.

Another deep breath and another sip of whiskey. I'd lied to him tonight. Lied right to his face.

But he'd known me—said my old name. That had been such a shock. I looked different than I had thirteen years ago. The altercation that had prompted me to run away had left me with a broken nose and a scar on my cheek. I'd had surgery to repair my nose, but it was more sloped now. And I hadn't received medical attention right away, so there hadn't been much they could do about my cheek.

Between that, my dyed hair, and aging from sixteen to

twenty-nine, I'd thought I looked different enough that I wouldn't be recognized so easily.

Apparently I was wrong.

That meant I needed to leave. Get myself out of West Virginia as quickly as I could. Even after all these years, I wasn't safe here. Not as Callie Kendall.

The postcards I'd sent to Jonah Bodine had been the one thing I'd allowed myself—the last connection to my old life. He'd done so much for me. As the years went by and I healed, I'd wanted him to know that I wasn't just okay. That with the loving help of my new family, I'd put the pieces of a shattered girl back together. I'd wanted him to be proud. To know that the risk he'd taken for me—a girl he hadn't even known—had been worth it.

Jonah Bodine was dead. The man who saved my life—my hero—was gone. And there were no more ties to the town I'd once loved.

Until I'd heard Gibson Bodine's voice.

Damn it.

I looked up his video on my phone and played it for about the millionth time. Whoever had recorded it had been sitting to the side, leaving parts of the crowd visible in the frame. There were faces I recognized in that crowd. People I hadn't seen in years. Not since I'd been Callie.

They were adults, now. What were their lives like? So many seemed to still be there. I caught a glimpse of Scarlett Bodine, dancing with someone. God, she wasn't a little girl anymore. Neither was Cassidy Tucker. Was that Bowie Bodine's arm draped around her shoulders? And a woman who had to be June Tucker crossed the corner of the frame for a few seconds. She held hands with a tall, muscular guy.

How many of them were married now? Starting families? They were planting roots, and half the time I didn't know what time zone I was in.

A tear trailed down my cheek. I missed them. The stupid box wouldn't stay closed.

And what about Gibson? Was he with someone? Seemed crazy to think he wouldn't be. He'd be in his thirties now. Some Bootleg girl had no doubt snatched him up. There were probably three or four little Bodines running around that town—little boys and girls with their daddy's blue eyes.

Why did that notion make me so sad? This place was messing with my head. I hoped Gibson was happily married with a family of his own. Maybe that was why he wasn't interested in a record deal. He had responsibilities at home. Made sense.

It also made my stomach hurt. Or maybe that was the cheap whiskey.

I glanced at my phone. I hadn't called Quincy and Henna since I'd been here. It was late, but I knew hearing their voices would help me calm down. I brought up their number and hit send.

I waited while the phone rang several times. My adoptive parents eschewed a lot of modern technology, including cell phones. They had one house phone in the kitchen. It looked like something out of a movie from the eighties, with a long twisty cord so they could walk around while they talked. I'd tried to convince them to get cell phones a few times, but they said the radiation was bad for their auras.

It was the same reason they didn't own a television or a microwave.

"Hello?" Henna answered.

"Hey, it's Maya."

"Hi, sunflower," she said. "It's so nice to hear your voice."

"Sorry to call so late."

"Is it late? I hadn't noticed."

I laughed. Of course not. Henna had always lived by her own calendar—one that had little to do with actual time. "Good, I'm glad I didn't wake you."

"Not at all, sweet girl. I've been on the porch, painting in the nude by moonlight. It's wonderful."

"That sounds awesome. Is Quincy home?"

"Oh yes, he's around."

"How's Blue Moon?" I asked and finished off the whiskey.

"Well, there was a nude protest at the farmer's market last weekend. At least until everyone got sunburnt. Then there's the Pierce's goat. You remember Clementine?"

"Of course."

"Well, a while back she escaped the farm and disappeared for a week or so. She came wandering back like nothing had happened. Turned out she got herself knocked up."

I laughed. "Really?"

"She had three little goat babies last week on Jax's side of the bed. They're still trying to figure out how she let herself into the house."

Only in Blue Moon. "I bet that didn't make him too happy."

"I suppose not. The baby goats sure are cute. Where are you now? Costa Rica? Japan? Maybe Australia?"

"No, I'm back in the States."

"Welcome home, then. But your aura is vibrating so loudly. What's bothering you?"

I took a deep breath. "I'm in West Virginia. It's for work, but... I saw someone I used to know."

"Did you? How did that feel?"

"Honestly, it scared me. I thought I was past this, but it's making me feel like a kid again."

"You're not a child anymore, sunflower," she said, her voice soothing. "I'm sensing a lot of imbalance in your divine energies. Have you been meditating?"

"Not as much as I should."

"That will help. Find your center and unwind the flows of energy that are twisted inside of you."

I smiled. Of course Henna would suggest meditation. It was her solution to most problems. Facing an important decision? Meditate. Fighting with a friend? Meditate. Stuffy nose? Meditate.

"You're right. I'll do that."

"Good. I'm lighting my candles for you right now. They'll send their light into the universe for you."

"Thanks, Henna. I appreciate that."

"Sunflower, remember, the past is the past. It can't hurt you anymore. But dwelling there is just going to reopen old wounds that don't need to be opened. I'd feel a lot better if you weren't in West Virginia."

I sat up straighter. All her talk about meditation and energies was what I expected to hear. But why was she worried about me being in West Virginia?

"Why?"

"People are looking for you again. For Callie."

I clapped my hand over my mouth to keep the whiskey down. My stomach turned over and it took me a second to answer. "What are you talking about? The case went cold years ago."

"They reopened it," she said. "I thought you'd know about that."

"What? How would I know? Is this recent? You never said anything."

She kept talking in the same breezy voice, as if she hadn't just dropped a bombshell on me. "I don't know much about it. Just things I've heard here and there. I thought you might have seen something on the neterweb."

"The internet?"

"Yes, that."

For the most part, I'd always loved Henna's spacey obliviousness to the outside world. She and Quincy had naturally insulated me from the fallout of my disappearance, at a time when I'd needed to be protected. And they'd been the ones to tell me Jonah Bodine had passed away.

But my case had been reopened? If there was an active investigation, I really needed to get out of West Virginia.

"No, I had no idea."

She was quiet for a moment. "Sunflower, don't go looking for trouble. Those old hurts are just going to weigh your spirit down. Let it go."

I thought about Gibson. His gravelly voice had taken root inside me. "I don't know if I can."

"The choice is yours, but you need to be careful. Ask yourself whether this is a road you want to go down. If you're prepared to see what's at the end of it."

"I know." I smiled again. "Let me guess. Meditate on it?"

"Mm-hmm," she said. "And make sure you're taking your wheatgrass shots. Oh, Quincy waves hello. He took a vow of silence until the full moon is in Aquarius."

"Tell him I said hi. And thanks, Henna. I'll let you know when I can come see you."

"I look forward to it, love."

"Me too. Love you."

"Love you too, sunflower."

I ended the call. Usually talking to Henna left me feeling

calm and relaxed. Her soft voice was so soothing. But my case had been reopened? How was that even possible?

I got my laptop out of my bag, set it on the bed, and powered it on. Anticipation tingled in my tummy as I Googled my old name.

Oh god. I was going to need another bottle of whiskey for this.

6

GIBSON

I drove home, feeling like a fucking disaster.

Ever since Scarlett had found that damn sweater, I'd been stuck on the Callie Kendall roller coaster, and I couldn't get off.

My gut churned and my shoulders were knotted with tension. I sped down the empty highway, my headlights flashing against the trees, lighting up the lines on the road. I rolled down the window to get some air—Gus Porter had gotten me in to fix the window Misty Lynn had broken—but it didn't help.

Callie Kendall had died. I'd been certain of it.

She'd been a sweet girl and I hated the thought that something terrible had happened to her. Wondering if my father had been responsible, though—that was what had been eating me alive for the past year.

But Callie wasn't dead. And my father had helped her. He hadn't killed anyone, accidentally or otherwise. But he had kept a big fucking secret for a long time. A secret that could have saved a lot of people from a lot of pain.

That woman in the bar. Why had I called her Callie? What was it about her that had grabbed me so hard I'd followed her outside?

Jenny Leland. I hadn't seen Jonah's mom since the day I'd been taken in for questioning. I'd been avoiding everyone. But she swore she'd seen Callie a year ago. She was the one person who might be able to sort this out. She knew what Callie looked like now.

"Maya," I said aloud, trying out the name. Was Maya Callie? Clenching my teeth, I punched the steering wheel.

It was late, but first thing tomorrow, I was going to have a little chat with Ms. Jenny.

JENNY WAS ALREADY SITTING in a booth in Moonshine. I nodded to Granny Louisa and Estelle on my way in. Half the people in here took one look at me, then started whispering. I rolled my eyes, ignoring them, then took a seat across from my brother's mother.

"Morning." She pushed a full cup of coffee toward me. "I'm glad you called."

"Thanks." I took a sip of coffee—strong and black, just like I liked it. "You've probably heard by now why Sheriff wanted to talk to me."

She nodded. "You were friends with Callie."

"Yeah."

"I had a feeling there was more to this story than I knew," she said.

I appreciated that she didn't press me for details, or ask if I'd been doing something with Callie that I shouldn't have. Jenny gave me the benefit of the doubt, which was more than I could say for the rest of the whispering gossips in the diner.

"I want to know more about the time you met her."

"Okay." She took a sip of coffee. "Like I said, she contacted me after your father died. She was in Seattle for work, so she asked if we could get together."

"What does she do for a living?"

"I don't know. She didn't tell me anything specific about her life now, and I didn't ask."

I shook my leg under the table and stared into my coffee. "Why did my dad lie about it?" I asked, then clamped my mouth shut. I hadn't meant to ask that right now.

"Gibson..." She paused and reached across the table to put her hand over mine. I didn't pull away. "Your father believed Callie would be in danger if her parents ever found her. And your mother's death sealed his silence. He didn't think it was an accident. He told me a hundred times I was never to utter a word about any of this to anyone. I think he was afraid he'd be next."

I shook my head. This was so fucked up. My father, so afraid of Judge Kendall he'd kept the biggest secret in Bootleg Springs until he died. And my mother's death was probably tied to Callie. Had the judge really had her killed?

"Did he say why?" I asked. "Why he thought my mom's accident was connected?"

"He did, but I didn't realize what he'd been talking about until I found out that the last place your mom had gone was that hotel. You have to understand, he was very distraught when he came to see me. It was hard to put together everything he was saying."

"What did he say? Why did Mom go out there?"

"I can't be sure, so don't take this as gospel. But I think

the two of them fought about keeping Callie's secret. She wanted Callie's mother to know that Callie was all right. Your dad disagreed—vehemently. But it sounds like Connie went to talk to Mrs. Kendall anyway."

"Sounds like Mom. She always did what she wanted." I took a deep breath. "Guess she should have listened to him that time."

Jenny squeezed my hand. It felt good. "I'm so sorry, honey."

I didn't meet Jenny's eyes. Talking about my mom had always been rough, but talking about her with Jenny was harder. "If Mom told Mrs. Kendall, the judge could have found out and decided to get rid of her so she wouldn't tell anyone else."

"It's possible."

"Fuck," I muttered.

She squeezed my hand again. "I couldn't agree more."

I didn't want to talk about my parents anymore. It was such a confusing mess. I pulled my hand away and took out my wallet. Grabbed the photo strip and put it on the table.

Jenny turned it so she could look at them right-side up. "So this is what the fuss was all about."

I grunted.

"You're both so young."

"You're sure the woman you met is Callie?" It wasn't that I didn't trust Jenny. But I had to be sure.

She nodded, her eyes still on the photos. "She looks different now, but some of that is age. She has a baby face here. But I can tell it's her."

How was I supposed to ask if she'd had rainbow hair and a scar on her cheek? I didn't want to talk about what had happened last night.

"Different, though?" I asked. "Different how?"

Jenny shifted in her seat. "Well, she had pink hair, like she's blond but dyed it. It was very cute. There's something else about the shape of her face that seems different in these photos, but it could just be her age. Maybe her nose? And she has a scar on her cheek now. I suspect she got it the night she disappeared."

My chest tightened. Scar on her cheek. The woman last night had a scar.

But I didn't say anything to Jenny. I wasn't sure if I was ever going to tell anyone I'd seen her. If Maya was Callie, she hadn't wanted me to know. That stung. But I didn't want to talk about that either.

I slid the pictures back across the table and put them in my wallet. "Thanks. I guess... I just wanted to make sure it was really her."

"Of course you did," she said. "Tell you what, honey, let me buy you breakfast."

"Thanks, but I have a lot of work to do."

I stood and she followed. Before I could turn and head for the door, she wrapped me in a hug. I was so startled, I just stood there for a second, not sure what to do. Then I put my arms around her and patted her on the back before she let go and stepped back. Great, now I had two women in my family forcing hugs on me.

"Have a good day, Gibson," she said with a smile.

I cleared my throat and gave her a short nod. "You too."

Ignoring the whispers of the other diners, I left and drove home. I knew people were talking, but fuck 'em. They could say what they wanted.

I hadn't been lying; I did have work to do. My workshop was in a metal pole building I'd constructed next to my house. It smelled of sawdust and wood stain. Granny Louisa was finally replacing her kitchen cabinets. Devlin had hired Scarlett to do a lot of work on Granny Louisa's outdated house already, but they were just now tackling the kitchen. They'd chosen a nice maple, the design simple and classic.

My stomach growled while I worked. I probably should have taken Jenny up on that offer of breakfast or grabbed something on the way home. But I had too much on my mind. I felt on edge, like a rubber band pulled too tight.

I worked until lunch, then took a break. By the time I got back to it in the early afternoon, I'd buried most of my feelings in sawdust and sweat. If Maya was Callie, at least I'd gotten a glimpse of her. She was alive, and there was relief in that.

And why did it matter? She wasn't an ex-girlfriend—not the one who got away. She'd been my friend for a couple of summers when we were both young. Whether or not I had the chance to see her again didn't impact my life. I didn't know why I was so bent out of shape about it.

I put the sander down and took off my goggles. The cabinets were coming along nicely. I brushed the sawdust off my hands—some of it, anyway—and shook out my shirt. I needed some water.

There were two reasons I'd become a custom cabinetmaker. One, I could be my own boss. I'd discovered early on that me and authority didn't get on so well, and I was smart enough to realize I needed a way to make a living where I didn't have to answer to someone else. Just my apprenticeship had nearly killed me.

Two, I could work alone, in a workshop at my house. Work with my hands, only have to leave to do client installations, and no boss to answer to? Dream job.

I went inside the house and got some water. While I was there, I checked my phone. I had a text from Scarlett telling me—not asking—to come to breakfast at Moonshine in the morning. I didn't bother replying. I'd go if I felt like it.

A faint sound came from outside, a car pulling up my driveway. I groaned. Now what? I really needed to put a gate at the entrance to my property. With a lock.

I debated whether or not to answer. The engine stopped. Car door closed. Whoever it was, they'd be knocking in a few seconds. It might be a reporter wanting the dirt on my visit to the sheriff's office. Or another one of those record company dipshits. I had nothing to say to either of them.

But no one knocked.

I put my empty glass down and glowered at the door. What were they doing out there? Wandering around my property? Maybe it was a nosy reporter. They might be walking around, taking pictures. I hadn't locked my workshop. Damn it, were they over there? I didn't like people in my space, especially people I hadn't invited.

In a few strides, I was at the front door. I threw it open, ready to rush outside and kick the nosy son of a bitch off my land.

It wasn't a reporter.

The woman from last night—Maya—stood on the step, her eyes wide. Her multicolored hair was wild around her face, blowing in the breeze.

We stood for a long moment, staring at each other, like we were frozen in place.

Without warning, she hurled herself at me, jumping up and throwing her arms around my neck. "Gibson."

The air rushed from my lungs and a lump rose in my throat. She dangled against me, her feet lifted off the ground, so I wrapped my arms around her to hold her up.

I knew it. Deep down, I'd known it was her. I spoke low into her ear. "Hey, Callie."

Her body shuddered, but I had no idea if she was laughing or crying. Felt like both. Closing my eyes, I held her while she laughed, then sobbed, then laughed again. I didn't give a crap what she did. She was here. She was alive.

Oh god, I never wanted to let go.

Eventually, she seemed to calm. I let her slide down until her feet touched the ground, then reluctantly dropped my arms.

"Oh my god, I'm so sorry. I'm such a mess," she said, sniffing. She swiped her fingers beneath her eyes, then glanced behind her. "Can I come in? Maybe I shouldn't. I should probably just go."

"No." Before I could stop myself, I grabbed her wrist. "No, don't go. Jesus, Callie, don't disappear again."

She glanced over her shoulder again, then met my eyes. "Okay."

I gently tugged her inside and shut—and locked—the door behind her. Kinda still felt like she was a flight risk. She glanced behind her and touched the lock a few times, like she was checking it, then turned back to face me.

"I got mascara on your shoulder." She reached for my shirt, but jerked her hand away, like she was afraid she'd get burned.

I couldn't seem to get any words out. I just stared at her. At that crazy-ass hair. The scar running down her cheek, leaving a little notch in her upper lip. She wore a loose shirt over a black tank top with a pair of cut-off jeans that showed a hell of a lot of leg—not that I was looking—and beaded sandals. Her shirt gave me a peekaboo glimpse of the tattoos down her arms.

"You're really standing here, aren't you?" I said, finally.

She chewed her bottom lip and nodded. "I'm so sorry

about last night. You caught me off-guard and I didn't handle it very well."

"Goddamn, I thought you were dead. This is freaking me the hell out."

A few more tears broke free from the corners of her eyes. They were a pretty shade of hazel. "I don't even know what to say. I'm sorry isn't enough. It's just so good to see you again."

She covered her mouth, her shoulders shaking with renewed sobs.

It took me a second to react. I didn't understand women on a good day. I had no idea what the fuck to do right now.

"Come on, let's just sit down."

I was almost afraid to touch her again. That hug had felt good—too good. And I didn't even like hugs. With my hand on her back, I guided her to the couch and sat down next to her.

"I have no idea what's wrong with me," she said. "I never cry like this."

"It's all right. Just... breathe or something."

She took a deep breath. "That's better. Thank you."

"You want to tell me what's going on? Who's Maya?"

"Me. I'm Maya." She took another breath. "I am now, I mean. I changed my name."

I nodded. A name change made sense. "Why were you in that bar? Don't tell me you live fifty miles outside Bootleg."

"No, I haven't been in West Virginia since... well, since I left. I'm a producer for Attalon Records. My boss saw a video of you online and he wanted me to talk you into signing a recording contract. I wasn't going to come, but he had me listen to you sing. And it felt like the next thing I knew, I was sitting in that bar."

I grunted. "Huh. So that guy wasn't fucking with me."

"Oliver? No, he was serious."

"I still don't want a record deal."

She cracked a smile, her cheeks still wet with her tears. "I know. That's not really why I came, anyway."

I had so many questions. What had happened the night she disappeared? Had my dad really helped her? Where had she been all these years? But there was one thing I had to know above all else.

"Why didn't you tell me you were okay?"

The smile disappeared from her lips and she looked down at her hands. "I was afraid. The fewer people who knew the truth, the safer everyone would be. I didn't want to put you in danger. I still don't."

"Fuck danger. I thought you were dead."

"I know this is hard to understand, but it was something I had to do. I had to leave, and I couldn't come back."

A battle raged inside me—anger warring with relief. I was pissed at her for disappearing. Pissed that it had hurt me so much. I was mad that she was alive and my dad had known. But god, it was good to see her. Things had changed —we were both older and had been through our own shit— but she was still familiar. I felt like I could pick up my guitar and strum a few chords, and we'd be right back where we were thirteen years ago.

"Well, here you are."

She nodded slowly. "Yeah. Here I am. But Gibs, you can't tell anyone I'm here. If word got out... I don't want to think about what would happen."

I had an inexplicable urge to scoop her into my lap and cradle her against me. But I didn't.

"Don't worry. Your secret is safe with me."

7

MAYA

This place—and Gibson Bodine—had me completely unhinged.

I was surprised he hadn't kicked me out for acting like a crazy person. I'd thrown myself at him before he'd even invited me inside. I didn't know what had come over me. I'd spent the drive here working out what to say—in between arguing with myself over whether to turn around and speed to the closest airport.

When he'd opened that door, his face like a storm cloud, my carefully crafted speech had disappeared. And I'd jumped right into his arms.

As soon as he'd murmured my name, his low voice gravelly in my ear, I'd crumbled. With a flood of tears that smeared makeup all over his shirt, I'd alternated between laughing and crying. It was like I'd gone hysterical.

And now all I could think about was the fact that there was no sign of a woman here.

The only décor was a metal sculpture above the wood stove and a single framed photograph on the mantle. No candles or vases. No knick-knacks or artwork. He had some nice furniture, a TV on the wall, and a stack of wood near the wood stove. Certainly no signs of a family.

No ring on his finger either.

It probably meant he wasn't married. Had he ever been married? Was he dating someone? He probably was. What would I find in his bathroom? An extra toothbrush for when she spent the night?

What was wrong with me? Gibson's relationship status had nothing to do with me. It wasn't like I was staying.

And there were bigger issues at play here.

"I know you probably have a million questions." I tucked my legs beneath me.

"I do, but..." He rubbed the back of his neck. "I think I can put most of it together at this point. Things at home must have been real bad."

Tears welled up in my eyes again and the damn demons in the box howled. I nodded, trying to swallow past the lump in my throat.

"Shit, don't cry again," he said. "We don't have to talk about that. So, you ran."

I nodded again. It was like my mouth was glued shut. I couldn't talk about that night.

"My dad really helped you?"

"Yes." I barely managed to croak out the word.

He was quiet for a long moment, opening and closing his fists. "All right, so you got away. And you didn't think it was safe to come back. I get that, but... why are you here now?"

That was a very good question. I brushed a tear from my cheek. "I don't know. There's a part of me that wants to run and never set foot in West Virginia again. I've worked really hard to move on and live my life. But ever since I heard your voice in that video, it's like the past keeps trying to grab hold of me."

He grunted, but I could tell he wasn't satisfied with my vague explanation.

"Seeing you last night dredged up a lot of stuff for me. And then you recognized me." I glanced up and met his gaze. "I'm sorry I didn't admit it was me, but I wasn't prepared for that."

"I wasn't sure it was you. I don't know what made me say your name. You look different. And your hair is distracting."

I fingered a lock of my hair, glad he hadn't pointed out the scar on my face. "Not different enough, apparently."

"Most people wouldn't know," he said. "I bet you could walk down Lake Drive at high noon and the most you'd get are some funny glances."

Then how did you know, Gibs?

"Maybe." I took a deep breath. "After I saw you last night, I called Henna. She's my adoptive mom. She casually mentioned I should be careful because my case had been reopened. I Googled it and god, I still don't know what to think."

"You didn't know?"

I shook my head. "I've been out of the country for most of the last year. And my parents are... they're unique. They live off-grid, no TV. To them, keeping up with current events means tracking celestial phenomena and horoscopes. They didn't tell me, and I had no reason to go looking."

Gibson stood and started pacing around the room. "It's been a shit show around here."

"I'm sorry—"

"Don't. It's not your fault my dad kept your damn sweater."

"I still feel awful that people think he..."

He stopped and met my eyes. "That people think he killed you."

I shrugged. "Obviously he didn't. I'm right here."

Gibson cracked a smile. "Yeah, no shit."

That smile made my tummy do a little flip. "So I guess... I'm here because I'm sorry about last night. And after seeing all those news stories, I wanted you to know it was me, and that I'm okay."

"How did you know where I live?"

"It wasn't hard to find. Property records are public information and Bootleg is a small town."

"Fair enough. So what happens now?"

Another good question. "People think Callie is dead, right? That forensics report said the body they found is me. She needs to stay that way."

"What?" His brow furrowed. "Why would you say that?"

"Because it's safer for everyone. I've stayed alive this long because people kept me hidden. And then because my case went cold. If it's closed now, I can just go on living my life as Maya."

"There are people who know, Callie," he said. "Jenny Leland is here, in Bootleg. She told us you're alive."

Dread swept through me and I covered my mouth with my hand.

"She didn't say anything for a while, but I guess she couldn't watch everyone grieve over a death that hadn't happened. Not when she'd seen you with her own eyes."

"Who else knows?"

He rubbed his chin. "My family. Sheriff Tucker. Rest of the cops in town, I'd imagine."

I stood, the sudden urge to run almost overwhelming. I was Callie all over again. A terrified girl, hurt and alone. Huddled in a cabin in the woods. Certain they'd find me.

"Hey, slow down there." Gibson was suddenly behind me, his big hands on my arms, his grip gentle. "No one knows where you are. And they won't. You're safe here."

Closing my eyes, I took a long, slow breath. He didn't let go, and I certainly didn't want him to. His strong hands anchored me.

But the box in my mind rattled violently. Quincy and Henna had always told me that the past needed to be left behind. That peace could only be found by living in the moment. I'd breathed and cleansed and meditated my way through the last thirteen years, trying to believe they were right—trying to *make* them right. And yet, the box had never disappeared. My past was locked inside, but it was still a part of me.

Callie lived on.

"I don't know what to do," I said, finally.

"People are gonna dig," he said. "The sheriff knows you aren't dead. He knows someone falsified that forensics report so they'd say that body in New York is you. And it's not just him. Hell, it was June Tucker who exposed that woman claiming to be you earlier this year."

"Do the Kendalls know that? Do they know about Jenny?"

"I don't think so." He dropped his hands. "But they probably know about me."

I whipped around to face him. "What about you?"

He rubbed the back of his neck again. "Do you remember when I took you to that concert over in Perrinville?"

"Yeah."

"We hopped in that photo booth on the way back to my truck." He walked over to the kitchen counter and picked up his wallet, then pulled something out.

I took a faded photo strip from his hands. A fresh wave of tears stung my eyes. "Oh my god. I forgot about these."

"Misty Lynn Prosser stole my wallet out of my truck after I told her off. She found those and turned them in. Sheriff hauled me in for questioning. The whole town knows now."

I remembered Misty Lynn. She was a few years older than me, and basically a nightmare. "Why did Misty Lynn steal your wallet?"

He groaned. "I don't want to talk about it."

"Why not?"

"She's crazy, all right? I dated her for a little while about a million years ago and she's been trying to worm her way back into my life ever since."

I gaped at him. "Oh my god. Please tell me you're kidding. You dated Misty Lynn Prosser?"

His expression clouded over. "It's not like I'm proud of it. Fuck's sake, I was twenty-one. Everybody makes mistakes, especially at that age."

I didn't know why I found it so funny. Maybe it was because he was getting so defensive. "Sure, but not everyone makes a Misty-Lynn-sized mistake."

The veins in his forearms popped as he clenched his fists.

God, he had nice arms.

"I'm never gonna live that shit down, am I?"

"It's Misty Lynn." I tried to suppress my smile. "Probably not."

He spun around and stomped down the hallway. Before I could react, he stomped his way back. "I want to yell at you to get out but if I do, I'll probably never fucking see you again."

I covered my mouth again, trying not to laugh, but I couldn't help it. Callie was retreating back into the recesses of my psyche, and I felt like Maya again. "I'm sorry. I'm just giving you a hard time. I wouldn't want you to meet some of my mistakes."

He narrowed his eyes at me, but I couldn't tell what that expression meant. "All right, you can stay."

I tucked my hair behind my ear. "We both know I really can't."

"What if you just stayed for a little while?" he said, his voice soft again. "If you have to disappear again, fine. I get it. But it's been thirteen years. You really gonna show up here after all that time and stay for half an hour?"

"Like I said, I don't know what I should do."

With his hands on his hips, he looked down at the floor and took a deep breath. Some of the intensity in his posture seemed to melt away. When he lifted his face to meet my eyes, he looked so much like the Gibson I remembered, it nearly made my heart stop.

"How about a song?"

I bit my lower lip. I didn't think I could refuse him anything when he looked at me like that. "You want to play with me?"

"It was our thing, right?"

"It was." I glanced down, the question leaving my lips before I could stop myself from asking. "You don't have a girlfriend who'll show up and get mad because I'm here, do you?"

He scowled. "No."

I had to fight to keep the smile off my face. "I was just making sure. I wouldn't want to make more trouble for you."

He took a few steps closer. His arm moved a little, as if he was going to touch me, but changed his mind. "Look, this mess is bigger than both of us. All I know is right now, I have my friend back. I'd kinda like to make the most of it while I can."

I met his eyes. They were so blue. "Okay. I'll stay a while."

He went into another room and came out with an acoustic guitar. I took one corner of the couch and he sat on the edge of the other. After plucking the strings and making a few small adjustments to the tuning pegs, he strummed the opening chords to "I Fall to Pieces," a classic Patsy Cline song.

God, it felt good to sing with him again.

One song turned into another. Soon we were singing and talking like we used to. Not about Callie, or investigations, or the Kendalls. About music. I told him about some of the artists I'd worked with. The things I'd seen. Places I'd been.

And he told me about Bootleg. About the tourism boom. The new vacation rentals and spas in town. The things that were different, and the things that were the same.

He talked about meeting his half-brother, Jonah, last year. About Scarlett's mini real estate empire, and the unlikely man who'd captured her heart. He told me about his brother Bowie finally marrying Cassidy Tucker. About Leah Mae Larkin coming back to Bootleg and getting engaged to Jameson. About Jonah's girlfriend, Shelby, and her brother George, the big football player who was dating June Tucker.

There was so much I'd missed. The kids I'd known had grown up and started their lives. So many were still here.

Bootleg Springs was that sort of place—the kind of town that drew people in and made them want to stay.

A lifetime ago, I'd daydreamed about living here. Making this my home. I hardly remembered what it was like to have a home, now.

We talked and played well into the night. Gibson produced some snacks from the kitchen, and neither of us said anything about the time. I needed to go. It was a long drive on winding roads to get back to my motel. But I couldn't seem to make myself leave.

Finally, my eyes were getting too heavy for me to deny how tired I was. "I should probably get going."

Gibson rubbed his chin and seemed to consider something for a moment. "It's late. You should just crash here."

Every bit of me wanted to take him up on his offer. But I couldn't stay here. "Thanks, but I shouldn't."

"Sweetheart, it's three in the morning and I'm not gonna let you leave just so you can run off the road on the way back to your crappy motel." He stood. "Come on. You can sleep in my room. I'll take the couch."

"You don't have to—"

He turned and leveled me with a glare. Apparently he wasn't taking no for an answer.

And really, I didn't want to go.

"Thanks."

"Mm-hmm," he mumbled. "I'll get you some fresh blankets."

I followed him to his room and Callie made a momentary reappearance, my heart fluttering and cheeks flushing at the thought of being in Gibson Bodine's bedroom. I tried to tell myself I was being silly. I was far from the teenage virgin of thirteen years ago.

But being with him in his bedroom, even while he was

making up the bed for me to sleep in alone, felt a little thrilling. Even dangerous.

I liked it.

He said a gruff goodnight and left me there. I glanced around at the tidy room. The walls made of logs and the bed with a quilt that looked homemade. It was so very Gibson. And I still couldn't quite believe I was here.

_____

8

GIBSON

*T*he sound of someone knocking on my door woke me with a start. It felt like I'd fallen asleep about five minutes ago, but sure enough, light peeked in through the curtains. Whoever it was knocked again. I groaned, hauling myself off the couch. Why the fuck were so many people banging on my door these days?

I ran a hand through my hair, still blinking the sleep from my eyes, and opened the door.

Scarlett stood on the step, an accusatory look on her face. "Mornin', sunshine."

"What do you want, Scar?"

She crossed her arms. "Well, you weren't answering your phone, so I came by to find out why you weren't at Moonshine this morning. But I think the reason is pretty obvious."

I scratched the back of my neck, still trying to wake up. "What reason?"

"Oh, I don't know, maybe the owner of the car out front

and those pretty little sandals in there." She pointed at something behind me.

Oh, shit.

I glanced over my shoulder. Sure enough, Callie's sandals were right there in plain sight.

"That's none of your business," I snapped.

"Trust me, Gibs, I don't want to know the details. But you're an ass for missing breakfast because you brought some hussy home last night."

Anger flared, running hot in my veins. I pointed a finger in my sister's face. "Don't you fucking call her that, you hear me?"

Her eyes widened, but instead of attacking me like a feral cat, her mouth turned up in a wide grin. "Oh my god."

I'd rather face the feral cat—and Scarlett was a biter—than that smile. Crap, why had I said that? "What?"

"I know you have a girl in there, but Gibson Bodine, is it a girl you actually *like*?" She stood on her tiptoes, trying to look past me. "Who is she? Do you have a secret girlfriend?"

Damn my nosy sister. Why'd she pick today to stop by unannounced? It was like she was drawn to family drama.

"No." I moved forward, bracing an arm against the door-frame to block her access. I didn't want her trying to slip inside. What could I tell her? Callie Kendall's alive and sleeping in my goddamn bed? "It's not like that. She's just a friend who needed a place to crash last night."

Inwardly, I congratulated myself on that one. It wasn't even a lie.

Scarlett, however, clearly wasn't buying it. "Since when do you have friends?"

"I have friends."

"Like who?"

I glowered at her. "I'm not telling you who she is."

She grinned. "Because she's your secret girlfriend."

"Jesus, Scar, no she's not. Go the fuck home."

"Fine. But tell your secret girlfriend I like her shoes."

I rolled my eyes, stepped back, and shut the door in her face.

"If your secret girlfriend needs a place to stay, let me know," she said through the door. "I might have a last-minute cancel on one of my lake cabins."

"Go away."

I ran my hand over my face. I needed coffee so I could think.

What was going to happen now? Would Callie say goodbye and I'd never see her again? Maybe I could convince her to start up the postcard thing again, but send them to me. At least I'd keep some connection to her. I could keep a secret; that clearly wasn't an issue. I'd just burn them after I read them. Then there'd be no evidence of her.

I hated that idea. Not because I'd want to keep the post-cards, or because I was worried about people finding out. It was because I didn't want her to leave.

The floor creaked behind me. I looked over my shoulder and it felt like the wind had been knocked out of my lungs.

Callie crept out from the hallway, dressed in one of my flannel shirts. Her crazy hair was a mess, and I couldn't tell if she was wearing anything underneath. The shirt was long enough on her, it might have been hiding her shorts. But her legs were looking awfully bare.

I cleared my throat. "Mornin'."

"Hey." She brushed her hair back from her face. "Was that your sister?"

"Yeah. Don't worry, she doesn't know you're here."

"Thanks." She glanced down at the shirt she was wearing. "Oh, sorry, I found this in your closet. I hope you don't mind. I left my bag in the car last night."

I didn't mind. The problem was, I liked the way she looked in my shirt a lot more than I should have. "It's fine. Hungry?"

She covered her mouth to stifle a yawn. "A bit. Sorry, my body still hasn't figured out what time zone it's in."

I glanced toward the kitchen. "I don't have much here. I don't have people over that often. Or, you know, ever."

"That's okay. Just coffee would be great."

"Sure." I paused for a second, waiting for her to say she didn't need breakfast because she was leaving anyway. The thought made my chest hurt. I felt like I was on borrowed time with her. Like if I didn't say something fast, she'd be out the door. "I'll run into town and get some food. You can just hunker down here."

Her lips parted, like she was about to say something, but she closed her mouth again.

"You got somewhere you need to be?" I asked.

She lifted one shoulder in a shrug. "No, not really."

"Then I'll go get breakfast."

I didn't wait for her to reply. Just started some coffee, then went back to my room to throw on some jeans and a clean t-shirt. I wasn't going to keep her captive—she could walk right out that door anytime she wanted to—but if I could coax a little more time out of her, I was going to do it.

Why? Because seeing her again was messing with my insides in ways I both hated and couldn't get enough of.

When I came out, she was in my kitchen waiting for the coffee to brew. She looked damn good in my shirt. She'd been pretty as a teenager, but now? Holy hell, she was hot as sin.

I really needed to stop thinking like that. This was Callie

Kendall. She wasn't standing in the kitchen wearing my shirt, her hair a mess, because I'd spent last night fucking her senseless. Although that's exactly what she looked like, and I was hard as steel just thinking about it.

Damn it, Gibson, knock that shit off.

Tearing my eyes away from those ridiculous legs, I grabbed my phone and keys. "I'll be back. If anyone comes over, don't answer."

She said goodbye as I was walking out the door. I just grunted, shutting the door behind me. Then I checked twice to make sure it was locked before heading to my truck.

I drove into town and stopped at the Pop In. Of course it was busy. The tourist season was winding down, but there were still a lot more people around than I liked. I just needed to get in and get out, preferably without any of my nosy family seeing me.

At least Scarlett wasn't here.

I got some eggs and bread, but realized I had no idea what she liked. Shit. Inexperienced with women I was not, but I had no idea what to feed one. What if she was a vegetarian or something? Maybe I should have just gone to Moonshine and ordered one of everything to go.

Moving through the store, I dodged the other customers and grabbed a random assortment of stuff. Packaged pastries, a pint of strawberries, some cheese, a few cans of soup, crackers, orange juice.

I paused in front of the shampoo and body wash. Maybe she'd want a shower. What did girls use? Even in this little store, there were basically ten thousand different options. I grabbed a bottle with flowers on it and flipped open the lid. Did they go by smell? This one wasn't bad.

"Whatcha doin' there, Gibs?"

I froze, like I'd just been caught stealing. Cassidy stood next to me, tilting her head, a little smile on her face.

"Nothing," I said, putting the bottle back on the shelf.

"Looking for something to make your hair softer?" She took a different bottle and held it out to me. "Might I recommend this?"

I glared at her, but took the bottle out of her hand. "Shouldn't you be on a honeymoon or something?"

"We were saving it for later anyway, but we're certainly not going anywhere now. Not with everything that's going on. Do you need conditioner?" She handed me another bottle.

Great. She'd obviously talked to Scarlett. And me buying girl shit was making it look like I *was* hiding a secret girlfriend at my place.

But she was being kinda helpful...

I tossed the conditioner in with the rest of the stuff and hesitated, not quite meeting Cassidy's gaze. With her mouth still turned up in a grin, she shook her head and rolled her eyes. She glanced up and down the aisle, then grabbed body wash, a package of pink razors, a toothbrush, deodorant, and a hairbrush.

"Thanks," I muttered, then took my stuff to the front. I didn't want to give her a chance to ask any questions.

Opal Bodine—no relation—was behind the front counter. She sat on a stool, her nose in a book. I waited for a few seconds, but she didn't look up.

I cleared my throat and she just about jumped off her stool.

"Sorry." She put a bookmark in the book and set it down. Was she blushing? That was weird. "Didn't see you there, Gibs."

I grunted something non-committal, then glanced

around while I set my stuff out for her to scan. A couple of summertimers got in line behind me and I noticed Buck wandering around with a package of donuts. No worries about gossip there. But then Zadie Rummerfield walked in, stopped, and looked right at me. Her eyes tracked my purchases, and she lifted an eyebrow.

Well, shit.

As quickly as I could, I paid and grabbed my bags—why the hell did I have so much stuff?—and got out of there. But I could practically feel the rumor mill sparking to life. It was like a fuse on a big stick of dynamite—one that was going to light up the whole town.

9

MAYA

$\mathcal{C}$offee was perking me up. I sat nestled in the corner of Gibson's couch, cradling the mug in my hands, my legs tucked up beneath me. I hadn't been able to resist slipping on one of his shirts before I came out of his room this morning. The dark blue plaid was soft against my skin. And I really had left my bag in the car last night. It wasn't like I'd come here planning to stay over.

Plus, his shirt smelled good. Really good. I lifted the collar to my nose and inhaled. It smelled like fresh laundry, but even clean, right out of his closet, there was a hint of Gibson on it.

It was the silliest thing, but I wondered if he'd let me keep it.

Waking up here, in Gibson Bodine's house—in his bed, no less—felt like something out of a dream. And amazingly enough, not a nightmare, considering I was on the outskirts of the town I thought I'd never be able to see again.

However, I still felt unbalanced. I'd kept all things Callie locked away for so long, I didn't know what to do with her now. Last night I'd bounced back and forth between feeling uncertain and afraid—like I was Callie all over again—to calm and composed. I'd hoped I could sleep it off and face today feeling whole. Feeling like Maya.

But it was as if I'd cracked. I was two different people inhabiting the same body. Really, I always had been. I'd just put Callie away and never let her out. I'd lived thirteen years as Maya. But Gibson wasn't the only thing that had escaped the box and wouldn't go back in. Callie had, too.

And I had no idea what I was going to do about that.

For about the millionth time, I told myself I should go. This was beyond complicated. It wasn't safe for me here.

But Gibson wasn't the only one who knew I was alive. He was right, people were going to dig. If I wanted Callie to stay gone, I'd have to disappear—really disappear. No contact. No ties. I had plenty of places I could go. I knew how to drop off the map. I was good at it.

Maybe I should have been busy wiping down every surface I'd touched to get rid of my fingerprints. But I stayed where I was, sipping coffee on Gibson's couch. At the very least, I wasn't going to leave without saying goodbye. Not again.

But if I left, then what? The way rumors flew through this town, the Kendalls had to know about Gibson keeping those photos. That put a great big target on his back. And he'd said June Tucker had exposed the fraud posing as me. Did the judge know that? Who else had been poking around in my case? Cassidy? Gibson said she was a deputy. And Jenny Leland was here. If it got out that she'd said I was alive...

How many people were in danger because of me?

Closing my eyes, I took a few deep breaths, trying to

slow my racing heart. Maybe I wasn't prepared to face what was at the end of this road.

The front door opened, and Gibson came in, loaded down with grocery bags.

I set my coffee down and stood. "Do you need help with that?"

"I got it." He brought the bags into the kitchen and set them on the counter.

I followed him in and watched as he started pulling things out. I wanted to help, but I didn't know where anything went. And he was so gruff. It wasn't just his gravelly voice and furrowed brow. Even his movements had a rough edge to them. It made me feel like I should stay out of his way.

That, or climb him like a tree.

"I thought you were just getting breakfast?" I asked after he'd emptied the third bag.

"I didn't know what you'd want."

He pulled out a bottle of shampoo. Then conditioner, followed by a bagful of toiletries. Pinks, lavenders, flowers. A hairbrush. None of that was for him. He didn't have a girlfriend. He was stocking up for me.

I felt like a ping-pong ball, bouncing back and forth across the table of indecision. Run. Stay. Run. Stay.

Gibson looked over his shoulder and his eyes flicked up and down. His expression softened and one corner of his mouth lifted. "I kinda went overboard."

Like magic, that little smile calmed my thundering heart. "Thanks. I really appreciate it."

He muttered something that sounded like *you're welcome*, then went back to putting things away.

"How about this. You were sweet enough to go to the store, so I'll make us breakfast." I stepped closer and hip-checked him out of the way. His head whipped around and he gave me a look I couldn't read. That damn brow furrow he kept doing made me all melty inside. I had to stop myself from sidling up to him and threading my arms around his waist.

I needed to calm my hormones. Apparently my old crush on Gibson was another thing that hadn't gone back into the box. It was out in full force, as if it hadn't been thirteen years since I'd seen him.

But it was totally one-sided. Just like it always had been. He was being nice to me, but I wasn't getting a hint of attraction from him.

Unless he was trying to hide it.

I sighed and got to work on breakfast. Now I was just making things up. This situation was complicated enough. I didn't need a bunch of imaginary sexual tension making it worse. Even if the tension wasn't imaginary for me.

After breakfast, Gibson said he had work to do out in his shop. He brought my bag in from my rental car. He seemed hesitant to let me go outside. Or to leave me alone. Whether it was because he was afraid someone would see me or that I'd leave, I wasn't sure.

I showered, using the stuff he'd bought for me, and changed into clean clothes. I left his flannel shirt lying on his bed. I wondered if there was a way to get him to wear it for a little while and then let me put it back on. Probably not. There really wasn't a way to say *hey Gibs, can you wear this for a few hours so I can put it on and enjoy your scent* that wasn't weird.

While Gibson worked—I could hear the muffled sound of power tools coming from his shop—I checked my messages. I had a text from Oliver, wanting to know how things were going. What was I supposed to tell him? I'd slept at Gibson Bodine's house last night because he'd been my friend before I ran away and changed my identity?

Obviously I couldn't tell him the whole story, but I decided to call and check in.

"There you are," he said when he answered. "I was starting to worry."

"Why, because you sent me out to talk to a random singer who's... what did you call him? Hostile?"

"Pretty much. Do you have good news for me?"

"Well, I have *some* good news. He hasn't signed with another label."

"Great. But why do I get the feeling you have bad news, too?"

I twined a strand of hair around my finger. "The bad news is, he doesn't want to sign with us, either. He doesn't want to sign with anyone."

"Damn. Really? You couldn't talk him into it?"

I sighed. *No, because I got distracted by the fact that he thought I was dead and then we sang together like old times.* "Not so far."

"That's my girl. Wear him down."

"Don't expect any miracles, Oliver. He's talented, but he has a lot going on in his life right now."

"I have faith in you."

I laughed. "Thanks, I think."

"Keep me posted."

"Will do. Talk to you later."

I put my phone down, feeling a little shaky. Why had that left me so unsettled? I was still struggling to reconcile what was happening. Talking to Oliver felt so normal—so Maya. But I was sitting in a log cabin outside Bootleg Springs, with Gibson Bodine working in his shop outside.

Henna's soothing voice ran through my mind. *Meditate*

and let it go, sunflower. That was exactly what I needed to do. Center my energy. Be present in the moment.

I found a blanket, folded it neatly, and set it on the floor in front of the couch. Sitting cross-legged, I closed my eyes and breathed.

At first, my mind spun like a whirlwind, thoughts flitting in and out of my consciousness. I kept breathing. Centering. Gradually, the chaos diminished. I felt a familiar sense of peace and calm.

The box still made its presence known. Without trying to push it away, I acknowledged it. It wasn't a problem for right now. Not this minute. For now, I was in a holding pattern.

Gibson hadn't explicitly invited me to stay today. He'd just acted as if I would. And as I sat there, breathing deeply, my mind calm, I realized I was glad. He hadn't insisted I stay or pressed me to tell him what I planned to do. He'd just bought me breakfast food—and lunch, and dinner, and bathroom toiletries—and told me to make myself comfortable while he went to work.

He wasn't exactly warm and fuzzy, but I felt welcome. Like if I told him I wanted to hide out here for the next few days—or weeks, or even longer—he'd just shrug, like it wasn't a big deal.

The door opened, and I heard Gibson's heavy boots on the floor. Slowly, I let my eyes drift open. He stood just inside, as if he'd paused mid-step to look at me.

God, that brow furrow was sexy.

"You okay?" he asked.

I took one last cleansing breath. "Fine. Great, actually. I was just meditating."

"Huh. Hungry?"

"Is it lunchtime already?" I uncrossed my legs and stretched them out, wiggling my bare toes.

"Yeah." Something dinged and he pulled his phone out of his back pocket. With a roll of his eyes, he put it back.

"Everything all right?"

"Scarlett's just being... Scarlett." He went into the kitchen, so I got up and followed. "It's fine, I'll handle her."

"Handle her?"

He got out a loaf of bread and set it on the counter. "She saw your sandals this morning, so now she thinks I have a girlfriend I'm hiding from everyone."

Gibson's secret girlfriend? I bit my bottom lip to keep from smiling. Why did that thought make me so giddy? God, I wasn't a little girl anymore.

But it was still fun to imagine.

"Are you known for hiding women out here?"

He scowled down at the sandwich he was making. "No."

I nudged him with my elbow. "Uh-oh. Should I have checked to see if you locked me in from the outside?"

That earned me a smile. "Yeah, I barred the door so you couldn't get out."

"I had a feeling you were evil."

A knock at the front door made me jump. Gasping, I grabbed Gibson's arm. His solid muscle flexed in my grip and he looked down at my hand. I was about to snatch it away and apologize, but then he gently laid his over mine.

"Wait in the bedroom. I'll get rid of them." He squeezed my hand.

I nodded and he let go. I cast a quick glance around to see if there was anything obvious sitting out that someone might see from the doorway. The blanket I'd used for meditating was on the floor, but that wasn't incriminating. I picked up my sandals, letting them dangle from my grasp, and tiptoed down the hall to Gibson's bedroom.

A woman's voice came from the front of the house, but I couldn't quite make out what she said. *Hi, Gibson*, most likely. I stood by the bedroom door, leaving it open just a crack, and strained to listen.

"What are you doing here?" he asked.

"Um... well, I just..." She trailed off, her voice soft. "Here."

"What's this?"

"Brownies," she said.

"Why did you bring me brownies?" Gibson sounded genuinely confused.

"Oh, you know, just being neighborly."

There was a slight pause. "Did Scarlett put you up to this?"

"Scarlett? No, not at all. She might have mentioned something about you having company. And if you did—have company, that is—I thought she might enjoy some brownies. I baked four batches this morning, and they needed a home. So, there you are."

I could practically feel Gibson's irritation all the way back here. I bit my lip again to keep from giggling.

"Thanks, I guess?" he said.

"Sure, it's my pleasure. If y'all are needing anything else, you can just let me know."

"Bye, Millie."

"Oh, I almost forgot. Let your girlfriend know she's invited to book club. First meeting is at the library tomorrow."

"I don't have a girlfriend."

"Right, of course. *Secret* girlfriend. Sorry, I forgot. In that case, she can come in a disguise if she wants. And tell her not to worry if she hasn't read the book yet. Some of us haven't had a chance. We'll start by discussing the author, so there won't be any spoilers while the rest of the ladies catch up."

"Bye Millie," he growled, and I heard the door shut.

I hesitated a few seconds before coming out. "Is the coast clear?"

He stood near the door, a foil-covered dish in his hands. "Yeah."

"Was that Millie Waggle?"

"She brought brownies," he said, looking down at them, his expression bewildered.

"Is it unusual for Millie to bring people brownies?" I lifted the foil and inhaled. "Oh my god, these smell amazing."

"No, she delivers them all over town. Just never to me."

I pinched a bit of the crispy corner and popped it in my mouth. It tasted like chocolate heaven. "Wow, that's good. I guess having a secret girlfriend has some unexpected benefits."

"You're not my—" He growled in frustration and took the brownies into the kitchen. "This is how it starts. You know that, right? First it's Millie with brownies. Next it'll be someone with a casserole and pretty soon I'll be answering the door every hour to someone new with a dish in their hands."

"Why is this bad?" I followed him in and took another pinch of brownie—a bigger one this time. "That sounds like nice neighbors bringing food."

"They ain't doing it to be nice," he said. "They're doing it to get up in my business. And to find out who you are."

"Did Millie really hear the secret girlfriend thing from Scarlett already? She was here like four hours ago."

His eyebrows drew together. "You remember this is Bootleg Springs, right? Half the town knows by now, and the other half will by sundown."

I leaned against the counter, picking at the brownies. Why was I being so indecisive? I should go. I could figure out what to do about the investigation and the Kendalls from my motel fifty miles away. Or from L.A. I could put three thousand miles between me and this place. Disappear again. What was I waiting for?

"Look, don't worry about it," Gibson said. There was that softness in his voice I'd heard last night. It made me feel all gooey—like Millie's brownies. "We'll just keep your stuff in the bedroom, and if anyone comes knocking, you can hide back there while I get rid of them."

The question hung in the air between us, unspoken. *Then what?*

I didn't know the answer to that, and he didn't seem to either. And maybe for now, that was where we needed to be. Here, in his house, not knowing what to do.

Because the truth was, now that I was here, I couldn't seem to make myself leave.

10

GIBSON

I hated—*hated*—leaving Callie at my place alone. I'd given her Jameson's number—I trusted him to keep his mouth shut—in case of emergency. Closed all the curtains, checked the doors half a dozen times to make sure they were locked, and left her a crowbar and a hammer near the door.

What was I so worried about? Hell if I knew. There was a lot she hadn't said—hadn't needed to say. I could figure it out. She'd stayed away because she was afraid of her father. She still was; I'd seen the fear in her eyes. Jayme had said Judge Kendall was dangerous. Sheriff had too. I reckoned they were right. And the urge to protect her from him was overwhelming.

I'd failed her thirteen years ago. I wasn't going to fail her again.

I wasn't sure if the Kendalls were still in town. They were usually here during the summer, but the season was winding down. And with the recent announcement that he was up for a federal judgeship, they might have gone back to their main home in Virginia. It wouldn't be hard to find out. And I'd sleep better knowing they were gone. But until I could be sure, I wasn't taking any chances.

Reluctantly, I pushed open the door to the Lookout, my guitar case in hand. Noise spilled out into the darkness. Music. Voices. Hung and Corbin were already here, setting up. The fact that we were supposed to play tonight was the only reason I'd come. Otherwise, I'd have shut off my phone —shut out the world—and spent the evening at home with Callie.

We seemed to have an unspoken understanding, Callie and me. I knew she was still trying to work out what to do. Whether she could come forward, and what that would mean for her. I also knew she had one foot out the door, ready to disappear again. This time for good. But for now— however long *now* lasted—she'd stay. I hadn't told her she should, and she hadn't asked if I minded. That would have felt too much like making a firm decision.

Maybe I didn't understand women, but I understood this. She needed a little time to figure this out. The least I could do was give it to her.

Tonight, that meant showing up at the Lookout and acting like nothing was going on.

Nicolette nodded to me from behind the bar. She already had a water for me—mason jar, no ice, with a straw.

"Evenin'," she said, pushing the water across the bar. Tonight she was wearing a shirt that said, *I know what you did, sincerely, karma.* "Cutting it close tonight."

"I'm here, ain't I?" I set my guitar case down.

"Yeah, you are." She eyed me up and down. "Alone."

"I'm always here alone. What does that have to do with anything?"

She poured a beer from the tap for one of her customers. "Just an observation."

I didn't respond. Just grabbed my water and took a sip.

No surprise that it was packed on a Friday. A few grizzled old-timers sat at the bar, nursing whiskeys and faded memories. A group of summertimers took up a couple of tables. Locals—including a handful of Bodines—took up the others.

Rhett Ginsler sat on a stool at one end of the bar, hunched over his drink, his trucker hat pulled down low. Misty Lynn was here, too, unfortunately. Judging by Rhett's dejected posture and Misty Lynn's seat on the opposite side of the bar, those two were still broken up.

I gave it a week, two tops, before they were back together. As far as I was concerned, they deserved each other. Misty Lynn kept leading him on, but he kept taking her back. Wasn't my fault he was a dumbass and she was a shitty human being.

Misty Lynn glanced up at me and at least she had the decency to look guilty. I ignored her. I was still pissed she'd stolen my wallet—even more so that she'd turned it in—but I didn't want to talk to her, even to tell her off. Bad enough I had to share this town with her.

I picked up my guitar case and took it to the little stage where Hung and Corbin were setting up. Put my water on a table nearby and got out my guitar. Corbin looked past me a few times, like he was watching the door.

"You waiting for someone?" I asked, lifting the guitar strap over my shoulder.

"Me? No," he said. "I just thought you might have brought..."

"I might have brought what?"

He shut his mouth and shrugged. "Never mind."

As predicted, the rumor mill had been churning. After Millie had stopped by with brownies, Sallie Mae Brickman had brought over a loaf of fresh bread, followed closely by Tanya Varney with a bag of pepperoni rolls. She'd claimed she had extra, and why not go see if Gibson Bodine could use a hot meal?

I knew their game. No one brought me food. Most people stayed away from my place, if they knew what was good for them. Seemed the allure of my supposed secret girlfriend was enough to make people brave.

That was going to become a problem real quick. Now that Bootleg smelled a juicy story, they wouldn't leave me alone until they got to the bottom of it.

"That's not what I heard," someone said behind me. Sounded like Moe Daily. "I heard he rescued her out on the lake and carried her all the way back to his place. She's there recovering now."

What the... were they talking about me?

"Why would he carry her? He has a truck." That was Randy Jenkins.

"I don't know, that's just what someone was saying over at Build-A-Shine earlier."

"There ain't a lick of truth to that," Randy said. "I heard from a very reliable source that he got himself a mail-order bride."

"No shit?"

"Swear on my Granny Patsy's grave, god rest her soul."

"May she rest in peace. How does that even work?" Moe asked.

"Well, I don't know how Gibson did it," Randy said. "But my great-uncle Earl got a mail-order bride back in the day. He and my great-aunt were married forty-odd years 'fore he passed, god rest his soul."

"May he rest in peace. Ain't that something."

Mail-order bride? Where in the hell had he gotten that idea? I was about to turn around and set them straight, but Hung interrupted.

"Ready, Gibs?"

I scowled over my shoulder. Sometimes the men in this town were as big of gossips as the women. "Fine, yeah."

We started in on our set, but something was off. My guitar was in tune, and Hung and Corbin played well, as usual. It wasn't the music. Our songs felt right.

It was the crowd.

They were watching me, but not the way they normally watched us when we played. People leaned in to talk to each other, their conversations animated, their eyes focused on me.

Who else thought I'd brought home a mail-order bride? What other stories were circulating around town?

Scarlett sat with Devlin, Cassidy, and Bowie at a table off to the side. Three of them were having a good laugh about something, but not Scarlett. Nope. Her eyes were on me. Scrutinizing. What was that girl thinking?

We played some more songs, but my heart wasn't in it. I kept thinking about Callie. Was she still at my place? Had she decided to run again? Would someone recognize her if they caught a glimpse?

I didn't think so. If she came out and said she was Callie Kendall, I reckoned people would believe her eventually. But she looked different enough, she could get away with pretending to be someone else. I'd barely recognized her. Thought I was crazy until she'd showed up on my doorstep. People wouldn't know.

Problem was, my oh-so-neighborly neighbors were

gonna keep trying to find out the truth about who was staying at my place.

And if Scarlett was involved, she'd play dirty.

Our last song ended—finally—and I put my guitar away. Downed the rest of my water. I glanced over and Scarlett was glaring at me. She raised her eyebrows and curled her finger, motioning for me to come to her table.

Ah, hell.

I left my guitar behind the stage and went to the table she shared with Devlin, Cassidy, and Bow.

"Hey Gibs," Cassidy said, giving me what she probably thought was a subtle wink. "How'd that lavender shampoo and conditioner work out for you?"

I groaned. I already hated this conversation.

"Gibson Bodine, I'm ashamed of you," Scarlett said.

"What the hell did I do now?"

"How could you leave that girl all alone while you go out to a bar?"

"I don't know what you're talking about."

"Don't play dumb with me." She hopped off her stool and poked me in the chest. "I know she was there this morning because you had a strange car in front of your house, and I saw her pretty sandals in your living room. And I know she didn't leave because Cassidy caught you buying girly shampoo at the Pop In. So why on earth did you leave her at home?"

I glanced around. "For fuck's sake, Scar, lower your voice."

"Why are you trying to keep this from us?"

Damn it, she was going to make this a bigger deal than it already was. Half the bar was leaning closer, trying to pretend they weren't eavesdropping.

I could tell Scarlett the truth—I trusted her—but I didn't

want to without asking Callie first. "I'm not keeping anything from you. I told you already, she's just a friend. She's got some stuff going on in her life and she needed a place to crash."

"So you don't like her?" Scarlett asked.

Goddamn, I really fucking do. "Yeah, I do, but that's not—"

"See," Scarlett squealed. "I can tell. I know you better than almost anyone, Gibs. I can see it in your face. I don't care what you say, you're sprung on this girl."

Bowie was looking at me with a sly grin on his face. He and Devlin shared a meaningful glance. Cassidy had a very distinct *I know the truth about you* smile.

Grinding my teeth together, I clenched my fists. They were seriously pissing me off. Why couldn't they just leave well enough alone?

"Look, it's complicated—"

"What's her name?"

"Maya, but—" I closed my mouth. Damn it. At least I hadn't said Callie. Crap, I needed to calm down. I was getting too angry to think straight.

"That's pretty," Cassidy said. "Maya what? Or do you not know her last name?"

I glared at Cass. "Yes, I know her last name. It's Davis. And I don't appreciate what you're implying."

"I'm not implying anything," Cassidy said.

"But really, Gibson, what bar were you at last night?" Scarlett asked. "I didn't think y'all were playing out of town again this week."

"I didn't pick her up at a fucking bar," I said. "She works for a record company in L.A. And whether or not she's my secret girlfriend is none of y'all's business."

Damn it. Now I was making it worse. I needed to cut my losses and get out of here.

"Just stay out of it," I said and stomped back to the stage to grab my guitar.

Without bothering to look back, I muscled my way through the bar and out the door. Fuck, I was stupid when I was angry. I hadn't meant to say anything. I should've canceled tonight's gig and stayed home. Made it up to Hung and Corbin somehow.

I got in my truck and put my guitar case on the passenger's seat. My tires squealed on the pavement as I tore out of the parking lot, headed for home.

By the time I got back to my place, I'd calmed down. I parked in front of my house and let my head fall back against the headrest. I'd screwed that up pretty good. Now they really thought I had a girlfriend tucked away in my cabin. And it wouldn't matter how many times I denied it—especially as long as Callie was still essentially in hiding.

I had a feeling she wasn't going to like this. I'd just have to go in there and tell her I'd made a messy situation that much messier.

11

MAYA

a nudge to my leg and a quiet voice woke me with a start. I gasped, blinking, trying to see in the dim light. For a second, I had no idea where I was.

"Didn't mean to scare you," Gibson whispered.

Right, I was at Gibson's house. I'd fallen asleep on his couch, waiting for him to come home.

"It's okay. What time is it?"

"Almost eleven."

I sat up and stretched my arms overhead, the blanket I'd grabbed sliding down to my lap. "It's not even late. I must still be jet-lagged. How was your night?"

He lowered himself to the edge of the couch next to me. "Okay, I guess. But there's something I need to talk to you about."

His tone made me a little nervous. He sounded so serious. "Sure, what's up?"

"I told you people were gonna talk, and they were."

"About your secret girlfriend?" I reached over and poked his arm.

He scowled at me. "Yeah. Scarlett's convinced of it. She was asking me questions and I think I might have made it worse."

"What did you say?"

"I don't even remember, now. I said your name's Maya and you work for a record company. And I tried to tell them you're not my girlfriend, but I got frustrated and I don't think I did a very good job of it."

Could this man be any more adorable? He sat on the edge of the couch with his elbows resting on his knees, his head bent forward. It was like he'd just told me he'd blurted out that Callie Kendall was back.

I rubbed a few circles across his back. Maybe I was being a little too familiar, but he didn't flinch away or tell me to stop. Just glanced at me over his shoulder, a groove between his dark eyebrows.

"I'm sure it's not that bad," I said. "What's the worst that will happen? People will say your girlfriend is staying with you? There's no real harm in that."

He abruptly stood. "No, the worst that will happen is we'll have half the town camped out in front of the house by tomorrow afternoon, everyone waiting to get a look at you. Hell, Cassidy's probably already researching Maya Davis."

"She won't find much. I've never used social media and I try to keep my picture off the internet as much as possible."

He grunted and walked into the kitchen.

I fiddled with the edge of the blanket. I wasn't worried about the town's curiosity because I'd made a decision while Gibson had been out. I wasn't going to run again.

I was still afraid of where this road led, but as I watched him pace from the kitchen and back, I knew it was the right choice. People had protected me for a long time. They'd put themselves at risk to keep me safe. Gibson's parents, Quincy and Henna, even Jenny Leland.

And since my case had been re-opened, that list had only grown. All those people—the Bodines, the Tuckers, the others in town who were trying to find out the truth—had become targets. And most of them had no idea they were in danger.

There was no way I could leave them to face that alone. Not when I could help. It was time I did something to protect the people who'd done so much for me, regardless of the risks.

"Gibson, I need to come forward and tell the truth," I said.

Gibson stopped in front of me. "Tell people that you're Callie?"

I nodded.

"No."

"Yes." My hands trembled and I felt as if I were dissipating into mist. Maya morphing into Callie, then back again. Fear swirling with resolve. I balled my hands into fists to stop them from shaking. "You said yourself, people are going to dig. You have to understand, the judge is dangerous, and not just to me. He could... I don't want to think about what he could do to you. To a lot of people."

"I'm not worried about anyone else. I'm worried about you. You told me you stayed away because it wasn't safe. It's no different now. In fact, it's probably worse."

"That's exactly why I have to come forward."

He crouched in front of me, resting his elbows on his knees. "I don't want to put you in danger."

"Gibson, I have to do this."

His eyes held mine, his gaze intense. A part of me

wanted to shrink away, hide from his scrutiny. Another part wanted to wrap myself around him and beg him not to let me go.

He stood again and rubbed his chin. "Fine, but if you're going to do this, we need to be smart about it. You can't just show up on Lake Drive tomorrow and start saying hi to people."

"What do you suggest?"

"Start small. We'll tell my family first. We can trust them, and it'll get them off my ass."

There was reassurance in that idea. Safety. "Okay."

"That kinda means more than just my brothers and Scarlett. We'll have to tell Cass, and that means Sheriff Tucker. It also means Juney and George. And Shelby."

"That seems like a good start."

"But to the rest of the town, you stay Maya," he said, pointing at me. "At least until we figure out what to do about the judge."

"I can live with that. But if I go out, do you think people will recognize me? Or should I just stay hunkered down here?" Truthfully, the idea of hiding out in Gibson's cabin for a while sounded nice. I liked it here.

"No, if you stay here, it'll just make everyone more curious. They'll assume we're hiding something. We'll just need to sell everyone on the story that you're Maya Davis. People might think you look familiar, but you've changed. And after Abbie Gilbert, no one's gonna be quick to believe the real Callie is back."

Absently, my fingers went to the thin ridge of scar tissue on my cheek. It was the strangest thing. Gibson didn't seem to notice it at all.

"Okay, so we tell your family. And we tell the rest of the town that I'm Maya Davis."

"Right."

Without meaning to, I tongued the notch in my lip. I tended to do that when I was nervous. "And that Maya is your..."

He rubbed the back of his neck. "It would probably help if we went along with the girlfriend story. That'll be gossip enough for the town to chew on for a while."

I grinned at him. "I take it Gibson Bodine with a real girlfriend isn't something they're used to seeing."

He shook his head and grunted.

God, this guy. So adorable. I realized that probably meant his body count was high. A man like him would have no shortage of willing women. But it didn't bother me. I'd had my share of flings and brief relationships. It had been a while since I'd been with anyone, but I'd never stayed with one guy for long. Mostly because I never stayed in one place.

And there I went again, thinking about Gibson all wrong. This pretend girlfriend thing was already going to my head. But I couldn't help it. I didn't typically go for men who were so surly and brooding. Usually that was because they were a client I was trying to coax back into productivity.

But Gibson's gruff demeanor, brooding looks, and gravelly voice were irresistible. It was probably a good thing he'd gotten up from the couch or I might have crawled into his lap.

"I can play along," I said. "Record producer Maya Davis meets Gibson Bodine, sexy carpenter by day, country bar singer by night. Sparks fly and the next thing you know, Bootleg Springs has a new couple to whisper about."

He gave me a quick nod and I couldn't tell how he felt about this plan. Did he hate the idea of having to pretend we were together? Or was he just frustrated that his neighbors wouldn't leave him alone? It was hard to be sure.

"Don't take this the wrong way, but if we tell all those people, but keep it from the rest of the town, will it stay quiet? Like you said, this is Bootleg Springs. Secrets don't stay secret for long."

"Sometimes they do," he said. "And if they tell anyone, I'll..."

"You'll what?"

He scowled. "I don't know, but they won't like it."

GIBSON'S TRUCK bounced on the gravel road, the early morning light filtering through the trees. It wasn't long after dawn, but he'd said the Bodines always did their business over breakfast. I hugged his flannel shirt around me, my stomach churning with nerves. I'd barely slept last night. Seeing Gibson was one thing. But I was about to step in front of nearly a dozen Bootleggers and tell them the truth about who I was.

These people had kept hope alive for almost thirteen years. Left my missing-persons posters up long after the case had gone cold. Held onto the belief that I'd one day be found. This entire community had mourned when they'd heard I was dead.

It both broke my heart and made me furious at the Kendalls.

He stopped, although I couldn't tell why. There was nothing out here. Just trees.

"Where are we going?"

"Secret hot springs," he said. "I signed up for two hours, so we should have plenty of time."

"You have to sign up to go to the hot springs?"

He turned off the truck. "This one, yeah."

"Why?"

His eyebrows lifted.

"Oh," I said, letting out a nervous—and unflattering—giggle. "I get it. To prevent interruptions. So I guess people will just think you and your secret girlfriend are getting serious."

He grunted and opened the door.

We walked down a path in the woods, passing several large *No Trespassing* signs. The air grew heavy with moisture, a thin mist curling between the trees.

Voices up ahead broke the enchanted silence of the woods. Gibson clasped my hand in his and walked in front of me, blocking me from view. My heart rate kicked into overdrive, but Gibson squeezed my hand, leading me forward.

"There you are," a male voice said. "What in the hell are we doing out here?"

"Damn it, Gibs, you said there would be breakfast."

"I'm all for meeting your lady friend, but couldn't we have done this at Moonshine?" That sounded like Scarlett. "Where there's caffeine. And pancakes."

Gibson stopped and, without letting go of my hand, nudged me so I'd stay behind him. "No, we couldn't do this at Moonshine."

"Okay, well, we're all here." The first voice again. Maybe Bowie? "You gonna tell us what this is about?"

He took a deep breath. "I do have a woman staying at my place, but she's not my girlfriend."

"You mean Maya who works for the fancy record company ain't your girlfriend?" Scarlett asked.

"No, she's not. And her name isn't Maya. Well, it is now, but it didn't used to be."

It was as if the entire forest had gone silent. I didn't even hear a bird chirp.

"Gibs," Scarlett said, her voice tentative. "What are you talking about?"

Squeezing my hand again, he glanced over his shoulder and nodded. I met his eyes and nodded back. Here went nothing.

Gibson drew me out from behind him. I clutched his hand, suddenly afraid to let go.

Steam rose from the water of the nearby hot springs, shrouding the area with mist. A group of people stood, mostly in pairs, around the clearing. Most I recognized. A few were new faces, but it was easy to tell who everyone was. Gibson's brothers, Jameson and Bowie, with Leah Mae and Cassidy. June stood in front of George Thompson. A man who had to be Jonah Bodine was on the end, holding hands with a woman I took to be Shelby. Scarlett was with her boyfriend Devlin. And giving me a reassuring smile was Jonah's mom, Jenny.

All eyes were on me. I searched their faces for signs of recognition. Did they know me on sight? Would all of Bootleg know if I showed my face?

"Y'all, this is Callie," Gibson said. "The real Callie."

No one said a word. They stared at me, glanced at each other, and eyed Gibson with confusion.

"Bullshit," Scarlett said, finally breaking the silence. "Since when did you get a sense of humor, Gibs?"

"I'm serious," Gibson said, his tone thick with impatience. "Maya Davis is Callie Kendall."

Jenny stepped forward, her smile warm. "It's true. This is Callie. We met last year, just like I told you."

I struggled to find my voice, the vestiges of my old self warring with my identity as Maya. I wanted to sound calm and collected. At peace with who I was. But I was anything but.

"It really is me. I know I look a little different." I touched the scar on my face. "But I'm Callie Kendall. Or I was. I haven't been Callie for a long time."

"Oh my god. Jenny, you're sure this is her?" Scarlett asked, then turned back to me. "No offense intended, but we've been fooled by a lookalike once. And then there's all the misinformation, what with you supposedly being dead, and Jenny saying you're not."

"Pose a question only the real Callie would answer correctly," June said.

Bowie turned to her. "Juney, I think this is really her."

"We need proof," June said, her tone completely matter-of-fact. "I also intend no offense. But we need to be certain."

"None taken." I took a deep breath. It meant reaching into the box, but I could handle digging through memories of my summers with all the kids in Bootleg. "Go ahead. Ask me something."

"I have one," Bowie said. "The last summer you were here, who fell off the roof of the Rusty Tool?"

It took me a second, but the memory came to me. I smiled. "Nash Larabee."

Bowie nodded. "And how many bones did he break?"

"Zero," I said. "People said it was a miracle. But two days later, he tripped on the flat sidewalk and broke three. That night you drove him down to the lake in a recliner tied up in the back of someone's pickup."

"She's right," Jameson said. "I remember that."

"Yeah," Bowie said, his voice awed.

"There's still something I gotta see." Cassidy stepped

closer and lowered her voice. "Would you mind pushing your sleeve up a bit?"

Gibson shifted closer. Was he growling?

"Easy, Gibs," Cassidy said. "Like Juney said, we need to be certain."

I pried my hand from Gibson's and held out my arm, palm up. I knew exactly what she was looking for, although I had no idea how she would know this. With a deep breath, I pushed the sleeve almost to my elbow, revealing my tattooed forearm.

Tattooed, and scarred.

Cassidy gently held my wrist and looked closely at my arm. Touched it gently, feeling the ridges of my scars. She nodded and spoke quietly. "Your tattoos are real pretty."

"How'd you know what was under them?" I whispered.

"I've seen a picture."

My stomach felt like it had turned to ice, but I just nodded, quickly pushing down my sleeve.

"It's her," Cassidy said. "It's Callie Kendall."

"You're here?" Scarlett asked, her eyes brimming with tears. "You're really alive and you're standing right here."

My eyes started to sting. "Yeah."

"I'm hugging you now, that's just what's happening." Scarlett came forward and threw her arms around me.

I hugged Scarlett back, tears breaking free from the corners of my eyes. Cassidy was next, then Bowie, Jameson, and Leah Mae. They introduced me to the others—Devlin, Shelby, Jonah, and George. Jenny wrapped me in a tight hug and by the time we were finished, my vision was blurry from crying.

"I'm glad you're not deceased." June gave me an awkward pat on the shoulder.

"Thanks." I wiped the tears off my cheeks. "Me too."

"Wow," Cassidy said. "This makes a lot of sense, but I have even more questions than I did last night."

"What are you talking about, Cass?" Scarlett asked.

"After Gibs told us the friend-named-Maya story, I did a little digging. I found a Maya Davis on Attalon Records' website, but it was almost impossible to find any more information. No photos of her. And there's nothing prior to twelve or thirteen years ago—like she didn't exist. But I guess she didn't."

"I know you have so many questions—"

"Only like a million," Scarlett said. "Where have you been all this time? Why did you disappear? Why didn't you ever come back?"

"She did come back," June said. "She's right there."

"But why did it take thirteen years?" Scarlett continued. "Why did my daddy help you, and why did he keep your sweater?"

"Enough," Gibson said, his voice booming through the woods. "Scar, I think we all know why she left. And she couldn't come back for the same reason. It wasn't safe. It still isn't."

"The judge," Devlin said.

"You didn't give yourself those scars, did you?" Cassidy asked.

I shook my head. "No, I didn't."

"Did you ever try to tell someone?" Shelby asked. "A friend or maybe... a teacher?"

I started to say no, but that wasn't true. "Once. I told a teacher, but only because she was persistent. Nothing ever came of it, and I was too scared to try again. I hid the evidence under my clothes. As for your dad, Scarlett, he found me on the side of the road and agreed to help me get away. But I don't know why he kept the sweater."

"His drunk ass probably forgot he had it," Gibson said.

"I think he kept it as a reminder of something good he'd done," Jenny said. "He had a lot of regrets in his life. I should know; I'm one of them."

"Oh, Jenny, don't," Scarlett said.

"It's okay, I made my peace with that a long time ago," Jenny said. "But I really think that's why. Maybe it was something he felt he could be proud of."

My stomach churned with nausea. I needed to change the subject—stop talking about that night. There were hazy spots in my memory that made my vision seem blurry. Like something was trying to break free. I shied away from it. "I want you all to know how sorry I am for disappearing. I'm sorry you didn't know I was okay."

"She didn't have a choice," Gibson said, his voice uncharacteristically soft.

"Where did you go?" Scarlett asked.

"A little town in upstate New York called Blue Moon Bend. A couple, Quincy and Henna, took me in. They were friends of a friend. I think you'd have to meet them to understand why, but I knew I could trust them to help me. I went to them thinking they'd shuttle me off to the next place where I could hide, but they insisted I stay. They're amazing people. A little odd, maybe, but amazing. They took very good care of me. Helped me heal. I lived there until I was nineteen. Since then, I've been all over the world."

"Where do you live now?" Leah Mae asked.

I hesitated, not sure how to answer. "Well, I was just on tour with a band—Outbound Platinum. Before that, I was in Seattle for a little while. Before that, it was Nashville." I paused again, thinking back. My trips tended to blur together. "I was in London for a few months. I don't have a permanent place to live, really. I stay in hotels a lot. Sometimes rent a temporary apartment. If I'm in L.A. for more than a few days, I crash with a friend. And I try to get out to Blue Moon every so often to see Quincy and Henna."

"Always running," Jenny said.

I'd never thought of it as running, but perhaps there was a bit of truth to that. My lifestyle made it easier to stay hidden. "Yeah, I guess so."

"But you can come back now," Scarlett said.

"Not so fast, Scar," Gibson said. "I need to make something perfectly clear. This stays between us. To everyone else, she's Maya. Anyone so much as *thinks* the name Callie in front of other people, I'll break them in half."

"Gibson, you know I can't do that," Cassidy said.

"That's okay," I said quickly. I could feel Gibson getting angry. "Your dad needs to know, too. I'm prepared to talk to him, as long as we can keep it quiet for now."

"Gibs is actually right about keeping her a secret," Devlin said. "We can't forget what we're dealing with here. There's a falsified forensics report, harassment, not to mention more than one mysterious death that could be tied to the judge."

Jonah stepped forward. "I'm seconding this. We need to be very careful."

"He's dangerous," I said. "Please don't underestimate him."

"Which is why y'all are going to keep your fucking mouths shut," Gibson said.

"Of course we'll keep her safe," Scarlett said. Her mouth turned up in a little grin. "But y'all realize you'll have to keep up the pretense that you're dating, right? People might look at you twice, but if we all stick to the story that you're Gibson's girlfriend Maya, it'll work."

My eyes darted to Gibson, but I couldn't read his expression. "Yeah, that's the plan."

"She's right," Leah Mae said. "We want to control the narrative. In this case, it means giving Bootleg Springs something else to talk about."

"A distraction," Devlin said, nodding.

"And let's be honest, Gibs," Bowie said, patting him on the back, a big grin on his face. "You walking around town with a girl on your arm is going to be one hell of a distraction."

12

MAYA

*G*ibson's family left the hot springs in small groups about ten minutes apart. They didn't want anyone in town noticing that we'd all been out there at the same time. I watched June and George go—the last of the group besides me and Gibson. June was telling George what sounded like a complicated plan to take a winding route back to town to throw off any pursuers. She didn't seem swayed by George's good-natured reminder that no one was actually in pursuit.

We left shortly after and went straight back to Gibson's house. Someone had left a tin-foil-wrapped dish outside the front door with a little note. Gibson brought it inside and tossed it on the counter, grumbling about nosy neighbors.

He got two calls and a text, all from different family members confirming that the Kendalls weren't in town. Their house had been vacant for at least several days, maybe longer. That was good news. There was a low risk that I'd run into them unexpectedly.

Which meant I could go into town.

After a late breakfast of scrambled eggs—Gibson cooked today—we decided it was time to see if we could pull off our plan. Either I was going to show up in Bootleg and cause an uproar, or they were going to buy our story that I was Maya.

We went outside and Gibson locked the door behind me. It was still warm summer weather here in West Virginia, the sun bright in the clear blue sky. We walked out to his truck, the gravel crunching beneath my sandals.

"What happened to your old truck?" I asked. "The blue one you used to have."

"It died," he said. "It was old when I got it, and I wasn't exactly easy on it. I've had this one for a few years. I got it mostly to haul lumber, but I've been driving it full-time for a while."

We both got in and I fastened my seatbelt. "Why?"

"I hit a patch of ice trying to avoid a deer last winter in my other car," he said. "Wound up hitting a tree instead. I had to save up to get the body work done. And now I have to wait because my guy's busy. But I don't trust my baby with anyone else."

"Your baby?"

"Nineteen sixty-eight Charger," he said with pride.

I could imagine him in a hot muscle car. "That's literally the perfect car for you."

"Yep." His lips turned up in a little smile. "She purrs like a kitten."

Shifting in my seat, I looked out the window. He really needed to stop being so effortlessly sexy. He was killing me.

We headed out the long drive toward the road, then down the twisting highway that led into Bootleg Springs.

I braced myself as the town came into view, expecting to

feel a rush of anxiety. The last time I'd seen this place was the day I left.

But instead of hitting me with a flood of bad memories, the sight of Bootleg Springs was comforting. It had changed in thirteen years, but not so much that it wasn't recognizable.

There were more stores and restaurants than I remembered, but the town still had a quaint lived-in feel. The buildings were worn, but friendly. A small knot of senior citizens sat on benches outside the Brunch Club. And a chicken strutted her stuff down the sidewalk, stopping to scratch and peck.

"Is that Mona Lisa McNugget?"

Gibson glanced over as he parked. "Yep. I think this is Mona Lisa the fifth, though."

"I guess I don't know the lifespan of a chicken. They just keep renaming them Mona Lisa?"

"It's tradition."

I really had missed this place.

He found a spot and turned off his truck, but paused, not reaching for the door handle to get out. "Are you sure you're ready for this?"

I fluffed out my hair and slipped on my oversize sunglasses. "I'm ready."

I'd decided to wear a tank top today, letting my tattooed arms show. Callie had always worn long sleeves to hide her wounds. But as Maya, I'd tattooed a delicate mandala pattern over my scars. Not only did it make them almost invisible, it had been my way of taking my body back.

Gibson got out and I followed him onto the sidewalk, shouldering my big handbag. I turned a slow circle, letting the moment sink in. I was back in Bootleg Springs.

A tingly feeling skittered up my spine. Henna would say

it was a premonition, or the energy of the universe telling me something. I decided it meant I was where I was supposed to be—that I'd made the right decision in staying.

Without quite looking at me, Gibson cleared his throat and took my hand in his. I couldn't tell if he was nervous or irritated at having to hold hands. Gibs had always been a little rough around the edges, and it was becoming clear that time hadn't softened him. If anything, he was harder now than he'd been when I'd known him before.

Not that it bothered me. He wasn't trying to hide anything. So many of the artists I worked with adopted a mask, an identity they showed the world. Usually it was the person they thought their fans expected them to be, but it wasn't really who they were.

I got the sense that with Gibson, what you saw was what you got. I liked that about him.

I also liked the way it felt to walk with him down the sidewalk, hand in hand. But I knew I shouldn't dwell on that.

He led me toward Yee Haw Yarn and Coffee. Heads turned as we walked, people's eyes darting between the two of us. It made me a little nervous, but it didn't seem like anyone recognized me. I doubted even Gibson would have known who I was if he'd seen me with big sunglasses on.

And they weren't really looking at *me*, anyway. They were looking at *us*. Maybe he'd been right—Gibson Bodine walking around town with a girl was gossip enough.

The scent of coffee and sugary baked goods filled the air as Gibson held the door open for me. I kept my sunglasses on for now—I figured it worked with my look, what with my wild hair and tattoos, and they made me feel like I could hide in plain sight.

"Hey, Gibs," the young lady behind the counter said. Her eyes flicked to me, then back again. "What can I get you?"

"The usual." He glanced at me and raised his eyebrows. "Maya?"

Hearing him say my name—that name—took some of the tension out of my body. "Coffee with cream, please."

"Sure," she said with a smile. "To go?"

"Yeah." Gibson let go of my hand long enough to take out his wallet and toss some cash on the counter. He stuffed a couple dollars in the tip jar, then clasped my hand again.

A guy I didn't recognize sat at a table near the window, staring at me. Gibson stepped in front of me, blocking me from the guy's view. I leaned slightly to the left to peek around Gibson's shoulder and caught a glimpse of the guy's face going pale.

Was Gibson growling at him?

I bit back a giggle while the guy turned away, almost knocking his coffee over in the process. I'd never been with a man who was so protective. Not that Gibson and I were actually together. But I was grateful for the way he seemed to guard me. Selling my identity as Maya to the people of Bootleg was important to keeping me safe. And with Gibson Bodine standing guard, I felt surprisingly secure.

We got our coffees and left. The late summer air felt good. It reminded me of long days spent at the lake. Swimming in the bath-like water. The smell of sunscreen and bonfire smoke. The good parts of the time when I'd been Callie.

"Hey there, y'all." Scarlett's chipper voice came from up ahead. "Good to see you, Maya. How do you like Bootleg Springs?"

Gibson groaned and muttered something under his

breath about not needing to yell. But the conspiratorial grin on Scarlett's face made me smile.

"It's such a nice town," I said. From the corner of my eye, I noticed a couple of the seniors sitting outside the Brunch Club leaning forward, like they were trying to eavesdrop. "So far I like it here."

"Course it's a nice town," Scarlett said. "Well, Maya, I hope you enjoy your visit. Nice to see you again, Maya."

"Jesus, Scar," Gibson said. "You don't have to keep saying her name."

Scarlett lowered her voice. "I'm just making sure everyone heard."

"So where are we off to next?" I asked.

"I need to run to the hardware store," Gibson said with a shrug.

"I have a better idea." Scarlett sidled up next to me and slipped her arm through mine. "Let's do a little shopping."

"No," Gibson said.

"Aw, come on, Gibs," Scarlett said. "Your sister needs time to get to know your new girlfriend. This is how things are done. Girl bonding and all that. We'll catch up with you later."

Scarlett tugged me forward and it took half a second for Gibson to let go of my hand. I glanced back at him and shrugged one shoulder. "I'll see you in a bit."

He glowered at us but didn't reply.

"I know the perfect place," Scarlett said. She kept her arm tucked around mine, like we were longtime best friends. "Leah Mae just opened up her own shop, and she has the cutest clothes. No pressure to spend money, but it's fun to look."

"Actually, I could use a few new things."

"See? I told you this was perfect."

Scarlett greeted people as we walked, waving and taking every opportunity to introduce me. She even shouted across the street. "Hey, y'all, this is Gibson's new girlfriend Maya."

I smiled and lifted my hand in a little wave each time. When we got to a small storefront with a sign that said *Boots and Lace*, we stopped. I glanced over my shoulder. Gibson was still standing in the middle of the sidewalk, his arms crossed over his thick chest, coffee in one hand.

Scarlett pushed the door open. With one last glance at Gibs, I went inside behind her, taking off my sunglasses and tucking them in my bag.

The air-conditioned store felt nice. It was small, but bright and cheery, with an eclectic mix of clothing and accessories. There were distressed jeans, flowing dresses, frilly tops, and tight skirts. Cowboy boots sat on a shelf next to stiletto heels. A display near the counter sparkled with earrings, necklaces, and bracelets, as well as some very cute handbags.

There weren't any other customers, but Leah Mae stood behind the counter, an open book in her hands. Her eyebrows were lifted, her mouth parted in a circle.

"Whatcha reading?" Scarlett asked.

Leah Mae startled, blinking as she looked up from her book. "Oh my god, you scared me. Sorry, I didn't hear you come in. It's that book for June's book club. Have you read it yet?"

"Not yet." Scarlett pulled on the sleeve of a blue shirt. "Is it any good?"

"Well..." Leah Mae's cheeks colored. She closed the book and tucked it beneath the counter. "Yes, it's really good. But... different. You kind of need to read it for yourself to see."

"Guess I'll have to start it tonight," Scarlett said.

"Hey, Maya," Leah Mae said. "What are y'all up to?"

"We're doing a little shopping while Gibson goes to the hardware store," I said. "Or, at least, I think he's going to the hardware store. Last I saw, he was still standing in the same spot, watching us walk away."

"Oh, Gibs is just being overprotective," Scarlett said. She grabbed a dress and held it up to me. "This would look adorable on you."

"It really would," Leah Mae said.

I took the dress from Scarlett and draped it over my arm. "Is he always so—"

"Grumpy?" Scarlett filled in for me.

"I was thinking guarded and serious, but yeah."

"He does have a temper on him, but he wouldn't hurt a fly," Scarlett said. She paused and pressed her lips together, as if thinking. "Well, he wouldn't hurt a fly unless it mouthed off to him at the Lookout and he was lookin' for a brawl. But that's all Bootleg men."

"True," Leah Mae said, nodding.

Scarlett glanced around. "There's no one in the dressing room, is there?"

Leah Mae shook her head. "No. I had customers earlier, but right now it's just us."

"Have you heard anything yet about..." Scarlett trailed off, nodding her head toward me.

"Oh yeah," Leah Mae said. "Jameson and I had breakfast at Moonshine after... you know. People are all aflutter about Gibson's new girlfriend."

"But just that, right?" Scarlett asked. "Gossip's all about *Maya*."

"Yep. There's talk about how y'all met. There's apparently a rumor going 'round that you were a mail-order bride, but I don't think many believe it. Mostly people are just surprised that Gibson has a real girlfriend."

"That's what I've been hearing, too," Scarlett said.

I took slow steps through the store, touching items as if my attention was on the clothes. But I was thinking about Gibson. "I take it that's big news? Gibson having a girlfriend?"

"Is it ever. I can't remember the last time he admitted he was dating someone. Maybe not since..." Scarlett paused and made a disgusted face. "I won't even say her name. Anyway, he takes his lone wolf status seriously. Mostly just occasional hook-ups with random girls he meets when he's playing."

"Scarlett," Leah Mae hissed.

I bit my bottom lip to keep from laughing.

"Well, it's true," Scarlett said. She held up another dress, first in front of herself, then on me. "This one's more my color. Anyway, when it comes to Gibs, there's no point in sugar-coating it. But don't let that put you off. My brother's a good man, deep down."

"That is your color. And his relationship history isn't my business anyway."

"Speak of the devil," Leah Mae said, pointing out the window.

I glanced outside. Misty Lynn Prosser paused, snapping gum between her teeth. Her eyes roamed over the window display. She was dressed in a hot pink tube top. Maybe it was just the angle, but it looked like her boobs might be crooked.

"Oh hell no," Scarlett said. "If she comes in, can I kick her ass out?"

"Yes," Leah Mae said.

"Good."

A flash of anger burst through me. She'd stolen Gibson's wallet and turned in the photos he'd kept. Photos of me and him. It didn't bother me that he'd dated her. That had been a long time ago, and he wasn't really my boyfriend anyway. But it did bother me—deeply—that she'd used me to try to hurt him. It made me want to march out there and give her a piece of my mind.

Misty Lynn flipped her bleached-out hair over her shoulder and walked by without coming inside.

"Damn," Scarlett said. "I was hoping I'd get to escort her out."

"She never comes in," Leah Mae said. "Which is fine by me. I know you're supposed to be courteous to your customers no matter who they are, but I think Misty Lynn is the universal exception to that rule."

"I agree," I said.

"Not that you need a reason, but do you have bad blood with Misty Lynn?" Scarlett asked.

I glanced toward the window again. "Not from before. But she turned in those pictures of me and Gibs. Am I wrong in assuming she did it to hurt him, and not because she thought it was the right thing to do? Maybe I'm jumping to conclusions."

"You're not jumping to anything," Leah Mae said. "Bex told me Misty Lynn sashayed into the sheriff's office like she was expecting a blue ribbon. She didn't even show a lick of remorse that she'd broken Gibson's window, or that she'd committed theft. She wanted to get him in trouble."

"God, that pisses me off."

"She cheated on him, too," Scarlett said.

"She what?"

Scarlett nodded. "Back when they dated. It was right after our mom died. That's mostly why I hate her so much. I didn't like her before—let's be honest, she's never been very likable. But after she cheated on my brother? She made an enemy for life."

I decided in that moment that I hated Misty Lynn, too. *Hate* was a strong word, but no one hurt my Gibson and got away with it. I didn't care if he wasn't my boyfriend. He was still mine, in a way, even if we were just friends.

"That woman needs a solid dose of Bootleg Justice," Leah Mae said.

I couldn't have agreed more.

Leah Mae and Scarlett chatted a while longer—mostly about Leah Mae and Jameson's wedding plans. I wandered through the store, looking at clothes. I really did need a few new things. I didn't own a lot of clothes, mostly because I hadn't had a permanent place to live for so long. I didn't own a lot of anything. Living out of a suitcase didn't leave room for many belongings.

Running my fingers over the soft fabric of a floral dress, I imagined my clothes hanging in a closet, my things folded neatly and tucked away in drawers that smelled like cedar. What would that be like? To have a home again? To belong somewhere?

I liked my life. I'd made a career for myself in music, which wasn't an easy thing to do. I enjoyed traveling, touring, meeting new people, seeing new places.

But Jenny had been right. I'd spent a long time running.

The door swung open and Gibson poked his head in. "Finished. You ready?"

"That was fast." Scarlett smirked at him. "I guess you couldn't wait to get back to your girlfriend."

He glared at her.

I laughed softly. "Almost ready. I'm just going to get this."

Gibson stepped inside and let the door shut behind him.

He had a bag that said *The Rusty Tool* in his hand. Leah Mae and Scarlett seemed to share a look, but Leah Mae just took the dress and scanned the tag.

"I'll give you the family discount," she said with a wink.

"Thanks." I paid and she handed me a cute little shopping bag.

A group of girls—probably high school age—came in, giggling and talking. Gibson appeared to ignore them. In fact, he appeared to be ignoring everyone except me.

"Bye, ladies," I said and headed for the door.

"See y'all later," Scarlett said. "Thanks for the mini-shopping trip, Maya. Have fun with your girlfriend, Gibs."

Gibson grumbled as he took my hand and led me out the door.

13

GIBSON

*T*he trip into town yesterday had done its job, solidifying Callie's identity as Maya. Grudgingly, I had to admit that Scarlett loud-mouthing her name on the street had been effective. And with my family all confirming the story, Bootleg Springs was not only convinced, they were too distracted by the fact that I supposedly had a girlfriend to question her name.

It also seemed to have taken the attention off my visit to the sheriff's office, and those pictures I'd been carrying in my wallet.

Her secret was safe, for now.

Cassidy had passed the truth about Callie on to her dad, and he'd called me to ask some questions. He told me straight that his first priority was keeping her safe. Made me feel better about cooperating with him. We'd agreed that it would be best if he met with Callie at his house, under the auspices of dinner, rather than at the station. Dinner with the Tuckers wouldn't raise eyebrows, whereas the new girl in town meeting with the sheriff in his office would.

For now, we just needed to lay low and keep up the pretense that we were dating. I'd have been happy to hunker down here and ignore the town. But I knew that if we didn't show our faces, it would start feeding the rumor mill again. I didn't need half the town claiming I was holding her hostage.

Which was why I was standing in my living room, wearing my best jeans and boots, waiting for a girl I wasn't dating to finish getting ready. For our date.

I looked out the window, my arms crossed, feeling nervous as hell. Why? No idea. We were just grabbing dinner at Moonshine—not even a fancy date. Then Scarlett was having a bonfire out at her place. The new house she and Devlin were building would be done before next summer, so she wanted to get in some more bonfires at her lake cottage while they were still living there.

Nothing to be nervous about. It wasn't even a real date. And since when did I get nervous about a girl? Since never.

Callie came out of my room wearing a floral dress. It had thin straps and stopped just above her knees, showing a lot of tanned skin—not to mention those sexy-ass tattoos. Her thick, multicolored hair fell in waves down her back and she'd put on bright lipstick and a pair of dark-rimmed glasses.

"I didn't know you wore glasses."

"I don't," she said. "They're not prescription. They just have a blue-light filter."

"A what?"

She adjusted the glasses. "Electronic devices emit blue light, and some people say it's bad for us to be exposed to so much. Someone in Blue Moon told Quincy and Henna, and they insisted I get some special glasses. The ones they suggested looked more like safety goggles so I found these as a compromise. I figure they might help me look different, since I won't be wearing sunglasses in the dark. It worked for Superman, right?"

"Huh."

"You don't like them?"

There was a hint of a smile on her lips and I had a feeling that if I said no, I hated them, she'd just smile that big pretty smile of hers and go on wearing them. But I didn't hate them. They looked adorable on her.

"They're fine."

"Okay, good. Are we ready?" she asked. "How do I look?"

She did a little twirl and I swallowed hard. She looked sexy as hell. Like the sort of girl I'd have been proud to introduce to my mom. And the sort I'd hope I'd get to bring home with me after a night out.

But she wasn't. She was Callie, and this wasn't a real date. But damn it, she looked amazing.

"You look all right," I lied.

"I guess that's good enough." She grabbed her giant handbag and slung it over her shoulder.

"Do you really need all that? What do you even keep in there?"

She glanced down at her bag. "No, probably not. I'm just used to carrying it around."

"Looks like you could live out of that thing."

"I have lived out of it." She patted the bag. "More than once."

"Fine. Let's just go." I turned for the door.

"We don't have to go out if you don't want to," she said.

I paused with my hand on the doorknob. "What makes you think I don't want to?"

"I don't know. You just seem kinda grouchy tonight."

She wasn't wrong. I was wound up so tight I felt like I might snap. Flexing my fist, I took a deep breath. I needed to calm my ass down. I didn't even know what had me so fucking irritable.

"I don't mind," I said without turning to look at her. "Dinner at Moonshine sounds good."

"Okay, if you're sure. Because dinner at Moonshine sounds amazing. I haven't eaten there in so long."

I cracked a smile and glanced over my shoulder. "It's the best."

She smiled again, so pretty it almost hurt to look at her. The scar on her face made her lip curl at an odd angle, but it was cute. Distinctive.

And right there was a part of what had me so edgy. Looking at her sent my emotions spinning out of control. She was beautiful in ways I'd never expected. But that scar on her face was a constant reminder of what her father had done to her. The mix of desire and anger was potent, almost intoxicating.

I didn't have an outlet for any of it. And it was making me a grumpy bastard. Grumpier than normal, anyway. But none of that was her fault.

"You don't look *all right*, you look beautiful," I grumbled. "The dress is nice."

"Thank you, Gibs." She stuck her hands in little openings in the dress and twisted back and forth a few times. "It has pockets."

I chuckled. She really needed to stop being so goddamn adorable. She was killing me.

We went out to my truck and I opened the door for her. Figured I could drum up some manners. I drove us into town and parked outside Moonshine. She waited while I got the door for her again. Took her hand to help her out. There was that smile again, making my insides feel all twisted.

Without really thinking about it, I clasped her hand while we walked. It was small and soft against my calloused palm.

It felt good.

Moonshine Diner had been a staple in Bootleg Springs for as long as I could remember. Hadn't changed much, either, which I appreciated. Still filled the block around it with the scent of good cooking.

Most of the tables were full tonight, but there was an open one near the back. The din of conversation hushed for a few seconds when we walked in. Heads turned. People watched. Some whispered to each other.

I held Callie's hand and ignored them. It only took a few seconds for people to go back to their dinners, the noise level rising again.

It was working. We were hiding her in plain sight.

Clarabell appeared next to our table half a second after we sat down. "Hey, y'all. This must be Maya. I'm Clarabell. So nice to meet you, sweetie."

"Thanks," Callie said. "Nice to meet you too."

"Gibson Bodine, I'm plum tickled you brought her in," Clarabell said. She turned back to Callie. "I've been dying to meet the girl who finally tamed this one. What with everyone else in his family pairing off, gettin' themselves engaged and whatnot, it's high time he settled down too."

Callie gave me an amused smile. "You think he's ready for that?"

"Oh sure. They all are, sweetie; it just takes some of them longer to figure out what's best for them."

"All right, Clarabell," I said. "Can we just have our menus?"

"Of course." She handed us each a menu.

I put mine down without looking.

"Can I get you anything to drink to start?" she asked.

"Water."

"I'd love a sweet tea," Callie said.

"Coming right up," Clarabell said, then walked away.

Callie leaned across the table and lowered her voice to a whisper. "She looks exactly the same. Do they still have those huge waffles with the whipped cream topping?"

"For breakfast, yeah."

Her eyes lit up. "Can we come back in the morning?"

God, that smile. "Sure."

She scrunched her shoulders and went back to her menu.

Clarabell came back to take our orders and thankfully left out any more relationship commentary. Our food didn't take long to come out—an open-faced turkey sandwich for me, roast beef with mashed potatoes for Callie.

Sallie Mae Brickman walked by our table no less than eight times during the course of our meal, pretending like she'd forgotten how to get to the restroom. And I heard people whispering things about us, as if they didn't realize we could hear them.

'BOUT TIME *that Gibson got himself a woman in his life.*

WITH ALL HIS SIBLINGS FIXIN' *to get hitched, it's a good thing he found her.*

THEY MAKE A CUTE COUPLE, *don't they?*

. . .

I STILL SAY she's a mail-order bride.

CALLIE STIFLED a giggle with her hand. "Mail-order bride?"

I rolled my eyes. "I don't know where they got that one."

"About that. I've been meaning to ask, did you find me in the online catalog, or the print version?"

"Print," I said, not missing a beat. "Your hair really stood out on that glossy paper."

She fluffed her hair out. "Ah, so it was my mermaid hair that sucked you in."

God, Callie, everything about you is sucking me in. "Must have been."

"Well, I'm glad you picked me. Although if I'm a mail-order bride, where's my ring?" She held out her left hand, fingers splayed.

Clarabell stopped at our table right as Callie said *where's my ring*. "That's a good question, sweetie." She lowered her voice, as if somehow that was going to keep Callie from hearing. "Gibs, if you're fixin' to pop the question to your lady, let me know. We can hide the ring in her dessert."

"Simmer down, Clarabell, that won't be necessary."

Callie stifled another giggle.

Clarabell shrugged. "Suit yourself. But if you ask me, not enough of y'all are getting engaged in my diner. It's a perfectly romantic spot."

"Has anyone gotten engaged here?" Callie asked.

"Sure have. Ricky Grant proposed to Susannah Varney right there where you're sitting."

"That must have been twenty-five years ago," I said.

"Most likely," she said with a smile. "It was an exciting day."

"That's sweet," Callie said.

Clarabell took our empty plates. "Sweet as my strawberry rhubarb pie. Speaking of, can I get you two lovebirds some dessert?"

Lovebirds? Jesus. "No. Just the check so we can get out of here."

"All right, don't get your britches in a bunch." She glanced at Callie. "You sure, sweetie? I have some lemon meringue pie that's a little slice of heaven."

"Thanks, but dinner was so good, I couldn't eat another bite."

Clarabell smiled and went to get our check. I took some money out of my wallet and dropped it on the table. It was more than enough for dinner and a nice tip. Too big of a tip, what with Clarabell's questions about rings and engagements. But I just wanted to get out of Moonshine.

Callie put a hand to her stomach while we walked to my truck. "I'm so full, but it was so worth it."

"Glad you enjoyed it."

"What's next? Bonfire at Scarlett's?"

"That's the plan." I opened the truck door for her again. Kinda wished it was my Charger. She'd look damn good in the front seat of my baby.

We drove down to Scarlett's place, a little postage-stamp-sized cottage on the lake. Because she was Scarlett, it was cute. And although she and Devlin were pretty cramped living there together, her little scrap of beach was great for a bonfire.

I parked among the cars and trucks already here. We got out and wandered down to the beach. Music played from someone's stereo, there were two coolers full of beer, and a whole mess of people stood, sat, laughed, danced, and drank around the fire.

Jameson was dragging what was basically a tree trunk toward the already large bonfire. Bowie and Buck helped him hoist it onto the pile, sending a flurry of sparks into the sky.

I said the requisite hellos to my sister and Devlin. Scarlett squealed with excitement and made sure to address Maya by name—loudly. Leah Mae and Cassidy were more subtle, greeting her with friendly hugs.

June and George arrived with June's pet pig, Katherine. George joined Bowie and Jameson while June found a spot off to the side and opened a book, using her headlamp to light the pages.

Callie and I sat on one of the old logs that served as a bench. I hesitated for a second, glancing around, then gently put my arm around her. It was what a boyfriend would do. I expected her to stiffen or shy away. But she didn't. She nestled in closer, letting her arm drape over my leg, and rested her head against my chest.

The lavender smell of her hair was strangely relaxing, and her warm body felt good tucked up against mine. There was nothing awkward. Nothing forced. This didn't feel like pretending. It felt like she really was my girl. And the craziest part was how much I liked that idea.

I was about as anti-relationship as a guy could get. Somehow my siblings had sailed into adulthood still willing to take a chance on love. Not me. Maybe it was because I was the oldest. I remembered too much of what my parents had been like. Sure, they'd had their moments. Dancing in the kitchen. Smiling together. Acting like they didn't feel trapped by marriage and family.

But those moments weren't what had stuck in my

memory. When I looked back, I saw the fighting. The resentment. The regrets. I'd decided a long time ago that I wasn't going to do that to myself. And I wasn't going to drag someone else down with me, either.

But ever since Callie had shown up at my door and jumped into my arms, I'd been thinking things. Dangerous things. And with her leaning against me like this, soft and familiar, it felt like all those reasons I'd held onto didn't matter nearly as much as I'd thought.

"Hey Gibs, how about a song?" Buck asked. He held an old acoustic guitar out toward me.

Callie sat up and I reluctantly dropped my arm to take the guitar. I settled it in my lap and strummed a chord. Out of tune. Took me a minute to tune it, but when I was done, it didn't sound half bad.

I plucked the strings, letting a song come to me. "Mamas Don't Let Your Babies Grow Up to Be Cowboys" felt right. Long title, but a damn good song. Someone turned off the music as I strummed the opening chords and sang the first line.

A few bars in, a voice joined mine. Callie's. We'd sung this song together a hundred times. Of course, no one else knew that. No one else in Bootleg had really known she could sing.

She found the harmony easily, and I shifted so I could see her while I played. The firelight reflected off her glasses and made her skin glow. Her sultry voice mingled with my deeper tone. She sounded different now. I'd noticed it the other night. Teenage Callie's voice had been soft and pure, like a bell. Maya's voice was richer, sexier. It was mesmerizing.

I lost track of everything but the music. The heat of the fire, the people dancing, talking, laughing—it all went away.

It was just me and Callie, alone in the woods again. Singing an old favorite.

The song ended and the party erupted in whoops and hollers. My eyes stayed locked with hers. She smiled at me and my heart nearly beat right out of my chest.

I was in big fucking trouble.

14

MAYA

$\mathcal{L}$ ife in Bootleg Springs moved at a different pace. It was slower. More relaxed. People lingered on the street corners to catch up on the latest gossip. Stopped to help their neighbors bring in groceries. Brought people homemade muffins and jam in a basket, just because.

It was a far cry from life in the music business. Touring, moving from city to city. Waking up in a new place every few days, sometimes without really knowing where you were. Long hours spent in the studio with the constant pressure to deliver.

I'd been here less than a week, and I could already feel myself acclimating. It helped that I wasn't working. I checked in with Oliver again and let him know I was staying in the area to take care of some personal business. He said he was glad I was taking a break.

Gibson had an order to fill, so I'd spent the last couple of days happily relaxing at his house while he worked. As promised, he'd taken me to Moonshine for breakfast—twice —and their waffles were just as delicious as I remembered. In addition to eating too much, I'd watched a baking competition show—and subsequently ruined three batches of macarons thinking I could duplicate what I'd seen—practiced yoga in the field outside his house, and painted my nails to match my hair.

It was the most downtime I'd had in ages, and it was surprisingly nice. I didn't usually slow down like this. I went from project to project. City to city. Always moving, never sitting still.

The sun was shining this afternoon, so I grabbed my handbag and went outside. Gibson had a single chair out on the back porch, facing a view of the woods beyond. I settled in, sitting sideways so I could drape my legs over one arm. The air was fresh and clean, a light breeze easing the heat of the late summer day. The sound of Gibson's power tools carried from his workshop.

Gibson Bodine. He was such an enigma. Usually I was adept at getting to the heart of a person—at figuring out what made them tick. It was what made me good at my job. But Gibson was hard to crack. One thing I knew for sure. He was hiding a lot of pain behind that angry façade.

What happened to you, Gibson? Who hurt you so badly?

When I worked with a struggling artist or band, I liked to leave them with something that would keep them on the right track after I'd gone. I couldn't be there forever to make sure they didn't drift back into conflict or malaise or self-doubt.

Sometimes I taught them meditation techniques to stay calm. I'd done conflict resolution role-playing, left a box of notes with things to spark creativity, and helped brainstorm ideas for hobbies that would give them some downtime. No one would ever believe how many badass rock stars I'd taught to crochet.

I felt like Gibson needed something else in his life. Something to soften him up a little. Bring him some happiness. But what would make Gibson happy? He wasn't exactly a people person, that was obvious. His work seemed to be fulfilling, and he had his music.

I thought back on Oliver's offer, but it was impossible to imagine Gibson as a rock star. He had the talent for it, no question. And the looks. Fans would eat up Gibson Bodine with a spoon. Even his prickly personality wouldn't be a problem, not from a popularity standpoint. His gruff demeanor combined with that husky voice of his—not to mention his rugged sex appeal—would be absolute catnip to millions. With the right backing, he'd be huge.

And he'd hate it.

Oliver would sign him in a heartbeat. And just to be sure I wasn't making the wrong assumption, I'd ask Gibson about it again. But I was almost positive I knew the answer. He didn't want that life.

Some people did. They wanted fame and fortune and the rush of playing for a packed house. Thousands of people screaming their name, singing along to their songs. They lived for it. And you could tell those people from the ones who didn't. The ones who loved music, but didn't want the trappings of a life in the spotlight.

Gibson was one of those. I was almost certain of it.

I wondered if he'd ever considered getting a pet. Maybe a dog. I could see him with a sweet dog at his side. A loyal companion, jumping in the passenger seat of his truck, tongue hanging out. Curling up at his feet at the end of a long day. And the thought of Gibson with a puppy was ovary-melting.

Maybe a dog would help. I'd have to see what he thought about the idea.

Although thinking about leaving him with something made me think about *leaving*. Which made my heart hurt.

This little unrequited crush I was nursing kept growing. The fact that we were pretending to be together in public only made it worse. I found myself living for those moments when he'd hold my hand or wrap an arm around my shoulders. Snuggling with him at Scarlett's bonfire the other night had been like a daydream come true. I'd nestled into him, and for a little while, allowed myself to pretend it was real.

I knew I was setting myself up for disappointment. We were just friends. That was how it had always been between us. He played the part well, when other people were watching. His touches felt awfully real; I was sure they looked convincing from the outside. But when we were alone, he kept his distance. It reminded me that this wasn't my home, and Gibson Bodine wasn't my boyfriend.

The noise of power tools quieted. This little fantasy I harbored wasn't realistic anyway. Even if Gibson did see me that way, what would I do about it? My life wasn't here. As nice as it had been to visit Bootleg Springs again, that was all it was. A visit. It wasn't like I could stay.

I pulled my song journal out of my bag and flipped through the pages. Snippets. Unfinished lyrics. Hastily scrawled melodies. I rarely jotted down more than a line or two. I wrote songs with other artists. I helped them get past their self-doubt to find the words and melodies that were waiting to come out. But writing my own songs had fallen by the wayside in the busyness of life on the road.

But really, lack of time wasn't why I'd stopped writing. The songs in my head were too close to the truth. My truth.

Every time I'd sat down with this book and a pen in my hand, I'd stalled out. Just like the artists I was so good at helping.

There was that hazy spot in my memory again. The box in my mind shook. Maybe being here would allow me to face whatever was inside, rattling around with so much noise.

But whenever I tried, there was nothing. It was like a foggy night, nothing but darkness and mist.

I closed the journal and put it back in my bag. I'd put all those things in the box for a reason. Maybe I just needed to let the rest stay there.

I heard the noise of a door shutting, interrupting the quiet stillness of the afternoon. It sounded like Gibson had emerged from his workshop. A minute later, he stuck his head out the back door.

"Hey. I need a shower. Then we can head to the Tuckers' place."

He had sawdust in his hair and a few flecks in his beard. I could smell the faint scent of wood from here.

"Okay. I think I'll change into something a little nicer."

His eyes flicked up and down. "If you want."

Without another word, he went inside.

To the outside world, Gibson and his girlfriend Maya were having dinner with Harlan and Nadine Tucker. In reality, this was a chance for the sheriff to interview me without blowing my cover. I appreciated that they were willing to do this for me, but I was nervous. This was the next step in not only revealing who I really was, but hopefully bringing the truth about Judge Kendall into the light. Which scared me to no end.

I couldn't keep my real identity hidden forever. I'd already noticed a few people giving me curious looks in town. For now, our story was working, but news of who I really was would get out eventually.

Plus, I didn't want to keep it from Bootleg much longer. This town had held out hope for me for so long, and I wanted more than anything to tell them I was alive. To thank them for never giving up on me. I loved them for that, more than I knew how to express.

I went inside to change and paused outside the bathroom door, listening to the sound of the shower. The thought of Gibson in there, hot water streaming over his body, made me tingly between the legs. I had a momentary urge to strip off my clothes, jump in, and surprise him.

If I'd thought he wanted me, I'd have done it. Right there and then. There was nothing wrong with a little friendly sex between two people who weren't exactly dating. I wasn't an innocent girl anymore. I'd had a fling or three.

But I wasn't getting an *attracted to you* vibe from Gibs. He was protective—which I enjoyed—and did his part to make it look like we were together. But despite those little moments—like his arm around me at the bonfire, or the way he'd looked at me when we'd been singing together—I felt the force of his friend-zoning.

So I let it go.

I went into his bedroom, where I'd been keeping my things, and changed into a cute summer dress. It was one of my favorites because it never wrinkled, no matter how scrunched up it was in my bag.

Gibson pushed the door open behind me and I turned. Oh dear sweet lord, he was in nothing but a towel, slung low around his hips, his skin damp and glistening. My eyes traced down the length of his body. Past a dusting of chest hair. Solid abs. A trail of body hair that disappeared beneath that towel. A droplet of water slid down his chest, between his pecs, tracing a wet path to his belly button.

Holy shit. With clothes on, Gibson was ruggedly handsome in a *don't approach me* kind of way. But half-naked, he was stunning. A glorious specimen of rough, powerful man that sent my hormones into a tailspin of unbridled lust.

"Sorry," he said, backing out the door. "Didn't realize you were in here."

"No, it's fine," I choked out, then cleared my throat to try to cover. "I'm done."

We stood there for a long moment, staring at each other. A slip of his hand and that towel would drop right to the floor. As if powered by a force I couldn't control, my eyes slid down his body again. Was he hard underneath that towel?

I felt my cheeks warm, and I was not a blusher. He cleared his throat and moved aside. Tucking my hair behind my ear, I darted past him. I needed to get him out of my line of vision before I did something embarrassing. Like licked the water off his neck.

The bedroom door shut behind me and I sank down onto the couch. What was I doing? Gibson and I had been good friends, but I'd never been so crazy around him. When we were younger, even my little teenage crush hadn't been that big of a deal. I'd liked him, but it hadn't bothered me that we couldn't be more. I hadn't thought about it all that much. Just enjoyed spending time with him.

And that time sure had been special.

15

CALLIE

Thirteen years ago

*M*oonshine Diner was packed, the smell of sunscreen thick in the air. It seemed like half the population of Bootleg Springs High School had decided to come in from the midday heat, piling into booths for the lunch special—a pepperoni roll and a Pepsi.

I sat with Tanya Varney and Lacey Dickerson, sipping what was left of my Pepsi. It was mostly ice, now. They leaned close to each other, whispering and giggling about the boys in the booth behind us. They lived here year-round, so they knew each other well. But like all the kids in Bootleg, they were always nice to me when I was here summers. Included me like I was one of them. It was one of the reasons I liked it here.

"What about you, Callie?" Tanya asked. "Do you have a boyfriend back at school?"

"No, there aren't any boys I like enough." That was partially true. There were plenty of boys at my high school in Virginia who were cute, but none that I liked that way. But it wouldn't have mattered if I had. My parents would never allow me to date. However, I didn't like talking about my parents unless I had to, so I left that part out.

"Really?" she asked. "Not a single one?"

I shrugged. "Not really."

"I bet you could date Amos Sheridan if you wanted to," Lacey said, lowering her voice. He was sitting right behind us. "He's so cute and I bet he likes you."

My eyes flicked to the boys in the other booth. Amos was cute. A lot of the boys in Bootleg Springs were cute. It made hanging out at the lake with all the local kids more fun. The other girls mooned over them, and the boys loved to show off.

Fun or not, I was more of an observer than a participant. I had to be.

"I don't know, Lacey," I said. "I bet he likes you more than me."

"Oh my god, Bowie Bodine just walked in," Tanya whispered. "He's so gorgeous."

Bowie sauntered in, wearing a battered baseball cap and a t-shirt that showed his athletic frame. Like all the Bodine boys, he was nice to look at. He paused at a small table near the window and said something to his brother, Jameson.

Jameson was my age, but I didn't know him very well. He was quiet and mostly spent time with Leah Mae Larkin. They weren't dating as far as I knew. They acted more like friends—friends who'd known each other since they were little. She spent summers here now, kind of like I did, except it was because her parents had divorced and she'd gone to live with her mom in Florida. I liked Leah Mae, but we didn't hang out much. She was always off somewhere with Jameson.

"Bowie's eighteen," Lacey hissed. "That means he's like a grown-up."

"What does that have to do with anything?" Tanya asked. "He's only two years older."

"Are y'all talking about my brother again?" Scarlett Bodine squished into the booth with Lacey and Tanya, and her best friend Cassidy Tucker slid in next to me. Scarlett and Cassidy were a couple of years younger, but they were nice girls. I'd always liked Scarlett's sass.

"No," Tanya said, but Lacey gave her the side-eye. "Okay, yeah. But I can't help it. He's so cute."

Scarlett rolled her eyes. "I guess. He's a pain in the ass, though. All my brothers are."

"Shh, he's coming," Tanya said.

Bowie paused by our table. He grabbed Cassidy's pony-tail and gave it a little tug. "Hey, trouble." Then he playfully punched Scarlett's shoulder.

Scarlett rubbed her arm while Cassidy grinned up at him.

"Don't punch me, you big fart face." Scarlett socked him in the arm.

"Ow," Bowie said, grabbing his arm. "What gives, Scar? I barely touched you."

Scarlett gave him a smug smile. He grumbled something and walked away, heading for a table near the back. I noticed Cassidy didn't take her eyes off him.

"You're so gonna marry him," Scarlett said.

"Shut up, I am not," Cassidy said, but her smile said otherwise.

Amos turned and leaned over into our booth. "Y'all done? We're heading back to the lake."

"Sure," Lacey said with a giggle.

"We'll see you down there," Scarlett said, standing to let Tanya and Lacey out. "Cass and I wanna get some lunch."

Cassidy stood so I could get out. We said goodbye, then I followed Tanya and Lacey out the door. The knot of boys came out right after us.

I pulled on my sleeves, even though it was hot out today. Maybe I'd dip my feet in the lake to cool off. The water was bathwater warm, but it still felt refreshing. And wearing short sleeves wasn't an option.

An engine rumbled behind me. I glanced over my shoulder and my heart did a little flip. Gibson Bodine drove by slow in his beat-up old pickup truck. He had his windows rolled down, music turned up. He wore a black muscle shirt that showed off his muscular arms and a pair of dark sunglasses.

The other girls stared, open-mouthed. Gibson Bodine was equal parts fascinating and intimidating. The type of guy the girls my age were both afraid of, and drawn to like flies to honey. The big, bad older guy, with stubble on his square jaw and a heart-stopping smile. A little scary. A little dangerous. A lot sexy.

And these girls had no idea he was my friend.

I held that secret like a treasure. I had a lot of secrets—far too many for a sixteen-year-old girl—but this was the one I cherished. A happy secret, instead of a terrible one. But still something I had to keep to myself.

So I didn't wave when he drove by. He didn't acknowledge me, either. He didn't need to. We both knew.

"Last one in the lake is a bug-eyed catfish," Amos yelled, then took off running down the street.

The rest of the boys followed, yelling insults at each other as they went.

Tanya and Lacey started to follow. "You coming, Callie?"

I made sure not to glance in the direction Gibson had gone. "I'll catch up with you later."

"Okay, see ya."

I turned in the opposite direction, walking up Lake Drive while the girls headed toward the lake. Sneaking away was easy. The kids and teens of Bootleg Springs roamed the town until dusk all summer long, everyone coming and going. Forming small groups, then breaking off to form new ones. No one seemed to miss me when I wandered off.

Technically I wasn't violating any of my parents' rules. Although there was no way they'd approve of me hanging out with Gibson Bodine. He was twenty, and most people thought of him as the bad boy in town.

I knew better. He wasn't bad. Misunderstood, maybe. But not bad. But I still couldn't let my parents find out.

Making sure no one was watching, I cut between two buildings and made for the woods. Not far into the trees, I left the trail. I knew my way. Gibson had showed me a clearing that was deep enough in the forest that it was secluded and quiet, but close enough that I could easily make it home by dark, even if we lost track of time.

We did that pretty often.

I picked my way through the trees, careful not to stub my toe on the forest debris. As much as I worried about getting caught, I never hesitated to come. I couldn't resist.

Gibson was already there, sitting on a fallen log, tuning his guitar. He usually parked on a dirt road and came in from the opposite direction.

He looked up at me and smiled. "Hey, Cal."

I tugged on my sleeves, making sure they were pulled all the way down. Gibson and I shared a secret, but he didn't know my other ones. "Hey, Gibs."

"I learned a new song." He strummed a chord. "Worked it out by ear, but I think I have it right."

"What song?" I lowered myself onto the log next to him.

"Let's see if you can guess." He strummed a few more times.

I picked up on the melody instantly. "That's 'It's Your Love.' It's a duet."

"I thought you'd like that."

Smiling, he continued playing. I listened for a minute, letting the music wash over me. I never felt as peaceful as I did when I was out here in the woods with Gibson. It wasn't his bad boy reputation or his formidable good looks that made me risk my parents' wrath to spend time with him. It was the connection we shared. The blissful relaxation of being away, alone in the woods, nothing but our voices and his guitar.

He looped around and started the song again, this time adding the words. His voice was like warm maple syrup, smooth and rich. I listened for a few bars, then found the harmony, singing along. He smiled as he sang, nodding to me in approval.

There was magic out here. The secrets I kept locked up so tight didn't exist. The weight on my shoulders lifted as I sang, as if our music wove a protective cocoon around us both.

I was never as happy as when I was singing in the woods with Gibson Bodine.

16

MAYA

*G*ibson pounded his fist against the Tuckers' front door. I stood next to him, resisting the urge to slip my hand in his. We weren't pretending to be together, tonight. I hadn't seen the Tuckers in person yet, but they already knew the truth about me, so there was no need to perpetuate the *Gibson's girlfriend Maya* story. So I kept my hand firmly by my side.

But I was riddled with anxiety. I felt like Callie again. A girl with too many secrets, trying to hold the threads of her life together. Afraid of what it would mean to reveal the truth.

I took a deep breath. I'd be safe here. We weren't in public where someone could overhear. And I knew the Tuckers were trustworthy. But the box in my mind bumped, as if the demons inside could sense their time was coming.

There were so many things inside. Things I still couldn't see.

Gibson took my hand and squeezed. That little gesture

of reassurance calmed my racing heart. Glancing up at him, I squeezed back.

Harlan Tucker opened the door, greeting us with a smile. His mustache had gone white, as had his hair, and he wore a flannel shirt with jeans. His wife Nadine appeared at his side, looking just as pretty as I remembered. Her silvery blond hair was pulled back and her green eyes were bright.

"Oh sweet heavens, look at you," Nadine said. "Come in, come in."

They ushered us inside and shut the door. It wasn't quite dark out, but I noticed the curtains had been drawn. I didn't know if that was on purpose, but I appreciated it nonetheless. Made me feel a little more secure.

Nadine wiped a tear from the corner of her eye. "My goodness, Callie Kendall. Is it really you?"

I nodded and before I could answer, she wrapped me in a tight hug. I hugged her back, blinking against the sudden sting of tears.

"Now, now, let's not smother the poor girl," Harlan said.

Nadine didn't let go. "I haven't seen her in thirteen years, Harlan. I'll smother her all I want."

I laughed. Her motherly hug was nice. "Smother away, Mrs. Tucker."

She pulled back, but held my arms. "Call me Nadine. It's so good to see you. I almost didn't believe it when Harlan told me the news. I've been dying to get a proper look at you. What a lovely woman you've become."

"Thank you." A part of me wanted to shy away from her scrutiny. The scar on my face was a frustrating reminder of what I'd been through, and I knew it was often the first thing people noticed. But her eyes didn't linger there. She seemed to take all of me in, looking at me like an aunt who hadn't seen her niece in a long time.

"Mom, are you going to let them come inside, or should we move the table to the front door?" Cassidy asked. She stood in the living room with Bowie, his arm wrapped around her shoulders.

"Oh, don't get your knickers in a twist." Nadine let go of my arms. "I'm just so darn excited to see you."

Gibson stood to the side, his arms crossed, his eyes never leaving me.

Bowie patted him on the shoulder. "Calm down, Gibs. It's just us here."

He grunted, dropping his arms to his sides, but he didn't move. Or take his eyes off me.

"Dinner is just about ready," Nadine said, ushering us in. "Let's have a good meal before things get too serious."

I felt Gibson's hand on the small of my back while we walked into the dining room. Why was he doing that? Not that I minded. The gentle pressure of his big hand was calming. But also a little bit confusing. Maybe touching me when other people were around had simply become a habit already.

We sat together at their cozy table while Bowie and Cassidy helped Nadine bring in dinner. The scent of roasted chicken and gravy filled the air, making my mouth water.

The meal was amazing. Home cooking at its finest. Nadine kept the conversation light and lively, asking easy-to-answer questions of me and the others at the table. Gibson didn't say much, but he was very polite to the Tuckers. I had a feeling it meant he liked them. He certainly respected them.

We finished eating and Bowie helped Nadine clear the table.

"I suppose we should get down to business." Harlan

folded his hands together, resting his elbows on the table. "Callie, we're going to need you to take a DNA test."

"It's not that we don't believe you," Cassidy said. "I know you're who you say you are. But we're going to need proof."

"Of course. I expected that."

"Good," Harlan said. "Cassidy filled me in on your story, but let me see if I have this right. You left home because you were being abused."

I nodded, feeling Gibson stiffen beside me. "That's correct."

"And Jonah Bodine Sr. found you, and helped you get out of town."

I looked down at the table, my throat suddenly thick, my heart racing. It was so hard to talk about this. I felt raw and exposed, like the old wounds on my arms would break open and start bleeding again.

"It's okay, dear," Nadine said, returning to her seat. "Take your time."

Bowie quietly took his chair next to Cassidy.

"Yes, he helped me. I was injured, and he took care of me as best he could. The next day, he and Mrs. Bodine helped me reach out to a friend I knew I could trust and arranged for a place to go. Mr. Bodine drove me there."

"Did you ask him to keep your whereabouts a secret?" Harlan asked.

"We came up with the plan together. He didn't want to put his family in danger, but he also wasn't willing to send me back. We decided I needed to disappear."

"I see," Harlan said, nodding thoughtfully.

"I have a question about your new identity," Cassidy said. "How'd you manage to get ID? You said you traveled a lot, but you'd need a passport for that."

"Someone in Blue Moon arranged it for me. He said he

knew a guy who knew a guy, or something like that. I realize that's not exactly legal." I winced.

"I was just curious," Cassidy said.

"I reckon your passport and whatnot aren't really our concern," Harlan said. "We have bigger issues to deal with, here."

I tucked my hair behind my ear. "I want you to know, I'm ready to come forward."

Gibson put up a hand. "No, she can't—"

"Gibson," Harlan said, his tone gentle. "We're not going to make any rash decisions. I agree with y'all keeping her identity a secret for the time being. It was the right thing to do, and I don't think that's changed. Callie, if you come forward now, it's your word against theirs. They'll claim your injuries were self-harm, and you ran away."

"What about the forensics report?" Bowie asked. "She's sitting right here. Clearly that body ain't her."

"We have to prove the judge was behind it," Harlan said. "It's damn suspicious, but that's not enough. And you need to understand, I don't have the jurisdiction to run a proper investigation against Judge Kendall. Not when it crosses state lines. I need to get the FBI involved."

"So how do we do that?" Gibson asked.

"We, meaning *law enforcement*," Harlan said, "need to find enough evidence that they'll take over the case. Right now we have theories and suspicions, but not enough to go to the feds."

"He's a high-profile man," Cassidy said. "Even more now that he's up for a federal position."

"Which makes our job harder," Harlan said. "It'll be too easy for him to argue it's a baseless smear campaign designed to lose him his federal appointment."

"And it also means he has a lot to lose," Nadine said.

"Exactly," Harlan said. "Which is why I'm glad y'all kept Callie's identity quiet. We don't want this to get out too soon. Believe me, I'll do everything in my power to get the right people involved."

Flashes ran through my mind. Old memories, long since locked away. Things I hadn't thought about in years. "Judge Kendall was involved with some terrible people. I think you should assume he still is."

"What kind of people?" Cassidy asked, her voice gentle.

"Organized crime type of people," I said, searching those old memories for meaning. "I heard things sometimes that I wasn't supposed to. He had agreements in place. He'd make sure their people went free or received reduced sentences. I think in exchange for money, or sometimes favors."

"Could you identify any of those people?" Harlan asked.

"I'm not sure. It's been a long time. A lot of my memories are... fuzzy. But if I saw them, I think I could."

Harlan smoothed his mustache with his thumb and forefinger. "I see. I'll keep that in mind."

"Here's what I don't understand," Cassidy said. "Your parents always claimed you were depressed. Your mother even showed me a photo of the cuts on your arms, claiming it was self-harm. Did she know that it wasn't? Is that why she didn't show it to the authorities at first?"

"Maybe that was a cry for help," Nadine said. "She's been married to that monster for a long time. Maybe she was hoping you wouldn't believe Callie had done it to herself, and that you'd uncover the truth."

"That's possible, I suppose," Cassidy said, her expression pensive. "Callie, do you think your father was abusing your mother as well?"

A rush of anxiety hit me like a truck. The box in my mind howled and shook, banging against the floor. Memories pushed at the edge of my consciousness, but when I tried to bring them forward, there was nothing but darkness and mist. I could almost feel the pain in my arms—the scars I'd covered with ink, red and bleeding. But I couldn't remember it happening. I'd locked it away too deep.

"Hey," Gibson said, putting an arm around my shoulders. "You all right?"

I nodded. "I'm sorry. Some things are just so hard to remember. But I don't think I ever saw him do anything to hurt her."

"I know it's been a long time, but if there's anything else you can tell us, maybe it'll lead us to the proof we need," Harlan said.

"I wish I could remember more specifics," I said. "I know I heard him threaten people. And he talked about bribes and blackmail. Once in a while that was dinner conversation. I don't remember what my mother had to say about that."

I paused again, reaching back. There was so much more, I could feel it.

"You're doing good," Gibson whispered.

His soft encouragement helped. "I always had the sense that my father was like a spider, with a big web of contacts and associates. A lot of them were political, but some were criminals, and he was at the center, directing all of it."

"People working for him, probably with degrees of separation," Harlan said.

"Keeping his hands clean," Cassidy added.

Harlan nodded. "One thing I'm certain about, he doesn't want his daughter turning up, especially now. I suspect he has concerns about how much incriminating evidence you have against him. And they're still watching our investigation."

I blew out a frustrated breath. I had no doubt the judge was worried about what I'd tell the authorities. Deep inside, I knew the reason for the scars on my arms had something to do with punishing me into silence. I'd heard things he didn't want me to tell. But there was still a piece missing.

"They're still watching?" Cassidy asked. "How do you know?"

"Their lawyer called the station this morning. He said he'd gotten word that we might have discovered a new witness. He was clearly referring to Gibson."

Gibson made a low noise in this throat. A sick feeling spread through my stomach and I took a sip of water to wash down the taste of bile.

"The whole town knows you brought him in, and why," Cassidy said. "They could have heard it from anyone."

"They could have," Harlan said. "But it's a reminder that we need to tread carefully. This is a man who's avoided the law for a very long time. We might only get one shot at him. That's why I don't think we should have Callie come forward yet. Child abuse is serious, but after all this time, it'll be hard to prove. Especially against a man like him, who knows how to work the system."

"So what do we do?" I asked.

"For now, we keep your secret," he said. "You're Maya Davis. You keep doing what you're doing, and we'll keep doing our job, looking for enough evidence to get the right people involved."

"I wish there was something more I could give you," I said.

"It's all right," Harlan said. "You were just a child. I'll tell you one thing, it's a pleasure to no longer be investigating your disappearance. Now we're finally focused on bringing down the monster who hurt you."

I nodded. "Thank you."

"All right, everyone, we need to clear out all this bad juju," Nadine said, getting up from the table. "How about some pie?"

"Bad juju, Mom?" Cassidy asked with a laugh, and got up to follow Nadine into the kitchen.

"Y'all know what I mean," Nadine said with a wave of her hand.

I glanced at Gibson and he met my eyes. There was a softness there—reassurance. It sent a warm, tingly feeling through me, chasing away the fear. I was still worried— about him, the judge, whether we could find enough proof. But when he looked at me like that, his gaze gentle, the corner of his mouth turned up in the barest hint of a smile, it was easier to feel brave.

And harder to keep from feeling a whole mess of other things.

17

GIBSON

*S*till blinking the sleep from my eyes, I poured myself a cup of coffee. I heard soft footsteps coming down the hall and my back prickled, like a cool breeze had brushed my neck.

Callie came into the kitchen, showing way too much skin in a little tank top and shorts. She gave me a sleepy smile, but it was hard to know where to look. The soft lines of her neck curved into her shoulders and a tendril of hair hung across her collarbone. Without really meaning to, my eyes dipped to her chest, to the tempting roundness of her tits.

I tore my eyes away, hoping she hadn't noticed. *Damn it, Gibson.*

"Morning." She grabbed a mug out of the cupboard and poured herself a cup. "Did you sleep okay?"

"Fine," I muttered.

"Are you sure? Because I keep telling you, I'll take the couch and you can have your bedroom back."

"Don't worry about it."

She'd been here a little over a week, and she said that every morning. But I wasn't having it. I couldn't do much for her, but keeping her comfortable was something.

Besides, I kind of liked having her in my bed, even if I wasn't in it with her. Made no sense, but a lot of things didn't make sense since she'd reappeared. Like why I couldn't stop seeing her every time I closed my eyes. And why those images kept turning to her getting naked.

I sat down with my coffee, but it was hard to be still. I had too much adrenaline in my system lately. Made me edgy. Truth be told, I was itching for a fight. A good fuck would do it, too, but that certainly wasn't happening. I needed something to take the edge off. I had too much on my mind, too many feelings swirling around my gut.

Maybe I'd go to the Lookout tonight. There was always someone looking to start shit with me there. Sure, I'd be coming in hot, looking for trouble, but I just needed to feel my knuckles crunch against something solid. Maybe take a good hit across the chin. Taste a little blood. A little bar brawl among friends was a great way to blow off some steam.

Callie's lavender scent reached my nose a heartbeat before she joined me at the table. God, that girl. She was riling me up in ways I was having a hard time containing. My eyes drifted across the smooth skin of her shoulder, imagining my lips there. My teeth.

I tore my eyes away. Again. Looked into my mug like my black coffee held the secrets of the universe.

"Have you ever thought about getting a dog?"

"What?"

She took a sip of coffee and grinned. "A dog. You know,

man's best friend. Loyal companion. Tail wagging all over the place."

I was glad for something else to focus on, although it still felt like an effort to keep my ass on this side of the table. I wanted to toss her over my shoulder and haul her to my bedroom like a cave man. "I know what dogs are."

"You seem like a dog person," she said. "I'm kind of surprised you don't have one."

"I like being alone."

"Do you, though?"

Like a knee-jerk reaction I couldn't control, I stood and walked a few steps away. Why the fuck was she analyzing my life? I needed a dog? I was doing just fine. If I needed anything, it was to bury my fist in someone's face.

Damn it, I needed to stop. I didn't want to yell at her when she hadn't done anything wrong. And I was still a little bit afraid she'd up and disappear again.

Another reason I was on edge. Every time I left, I kept wondering if she'd be gone when I got back. Or if I'd imagined the whole thing, and she'd never really been here at all.

I clenched my fists and took a deep breath. "Why do you want to know if I've thought about getting a dog?"

"Just wondering," she said, her voice casual. She either couldn't tell I'd been about to snap at her, or it didn't bother her. "Like I said, you seem like a dog person."

I turned toward her and rubbed the back of my neck, but didn't sit down. I felt like I couldn't get too close to her right now. It was hard enough just breathing the same air. If I kept smelling that lavender scent, I was going to lose my mind. "I like dogs fine. Just don't know if I'm cut out to take care of another living thing."

"Really? You've been taking excellent care of me."

Turning away, I grumbled something incoherent, but

hearing her say that made a warm, contented feeling spread through my chest. "I need to go into town. Wanna come?"

"I'd love to. Do you mind waiting, though? I need a shower."

I had to stop myself from groaning. *No, it's fine, I'll just be out here dying of this perpetual hard-on while you're naked in my shower.* "I can wait."

She finished her coffee and went into the bathroom. I paced around the house, listening to the water run. I felt guilty for the way my dick ached with unrelieved tension. Callie was a friend. Even after everything she'd been through, she trusted me. I couldn't let all this shit I was feeling mess that up.

I thought about calling Jonah to see if he wanted to go for a run today. It was a testament to how keyed up I was. I hated running. But maybe it would help me burn off some of this fucking energy.

After she came out of the bathroom, I took a quick shower and threw on some clean clothes. By the time I finished, she was ready to go. Her colorful hair was wavy and still a little damp and she'd put on a tank top and denim shorts. Her purple toenails matched her hair.

She was all smiles and idle chitchat on the way into town. I still felt like I had a seam about to burst open. She looked good and smelled good and as soon as we were in public, I'd be reminded that she felt good too, even if it was just her hand in mine.

Sure enough, we got out of the truck, and she slipped that soft little hand of hers into mine. The skin contact was both soothing and arousing.

I didn't even think about letting go. I wanted to surround her—cocoon her in my arms so I could protect her. Being in public made me edgy, like I half-expected the Kendalls to pop out around every corner.

She squeezed my hand. "How about this. I want to stop in and say hi to Leah Mae, then go grab a few things I need at the Pop In. Girl stuff." She winked. "If you're still busy when I get done, I'll wait for you at Moonshine."

My brow furrowed and unconsciously, I pulled her a little closer to me. I didn't like this plan.

"I have my phone," she said, as if she could read my thoughts. "I'll be fine."

"All right," I grumbled. "I'll walk you to Leah Mae's shop."

Reluctantly, I left her at Boots and Lace. Leah Mae had other customers, but Callie still wanted to stay. Maybe the upside was that she might buy another dress. The one she'd worn the other night had looked damn good on her. Nothing wrong with a beautiful girl in a pretty dress.

And there I went again, thinking about her all wrong.

I had a meeting with a client around the corner. Betty Sue Wheatfield owned a little bookstore, tucked in an old storefront that had once been someone's house. She and her husband were looking to fix up the place. Wanted me to make built-in shelves to replace the rickety freestanding ones they had.

I pushed open the door and inhaled the scent of old paper and leather. Bookshelves crowded the tiny space, books packed tight. There was a shabby old armchair below a four-paned window, the glass so old it was starting to warp. A small digital screen sat on the counter where the cash register used to be. The modern device looked odd in this throwback of a store.

Puck, the shop's cat, came around a corner to eye me curiously. He was all black except for his white feet and a patch of white on the end of his long tail. I crouched down to scratch him behind the ears.

"Hi, Gibson," Betty Sue said, her voice cheery. She was in her fifties, with smile lines around her eyes and graying blond hair pulled back from her face. "Sorry, I didn't hear you come in."

I straightened, leaving Puck to rub up against my legs, probably looking for more attention. "I just need to take some measurements."

"Have at it."

I pulled the tape measure off my belt and got to work. It was tough to get around all the existing shelves and clutter, and Puck kept trying to walk under my feet. But I got what I needed, scrawling numbers on my little spiral notepad. When I finished, I tucked my pencil behind my ear and clipped the tape measure back on my belt.

"All done."

Betty Sue poked her head out of the back. "How're we looking?"

"I'll run the numbers and get you a quote." I glanced around at the room, looking past the shelves to the building itself. "Y'all have some wall damage and loose trim. Since you're clearing out to get new shelves anyway, you could fix all that, and the loose floorboards. Get Scarlett on in here and she'll take care of you."

She smiled. "Much obliged. I'll do that."

I tipped my chin to her and left, squinting in the summer sunshine after the relative dimness of the old shop. I needed some new clamps and a package of sandpaper for my sander, so I headed over to the Rusty Tool. Found what I needed—I knew this store like the back of my hand—and went to the front to pay. I hadn't been gone long, but I wanted to get back to Callie. Didn't much like leaving her alone in town.

It was only because I was concerned for her safety. Not because I liked being around her so much.

Jimmy Bob Prosser was at the front dressed in a Rusty Tool t-shirt and jeans. The fact that his daughter was the spawn of evil had never made me dislike him. It wasn't his fault. I didn't know why Misty Lynn was the way she was. Maybe the bad genes had come from her mama. Jimmy Bob had always been a good guy.

"Hey, there, Gibson," he said. "This all for you?"

"That'll do it."

Jenny came in wearing a sundress that made her green eyes stand out. She smiled, first at me, then at Jimmy Bob.

"Well, if it isn't two of my favorite guys."

I was one of her favorites? I was the son of the man who'd left her, pregnant and alone, after he'd cheated on my mother. And I looked almost exactly like him. But Jenny had always been nothing but nice to me. Especially since she'd come clean about Callie being alive.

"Hi, Ms. Jenny," I said.

"Look at you, pretty as summer sunshine," Jimmy Bob said.

She beamed at him. "Sorry I'm early. I can wait until you're ready to go to lunch."

"What time do you have to work?" he asked.

"Not until two."

Jenny was working with Whit and Clarabell over at Moonshine now. Word in town was that she'd be taking over the diner when they retired.

Jimmy Bob leaned to the side, turning to yell toward the back of the store. "Hey, Carl. Can you come on up here?"

Carl scurried out, his skinny arms so pale it looked like he'd never seen the sun. The crop of red hair on his head stuck out at odd angles, and the only thing that made him look his eighteen years was his height. Kid was tall but still had a baby face. He'd started working for Jimmy Bob last year.

"I need you to work the front while I go to lunch," Jimmy Bob said.

"Sure thing," Carl said with a nod.

Jimmy Bob took my cash, gave me some change, and handed me a bag. He looked over at Jenny. "I'll be right back."

She smiled again. She was always smiling. "I'll be right here."

I put away my wallet and nodded to Jenny. "Ma'am."

"Oh, don't *ma'am* me, Gibs." She opened her arms. "We're not strangers. Come here."

I gave her a stiff hug, feeling awkward. She gently patted me on the back and pulled away, putting her hands on my arms.

"How're you doing, honey?"

"Fine."

"How's Maya?"

"She's fine."

She raised an eyebrow. "Fine? That's it?"

"Yeah."

"Okay, I'll take that for now," she said. "It's good to see you, honey. We should have coffee again sometime. That was nice."

I was a little surprised to realize she was right. It *had* been nice. I'd been a mess of confused feelings at the time— still was, really—but Jenny had a way about her. She'd made me feel better. I could tell why Jonah was such a steady guy.

"Yeah, that'd be all right."

"Good. I'll see you around."

I nodded to her and left, feeling a bit off-balance. I liked Jenny. Nothing wrong with liking your half-brother's mom.

But I didn't really like many people, and it surprised me a bit that she was one of them.

I needed to get my head together. I stopped outside the store to text Callie—she was *Maya* in my contacts—to see where she was.

Me: *You about done? Where are you?*

Maya: *Little change of plans. Ran into Shelby. Going to get our nails done. Do you mind?*

A flash of irritation made me growl. I didn't mind that she was with Shelby, or that she was getting her nails done. Girls were weird about that stuff, it wasn't anything to me. But I couldn't exactly park myself in the little nail salon and watch them get manicures. The desire to be with her—just to make sure she was safe, of course—was making my back prickle.

Me: *Let me know when you're done.*

I pocketed my phone. I'd just have to kill some time while I waited. And if that meant I happened to wander around by the nail salon, who could blame me? Made sense to stay close.

People meandered up and down the street. Summer-timers wandered with shopping bags and ice cream cones. Locals waved to each other or stopped for a chat. Trent McCulty lumbered by on a big green tractor. He had to stop for Mona Lisa McNugget. She bobbed her way out onto the road, then stopped right in front of the huge tire to peck at something on the concrete.

Scarlett came around a corner, dressed in a dark blue tank top and jean shorts. A dog tugged on a leash in her hands. She gripped it tight and leaned backward, like she was having a hard time hanging on.

"Who the hell's dog is that?" I asked.

"Oh, hey Gibs," she said, breathing hard. She shoved the leash toward me. "Take him for a minute, will you?"

I grabbed the nylon leash just as it went taut, the dog pulling hard. Wrapping it around my hand twice for a better grip, I gave it a solid tug. I pursed my lips and let out a shrill whistle. "Hold up, there."

The dog stopped, turning to look at me. He had tan fur with a white patch on his face. He looked like a pit bull, but on the small side, with a turned-up snout and only one eye. He regarded me for a moment, like he was deciding whether to listen to me. I stared him down.

His tongue lolled out of his mouth and he plopped down onto the sidewalk.

"How'd you do that?" Scarlett asked. "He won't listen to a word I say."

I tilted my head at the dog. "I guess he knows what's good for him. But Scar, please tell me you didn't get a dog. Between you and Dev and that demon you call a cat, your house is cramped as it is."

"I didn't get a dog."

"Then where'd he come from? You dog-walking on the side now?"

"You're not going to believe this." There was heat in her voice. "Some asshole summertimers left him. Abandoned him at one of my rentals."

"Are you sure he's not lost?"

"I'm sure all right. I've been trying to get a hold of them to tell them he's still here. Finally did, and the guy claimed they'd never had a dog. I called him on his bullshit and got him to admit they'd left him on purpose. Said they thought they were doing him a kindness, since they weren't cut out to be dog owners."

A flash of anger hit me. "The fuck?"

"I know, it's horrible. They're blacklisted from this town for life. But now I gotta figure out what to do with him."

I eyed the dog for a second. He watched me with his one eye. It was a clear bluish-green, so light it almost lacked color. He cocked his head, the tips of his ears flopping forward. The little guy did something weird to that tangled knot of feelings I was carrying around. Poked at it. He was awfully cute, and Callie had said I seemed like a dog person. Kinda made me want to—

"I'll take him."

"What?"

Shit, I'd said that out loud. I crouched down and he got up to sniff my hands. His nose was wet and his fur soft.

I glanced up at my sister while I absently petted the dog's head. "I said I'll take him. Been thinking about getting a dog anyway."

"All right," she said with a smile. "He ain't very big, but he's strong and he has a mind of his own."

"Sounds like someone else I know." I winked at her.

"Very funny," she said. "So, what's his name?"

"Doesn't he have one?" I checked his collar, but it looked new and there wasn't a tag.

"I didn't ask the pieces of crap who left him. They don't deserve to name a sweet boy like that. Although now that I think about it, maybe if I'd known his name, he would have answered to it."

He licked my hand. "I'll come up with something."

"Okay, you are now the proud owner of this very cute dog." She brushed her hands together. "I'll dump the dog stuff I bought for him in your truck."

I scratched his head one last time and stood, keeping the leash tight in my grip in case he decided to run off. "Thanks, Scar."

"I'll see you later. I'm gonna go tell Dev we're done dog-sitting."

I watched my sister go, the leash dangling from my hand. Damn it, what had I just done? I looked down at the dog. He lifted his chin, his tongue hanging out. He was cute, all right.

Apparently I had a dog now.

18

GIBSON

*C*allie was still getting her nails done with Shelby, so I waited outside. I'd stopped at the Pop In for a couple of bottled waters and a plastic dish. It was hot out and the dog—little guy really needed a name—had been thirsty. He'd happily lapped up the water, his big tongue slapping against the dish.

I sat on a bench outside the salon, the dog's leash still firmly in my hand. Scarlett had been right, he was stronger than he looked. For the most part, he sat near my feet, but once in a while, something would catch his interest and he'd try to dart away.

"Come here, buddy," I said, patting the bench beside me. "Come on up."

He jumped up, his tail wagging furiously, and stood in my lap.

I leaned back and shoved his butt down so he'd sit. "Not in my face, buddy. Sit. That's right, sit."

He plopped down on my lap and rested his chin on his front paws. I shook my head, scratching behind his ears. Weird dog.

Callie and Shelby came out of the shop, laughing together. The dog sat up and his tail started smacking against the bench.

"Hey, who's this?" Callie sat on the bench next to me and the dog went right to her, his tail wagging so hard his back-side wiggled back and forth. She laughed, petting his head.

"Aw," Shelby cooed. "He's so cute. Whose dog is he?"

"Mine."

"What?" Callie asked, still laughing softly. The dog kept trying to sniff her boobs.

Couldn't say I blamed him.

"He's mine, I guess." I shrugged one shoulder, crossing an ankle over my other knee. "Someone abandoned him at one of Scarlett's rentals."

Callie grabbed both sides of his face and rubbed them, bringing her nose close to his. "Oh my god, I love him. What's his name?"

"Doesn't have one yet."

"Aw, Gibson, he's adorable," Shelby said. "Maya, we need a puppy playdate. He and Billy Ray can be best friends."

"They'll be so cute together," Callie said.

Shelby took a turn petting his head. "I have to run, but thanks for hanging out. It was fun."

"It was." Callie smiled at her and the dog nudged her face. "Okay, big guy, I'm still paying attention to you. We'll chat later, Shelby."

"Bye, Gibson."

I nodded to Shelby. Her ponytail bounced as she walked up the street to her car.

"You really got a dog," Callie said.

I wasn't sure if she meant it as a question. "I didn't go looking for him. Scarlett walked up the sidewalk with him tugging on his leash and... I don't know. He needed a home."

"Who would leave you out here, huh?" she asked. "Good thing we found you. Who's a good boy? Yes, you are."

"What should—" I paused, clearing my throat. I'd been about to say *what should we name him*, like it was *our* dog. Like Callie and I were a real thing. "He needs a name."

He turned and jumped back in my lap, whacking Callie with his tail a few times in the process. I sputtered as he licked my face. "Down, boy. Sit."

Callie laughed. "Looks like you taste good."

My eyes darted to her and she glanced away quickly. She hadn't meant it like that, but it still made me think of what it would be like to have her tongue on me.

Fuck's sake, even an unplanned dog adoption couldn't distract me enough to stop thinking dirty thoughts about her.

"Come here, buddy." She took his face in her hands again. "How about Cash?"

"As in Johnny?"

"Yeah. I think he looks like a Cash."

The first song Callie and I had ever sung together was "I Walk the Line" by Johnny Cash. Did she remember that? Thinking back on that made me smile.

"Works for me," I said. "We should get back. I have more work to do today."

I took them home and left Cash in the house with Callie while I went out to my workshop. A couple of hours later, I heard her voice outside. She was tossing him a ball out back. I stood by the house and watched them for a few minutes.

Cash happily ran back and forth, bringing the ball back and dropping it at her feet.

Callie's colorful hair blew in the breeze and she smiled while she played with Cash. I was still coming to terms with the fact that it was her. That thirteen years of wondering what had happened to her had come to an end. Thirteen years of assuming I'd never see her again.

My insides were still all twisted, but at least I didn't feel like I was about to pop a blood vessel. Wasn't quite sure when I'd calmed down. Working for a few hours had helped. Maybe Cash had, too. I still didn't know how to deal with all the fucking feelings I was having, but I didn't want to punch something anymore. Seemed like progress.

I went back to my workshop to finish up and when I went inside the house, I found Callie curled up on the couch with Cash's head in her lap. They were both asleep. Looked like they'd worn each other out.

Scarlett had given me a small bag of dog food and a couple of toys, but that wasn't going to last long. And the little guy could use a bed of his own, and some sturdier dishes. Some more toys. Probably another leash, in case we needed a spare.

I didn't want to wake them—they were awfully cute sleeping on the couch like that—and I felt better leaving Callie with Cash here. He wasn't very big, and if someone did come creeping around, he'd probably just try to lick them. But at least he'd bark. I grabbed my keys, made sure both doors were locked, and went out to make a quick trip into town.

Pet Paradise was in downtown Bootleg with a colorful sign out front. The window display had a tall carpet-covered cat tree and a stack of pet beds marked twenty-five percent off.

I rolled on in and made a quick sweep of the store, grabbing dog stuff I figured we'd need. Or *I'd* need. I had to quit thinking like that—like Cash belonged to both Callie and me. Despite how comfortable I was having her there, she didn't live with me. Not really. And we weren't a real couple.

Besides, Callie's life wasn't one that involved things like sweet little one-eyed dogs with stocky legs and happy tails. She traveled too much. Didn't even have a real home.

I wasn't sure why, but thinking about that made me sad.

Shrugging off another rush of stupid feelings, I paid for my purchases and hauled them out to my truck. For a guy who'd always insisted on solitude, I sure was setting up to share my space these days.

"How's it going?" a voice behind me said.

I shut the passenger's side door and glanced over my shoulder. A guy in a dark shirt and slacks stood a few feet away. Looked older than me. Maybe in his later forties. Had a crooked nose.

"You need something?" I asked, my voice low.

"Nice town," he said. "You're Gibson Bodine, aren't you?"

Great, this again. Now they were coming to town to bug me? It was bad enough when it was just phone calls. "If you're another record company asshole, I'm not interested. Save us both some time and move on."

"I don't work for a record company."

Something in his voice rubbed me wrong, my instincts flaring to life. He looked nondescript. Just a regular guy in street clothes. But he had that look some men had—danger in his eyes.

"Then what are you doing here?"

"Like I said, this is a nice town." He put his hands in his pockets, but his body language was anything but casual. "Interesting history."

"Yeah."

"I've been to a lot of small towns and you know what they all have in common?"

"What?"

"They can't let things go," he said. "They tell the same stories, over and over. You ever notice that? The old-timers sit in their rocking chairs telling tales. Same stuff they've been talking about for years. Same gossip passed around."

"Do you have a point, or you just making conversation?" I asked. "Because I don't like conversation."

"The other thing about small towns is that people talk," he said, ignoring my comment. "Everybody knows everybody's business. Isn't that right?"

"I guess."

"Have a good chat with the sheriff?" he asked.

Oh, fuck. Was this about Callie? Did someone know she was here? Or was this just about the fact that I'd been questioned? "Who the fuck are you and why are you asking me shit?"

"Like I said, people talk. And this town seems to have a problem letting things go."

"Yeah, they talk," I said. "Even when there ain't shit to talk about."

"I don't know about that," he said. "Are they questioning everyone who lived here thirteen years ago, or are you special?"

I hesitated for a beat, not quite sure how to answer. "It was a misunderstanding."

"Was it?" he asked, looking oddly thoughtful. "I guess if you'd dropped a new piece of evidence in the biggest case in your town's history, everyone would know about it."

"So?"

"You knew her?" he asked. "The girl who disappeared?"

I narrowed my eyes at him. I did not like him talking about her. "It was a long time ago."

"Damn shame." He shook his head. "A girl just up and disappears like that without a trace. Makes you wonder what kind of world we live in, doesn't it?"

I didn't answer.

He took a step closer and lowered his voice. "I'll tell you what kind of world it is, Mr. Bodine. A dangerous one. More than any of you backwoods hicks in this podunk town realize."

"You threatening me with something?"

"No. But some things are meant to stay buried."

He turned and started to walk away. I was about to say something when I noticed a subtle bulge just above his waist, beneath his shirt. Looked like he was carrying a concealed handgun.

Some things are meant to stay buried. Had he been threatening me, or Callie?

Fuck. Callie.

I hit my back pocket, looking for my phone, but it was empty. Shit. Where had I left it? I wasn't careful about carrying it with me. It was probably sitting on my workbench. But right now I could have punched myself in the damn teeth for leaving it.

I hopped in my truck, wishing I had my Charger back. It was faster. The truck revved to life and I took off out of town, my heart thumping hard.

She was fine. I'd find her on the couch, still napping with Cash. Or maybe taking him outside so he could do his business, or sitting cross-legged on the floor, doing her weird meditation thing. Whoever that guy was, he hadn't sounded like he knew she was here. But he'd definitely been talking about her.

Some things are meant to stay buried.

I tore around the hairpin turns to my property and kicked up gravel all down the long driveway. Slammed on the brakes and came to a stop. Her rental car was still here, but she wasn't outside.

Cash didn't bark when I rushed up to the front door and shoved my key in the lock. So much for his guard dog abilities. I threw open the door and looked around. Empty.

"Callie?" I called out, barreling through the house. It wasn't very big. Took me all of a few seconds to check every room. No sign of her, or my dog.

"Shit." I stuck my head out the back door, finding an empty porch. No pretty girl out back tossing a ball or walking the dog. "Callie? You out here?"

Maybe Cash had run off and she was hunting for him in the woods. I jogged out to the trees, but there weren't any real trails out here. Henrietta seemed to move through the forest without disturbing a single branch, and the game trails didn't lead this close to my house. If they were out here, they couldn't have gone far. Not past shouting distance.

I called for her, called for Cash, whistled to see if he'd come. Nothing. Just the breeze whispering through the branches.

There was a sickening familiarity to it. To the silence in the woods and my heart trying to beat its way out of my chest, fear spreading through my gut.

I'd only been scared—really, truly scared—three times in my life. The first was when Scarlett was a kid and tumbled out of a tree. I'd thought she'd broken both legs. Turned out it had just been the one. The second was when

Jameson had fallen through the ice and almost drowned. We'd made a human chain to pull him out, but that could have gone very, very wrong. The third was the day I found out Callie had disappeared.

Right now was number four. And it was feeling a hell of a lot like number three.

19

GIBSON

Thirteen years ago

I kicked my aching feet up onto the crate I used as a coffee table, next to a half-eaten greasy pizza still in the box. I'd worked late, eaten dinner late—that pizza was sitting like a rock in my gut—and now I couldn't sleep.

I flipped through the channels, idly looking for something to watch, caught between not tired enough to go to bed and too tired to do much else. I settled on a rerun of some cop show, and tossed the remote on the couch next to me.

My phone rang and I picked it up. Why were my parents calling? It was getting close to midnight.

"Yeah."

"Gibs, it's Mom."

"I know it's you, Mom. Your number comes up when you call."

"Right. Listen, sugar, I need a favor."

The hitch in her voice got my attention. She sounded upset. And she hadn't called me *sugar* in years. "What's up?"

"Can your brothers and sister come stay with you tonight?"

"I s'pose. Why?"

"It's nothing," she said quickly. "It would just help me out."

I rolled my eyes. My mom upset, asking for a favor, trying to get my siblings out of the house? She and Dad were fighting again. I didn't bother asking what it was about. It wasn't like it mattered; they were always fighting about something.

"Sure. You need me to come pick 'em up?"

"No, Bowie's gonna drive 'em over," she said. "Thanks."

"Uh-huh."

I hung up and put my phone down. *Damn it, Dad, what did you do this time?* He'd probably come home drunk again and Mom didn't want Scarlett to see. As if we all didn't know. I hoped there hadn't been too much yelling. It was like they didn't realize half the town could hear them.

Even though it was late, I wondered if they'd eaten any dinner. I got up and checked the kitchen cupboards. I kept a few things on hand—easy stuff—for times like this. Tonight was going to be boxed mac and cheese, unless Mom had already fed everybody before Dad fucked up everyone's night.

Not more than five minutes later there was a knock on my door. My feet hurt and I wanted to sit and stare at the TV, doing nothing. But instead, I had to play fucking babysitter to a bunch of teenagers.

"It's open," I said.

Bowie came in first, wearing a baseball cap and a

Bootleg Springs High School t-shirt. Scarlett was right behind him, her long hair in a ponytail. Her freckled nose was scrunched up, like she was annoyed about something. Growing up with three older brothers, she was probably annoyed more often than not.

Behind her was Jameson. His hat was pulled low over his forehead, as if he was trying to hide under it. He towered over Scarlett, and I realized he'd somehow gotten to be almost as tall as me and Bow. Made sense. He was sixteen, now.

Jameson shut the door with his foot, then he and Scarlett put their fingers on their noses and simultaneously said, "Not it."

"Dang it, you guys," Bowie said.

"Bowie gets the floor," Scarlett said. "Jame, you wanna flip a coin for the couch?"

"I got it." I pulled a quarter out of the change jar I kept on the counter. "Heads or tails, Scar?"

"Tails."

I tossed the coin in the air, caught it, and flipped it onto my forearm. Removing my hand, I let them both look.

Scarlett did a fist pump. "Yes. Tails."

Jameson just shrugged, like he didn't care either way.

"Y'all hungry?" I asked, dropping the coin back in the jar.

"Starving," Scarlett said.

No dinner, then. I met Bowie's eyes and he raised his eyebrows. He followed me into the tiny kitchen, and I got out a pan.

"What happened?" I asked, keeping my voice low. None of us liked talking about it when they fought. What was the point? And it just upset Scarlett more.

"I'm not sure," Bowie said. "Dad got home real late and

then they went upstairs for a long time. I heard raised voices, but not like they were yelling. I don't know what's going on."

I filled the pan with water, put it on the burner, and turned on the heat. "Whatever. Y'all can crash here. It's quieter at least."

He got the milk and butter out of the fridge and set them on the counter. "Yeah, thanks."

Anger at my dad ran hot through my veins. Why did he have to make things so goddamn difficult? Why couldn't we just be a normal family?

"Go play cards or something with Scar, will ya?" I asked. "I've got this. And y'all can have a piece of pizza if you want, too. It's from earlier."

Bowie nodded and dug out the pack of cards I kept in the junk drawer. Like the boxed mac and cheese, they were here for nights like this. When my siblings had to sleep over because my parents were making the whole family miserable.

I glanced out into the other room. Jameson was huddled up in the corner of the couch, his legs bent, drawing something in that notebook of his. He hadn't said more than two words since he got here, and I'd probably be lucky to hear two or three more before he left tomorrow. Looking at him over there made my chest hurt a little. He was a good kid. He deserved better.

Bowie was dealing cards on the crate while Scarlett sat across from him, perched on the edge of the couch. Her purple cardigan hung off one sunburned shoulder. I noticed she'd replaced the top button with a yellow butterfly. All the girls Scarlett's age had started doing it. Callie had started the trend.

Thinking about Callie made me crack a smile as I

ripped open the boxes of mac and cheese. That girl was something else. Sweet as sugar with a voice like an angel. I wondered if Scarlett, or any of the other kids in town, knew she could sing. I bet they didn't. Callie was like that, only showing certain parts of herself to the people she trusted.

And I was one of them. That was pretty fucking cool.

I'd missed her today. She'd probably been hanging out at the lake with Scarlett and Cass and the rest of the kids in town. Not only had I been busy at work, we'd taken too big of a risk yesterday to chance being seen together for a little while.

It was an unspoken thing, the way Callie and I hung out without telling people. She didn't have to explain to me why it was necessary to keep it a secret. She was sixteen, for one. I wasn't about to make a move on a girl so much younger, but other people wouldn't know that.

It wasn't about that anyway. Had she been older, sure, I might have seen her differently. She was pretty as a summer day. And who knew, maybe someday, when she was a proper adult...

But I didn't let myself think like that. It felt disrespectful to my friend. Because that's what she was—my friend. We shared something, and the afternoons we spent together—playing music, singing, daydreaming—were some of the best times I'd ever had.

She didn't look at me like everyone else, like she already knew exactly where my life was going and was unimpressed. Disappointed, even.

She looked at me like maybe I was worth something.

And yesterday, seeing her face at that outdoor concert, had been worth the trouble to smuggle her out of town. I'd made damn sure to get her back in plenty of time so she'd have a solid alibi in case her parents asked too many questions. But man, we'd had a good time.

I dumped the macaroni in the boiling water and gave it a stir. Scarlett slapped her palm on the stack of cards on the table. Apparently she and Bow were playing slap-Jack.

When I had some more money, I needed to get a bigger place. Of course, Bowie would be off to college soon. And it wouldn't be long before Jameson would be on his own, too. Few years from now, I wouldn't be hosting my siblings when things were rough at home anymore.

Things changed.

By the time we finished up dinner, it was getting on toward one, so we all hit the sack. I didn't have to work in the morning, so maybe I'd take them all to Moonshine for breakfast. A stack of pancakes would make Scarlett happy. Jameson, too. I probably had enough pocket money to cover it. Wouldn't make up for the shitty night, but it was something.

～

I GOT up and headed straight for the coffee maker. Bowie and Jameson were already awake, sitting on the floor with their backs to the couch, playing video games with the sound turned down. Scarlett was curled up on the couch, her eyes open, but only just, like she wasn't quite ready to be awake yet.

"Morning," Bowie said without looking away from the screen.

My phone rang. I figured it was Mom, but I saw the Tuckers' number on the screen.

"Yeah."

"Gibson? It's Cass. Is Scarlett there?" There was urgency

in her voice. That was weird.

"Yep," I said. "She doesn't look awake yet. Wanna talk to her?"

"Yeah, but Gibs, something happened."

My spine straightened, my back muscles clenching. In that split second, I prepared myself to hear it. Probably a car accident. Had it been one or both of them? Jesus, I hoped Mom was okay. "What?"

"Callie Kendall is missing. She didn't go home last night."

It felt like I'd been kicked in the gut, all the air rushing from my lungs, and I almost dropped the phone. "She what?"

"I don't know what's going on, but it's scary," she said. "My dad left to start organizing a search."

"Shit," I muttered. Keeping my face carefully neutral, I walked into the other room and handed the phone to Scarlett.

"What's wrong?" Bowie asked.

I hesitated for a second, not sure I could get the words out.

"What did you just say?" Scarlett shrieked into the phone. "Callie Kendall's missing? You can't be serious."

"That," I said, gesturing toward Scarlett.

Fear turned my blood to ice. She hadn't made it home? It was morning. Did that mean she'd been out somewhere all night? Where the fuck would she have gone? Who would have...

Oh god, no. No, no, please no. Not Callie.

Scarlett hung up and the three of them looked at me, like I was supposed to have an answer.

"What do we do?" Scarlett asked, her voice unusually quiet.

"Y'all go on home," I said, surprised I sounded normal. "She probably just spent the night at someone's house and forgot to check in with her parents. She'll turn up, or the cops will find her."

"Hope so," Scarlett said, pulling the blanket up to her chin.

It seemed to take forever and a fucking day for them to clear out. I griped at them that I had shit to do, but that didn't make anyone move faster. I felt like I was crawling out of my own skin. I watched my phone, willing it to ring. For Cassidy to call back and say Callie had turned up. It was all a big misunderstanding and she was fine.

But the call didn't come.

And what was I supposed to do? Tell my siblings they had to get home so I could look for her? How would I explain that? If word got out that I'd been hanging out with her—in secret, no less—nothing good would come of it. I'd just get her in trouble with her parents, not to mention what the rest of the town would think. Her daddy was a judge, and he didn't seem like the kind of man you wanted to cross. Especially not where his sixteen-year-old daughter was concerned.

So I waited, feeling like a tornado raged inside me, until Bowie took Jameson and Scarlett home. As soon as Bow drove out of sight, I hopped in my pickup. I knew where I'd look first. I had no idea why she'd have gone out there last night, or why she'd still be there now if she had, but I hoped to god I'd find her.

I drove out of town and turned onto a dirt road. I parked in the usual place and rushed out to our spot, desperately hoping I'd find her curled up in a sleeping bag or sitting in front of a little campfire. Maybe she'd had a fight with her parents and spent the night out here. She didn't talk about her family—and I didn't talk about mine—so who knew. It could explain why she hadn't gone home.

But if she was in trouble, why hadn't she come to me? She had to know I'd help her. I'd do just about anything for that girl.

Debris crunched under my shoes as I ran. I burst into the clearing, but it was empty. Silent. No sign of a fire. Just the log she and I always sat on.

"Callie?" I called, turning in a slow circle. "Callie, you out here?"

I spent an hour searching the woods, tracing the route she usually took. I walked toward her parents' house, calling her name. Maybe she'd been out here last night and fallen. Hurt herself and couldn't get home.

I didn't find anything but trees.

By the time I drove back into town, I knew it was serious. She hadn't been found. She hadn't slept over with a friend and carelessly forgotten to check in. I could tell without even stopping to ask. Knots of people stood on the street, talking to each other, their faces etched with concern. A deputy cruised past, his window rolled down, like he was making the rounds, searching.

And there wasn't a single kid to be seen. The sun shone bright and the air was warm, but no scabby-kneed Bootleg kids ran down the sidewalk with lemonade or ice cream cones. No packs of teenagers strolled to the lake with beach blankets slung over their arms. I did a loop past the beach and it was almost empty. Looked like a few summertimers had set up a picnic, but there was no one I recognized.

I circled the town in my truck, driving past Callie's house about a dozen times. Sheriff Tucker's car was there at first. When I passed again, maybe ten minutes later, it was gone. I slowed down, staring at the big front door. It was like that driveway led to another world, with judges and money and important people. A world I couldn't reach. As much as I wanted to go in there—talk to her parents and offer to help —I couldn't.

So I kept driving. I took the highway out toward Perrinville. Stopped along the way and checked the trails. My mind raced, coming up with explanations, each one worse than the last. Had she hurt herself on the way home and couldn't get help? She walked everywhere. Had she been hit by a car? The cops had to be checking local hospitals.

But what if she got hit and whoever did it tried to hide it? Dumped her body in the lake?

Or what if someone took her? She wasn't stupid enough to get in a car with a stranger offering a ride. Unless it wasn't a stranger. But why would someone she knew kidnap her?

I didn't have a single answer. The day wore on, the sun moving relentlessly toward the horizon. I only stopped searching to make a pit stop at the Pop In. Partly because I was hungry as shit, and partly because it was the easiest way to find out what was going on. People talked in this town.

Search parties had been organized. They'd been sweeping the town, the woods, the beaches, the hot springs. People were already speculating—everything from she'd run off with a boy to she'd drowned in the lake. But no one had seen any sign of her since last night. She'd said goodbye to the kids at the beach, and no one had seen her since.

I wandered back to my truck, the ache in my chest threatening to swallow me whole. I'd never felt so helpless in my entire life. My eyes burned and a single tear broke free from the corner of my eye. Something terrible had happened to her. I felt it, deep in my bones. Something awful, and there was nothing I could do to help her.

20

MAYA

*S*helby and I sat in the almost-empty Yee Haw Yarn and Coffee sipping our sweet tea. Billy Ray was curled up beneath her chair, chewing on a toy, making cute puppy-growl noises. Cash was asleep next to me, tuckered out from playing fetch earlier and his excitement over meeting Billy Ray.

She'd called, waking me from my nap, and asked if I'd like to hang out with her and the girls tonight. She was already out and about, so she'd offered to come pick me up. We were currently killing time while we waited for Scarlett, Cassidy, June, and Leah Mae. Then we were going to head down to the lake with a take-out picnic.

Just like old times, the girls of Bootleg were happy to tuck me right into their circle.

Gibson's truck hadn't been outside—he'd probably gone into town again—so I'd sent him a text to let him know what we were up to.

Shelby and I had been chatting over our drinks—mostly

small talk—but she kept eying me, like she had something else she wanted to talk about.

Finally, she leaned closer and lowered her voice, although there wasn't anyone close enough to overhear. "Can I ask you a question?"

"Sure."

"How does it feel to be back?"

I took a breath. "Good and strange and familiar and a little bit scary all at once. I've been having a lot of feelings."

"I can imagine."

"I've been Maya for thirteen years, and I really thought I'd be her forever. I didn't think anything in my past would be a part of my life again. It hurt to let the good things go, but..."

"But you had to."

I nodded. "Back then, it was about survival. I was a very broken girl."

She tilted her head, like she was scrutinizing me, and adjusted her glasses. "You don't seem very broken anymore."

"I did a lot of healing, especially in the first few years when I lived in Blue Moon. And I found my strength. Henna, the woman who took me in, looked at me one day and said, *You survived, but now it's time to decide who you are. And that isn't up to anyone but you.*"

"A powerful statement."

"It was. I learned how to stand up for myself. And I realized that I'd never been weak. I'd survived because I had strength inside me."

"That's absolutely true."

"But I have to admit, being here is messing with my head a little bit." *Not to mention being with Gibson.* "I keep waiting for people to recognize me or to run into... well, you know."

"They're not in town, though, right?"

I realized I was tugging on my sleeves. An old reflex. I grabbed my tea to give my hands something else to do. "No. And I'm sure we'll hear about it if they come back."

Shelby smiled. "I think June and GT are running surveillance on their house."

"That's the craziest part. They don't have to do that for me, but they are anyway. None of you have to help me. And no one seems angry that I disappeared and they didn't know what happened. No one's blaming me for that."

"That's because they understand," she said. "We all do. Even before you turned up, we all realized your father is dangerous. We knew this was a lot bigger than just a girl who went missing."

I nodded. "I wish there was more I could do. I talked to the sheriff, but like he said, even if I come forward, it's my word against theirs. We can't prove anything yet."

"Exactly." Billy Ray popped up and she reached down to scratch his head. "I think we're doing the right thing by keeping quiet for now."

"I just hope the sheriff finds something they can use."

"He will," she said. "I'm sure of it."

"Can I ask you a question now?"

She smiled. "Of course."

"How did you wind up in Bootleg Springs?"

"In a way, because of you. After the case was reopened, the media descended on this place like locusts. I found it fascinating the way the town came together to get rid of them. I've always been interested in community dynamics, so I came here to do my dissertation research."

"And now here you are."

"I met Jonah, and those Bodines are hard to resist."

You're telling me. "I'm glad Jonah found his way here. Jenny, too."

"So am I," she said. "He belongs here, even if he didn't always realize it."

Billy Ray jumped up and put his front paws on my leg. I scratched between his ears and his tongue lolled out to the side.

"Sweet boy. Who's a good boy? You are, aren't you, buddy?" I cupped his cute little dog face in my hands. "He's so handsome."

"I'm kind of stunned that Gibson got a dog," Shelby said. "Was that planned?"

"No. He told me just this morning that he's not cut out to take care of another living thing. But I guess I put the notion in his head and when he saw Scarlett with Cash, he took the leap."

"I think it'll be good for him," she said. "He's so..."

"Grumpy?" I asked with a soft laugh.

"Okay, I have to ask," Shelby said, straightening her glasses. "Is he like that all the time? Or just around other people? I mean, you're another person, but maybe he's different when you two are alone."

"No, he actually softens up when we're in front of other people. He's very closed off when we're alone."

"Are you kidding, or do you mean that?"

I laughed again. "I mean it."

"What was he like when he was younger?"

I took a sip of my sweet tea. "The same in a lot of ways. He did that brooding bad boy thing well."

"How did you become friends?"

"We knew each other by sight, of course. I'd been spending summers and holidays in Bootleg for years, and this is a place where everybody knows everybody else."

"Very true."

"One afternoon, I took a walk by myself down the beach. I found him sitting alone, quietly strumming his guitar. He was so intimidating—older than me with a reputation for being mean and causing trouble. But he just looked at me without saying a word. Didn't stop playing. Just kinda watched, like he was curious to see what I'd do. So I sat down next to him."

"That was brave."

"Yeah, I suppose so. I'm not even sure why I did it. I didn't usually feel very brave back then, but there was a spot on the log next to him, and I just sat. He started playing a Johnny Cash song, so I sang the words. We both kind of lit up. He came in on the second verse and I tried, and failed, to harmonize. We got a lot better after that. But that was how it started."

"It's so sweet," Shelby said. "And so un-Gibson-like."

"I keep wondering where that guy went. He was just as surly back then, but when we were alone, he was different. His edges weren't so hard."

"I think he's been through a lot."

"I'm sure he has." And how much of it was because of me?

"So have you," she said quietly.

"It hasn't all been bad. I learned to let go and be happy. And I've been all over the world, working with amazing people."

She rested her chin in her hand. "That does seem really exciting."

I nodded and took another sip of my tea. "Life on the road has its disadvantages, but it works for me."

The door opened and Scarlett came in. She smiled and Shelby waved her over.

"Hey, y'all," she said, pulling up a chair. "I've got food

out in my truck, but I think Cass is still waiting on June. Katherine got out again."

"Katherine?" I asked.

"June's pet pig," Scarlett said. "She's real sweet."

I decided it didn't surprise me that June Tucker had a pet pig. "Oh, of course. I saw her at your bonfire."

"We were just talking about Maya's glamorous life," Shelby said.

"I wouldn't call it glamorous," I said. "But I do travel a lot."

"Do you know anyone famous?" Scarlett asked.

I lifted one shoulder in a shrug. "Yeah, I've worked with a lot of artists over the years. Some are well-known."

She grinned. "Ever had a fling with a hot rock star?"

"Sure."

"That's all you're gonna say?" Scarlett asked. "Sure?"

I laughed. "I don't stay in one place very long, so yes, I've had flings with guys. Some were musicians. A couple were famous. Or they're famous now. They weren't when I was with them."

"Have you ever gotten serious with one of them?" Shelby asked.

"Not really. Like I said, I don't stay in one place. Long-distance is hard, especially in this business. I never wanted to get attached."

Shelby regarded me with interest, and I wondered what she was thinking.

"Sounds like someone else I know," Scarlett said, giving Shelby a pointed look.

"You never know," Shelby said. "Maybe things will change."

Scarlett looked me up and down and I got the distinct

impression that she was sizing me up as a potential match for her brother.

I didn't want either of them getting the wrong idea. I made sure to keep my voice quiet. "We're just friends, ladies. This whole *Gibson's girlfriend* thing is just a story."

"Uh huh," Scarlett said.

"Trust me," I said. "He's not interested."

"He's just too damn stubborn for his own good," Scarlett said. "It's a solid Bodine trait."

"She's not wrong," Shelby said.

I glanced at the door as it opened again and felt a sudden rush of irritation. Misty Lynn Prosser came in, dressed in a bright pink tank top over a leopard print bra, with cut-off jeans so short they were basically underwear. Her bleached blond hair was teased high and she snapped a piece of gum between her teeth.

"Oh, lovely," Scarlett muttered, rolling her eyes. "Don't make eye contact. Maybe it'll go away."

Shelby snickered behind her hand.

Misty Lynn's gaze swept the café, then landed on me. Her eyes narrowed and her gum chewing slowed. She sauntered over to our table and put her hands on her hips. "Hey, y'all."

"What a shame, our table's full up," Scarlett said, her tone full of mock sweetness. "Guess you'll have to be on your way."

Misty Lynn glared at Scarlett, then turned her attention on me. "So you're the famous Maya."

"And you must be Misty Lynn."

Her eyes traced up and down my face and for a second, I wondered if she'd recognize me. "I've heard so much about you."

I gave her a fake smile. "And I've heard plenty about you."

She snapped her gum. "Really. Well, I hope you enjoy your little moment with Gibson. It won't last."

"What's it to you?" Scarlett asked. "My brother has made it very clear how he feels about you."

"This ain't about you, Scarlett," Misty Lynn said with a sneer.

Scarlett started to stand up, but I put a hand on her arm to stop her.

"It's all right." I met Misty Lynn's eyes. "She's not worth the trouble."

Misty Lynn gaped at me. I stood, slowly, like I wasn't in any rush whatsoever. Shelby and Scarlett followed while Cash got up and stretched. We were done with our tea anyway, and despite what I'd just said, I had an overwhelming urge to punch Misty Lynn in the teeth. I figured I was better off walking away than starting a cat fight in a coffee shop.

Scarlett gave her a dramatic eye roll and Shelby clicked her tongue for Billy Ray to follow, his leash in her hands.

I tugged on Cash's leash and walked past Misty Lynn, but paused just before I got to the door and glanced over my shoulder. "I'll tell Gibson you said hi."

Misty Lynn ground her teeth together and her face flushed pink. I didn't wait to see if she'd reply. Just swept out the door with a little toss of my hair, Cash right on my heels.

"Oh my god, that woman makes me furious," Scarlett said when we got outside.

Shelby nodded. "She's the worst."

"She'll get what's coming to her," I said. "People like that always do."

We started walking down the street, heading toward the

lake. Cash got excited, pulling on the leash. Billy Ray tried to outrun him, but Shelby and I reined them in.

"Punching her in the nose is still one of the highlights of my life," Scarlett said wistfully.

"You punched her in the nose?" I asked.

"Sure did. Bootleg Justice."

I tucked my hair behind my ear as we walked. Bootleg Justice. God, I loved this place. "Apparently it wasn't enough."

"She deserves worse for everything she's done," Scarlett said. "I don't understand why she can't get over my brother. He didn't even date her for very long."

"And wasn't it years ago?" Shelby asked.

"Yep. He's told her, right to her face, that he's never giving her the time of day again. Dumbass can't figure it out."

My palm stung and I realized I was clenching my fist, digging my fingernails into my hand. Maybe I should have started a cat fight in the café.

But I had a feeling Bootleg Justice was coming for Misty Lynn. Somehow.

21

MAYA

*W*e got to the lake and sat on top of an empty picnic table, our feet on the bench. A warm breeze blew across the water, making little ripples and eddies on the surface.

It reminded me of the last time I'd been at this beach, sitting with the girls. I'd been looking out over the water, just like this, with no idea my life was about to change forever.

I let Cash's leash out all the way so he could run around with Billy Ray. Their playful snarls were adorable. The other girls weren't here yet and the smells coming out of the takeout bags behind me made my mouth water.

"By the way," Scarlett said, breaking the short silence, "have y'all been reading the book for June's book club?"

"I bought it, but I haven't started it yet," Shelby said. "I have some catching up to do."

"Okay, because it's not what I expected when June said

we all needed to read it. I mean, it's Juney. And y'all, this book is something else."

"Really? What's it about?" Shelby asked.

"Well—"

"Maya," Gibson called from somewhere behind me.

I turned and lifted my hand to wave, but he ran toward us like a storm thundering across the plains.

"Are you okay?" I asked.

"No, I'm not fucking okay." He stopped next to the picnic table, breathing hard. "I didn't know where you were."

"I'm fine—I've been with Shelby and Scarlett. I texted you."

Billy Ray jumped up, putting his font paws on Gibson, while his tail wagged furiously. Gibson reached down to absently scratch his head, but his brow was deeply furrowed, his eyes intense. Cash caught up, his tail rivaling Billy Ray's.

"We need to get home."

"Now? Don't you want to stay and enjoy some puppy love?"

"No," he snapped.

Billy Ray jumped back, retreating behind Shelby.

I stared at Gibson. What the hell was his problem? "What's wrong with you?"

"Wow, calm down, Gibs," Scarlett said.

He ignored his sister, his eyes on me. "We'll talk at home."

His voice was strained, like he was trying to keep himself under control. But I wasn't sensing anger simmering beneath the surface. Was that fear in his eyes?

"All right," I said, jumping down from the table. I retracted Cash's leash. "Thanks for hanging out."

"Is everything okay?" Shelby asked.

I slipped my hand into Gibson's and he squeezed back—hard. "Yeah. I'll text you guys later."

Shelby nodded, but eyed Gibson like she wasn't sure what to think. Scarlett looked worried. I was, too. There was something wrong. He wasn't just irritated that he'd had to look for me. He was upset about something.

We walked back to his truck in silence. Cash trotted next to him rather than trying to rush ahead, as if he could tell something wasn't right. Gibson kept glancing over his shoulder, like he thought someone might be following.

Maybe someone was. Or had been. Had he seen someone? The Kendalls? Who else would have him so on edge?

Cash and I got into Gibson's truck and I locked the door. He got in and did the same. My heart beat rapidly and a trickle of fear worked its way down my spine. I wanted to know what was going on, but I seemed to have lost the ability to speak.

He didn't take the shortest route back. We detoured on side streets, taking a crisscrossing path until we finally left town and made our way up the winding road to his house. The truck bounced on the long gravel drive, the crunch of the rocks the only sound. The silence between us was disconcerting, but I couldn't bring myself to break it.

We parked and went inside. A tired Cash went straight for the couch, curling up in the corner and putting his head on his paws. Gibson locked the door behind us, but I compulsively checked it several times before I felt like I could walk away. I checked the lock on the back door while Gibson closed the curtains.

"You're freaking me out right now," I said, finally. "What's going on?"

"Some guy in town started asking me questions," he

said. "I think he was trying to find out why I'd been brought in by the sheriff before you came back."

I could feel the color drain from my face. "What did he say?"

"A bunch of stuff about how people talk in towns like this, and how Bootleg can't let shit go. But it was the last thing he said. Something about how we live in a dangerous world and some things are meant to stay buried."

I swallowed hard and when I spoke, my voice shook. "What did he look like?"

"Probably in his late forties or so. Blond hair. Plain clothes. Almost forgettable. His nose was crooked."

"Crooked nose…"

"Do you think you know who he is?"

I nodded. "I might. He sounds like a guy who worked for my father when I was a kid."

"Why do I think you don't mean he was your dad's gardener?"

Memories ran through my mind, like a film reel. "No. I remember him. He was like a cross between a private investigator and a thug. I'm pretty sure he was one of the men doing my father's dirty work. He'd give him jobs and talk about how important they were. I can't think of his name."

Gibson waited while I struggled to remember.

"Lee Williams," I said suddenly. "That was his name."

"I'm pretty sure he was carrying a gun."

"Oh god," I said. "I'm not sure why I know this, but I think if he let you see it, he wanted to scare you."

"Well, it goddamn fucking worked," he said, almost shouting again. "Jesus, Callie, this fucking guy shows up asking questions and then I can't find you. I was losing my mind."

"I'm sorry. I texted you to tell you what I was doing. I didn't know he was here."

"I know, it ain't your fault." He raked his fingers through his hair, the veins in his forearms sticking out. "I didn't have my phone, and I just..."

"Do you think he knew I was here?"

He let out a breath and dropped his arms to his sides. "No. I think he was trying to figure out if I knew something, or if I'd brought in new evidence."

"If the judge's lawyer couldn't get information out of Sheriff Tucker, they'd send someone to poke around. It makes sense."

He nodded, but none of the tension had left his body. He had a groove between his eyebrows and his arms were flexed, veins bulging.

He took a step toward me and I took a step back. "You need to be careful."

"I know, but what do you want me to do?" I asked. "Stay tethered to you all the time?"

"No."

"Then what do you want?"

He moved closer, the intensity in his eyes making me feel raw and exposed. "I just don't want anything to happen to you."

I backed into the wall. "Why do I feel like you're mad at me?"

He put his hands on the wall on either side of me, caging me in. His imposing presence made me feel tiny by comparison, and his eyes never left mine.

"I ain't mad, Callie," he said, his voice husky and low.

"Then what are you doing?" I whispered.

"I'm trying to keep my fucking hands off you."

My breath caught in my throat. Was that why he'd been

keeping his distance? Not because he only saw me as a friend, but because he'd been holding back?

"Maybe you should stop trying."

He was so close. So big. Without a single inch of our bodies touching, he held me against the wall, immobilized. A low groan rumbled in his throat and I could almost feel the vibration in my chest, down my spine, between my legs. He smelled so good, I wanted to bury my face in his neck and breathe him in.

Gradually, as if he wasn't aware he was doing it, he inched closer. I stayed pressed against the wall, my chin lifted.

"I'm no good for you," he said, his voice suddenly quiet.

Our noses brushed and a hot rush of desire poured through me. My body lit up, nerve endings pinging. "You've always been good for me, Gibs."

His head tilted and his lips touched mine. So soft. So tender. My eyes fluttered closed as he exerted gentle pressure.

He trembled, like he was struggling to hold himself in check, or afraid to move too fast. Gibson was rough and brusque. Who would have thought he'd kiss like a butterfly?

I draped my arms around his shoulders and he stepped in closer, slipping his hands around my waist. His beard was rough against my skin, pleasantly contrasting with the softness of his mouth. He pulled my lower lip between his and I felt the brush of his tongue.

That little taste made me shudder. His hands flexed, drawing me against him, and finally, finally, we sank into the kiss. Our lips parted and his tongue dragged against mine. I slid my fingers through his hair, angling my head to let him take the kiss deeper.

He kissed me slow, like warm maple syrup. Sweet and

soft and a little messy. I melted against him, yielding to his gentle touch.

I wanted it all. I wanted him to devour me. But this wasn't the unleashing of bottled up sexual tension. This was saturated with emotion, as if he was saying everything he couldn't put into words with his kiss.

He pulled away slowly and rested his forehead against mine. "Shit."

I kept my arms around his shoulders. "That bad?"

"No, too good. I wasn't going to kiss you."

"Too late."

He nuzzled his nose against mine and I massaged his scalp with my fingertips. He seemed so much calmer. Like kissing me had drained all the stress and tension right out of him.

"I'm glad you're okay," he said.

I nodded, enjoying the closeness. The feel of his hands on my waist, his face next to mine. "I'm glad I'm here with you."

"Me too, Callie. I'm so fucking glad."

He drew me against him and wrapped his arms around me, holding me tight.

How long had it been since I'd been held like this? Strong arms surrounding me, protective and comforting. An embrace filled with emotion, not as a means to getting my clothes off. Although my body whispered soft suggestions— and we were certainly alone—this moment wasn't about sex. And I didn't want it to be. I didn't want to be another notch in his bedpost. And he was more than something to make me feel a little bit less alone for a night.

Truthfully, I didn't know what this was. He turned his face into my hair and breathed in deeply, his arms still wrapped tightly around me.

I wasn't the girl who stayed. I always moved on. There was always another project, another artist. Another tour.

But maybe Jenny had been right. Maybe I had been running.

And maybe I was ready to stop.

22

GIBSON

*R*ain pattered on the roof and against the windows. A storm had rolled in after sunset, and it had been dumping out there for hours. I lay on the couch, my head on a pillow, a blanket over my legs, and stared at the ceiling, listening to the rain. Cash snored softly on his dog bed in the corner.

I couldn't sleep. The memory of Callie's lips against mine was visceral, like she'd imprinted herself on me. Her mouth had molded with mine so perfectly, her lips soft and sweet. I'd been trying so hard to hold back—to keep my feelings from showing. Hell, I barely knew what all those feelings meant.

But I'd cracked.

Despite the way I wanted her—the primal urge I'd been fighting to rip her clothes off—once I'd touched her, all that animalistic lust had taken a back seat. I'd never experienced anything like it.

I'd kissed her, but carefully. Like if I made one wrong

move, she'd disappear. And it had felt better than any kiss—better than anything I'd had with a woman before. Sex was great; I enjoyed it as much as the next guy. But somehow kissing and holding her like that had been better.

It was really fucking with my head.

Because there was one thing that would explain what had happened to me today. One single reason that a simple kiss and a woman in my arms would have rocked my world like this. And it scared the living shit out of me to even think it.

I didn't do love. I wasn't cut out for it. I loved my family, even if I was terrible at showing it. But romantic love, relationships, commitment? That wasn't for me.

My mama had made Scarlett promise she wouldn't get married until she was thirty. She'd made us boys promise we wouldn't get married for any reason, except one. Only if we were stupid in love.

She'd emphasized the word *stupid*.

I hadn't kept to that promise because I felt obligated, like my sister. I'd kept it because it made damn good sense. People like Harlan and Nadine Tucker—happily married after so many years—seemed like the exception. My parents were the rule. Two people stuck together by circumstances they couldn't control, making each other miserable.

Maybe that was where the stupid came in. Because when I thought about Callie, it was hard to see a future of resentment and regret. In fact, I realized as I lay there, if I let her go, that might become the biggest regret of my life.

I was well and truly fucked. That was all there was to it. She hadn't been here that long, and she'd already turned me inside out.

But when I thought about it, I'd always loved her a little bit. All those years ago, I hadn't looked at her like a girl I wanted. She'd been young, and sweet, and innocent. Older or not, I'd been all wrong for her as a boyfriend. Still was.

But as a friend, we'd shared something special. That was how I'd loved her. With music. With songs and harmonies and the sound of my guitar.

The bedroom door whispered open. It was dark, but I could see Callie's outline as she padded down the hallway. She hardly made a sound, turning the corner into the kitchen.

Without really thinking about what I was doing—or the fact that I wasn't wearing anything except underwear—I tossed the blanket aside and got up. I found her at the sink, filling up a glass of water in the dark.

"You all right?" I whispered.

She turned around, still holding her glass, and even in the dim light, I could tell she wasn't.

"No."

I took the glass and set it on the counter, then brushed her hair back from her face. "What's wrong?"

Her voice shook. "I woke up after a bad dream and now I can't calm down. I keep remembering things, but they're all confusing flashes. It's like suddenly my brain wants to replay all the worst moments of my life, but none of them make sense."

Slipping my hands around her waist, I drew her close. Kissed her forehead. "Nothing can hurt you here. I won't let anything happen to you."

She leaned on my bare chest and I hugged her against me. I had no idea what I was doing. Comforting someone wasn't exactly in my skill set. But this seemed simple enough. Wrap my arms around her and hold her tight.

The best part was, it felt really fucking good.

There was so much happening inside me. My chest felt

warm and full, like I might burst. Her hair smelled like heaven and the feel of her in my arms was so right. Perfect, even. Like the roads we'd both taken had always been leading to this.

Was this what love felt like? A rush of euphoria and affection mixed with a healthy dose of terror? Had my brothers been through this? I'd never bothered to ask. Hadn't thought it would apply to me.

Callie wound her arms around my waist, her body trembling. I rested my cheek against her head and rubbed slow circles across her back. Right now, in this moment, I wanted nothing more than to make her feel better. To make things okay again.

"Let's go back to bed," I whispered.

"I don't want to be alone."

I kissed the top of her head. "Don't worry. I've got you."

With an arm around her, I led her back to my bedroom. She crawled into bed and I slid beneath the covers beside her. Gathered her in my arms so she could rest her head on my chest.

I took slow breaths, feeling her body gradually relax. She stopped shivering. Her arm draped across my rib cage and she tucked her leg over mine, nestling in closer. I traced my thumb over her soft skin and breathed her in as she sank into me.

I hated that she was scared. That her father had hurt her so badly, the pain echoed in her dreams even now. But holding her like this—warm and comfortable in my bed— felt so good, I couldn't help but smile. That was something I didn't do very often.

"Gibson?" she whispered.

"Yeah?"

"Thank you."

I squeezed her tighter. "Feel better?"

"So much better."

"Good." I kissed her head again.

She was quiet for a long moment and I wondered if she'd fallen asleep. "Everything is different now, isn't it?"

"Yeah, it is."

"Does that scare you?"

I thought about it for a beat. It did scare me. Didn't seem like there was any reason to keep that from her. "Little bit. You?"

She nodded, her head moving against my chest. "Little bit."

Oddly, that seemed like a good sign. I didn't know what I was doing, or where this was headed. But at least we were on the same page.

"Do you think you can sleep now?" I asked.

"Will you stay with me?"

I squeezed her again. "I'm not going anywhere."

"Good."

The last of the tension seemed to melt from her body, her limbs going languid. I closed my eyes, drifting in the warmth of her skin, the feel of her soft breathing. And I couldn't remember the last time I'd felt so at peace.

23

GIBSON

$\mathcal{T}$he smell of paint filled the air in the Bootleg Springs High School gym. Jonah and Jameson were each on a tall ladder, rolling on a coat of light blue in a band across the wall. Bowie, Devlin, and I were working on the dark blue at the bottom.

Painting the old high school gym. The things I did for my brother. At least we were just doing the stripes, not the entire walls.

Cash was at home. I'd spent the last few days building a fence around a good portion of the yard, right off the back porch. He had room to run, a bed on the porch to sleep on, food and water. The weather was nice, so he was a happy little guy. And we could let him run free without worrying about him taking off.

"I thought you said George was coming," Jameson called down from his perch above my head. "It should be his tall ass up here."

"I thought he was," Bowie said. "I texted him, but he hasn't answered."

"He better show up," Jameson said. "It ain't like we can toss him in the lake again if he doesn't."

I chuckled a little at that. George was too big for us to throw in the lake, even if we all took a limb. The guy could hold his liquor, too. It had taken an impressive amount of moonshine to get him drunk. But that trebuchet toss had become the stuff of legend.

"He'll show," Jonah said.

My phone buzzed, so I wiped a smear of paint on my jeans and took it out of my pocket. I had a text from Callie. She'd sent me a picture of herself wearing a fluffy white bathrobe. She was at the spa with the girls while the rest of us helped Bowie paint the gym.

Ordinarily, I'd have grumbled about that. We were busting our asses to help Bowie out, and they got to get massages and manicures and shit?

But I loved seeing Callie having fun, even if I was stuck here with these shitheads.

She'd been skittish about coming into town for a few days, but I'd spread the word about that Lee Williams prick to my family, and they'd been keeping an eye out. No sightings of him, so we figured he'd left town. Probably just been here that day. No one else remembered seeing him.

I didn't for a second think we could let our guard down. But she was with Scarlett today, so I wasn't worried. My sister was a force to be reckoned with.

All things considered, I was in a decent mood. Sleep helped. I'd spent the last week sleeping in my own bed again. My couch wasn't bad, but this was better, especially because Callie was in there with me. She snuggled up to me every night and I fell asleep to the feel of her breathing.

It was pretty fucking great.

Maya was still my girlfriend in public, and we acted every bit the couple. I'd even planted a kiss on her lips right in front of Myrt Crabapple and Old Jefferson Waverly outside the Brunch Club yesterday.

In private, when she was Callie, was where things were getting real. Instead of keeping my distance, I held her closer. Kissed her more. Slept cuddled in bed with her. Woke to her scent, and usually her long hair in my face.

That was pretty fucking great, too. Even her hair.

I dipped the roller in the paint and rolled it on the wall, leaving a wide streak of dark blue.

"How's progress on the house?" Bowie asked, glancing at Devlin.

Even in an old Cock Spurs t-shirt and paint-splattered shorts, Devlin looked like a suit. He and my sister were such a mismatched couple. But he made her happy, and he treated her like gold. She loved him, so that was good enough for me. Dev was on my short list of people I actually liked.

"Walls are going up on the second floor," Devlin said. "It's starting to look like a house. How's married life treating you?"

"Best thing ever," Bowie said, rolling more paint on the wall.

Weird shit was happening. Bowie was married. Jameson was planning a wedding. The only reason Scarlett lacked a ring on her finger was her stubborn insistence on keeping her promise to Mom. She and Dev were building their dream home together. Even Jonah had given up the bachelor life for Shelby.

A few weeks ago, I'd have left them all to their funerals.

Get hitched and tie myself to a woman? Hell, no. Why would anyone go and do a thing like that?

It was crazy how fast a man's perspective could change.

Less than three weeks. That's how long it had been since I'd opened my front door to find Callie Kendall standing there. Less than three weeks since she'd jumped into my arms and sent my entire world into a tailspin.

That wasn't enough time to know anything, was it? Not enough time to fall in love, even if I had known her before. When I thought about it like that, it seemed crazy.

My problem was, I had no idea what love actually felt like. Maybe I was still riding the high of seeing her again. Of having her reappear when I'd thought she was gone forever.

But that kiss. I could still feel it. The way her lips had pressed against mine. Her arms draped around my neck. I'd kissed her plenty of times since then, but that was all we'd done. Like we were a new couple, getting to know each other. Not wanting to rush it.

Was that normal? I had no idea what I was doing.

"Gibs?" Bowie asked.

I startled, realizing I'd been staring at the wall with the roller in the paint tray. "Shit."

"You all right?" he asked.

"Yeah, fine." I rolled off the excess paint and got out of his way.

"You sure?" he asked. "Everything okay with Maya?"

I rolled the paint on the wall, stalling for time. Damn it, I didn't want to talk about this. But I also wanted to know. I was flying blind, and I hated that more than I hated talking about shit. Even feelings.

"She's good." I set the roller on the edge of the tray and cleared my throat. "Things are, you know... not as pretend anymore."

Everyone stopped painting and looked at me.

"Shut your fucking faces," I snapped. "It's not a big deal."

Bowie grinned. "Well, holy shit. The final Bodine bites the dust."

"It ain't all that," I said. "She's only been back a few weeks and I don't know how long she's staying."

"Yeah, but this isn't just any girl," he said. "Y'all were friends before, and it doesn't seem like thirteen years did much to change that."

I grunted my agreement.

Jameson climbed down the ladder. "It's pretty cool, Gibs."

I rubbed the back of my neck. "Yeah, but I have no idea what I'm doing."

"Weren't you the one giving George relationship advice when he got in a fight with June that one time?" Jonah asked.

"That's different."

"Why?" Jonah asked, sounding amused.

"Because it wasn't me."

Jameson handed me a bottle of water, then passed a beer to everyone else. Apparently it was break time. They got comfortable—sitting on stools or the floor—and cracked open their beers while I took a sip of water. Jameson ripped open a package of cookies.

"I like her, okay?" I said, finally. "I like her a lot. I might even... shit. But how the hell do you know?"

"How do you know?" Bowie asked, repeating my question. "You can't stop thinking about her."

"You want to be with her all the time," Jameson added. "And you'd do just about anything to keep her."

Devlin sat on a stool and rested his elbows on his knees. "She makes you feel alive."

"Yep," Jonah said. "And her being happy makes you happy."

I took another drink. "Okay, if all that's true, then what?"

"Then you date her," Devlin said. "Spend time with her and see where it goes."

"Basically what you're already doing," Bowie said. "Have you had the talk?"

"What talk?"

"If you don't know, you probably haven't," Bowie said. "The talk about where things stand. If you're officially a couple."

"Girls like to put a label on it," Jameson said.

"Jameson's very sensitive, so he needed a label on it before Leah Mae did," Bowie said with a smirk.

Jameson glared at him. "Gee, Bow, how many decades did it take before you finally told Cass you were in love with her?"

"It was complicated," Bowie said.

"Don't listen to this guy," Jameson said, gesturing at Bowie. "Take it from me, if you see an opportunity, you gotta take it."

"Just maybe don't leave your truck running in the middle of the street so you can jump out and kiss her," Jonah said.

"I stand by that," Jameson said. "Best decision of my life."

I was actually proud of Jame for that one. I gave him a chin tip.

"Just be honest," Devlin said. "If you have feelings for her, tell her."

"Maybe it's too soon," I said. "And it ain't like she lives here permanently."

"Jesus, Gibs, tell her," Jameson said. "Trust me on this

one. I didn't speak up when I should have and I almost lost Leah Mae because of it."

We all went silent and I stared at the floor for a long moment. The way they put it, it didn't seem all that complicated. It wasn't like I was thinking about marrying her. Yet. Maybe this was just how real relationships happened.

The silence went on long enough to get awkward. I cleared my throat again. "Get back to work, lazy-asses. I don't want to be here all day."

Devlin took his beer back to the spot he'd been painting, and Jonah started climbing one of the ladders. Bowie shook his head at me with a little grin on his face. Kinda made me want to punch him—but not too hard.

Jameson patted my shoulder. "She likes you too, Gibs. I'd bet my poker money on it."

"Thanks. Now shut your pie hole about it."

He slapped me on the back, then went back to work.

"Hey guys," George said from the doorway. He came in dressed in an old t-shirt and torn jeans. "Sorry I'm late."

"What the hell happened to you?"

George looked a little rough. His hair was a mess, his beard hadn't been trimmed in a while, and he had dark circles under his eyes.

"It's June," he said. "She's killing me."

"Killing you how?" Bowie asked.

"I don't know what's gotten into her," George said. "She's insatiable lately. I'm talking multiple times a day, like meals and snacks, only sex. She woke me up in the middle of the night last night and... well, I won't go into detail, but suffice it to say, it was pretty great. But I'm exhausted. I haven't had a full night's sleep in a week."

"Slow your roll, George," Bowie said, wincing. "Hearing about June is like hearing about our sister."

"You better get some rest tonight," Jonah called down. "We have an eight-miler tomorrow."

"Ah, shit," George said. He grabbed a paint roller. "What's new with you guys?"

"Gibson has feelings," Jameson said.

Everyone laughed, including George.

"Go ahead, shitheads, laugh all you want," I said. "Next Cock Spurs game, y'all are gonna have to get your drunk asses on the bus to get home by yourself."

We all got back to work and a couple of hours later, we'd finished. Place didn't look half bad with some new paint.

Just as we were done cleaning up, the girls arrived, fresh from their spa day. Each of them, including June, darted for their significant others, jumping into their arms. Callie looked a little shy as she walked toward me, her tongue darting to the notch in her lip.

"Hey, you." I slipped my hands around her waist and drew her close. "Have a good time?"

"Yeah, it was nice."

I leaned in to kiss her—just a taste. But then kissed her again because it felt so damn good.

"I like it when you do that," she whispered, brushing her nose against mine.

"That's good. I like doing it."

Her lips were so delicious, and so close, I decided I didn't care that my sister was probably staring at us, and kissed her again. Scarlett knew I didn't have to do this here. We were all in on the truth, so kissing Callie now wasn't for show.

I pulled back and looked her in the eyes, ignoring everyone else. "Ready?"

"Sure." Her phone rang and she pulled it out of her bag. "Hang on a second. I should take this."

I nodded.

She held the phone up to her ear. "Hey, Cole. Are you still in the studio? How's it going?"

Bowie caught my eye and whispered, "Cole? She isn't talking to Cole Bryson, is she?"

I shrugged. Cole Bryson was a big deal—famous rock star with millions of rabid fans.

"Yeah, I know it's hard," she said, her voice soothing. "But you need to remember, you've done this before. Look at those platinum records on the wall. You've totally got this."

Holy shit. Maybe it was Cole Bryson.

She paused again, listening, and her posture changed. Crossing her arms, she widened her stance. "All right, Cole, I get it. But if the album doesn't feel right, is wallowing in self-pity going to fix it? No, it's not. The only thing that's going to fix it is you. So here's what you're going to do. You're going to peel yourself off the floor, grab that guitar, and get your ass to work."

I raised my eyebrows. She sounded like a coach giving her team a fourth quarter locker room pep talk.

"No more excuses," she said, her voice firm. "I'm serious, quit being a pansy. You're tougher than this. If I have to fly out there to babysit you in the studio, you're not going to like it. I will ride your ass day and night until you get that motherfucking album done."

Everyone stared at her, including me. She made *me* want to quit being a pansy. About what, I had no idea, but her tone didn't leave any room for argument.

She smiled and when she spoke again, she was all sugar. "That's what I like to hear. It's going to be amazing. I have faith in you. Okay, we'll talk soon." With a satisfied breath, she put her phone away. "Sorry about that."

I stared at her in awe. She'd gone from sweetheart to

hardass take-no-shit woman and back again in the blink of an eye. I was a fucking goner for this girl.

"Dang, you told him," Scarlett said.

Callie just smiled and slipped her hand in mine. "Shall we?"

"Yes, ma'am."

No one said anything, but all eyes were on us—or maybe just her—while we walked out.

We left the high school and drove back to my place. I thought about what my brothers had said. We hadn't talked. I didn't know where this was going, if anywhere. And the weirdest thing was, I wanted to know. I cared. A lot. And I hadn't cared about anything this much in a long fucking time.

I parked in front of my house and we both got out. Before we went inside, I stopped in front of my truck and cupped her face in my hands. Kissed her, deeply this time.

"What was that for?" she asked.

"I like you." I wasn't ready to start saying the other word, even if I'd thought it a few times. "I know you haven't been here long, and we aren't sure what's going to happen. But this means something to me. I want you to know that."

A slow smile parted her lips. "This means something to me, too."

There was that full feeling in my chest again. "So we see where this leads?"

"Yeah. We see where this leads."

I leaned in to kiss her again, but the crunch of tires coming down my driveway interrupted us. Instinctively, I put myself between Callie and the car, gently nudging her behind me.

A compact maroon two-door with a dent in the bumper

on the driver's side pulled to a stop. A big guy with a dark beard got out and walked toward us.

"Are you Gibson Bodine?"

"Yeah. Who's asking?"

He held out a manila envelope. "This is for you."

I took the envelope and watched him like a hawk while he got back into his car and turned around. Didn't stop watching until he'd driven out of sight.

"That was weird," Callie said.

"Yeah. It was."

The envelope had my name on the outside, typed on a white label, but nothing else. I ripped it open and pulled out a thick bundle of paperwork.

"What is it?" Callie asked.

I skimmed the first page, my brow furrowing as I read.

"It's a lawsuit," I said. "A wrongful death suit in the case of Callie Kendall. Your parents are suing my family."

24

MAYA

*T*he tension in Bowie and Cassidy's living room was thick as mud. One of their cats had disappeared at the first sign of company. The other—a fat orange guy—hadn't moved from his spot, curled up on a pillow. Jameson stood against the wall with his arms crossed, staring down at the floor. Leah Mae sat on the arm of a chair next to him, casting worried glances his way. Jonah had an arm around Shelby, his muscles bulging, the veins in his arms standing out.

Cassidy sat on the couch next to Bowie, rubbing circles across his back. She had her laptop open in front of her. Bowie leaned forward, elbows on his knees, reading his copy of the lawsuit.

Gibson alternated between standing with crossed arms and pacing. His jaw clenched tight, making the cords in his neck pop, and his face was dark with anger.

He and I had read through the paperwork back at his place. His father's estate was being sued, and he and his siblings were all named. There were parts of the legalese I didn't understand, but the bottom line was clear. The Kendalls were suing Jonah Bodine's estate and its heirs for my supposed death.

It hadn't taken long for the phone calls to start flying. The other Bodines had all been served. Bowie had told everyone to meet at his place. We were just waiting on Scarlett.

She burst in the front door like a tiny whirlwind. "What in the actual fuck is happening right now? Can you believe this?"

Devlin was right behind her, and put calming hands on her shoulders. "It's okay. No one needs to panic."

"Don't panic? Do you hear yourself? The stupid Kendalls are suing us for a death that ain't even happened."

"Can they do this?" Jameson asked.

"Legally speaking, yes," Devlin said. "Now that they supposedly have a body, she's no longer considered missing. She's dead."

"So they're suing the estate?" Jonah asked. "Let's forget for a second that Callie isn't dead. They can't have enough proof to implicate him."

"Do they know something we don't?" Shelby asked.

"Not necessarily," Devlin said. "This isn't my specialty, but I read over the Complaint. It alleges that Jonah Sr. aided Callie's disappearance and either failed to prevent or was complicit in her death. The burden of proof in a civil suit like this isn't the same as a criminal trial. They don't have to prove he did it to win."

"And think about it," Bowie said, ticking points off on his fingers. "There's the sweater. Callie's fingerprints in Mom's car. Dad's speeding ticket in New York putting him near the location of that body."

"And they aren't alleging he killed her," Devlin said. "Which means they don't have to prove that he did. Essentially, they're alleging he helped her run away, and as a result of that, she died, putting him at fault."

"It fits with their story that she had mental issues," Cassidy said, then glanced at me. "Sorry, I don't mean to talk like you aren't here. My point is, they've always claimed you were depressed and unstable. Adding that you were a runaway means they don't have to change their story. It all sounds plausible."

I nodded at Cassidy—she was right—but my shoulders pinched with tension. Their story had clearly been designed to paint me as the problem and them as the poor victims of a depressed teenager. It made me sick.

"What's their game?" Bowie asked, and I wasn't sure if he was talking to himself or expecting an answer.

"Are they trying to force her out of hiding?" Jameson asked.

"I don't think so," Devlin said. He squeezed Scarlett's shoulders and stepped around her. "I know we don't have proof, but if they're behind all those incidents—the forensics report, Shelby's attack, intimidating that retired teacher, even Abbie Gilbert's death—they're trying very hard to make sure the truth doesn't come out. They want her to stay dead."

"So why sue us?" Gibson growled.

"This is just my opinion," Devlin said. "But I think it's an intimidation tactic. I don't know if their case is strong enough to win, but I doubt they care. A lawsuit could bury all of you in legal fees, not to mention stress, for the foreseeable future. If they have deep enough pockets, they won't think twice about getting you all tangled up in the legal system."

"I think he's right," Cassidy said. "I think they realize things are happening and there's a chance the truth about Callie will come out. They're trying to keep y'all from digging."

"It wouldn't surprise me if at least one of you gets a call from their lawyer or someone who represents them," Devlin said. "I bet they try to get you to do something in exchange for dropping the lawsuit."

"Something like what?" Bowie asked.

"Probably a public statement confirming their story," Devlin said. "It would be a PR stunt. Something to make them look gracious and forgiving and get you all on record saying their story is true. Or I could be wrong, and they just want to ruin your lives by emptying your bank accounts."

I raised my hand, like a kid in a classroom. "Can I say something?"

Heads turned in my direction.

"This isn't really a problem. I'm not dead. I'm sitting right here. So all I have to do is come forward, prove my identity, and this lawsuit goes away."

Gibson stopped moving and stood, his posture defensive. "Hold on."

I put up a hand. "I know you're worried about what will happen when the Kendalls find out I'm here. I am, too. I won't lie, I'm scared. But I can't let y'all get sued."

"I'm with Gibson," Jonah said. "We need to think this through and remember who we're dealing with."

Gibson tipped his chin to him.

"This is some messed up shit," Bowie said, pushing the papers away. "But y'all are right—we have to think about what the judge will do if his dead daughter suddenly reappears."

"We have time," Devlin said and the professionalism in

his tone was calming. "You have thirty days to respond, and then the courts move slowly."

"But y'all are still going to have to pay your lawyer to file a response and start fighting this," I said, only half aware of the *y'alls* I was suddenly dropping.

"Don't worry about that," Gibson said. "I'll cover it."

"We'll all cover it, like we've been doing," Bowie said.

"Speaking of, has anyone called Jayme?" Jonah asked.

"I did," Bowie said. "I sent her a scanned copy. We're supposed to call her. Are we telling her about Callie? Because I really think we have to."

Gibson met my eyes and I gave him a short nod.

"Yes, tell her," I said.

Everyone else nodded and murmured their assent.

Bowie tapped his phone screen, then set it on the coffee table.

"Bodines," Jayme said. "Before you say anything, don't panic."

Devlin nodded his agreement.

"No one's panicking," Bowie said. "Mostly."

"Is everyone there?" Jayme asked.

"Yes, ma'am. And Devlin filled us in a bit on what this means."

"Good," she said, her tone clipped. "They don't have a strong case, but they don't necessarily need one. I don't think they care if they win. They're trying to put the blame for Callie's death as far from their doorstep as possible. This is a good way to do it."

"We're also wondering if this is an intimidation tactic," Bowie said. "Someone showed up in town and approached Gibson. Asked him about why he'd been taken in to talk to the sheriff. Seems like that could point back to the judge."

"Why am I just hearing about this now?"

"There's been a lot going on," Bowie said, casting a wary glance around. "There's another rather important development you need to know about. We know Callie's not dead."

"That's not new," Jayme said.

"That's not what I mean," Bowie said. "She's here."

The phone went silent for a few seconds. "Excuse me?"

"Callie's here," Bowie said. "In this room, right now."

"Are you fucking kidding me?" Jayme said. "Jesus. Get me her DNA."

"Already working on it," Bowie said.

"Good. And for fuck's sake, tell me you're all being smart and hiding her in a closet or something."

Gibson raised his eyebrows at me, as if to say, *see?*

"She's been living under a new identity, so that's what we've been going with," Bowie said.

"Okay. I'll believe it's her when we get her DNA results. Now, the judge is gearing up for his confirmation hearing, so we're walking on a very thin wire. He has a lot to lose. If you really have his daughter sitting there, it obviously helps answer a hell of a lot of questions. But without hard evidence, we still can't nail him for anything."

"That about sums it up," Bowie said.

"We're trying to track down the lab tech who confirmed the dental match on the body in New York, but so far no luck. Just voicemail."

"What about Abbie Gilbert's supposed accident?" Jonah asked.

A shudder ran down my spine.

"Dead end," Jayme said. "Late night hit and run with no witnesses. If you want to hire a PI to dig deeper, be my guest, but I don't think you're likely to find anything. And you need to remember, my job is to represent your family. Not prosecute the judge. There's only so much I can do."

"Understood."

"So you don't think we can prove the judge was involved in Abbie's death?" Jonah asked.

I nervously tongued the notch in my lip. My stomach was starting to feel queasy.

"Not without something other than what we have," Jayme said. "Tell me about the guy asking questions about Gibson. What was that about?"

Gibson cleared his throat. "He approached me in town. Said some weird stuff about small towns and gossip and not letting go of the past. He asked if everyone in town was being questioned again, or just me. Then he said something vaguely threatening about the world being dangerous and that some things are meant to stay buried."

"Did he know who you were?"

"Yeah, knew my name, I didn't give it to him. I'm also pretty sure he was armed."

Hearing that again made me shiver. The thought of being face to face with Lee Williams again was terrifying. I'd had nightmares about him when I was little.

"Fucking fantastic," Jayme muttered.

"Callie thinks she knows him," Gibson said. "A guy by the name of Lee Williams. Worked for her father."

"I've been doing some research," Cassidy said, turning her laptop toward Gibson. "It's a common name, but I found someone that might fit. Is this him?"

Gibson peered at her screen. "That's him."

Cassidy picked up her laptop and held it so I could see the screen. "Recognize him?"

My breath caught in my throat and the box in my mind rattled violently. It was an older photo, something that had been printed in a newspaper. But it was definitely him. "Yes. He worked for my father."

"Forward that to me," Jayme said.

"Doing it right now," Cassidy said, moving her laptop back in front of her. "This guy is sketchy as all get-out. Started as a cop about twenty-five years ago, but left the force after an investigation. I can't find much about it. If I didn't know better, I'd wonder if there was a cover-up."

"My father kept him out of jail," I said. It felt like sorting through file folders. Old memories that had been tucked away. "I'm not sure what he did; I was too young to understand it all at the time. But I know he did something and got fired. He went to work for my dad after that. I must have been eleven, so that would have been about eighteen years ago."

"That matches up with when he left the police force," Cassidy said. "But I've done some searching and I can't find anything that ties him to the judge."

"There might not be any direct connections," Jayme said. "We'll need to look into the Kendalls' lawyer and other people closely associated with the judge. We might be able to tie this guy to the judge through one of them. And we need that link. We could use it to show harassment, especially because he made threatening statements."

"On it," Cassidy said, already typing.

"Alleged-Callie, is there anything else you can give us on this guy?" Jayme asked. I didn't sense any malice in her tone. She just wanted proof before she believed me.

"My father used to meet with him in secret. Our house in Virginia had an alarm system with video surveillance. When certain people came over, he'd turn it off. Lee Williams was one of them." It was a clear memory. If the cameras were turned off, I knew to stay away. Hearing things got me into trouble.

"Make me a list of the rest of those cameras-off people," Jayme said.

"Okay, sure. I'll try."

"And I take it you rode in Connie Bodine's car," Jayme said. "Alleged-Callie's story explains the fingerprints?"

"The fingerprints, the sweater, and the New York speeding ticket," Bowie said. "He helped her escape."

"Abuse?" she asked.

"Yes," Bowie said.

Cassidy reached over to squeeze my hand and Scarlett sidled up next to me. She put her arm around my shoulders and gave me a reassuring hug.

"Well," Jayme said, and I imagined her crossing things off a list. "Since the forensic results on Connie's car were inconclusive, we're probably not going to find anything to tie her death to the judge, and..."

Jayme kept talking, but everything went fuzzy, especially her voice. I couldn't hear a word because she'd just said *tie her death to the judge*. Connie Bodine's death? I stared straight ahead, unseeing. I'd known Connie had passed away. But Jayme was saying my father might have been involved.

Oh god. Had my father arranged to have Gibson's mother killed?

The room slowly came back into focus. Jayme was still on the phone. Scarlett stood next to me, gently rubbing my back, but her attention was on the call. Jameson and Leah Mae listened quietly, as did Jonah and Shelby. Devlin was taking notes. Cassidy typed and clicked, searching for evidence and answers. Bowie spoke again, gesturing with his hands, but I couldn't make sense of what anyone was saying.

Gibson still paced, his path taking him toward the window and back again. He stopped and our eyes met.

I looked away, feeling like my chest was going to explode with grief and guilt. The pain of it smashed my lungs, making it hard to breathe. How many lives had been ruined? Jonah Bodine had risked everything to help a hurt little girl, and his wife might have been killed for it. Had four kids lost their mom because of me?

An entire town had spent over a decade holding onto hope for me, grieving me as a loss. And where had I been? At an off-grid farm in a hippie town, doing yoga and drinking wheat-grass smoothies. In recording studios, back-stage at concerts, flying around the world, living in hotels.

"I think we're done for now," Jayme said. "But for god's sake, get me her DNA."

Conversations rose around me, everyone rehashing, planning, venting their frustrations. It all blew past me like a strong breeze. Jayme's words replayed in my head, over and over. *Tie her death to the judge.* Why hadn't anyone told me?

Someone took my hand and pulled me forward. Gibson. He spoke soft words I couldn't hear through the blood roaring in my ears, but I let him lead me into the kitchen.

He touched my face, brushing my hair back. His thumb traced my bottom lip. "Callie, honey? Where you at? What's wrong?"

I lifted my gaze to meet his. "He had your mom killed?"

His eyes went stormy, worry lines creasing his forehead. "We don't know."

"But it's possible."

As if reluctant, he nodded slowly. "The last place she went before she died was a hotel in Baltimore. Your mother was there that day, at a charity lunch. We can't come up with another reason she would have gone out there, other than to see your mom. We always thought she'd been in an accident on the way home. But it might not have been an accident."

I covered my mouth, my stomach roiling. "Oh my god."

He put his hands on my arms. "If he did, it ain't your fault."

"How can you say that?" I asked. "How can you even look at me? I left, I abandoned everyone, and look at what happened."

"Jesus, Callie, you were sixteen," he said. "You didn't abandon anyone. You got away so you could live."

"Why didn't you tell me about your mom?"

"Fuck, I don't know. Because we don't know for sure. Because there's nothing we can do about it without proof."

Connie Bodine. I remembered her calloused hands bandaging my wounds. Her authoritative voice as she and Jonah patched me up and tried to make me comfortable for the night.

"Gibson, I'm so sorry." My voice broke and tears stung my eyes.

"Don't." He cupped my face. "It's not your fault."

Taking a deep breath, I straightened my spine and sniffed back the tears. Looking into Gibson's stormy blue eyes, a sense of resolve filled me, pushing away the guilt.

"I want to take them down, Gibs. We have to find a way."

"We will." His voice was hard. "We're going to end this, and we're going to do it together."

25

MAYA

*T*he Bodines had decided there was only one thing to do in the wake of this new crisis: eat our weight in comfort food and go drink at the Lookout.

I hopped out of Gibson's truck, feeling a little sleepy after such a big meal. We'd gone home to check on Cash and play with him a little before heading back to Moonshine for dinner. I'd devoured most of a huge pepperoni roll and I had zero regrets.

Gibson walked around the front of his pickup, dressed in jeans and a dark t-shirt. He gave me a lazy smile, then draped his arm around my shoulders. Even though the lawsuit was stressing everyone out, Gibson had seemed relaxed since our meeting with his family. Those edges of his weren't nearly so rough. I was starting to feel like I had my old Gibson back.

"Can I tell you something that's a little bit silly?" I asked.

"Sure."

"I used to daydream about my first time going to the Lookout."

"You've never been here before, have you?"

I shook my head. "Nope. I was too young."

We started for the door, his arm still around me. "What's silly about that?"

"This was kinda my daydream," I said, feeling a little sheepish. "Walking in here with you."

"You thought about that back then?"

I reached up and twined my fingers through his. "Um, yeah. I might have had a bit of a crush on you."

He paused and looked down at me, one corner of his mouth hooking in a grin. "You did?"

"Come on, Gibs. You were the sexy, intimidating older guy. And you can sing. Of course I had a little crush."

"And all this time, I thought you'd liked how I played guitar."

"Look who has a sense of humor all of a sudden," I said, nudging him with my hip. "A crush wasn't why I liked hanging out with you. I just indulged in a little daydream once in a while."

"Imagine that. Me, making a teenage girl's dream come true." He grabbed the door handle.

I looked up at him. "I'm not a teenager anymore."

His brow furrowed and heat smoldered in his eyes. With a low rumble in his throat, he looked me up and down, a predator sizing up his prey. My body responded to his fire, a tingle rushing straight to my core. For a heartbeat, I wondered if he'd turn us around, put me in his truck, and drive us back to his place.

Instead, he opened the door.

Noise spilled out into the warm night and I stepped into the once-forbidden realm of whiskey and moonshine. The lights were dim, the air just shy of stuffy. Most of the stools around the L-shaped bar were taken. A lot of the tables, too. There were pool tables, neon beer signs, and peanut shells on the floor. Country music mixed with the din of a dozen conversations.

I'd been in countless bars before, but never *this* bar. Never the bar in my girlish fantasies. I'd forgotten about those daydreams—boxed them up with all things Callie. And now, here I was. With Gibson Bodine's arm around my shoulders.

I hadn't planned for any of this. Coming back to Bootleg, reconnecting with my past. I certainly hadn't planned to fall hard for Gibson Bodine.

But falling for him was exactly what was happening. There was no denying it. The moment he'd kissed me, my entire world had changed. Truth was, that kiss had been a long time coming. It wasn't like he was a man I'd just met. We had a history, even if it hadn't been romantic. A history that had already primed my heart for him.

We said we'd see where this led, and that felt right.

But there was a part of me that already knew exactly where this led—right here, to Bootleg Springs. It led to a tiny four-letter word. Something I'd never considered in any place I'd been in the last thirteen years. A word I'd thought didn't apply to me.

Stay.

I wasn't ready to make a decision tonight. Or even soon. I felt like we were on the brink of a confrontation that could alter the course of a lot of people's lives. I was determined, come hell or high water, to find a way to bring my father to justice. Not just for what he'd done to me, but for all the people he'd hurt over the years.

That was a task so formidable, it was almost hard to see

past it. To imagine a time when I wouldn't live in the shadow of fear. When I could reconcile the two halves of myself and be one person, in private and in public. When I could be Callie again.

That time would come. And when it did, where would I go? Back to a life on the road? Living out of a couple of suitcases, in hotels and temporary apartments? Dipping into people's lives for a short time, only to leave again when I thought they were strong enough to stand on their own? Never staying in one place?

No. I wasn't about to call Oliver and tell him I was making a change—it was too soon for that—but I already knew that life would never be enough. I wanted home. I wanted family and friends. A place to belong. And for the first time since my teens, it seemed like that life was within my reach.

Had I found all that here in Bootleg Springs, with the sometimes surly and so damn sexy Gibson Bodine? I was almost afraid to hope that I had.

We'd see where this led. We had a long road to travel before we were in the clear.

Scarlett and Cassidy were playing a game of pool with Devlin and Bowie. At a glance, it looked like girls against boys. Jameson and Leah Mae were at a small table tucked in a corner nearby. George stood by the pool tables, watching with a beer dangling from his big hand, while June sat on a stool next to him, her nose in a book.

Jonah had Shelby in his arms, swaying to a slow song. They were one of only two couples dancing, but they didn't seem to mind. Or notice. I did a double take when I realized one member of the second couple was Jenny. She and Jimmy Bob Prosser looked adorably cozy. He had one of her hands tucked against his chest and she smiled up at him.

Gibson led me to a table on the outskirts of the bar, as if he'd scanned the room and chosen the least crowded spot. He probably had.

"You want a drink?" he asked.

"Apple pie moonshine."

"Part of the daydream?" he asked.

I nodded. "I've never had it before."

He scowled. "What kind of Bootleg girl are you? We're fixing that."

I waited at our table while Gibson went to the bar. The bartender—Nicolette, if I wasn't mistaken—was a petite brunette with her hair in a ponytail and a no-nonsense look about her. Gibson rested an elbow on the bar and leaned across to give her our orders. Her eyes flicked to me for a few seconds, then back again, but she was too far away for me to read anything in her expression.

A woman whose face seemed familiar came over to my table. She was slim, maybe in her fifties, wearing a plaid flannel shirt, cowboy boots, and a friendly smile.

"Evenin'," she said, raising a half-full mason jar. "Just wanted to pop on over and say hi. I'm Fanny Sue."

Of course, Fanny Sue Tomaschek. I remembered her from before. "Nice to meet you. I'm Maya."

Her eyes tracked my face, just long enough for me to notice, but not quite long enough to be rude. And there was something in her expression. A wistfulness, maybe. "I hear you work for a big record company."

"I do. Attalon Records. I'm a producer."

"Wow, ain't that something else," she said. "That make you happy?"

I blinked in surprise. I'd expected a question about why I was in Bootleg, or maybe how I'd met Gibson. "Oh—well, yeah, it does."

Her smile grew. "That's wonderful to hear. So good to see you, Maya. I mean meet you."

I watched her walk away, my lips parted, my heart suddenly pounding. Oh my god, did she know?

Gibson came back with our drinks. He slid a mason jar with an inch or so of amber liquid toward me and sat on the other stool.

"You all right?" he asked.

I leaned across the table and lowered my voice. "Fanny Sue Tomaschek just came over and said hello. I think she might know."

His expression went stony, worry lines etching into his forehead. "You sure?"

"Not positive, but she said it was good to see me, then corrected herself to meet me."

"She didn't come out and say it? Use your name?"

I shook my head. "No. Isn't she a deputy? Did Sheriff Tucker tell the department?"

"I don't think so. Not yet. But Fanny Sue's sharp. If anyone in this town was going to figure it out, it'd be her." He looked in her direction for a second. "I don't think we need to worry. She's one of the good guys, anyway."

With a deep breath, I released the tension in my shoulders. Gibson was probably right. There didn't seem to be any reason to panic.

I took a sip of my drink, my first taste of real Bootleg Springs moonshine. It tasted exactly like apple pie—tart with a bit of cinnamon. It had a nice bite to it, warming my throat as it went down.

"Wow." I put the mason jar down. "This is dangerous."

"Yeah, you gotta sip it slow."

"What are you drinking?" I gestured to his jar.

"Just water. I don't drink."

That was something I didn't know. Had alcohol been a problem for him, or was it simply a matter of taste? "Can I ask if there's a reason?"

He looked away and for a second, I wondered if I shouldn't have asked.

"Dad drank. So I don't."

"I can understand that. I don't need to, if it makes you uncomfortable."

"Naw," he said, meeting my eyes again. "If it bothered me to watch people get shitfaced, I'd have to move to another town."

I tipped my mason jar, looking at its contents. "Well, I don't plan on getting shitfaced. Although I have a feeling this stuff would make it easy."

"That is a fact. If you do, I'll get you home safe."

That made me smile, and a warmth that had nothing to do with the liquor spread through me. I knew he would get me home safe. I could drink myself into oblivion, leaving me completely vulnerable, and I'd wake up in his bed tomorrow, no harm done—save the wicked hangover I'd be nursing. I trusted him.

Who else in this world did I trust like that? Almost no one.

I took another sip. It was damn good. "Thanks."

A burst of laughter from near the pool tables carried over the music. Scarlett and Cassidy were cracking up at something. Devlin watched Scarlett, the end of his pool cue resting on the ground by his foot. Even from over here, I could see the adoration on his face. Bowie was looking at Cassidy with the same eyes.

I glanced around the bar again. At Shelby and Jonah,

who'd joined the others at the pool tables, standing close together like they didn't want to stop touching. At George and June, now the sole occupants of the dance floor, swaying to "Tennessee Whiskey." At Jameson holding Leah Mae's hand over their table, idly twisting her engagement ring while they talked.

They had a potential crisis on their hands, but I realized none of them were going to stop living. Watching Gibson's family, I saw smiles and laughter. Good-natured shit talking. Kisses and soft touches. These people were spilling love all over the place.

It made me want to tuck them into my pocket and keep them forever. And the notion that I could maybe one day be a part of this—really, truly a part of it—brought the sting of tears to my eyes.

It also sent another fierce jolt of resolve pouring through me. I wasn't going to let my family ruin these people. No matter what it took.

Gibson reached across the table and took my hand. He straightened my arm and traced his fingers over my tattoos. Across the subtle ridges on my wrist, up to my elbow on the inside of my arm. "This is why you always wore long sleeves, isn't it? Why you were wearing a cardigan, even though it was summer."

I nodded. "I always did. I found lightweight ones so I didn't get too hot. And I suppose I was used to it."

His brow creased and he kept caressing my arm. "You even had one of those swimming shirts, didn't you? One with sleeves."

I glanced at his hand against my tattoos, thinking back. Somehow with him touching me like this, I could draw on the memories without feeling like they'd drown me. "Yeah, a rash guard. The one I had that summer was pink and blue, with bikini bottoms to match. I always left the house with shorts on so my parents wouldn't object to it. Even though it had sleeves, it was cropped pretty high. Showed a lot of my midsection."

"Why didn't we ever notice?" he asked. "Why didn't any of us wonder why you always wore long sleeves?"

I slid my fingers along the back of his hand. "I was very good at hiding my secrets. I'd started early, so it was second nature. I knew exactly how to behave to make it look like I was a normal girl. How to draw attention away from any little clues that might tip someone off. And people see what they expect to see most of the time. If my face didn't show my fear or pain, people didn't know to look for it."

"I should have known."

"No, you shouldn't have," I said. "And Gibs, those days we spent in the woods meant more to me than I know how to say. You made me feel good, and safe, at a time when I needed that more than anything."

His face lifted, his blue eyes meeting mine. "Oh my god."

"What?"

"I didn't even think about it when you said your name. Maya Davis. Davis ain't your Blue Moon family's last name, is it?"

I nibbled my bottom lip, feeling that little tug of sheepishness again. "No. Theirs is Holly."

"Davis is my middle name."

"Yeah, I kinda borrowed it from you."

A slow grin spread across his face and he took my hands, bringing them to his lips. "You can keep it. Although maybe someday..."

He trailed off, but I knew what he was thinking. He didn't need to say it. Maybe someday he'd give me his last name, too.

Right then and there, it happened. There was no stopping it now. I felt light, like I could float off this stool, filled with a heady euphoria. I wasn't getting tipsy from the moonshine. But I was drunk, all right. Drunk in love with Gibson Bodine.

26

GIBSON

*T*he scars on Callie's arms weren't noticeable when you looked at her, not with those beautiful tattoos. But I could feel them beneath my fingertips. Small ridges marring her otherwise smooth skin.

They rekindled my anger at her father, but instead of giving into it—and probably taking it out on someone else —I turned away from the raging heat that burned in my gut. It was still there. That man needed justice—Bootleg or otherwise—before I'd ever truly let it go.

But tonight, I didn't want to simmer in rage, like a pot threatening to boil over. I wanted to have a good night with my girl. Wanted it more than I wanted to be mad.

And damn, she made it easy.

That smile. Those hazel eyes, so pretty and clear. Her long wavy hair hung around her shoulders—a wild mix of blond, purple, turquoise, and blue. Her flowy dress was a hippie sort of sexy, like she ought to be wearing a crown of flowers on her head. She had a thin gold ring on one index finger, and a ring with a purple stone on another.

It hit me, like a punch to the face, that she was here with me. This beautiful girl with a spine of steel and a survivor's spirit was sitting across from me, looking into my eyes, smiling.

She'd borrowed my middle name, taken it with her when she'd left. Truth was, she'd taken more than that. She'd taken a piece of me. But instead of wishing for it back, all I wanted was to give her the rest.

Suddenly all those old country love songs I'd played so often made perfect sense.

"Did that teenage daydream of yours happen to involve dancing?" I asked.

Her eyes lit up. "You dance?"

"I'm a man, ain't I?" I said, almost offended that she was surprised. "Every Bootleg man worth his salt knows how to dance."

I took her hand and led her to the open space we used as a dance floor. June and George were still there. Bowie and Cass had joined them. I slipped a hand around Callie's waist, to the small of her back, and pulled her close.

Truth be told, my dancing skills were probably a bit rusty—I rarely used them—but for a slow song, it didn't matter. I knew how to lead, and that was the important part. And simply having Callie next to me—the excuse to touch her—was enough.

The slow song ended, and it rolled into a new one. "Meant to Be." It was a little more upbeat, and too new for us to have ever played it together before. But I knew the words, and I was feeling it in my bones, so I quietly sang along. Singing it just for her.

I wasn't trying to make a show of it, but Callie lit up. She smiled and danced with me while I sang to her. So I turned it up a little. Sang a bit louder.

The song was a duet, and Callie came in on the next verse, her voice full and clear. That special magic we had together filled the bar. We sang lyrics about love and taking a chance and letting it be. Seeing where things led, just like we'd said before. Sang it for each other while we danced.

Applause erupted at the end of the song, but neither of us acknowledged the crowd. Just looked into each other's eyes, smiling. I was on some kind of high I'd never felt before and I didn't want it to end.

The cheers died down, a new song taking their place. "Die A Happy Man." It was whiskey-smooth with a slow beat. I pulled her in close and breathed in the scent of her hair. Felt her body pressed against mine. Felt those damn lyrics in my soul.

We moved slow and I leaned my forehead down to touch hers. The fabric of her dress felt thin beneath my hands, barely concealing the curves of her body. I touched her, running my hands over her, skimming the line of what was decent.

She tilted her chin up and I kissed her. Instead of meeting my kiss with softness, she ran her fingers through my hair and parted her lips. I delved into her mouth with my tongue, tasting a hint of apple pie moonshine. The desire I'd fought so hard at first came roaring to life. The music, the feel of her in my arms, and the taste of her lips made my blood run hot.

I was instantly hard for her and for half a second, I thought about shifting so she wouldn't feel my erection through my jeans. But she pressed herself closer, rubbing up against me. And all I could think about were her words when we'd walked in.

I'm not a teenager anymore.

No, she was not. She was all woman. A woman who was currently driving me crazy on the dance floor.

I leaned in to speak low into her ear. "You're doing somethin' to me. You know that?"

"Maybe you should be doing something to me."

"Honey, you have no idea how much I want to."

"Then what are you waiting for?" She nipped my earlobe with her teeth. "Take me home."

She didn't have to tell me twice. I grabbed her hand and led her straight for the door.

We tumbled out into the quiet night, the air warm and still. She giggled, hanging on my arm as I led her to my truck.

"I didn't finish my moonshine," she said.

I knew she was teasing, but I spun her around and pushed her up against the side of my truck. Took her mouth in a kiss. This wasn't soft or sweet. It was me—rough and untamed. Hard and demanding. I growled into her mouth, pinning her against my truck, and made her melt for me. Pressed my hard-on against her. I didn't stop until I was sure she knew I was fucking her tonight.

When I finally pulled back, her eyes were glassy and dazed.

"I'll buy you another one. Now get in the truck."

For the first time since building it, I regretted my house's location. It wasn't far from town, but my consciousness was filled with a haze of lust as I drove. More than lust. I wanted her, but not just for a quick fuck. I wasn't bringing her home to scratch an itch.

I wanted to love every inch of her.

Finally, we pulled down my long gravel driveway. I got out and she didn't wait for me to open her door. Cash was out in his yard, but it was warm and he had everything he needed, so I didn't worry about him for now.

We rushed inside and as soon as I'd slammed the front door behind us, clothes started falling to the floor. She kicked off her sandals and slipped out of her dress. I tore my shirt off and paused with my jeans halfway down my legs, getting my first real look at her.

She stood in front of me in nothing but a light pink bra and panties. Reaching behind, she unclasped her bra and slowly let it drop to the floor.

The sight of those full tits and hard pink nipples short-circuited my brain.

She bit her bottom lip and curled her finger at me. "Get those pants off and come here."

"Yes, ma'am," I said, stepping out of my jeans.

She backed up toward my bedroom, a wicked gleam in her eyes. I followed, like a man in a trance, devouring the sight of her. The air between us snapped with electricity, anticipation making my heart thump in my chest.

Stopping next to the bed, she beckoned to me again. I licked my lips and grabbed my cock through my underwear, giving it a short tug as I approached her.

"Ooh," she cooed, her eyes on my cock. "Big, dirty boy."

"You have no fucking idea," I growled.

I grabbed her waist and hauled her against me, feeling her tits press against my chest. Kissed her hard and deep, tasting the cinnamon on her tongue. She slid her hands across my shoulders, to the back of my neck. Her skin was warm and soft against mine, the contact making my nerve endings fire, lighting up the primal parts of my brain.

"On the bed," I said, giving her a light shove.

She grinned, falling onto her back and scooting up the bed. I climbed on and kissed my way up her thighs.

Grabbed her panties with my teeth and pulled them down her toned legs.

"Goddamn, you're beautiful."

"I'm on birth control, but we should probably still use a condom," she said.

"Don't worry, honey, I got us covered."

As much as I ached to be inside her, I took my time loving on her body. Kissed her hip bone and across the smooth skin of her belly. Made my way up to her tits. She moaned as I slid one hand down between her legs and licked her nipple.

Sucking on her hard peak, I teased her clit with soft strokes. Dipped a finger into her opening.

"Damn, Callie, your pussy's wet."

She moaned again. "Gibs, I've been wet for you all night. I need you to fuck me."

"Yeah?" I pushed my finger inside her and she shuddered. "You need more of this, sweet girl?"

Her only answer was a whimper.

"I'll give you what you need, darlin'." I slid a second finger inside her. Pumped them a few times to feel for what she liked. Her eyes rolled back with a groan and I knew I'd found the right spot.

"Gibs."

I sucked on her tits while I fingered her, getting her good and ready. Enjoyed the feel of her nipple in my mouth, the taste of her skin. She rolled her hips against my hand, soft moans escaping her lips.

I'd never been so turned on in my life.

She gasped as I pulled my fingers out. I brought them to my mouth and sucked off her wetness.

"You taste so fucking good."

Her cheeks were flushed a delicate pink. She reached down and grabbed my dick, giving it a solid squeeze.

I grunted at the pressure. "You need that, don't you? You need my cock inside you."

"So bad," she breathed.

I leaned down, our mouths meeting in a messy kiss. She squeezed my dick again and I was done playing. I tore off my underwear, grabbed a condom out of the nightstand, and rolled it on.

She opened her legs and pulled me on top of her. Without hesitation, I pushed my cock inside her, groaning as the heat of her pussy enveloped me.

There was no waiting. No long, slow thrust while we sank into it. The tension between us was pulled too tight. I could feel what we both needed. We needed to fuck, and we needed to fuck *hard*.

I was happy to oblige.

She reached overhead to brace herself against the headboard while I drove in deep. My hips thrust, my muscles flexed. Her pussy felt so good, the heat and pressure overwhelming.

"Yes, Gibson. Fuck, that's good."

I kept going. Hard, steady thrusts, making her tits bounce. The pressure in my groin rose fast, but I didn't let it unleash. Not yet. She needed more, and I was going to give it to her.

Leaning down, I found her mouth again. Kissed her. Sucked on her lower lip. She wrapped her arms around me, holding on tight, and drew her knees toward her shoulders. I drove deeper, slamming my cock into her, grunting with the intensity of it.

Her pussy tightened with a rolling tremor.

"That's it, honey. You want to come on my cock?"

"Yes, Gibs," she whimpered. "Make me come."

"I want this pussy," I growled into her ear. "It's fucking mine. You hear me?"

"All yours, baby." Her fingers dug into my back. "And that cock is all mine."

That was the hottest thing I'd ever heard in my life. "Only yours, Callie."

She moved her hands down to grab my ass, pushing me deeper inside her. For a second, I thought about pulling out and turning her over. Maybe getting her on her knees so I could pound her from behind, or lying down so she could ride me. Hell, she was pretty fucking flexible, we probably had a lot of options.

But tonight wasn't about sexual acrobatics or mixing up positions. Tonight was about one thing, and one thing only. Good old-fashioned dirty fucking.

I felt the tension ease in both of us—anger and fear burning away in the heat of our passion. It was an outlet. A primal release of pent-up emotions. She needed it. I needed it. And together, alone in my room in the dark of night, we made a new kind of magic.

Her body was new to me, but I let instinct be my guide. She was coming before me—or with me—no matter what I had to do to get an orgasm out of her. Hard and deep seemed to be working for her, but I slowed down, just a little. Enough that I could really grind against her each time I thrust inside.

That was what she needed. Her pussy tightened and her moans turned into uninhibited cries. Her fingers dug into my back while she chanted a breathy stream of *yes, yes, yes.*

"Yes, baby," I growled.

I drove in and held there, burying myself to the hilt. I needed to kiss her. To meld my mouth with hers while our bodies joined. Taste her and feel her tongue lapping against mine.

With our mouths still tangling, I resumed my rhythm. She kissed me like she was desperate. Like I was oxygen. I drove harder, faster, feeling her body respond, the heat in her pussy rising. So tight. So hot. Fuck, I was about to unload inside her. I didn't know if I could hold out much longer.

With a carnal moan, she came apart under me. Her pussy clenched, pulsing with her climax. I rode it out with her, feeling the pressure in my groin intensify.

Like a ripple through still water, all my nerve endings fired, the sensation in my cock staggering. And I came fucking undone.

The most powerful orgasm I'd ever had ripped through me. My cock throbbed inside her as I burst, exploding with a loud groan. I thrust deep, bottoming out. With my face buried in her neck, I growled, muscles clenching, overpowered by the sheer force of it.

My climax subsided, but I stayed inside her, breathing hard into the sheets. Her arms were wrapped around my back and she hooked her legs around my waist.

"I love you," I whispered, suddenly not giving a shit that it was too soon to say it. I felt it, deep in my soul, and I needed her to know. I knew all too well what it was like to lose someone before you'd had a chance to tell them how you felt. I wasn't taking that chance with her. "I fucking love you so much, Callie."

"I love you too," she said, her voice breaking. "I can't let you go, Gibson. I can't."

I picked myself up so I could look her in the eyes. "You'll never have to, you hear me? I'm yours. And we're going to fix everything so you can stay."

Tears leaked from the corners of her eyes, but she smiled, nodding. "Okay."

"Okay."

I leaned in and kissed her, soft this time. We were going to fix things. I wasn't sure how, but I was a Bodine. We were nothing if not stubborn bastards. I was going to find a way, for her, and for us. She was mine now, and no one was ever going to take her away from me.

27

MAYA

I woke slowly, coming awake with a deep, cleansing breath. It felt like I was floating—enjoying the lake on a lazy summer day. But I wasn't surrounded by warm water. Instead, I drifted in relaxed bliss on Gibson's sheets. I was tucked up next to him, my back to his front, his arm around my waist. His chest moved against me with his soft breathing, and his skin was warm against mine.

Still feeling a little loopy and sex-drunk, I nestled into him. He tightened his arm around me, a contented moan rumbling in his throat.

This man loved me.

He'd said it, his voice husky in my ear. I hoped the memory of those words never faded. I wanted to be a hundred years old and still able to recall his deep voice, whispering the most beautiful thing I'd ever heard.

I loved him right back. I didn't care what other people were going to think. Whether it seemed too fast to fall in love. I didn't believe in those kinds of rules anyway. Quincy and Henna had taught me that. They'd always told me that I needed to find my own path—live my life on my terms. Hell, they'd eloped after knowing each other for a weekend, and they were one of the happiest couples I'd ever known.

Gibson Bodine was mine, and I was his. And that was all there was to it.

The problem of my father, and my real identity, had taken on new meaning overnight. The danger hadn't gone anywhere. I couldn't stay here if he was free. He'd find out the truth about who I was, sooner rather than later.

Convincing Bootleg I was Maya Davis had been a temporary plan. I was convinced Fanny Sue knew who I was. And if one person did, others would too. It was only a matter of time before people looked closely enough to see me. Saw past my scar and my altered nose. Past my tattoos and dyed hair. They'd see the girl they'd lost. They'd see Callie.

And going back to my life as Maya wasn't an option. I'd liked a lot of things about that life. It had felt exciting, but still safe. Working with musicians—songwriting, helping them find their power or their peace or their confidence again—was fulfilling. I was good at what I did, and the people I worked with appreciated me. There was value in that.

But proud as I was for having built a life for myself, given where I'd come from, this was what I really wanted. Home. Family. The man I loved sleeping beside me, his arm tucked around my body. I wanted Gibson and I wanted him forever.

And it scared the shit out of me to think the Kendalls could take it all away. That the people who should have loved me could hurt me all over again.

Gibson had said we'd fix things so I could stay, and I'd felt his sincerity. Heard the determination in his voice. I'd have to trust that we'd find a way.

"Morning, love," he said, his voice rough with sleep. He nuzzled his face in my hair and kissed my head. "How do you feel?"

"Amazing." I closed my eyes and took another deep breath. I was pleasantly sore between my legs, my body still sated. "How about you?"

He curled in around me, hugging me with his whole body. "So fucking good."

We relaxed in bed for a little while. But life didn't stop because we'd fallen in love. Cash needed food and attention. Gibson had work to do, so I brought Cash inside and made us coffee and breakfast while he showered. He rough-housed with Cash a little, crouching down to pet his tummy, then kissed me goodbye in the kitchen before heading over to his workshop.

It was so easy to imagine this being our normal. Our forever. Sharing coffee in the morning. Kissing him good-bye. Hearing the muffled sounds of his tools in the building next door.

Living a life with him.

Oliver called shortly after I'd showered and dressed. He'd been talking with Saraya Lin, an artist I'd worked with before. She was writing songs for a new album, but running into trouble. It didn't sound like a full-blown emergency requiring a Maya-intervention. So after I took Cash outside, I got her on a Skype call.

I propped up my phone on the table in front of the couch and borrowed Gibson's guitar so I could strum out the melodies she was working with. Cash wedged himself behind my back for a snuggly nap.

Saraya was off to a good start, but she'd hit a creative wall. With probing questions, I coaxed the truth out of her. She'd lost her favorite grandma a few months back and she was still recovering from the loss. But instead of reaching into her grief and using it to fuel her creativity, she'd been trying to push it away. To separate her emotions from her songwriting. Her usual sound wasn't heavy or mournful. She was known for her upbeat, vibrant music, and she didn't know how these dark emotions fit.

I encouraged her to try writing a fresh song and let her love of her late grandma be the inspiration. She didn't have to delve into the darkness of her loss to find inspiration and meaning. She could draw on the good things. On love and happy memories.

Hours later, with my phone about to run out of battery, and Cash constantly licking my face, we had a song. A soft, beautiful, heartfelt song that made Saraya sound like the musical angel she was. It still needed work, but I knew she could handle it. And if she kept that up—allowing her true emotions to meld with her creativity—she'd be just fine.

Gibson came inside smelling of wood stain. He smiled and went into the kitchen to wash his hands, then got down on the floor to snuggle Cash. It was so cute, it made my ovaries ache. He got up again and came back with two glasses of water.

I took one gratefully and gulped down half of it. "Thank you. I didn't realize how thirsty I was."

"You all right?"

"Just worn out. I was on a call for most of the day, working with Saraya Lin. She's a singer and songwriter with Attalon."

His brow furrowed. "I've heard of her. Was she having trouble with something?"

"Yeah, but I think we broke through her wall."

"So they don't need you to go to..."

"She's in Nashville, and no. Besides, Oliver knows I need time. I told him I'm dealing with some big personal things."

He nodded and took a drink of water. "Is your boss still asking you about me?"

"About your record deal?" I asked. "No, he knows you're not interested. You're not interested, right?"

"No."

"I'm not asking this to push you, I'm just curious. Why not?"

He glanced away for a moment. "That's just not me. I like playing in little bars like we do now. But if it was something bigger, I don't think it would be the same anymore. And I don't want that kind of life."

I smiled at him. "I know you don't."

"So, you worked with her without going anywhere."

"Saraya? Yeah, why?"

"I'm just wondering if that means you could still do your job but stay in one place, at least some of the time."

"I think I'll have options going forward. I didn't travel so much because I had to, necessarily. I wanted to. I was always bugging Oliver to send me somewhere new as soon as I finished every project."

He rubbed his chin, his brow furrowing again. "I wouldn't hate traveling sometimes."

God, he was adorable. "No?"

"As long as I was here enough to take care of my clients. And we'd have to think about Cash."

"So, you're saying if I traveled less, you could come with me."

"I ain't saying I'd go on some world tour with a bunch of fucking head-up-their-asses rock stars. But if you need to travel to keep doing what you love, I think we can make it work."

My tummy tingled at this newfound and unexpected sense of contentment. "Are we sitting here planning out our future?"

One corner of his mouth lifted. "I reckon we are. I told you, you're mine now. I meant it."

There was nothing I wanted more in this world than to be his. But the shadow of my past still lurked, threatening to enshroud us in darkness.

"You know we have bigger things than my job to deal with. There are other ways I can make a living. But I can't stay with you if..." I trailed off. I didn't need to say it. We both knew.

"I've been thinking about that. The sheriff can only do so much until he can get the attention of someone with the right pull. Jayme's looked into things, but she's a lawyer, not a detective. We both know this thing is at a standstill until someone comes up with real evidence against the judge."

I nodded. That certainly summed it up.

"So we get some fucking evidence," he said.

Swallowing back the prickle of fear that tried to invade my thoughts, I nodded again. "Okay. But what?"

"I've been thinking about that, too. Seems like the first place to look is that forensics lab. Maybe proving the judge was responsible for that false report would be enough to get the right people looking at him. Jayme couldn't reach the lab tech, but a phone call's easy to ignore."

"True. What do you suggest?"

"A little visit." He shifted, making his broad shoulders and chest flex. "He won't ignore me."

"How do we find him? Wait, let me guess. You've thought about that, too."

"You got that right, sweetheart," he said. "I already got his name from Jayme and put Leah Mae on the case. If he uses social media, she'll find him. It's like her fucking superpower. That, and getting my brother to quit being a mute."

GIBSON HAD BEEN RIGHT—LEAH Mae's social media skills did seem on par with a superpower. The lab tech, Darren Covington, lived in upstate New York, not far from where the body had been found. He was currently on medical leave, and his social media accounts had been locked down. No recent posts or photos to be found.

But a couple of days later, she found him, tagged in a photo with a friend. It showed him posing in front of a shiny new black Tesla with a buddy, both giving a thumbs-up sign. And the post had a GPS tag. It had been taken at a hotel a couple of towns over. It wasn't a guarantee we'd find him there, but it gave us a place to start.

Gibs cleared his schedule for the next day and we left early, before the sun was up. We had a heck of a lot of driving ahead of us, so we took my rental car. It was easier on gas. Shelby and Jonah had happily taken Cash.

It was almost surreal to be on this road with him. Thirteen years ago, his father had driven me along this same route.

Shuddering, I watched the scenery go by. That blank space in my memory was still hazy. Like I was looking through thick mist, not quite able to see what lay beyond, but well aware that something was there.

I wasn't sure if I wanted to see.

We located the hotel easily. It was nice, bordering on

fancy, with a pool and overpriced room service. I'd been in places like it hundreds of times.

And in the parking lot—a shiny new black Tesla.

We parked in the lot and pulled out our phones, pretending to look at them, as if we were just a couple of people distracted by the screens in our hands.

"I did something like this once," Gibson said.

"What, a stakeout?"

"That's a better term for it, I guess. I kinda stalked Abbie Gilbert, trying to find out if she was you."

"Did you, really?"

"I knew in my gut she wasn't," he said. "Her whole story was such bullshit. But that wasn't why I knew."

"Then how did you know?"

He glanced at me. "I knew if you were alive and you could come back, you'd come see me. Even if it wasn't first. I knew you wouldn't reappear and then never show up in Bootleg, looking for me."

"You're right."

"But I still went looking for her. Needed to see her with my own eyes."

And now Abbie Gilbert was dead. The thought sent a chill down my spine.

A young guy came out of a side entrance and went straight for the Tesla. It was Darren Covington. A second later, Gibson was out of the car.

I scrambled out and followed Gibson. He intercepted Darren in front of his car.

"You Darren?" Gibson asked, his voice casual.

Darren stopped in his tracks, his forehead tightening. "Who are you?"

Gibson strolled up to him, his easygoing gait somehow more intimidating than an open threat would have been. He put his arm around Darren's shoulders. "I'm your new best friend. And we're going to have a little chat."

"What the fuck's going on here?" Darren asked, his eyes widening.

"Let me see if I can make this easy," Gibson said, his expression friendly. "You're going to talk to us and you're going to tell us the truth. We clear?"

"Are you threatening me?" Darren asked. "I'll call the police."

"Go right ahead," Gibson said. "I'm sure the police would love to see this nice, new car of yours. How did you afford that beauty, Darren? Do lab technicians make that kind of money?"

Darren didn't answer.

"And does your boss know you're living it up at this swanky hotel? You seem awfully healthy for a guy on medical leave."

"Fuck," Darren muttered.

"Yep, I'd say so," Gibson said, his voice going low. "Let's unfuck some of this situation, shall we?"

Darren reluctantly led us back to his hotel room. The king-sized bed had been made—housekeeping had obviously been here already—and a glass door behind a mostly-closed curtain led to a balcony. I peeked into the bathroom. Beige tile, neatly folded white towels, and a large soaking tub. A terrycloth robe hung on a hook.

Gibson's face was stony as he performed a sweep of the room before he nodded for me to sit at the small desk. He looked at Darren and pointed to the bed. "Sit."

Darren lowered himself onto the edge, his face tense with fear. "Are you going to hurt me?"

"Depends." Gibson's stance was relaxed, his arms

crossed loosely over his chest. But anyone with half a brain could see the tension he kept coiled inside.

"Depends on what?"

Gibson absently pressed his thumb against his middle finger, cracking the knuckle with a pop. "On whether you tell me what I want to know. And whether I think you're lying. See, Darren, I don't like it when people bullshit me. It's a waste of my time and that just pisses me the fuck off."

I watched Darren swallow hard, some of the color draining from his face. His eyes flicked to me a few times, as if he were trying to decide why I was here. I just stared back. I wasn't going to let Gibson actually hurt the guy, but I could tell it wasn't going to be necessary. I'd seen too many people on the brink of losing it. I knew what it looked like when someone was about to crack.

"What do you want to know?" Darren asked, his voice shaky.

"You signed off on a forensics report that identified the remains of a young girl recently," Gibson said. "I want you to tell me about that."

Another hard swallow from Darren. "My job was to determine the identity of the remains using dental records. I found a match."

"Did you, though?" Gibson asked.

A sheen of sweat broke out on Darren's forehead. "Yes."

Gibson cracked another knuckle. "Stop wasting my time, Darren. It's starting to piss me off."

Darren's eyes darted around wildly. "Look, it was a lot of money, okay. I had student loans up the ass. Who wouldn't have taken it?"

"Huh," Gibson said. Another knuckle crack. "Enough money to pay off your loans and buy you an expensive new car? Did they put you up in this hotel, too?"

"I'm supposed to lay low for a while. And come on, man, that's my dream car. You aren't going to smash it up or something, are you?"

"I wasn't, but now I might," Gibson said. "Who paid you off?"

"I don't know his name," Darren said. Gibson's gaze snapped to him and Darren flinched. "I swear. He never told me who he was. He showed up at my house after work one day and offered me money to fake the report. I said no at first, but it was a lot of money, and those loans were killing me."

Gibson pulled his phone out of his back pocket. Wordlessly, he tapped on the screen a few times, then held it out to show Darren. "Was it that guy?"

I could see the recognition in Darren's expression even before he nodded.

"Yeah, that looks like him."

Gibson pocketed his phone, then crouched in front of Darren, leveling him with a piercing glare. "You caused a big problem when you did that. And the people who paid you won't hesitate to get rid of you to keep you quiet."

Darren's face lost another shade of color. I wondered if he'd pass out. Or maybe piss himself. "What do you want from me? I don't have the money. I paid off my loans and bought the car and—"

"Shut your pie hole." Gibson stood. "Like I said, you're going to help us unfuck this. And when it's over, you might even get to keep that car of yours."

"I don't understand. What do you want me to do?"

"You said you need to lay low for a while?" Gibson asked. Darren nodded.

The corner of Gibson's mouth hooked in the barest hint of a grin. "I have just the place."

28

GIBSON

*L*eaning against Nicolette's bar, I chewed on a toothpick. My water sat near my elbow. The Lookout wouldn't get busy until after five. For now, it was me and a bunch of members of Bootleg's only biker gang, the Dirt Hogs. They weren't so much a gang as a group of balding, gray-haired old-timers who wore matching leather vests when they occasionally went out riding. They usually drank over at the Still while their wives played bingo on Tuesday nights. But this afternoon, half a dozen of them had gathered here, taking up a table nearby.

"Need something else, Gibs?" Nicolette asked.

"Nope."

She gave me a short nod. "I need to run into the back. Don't hit anyone while I'm gone."

I scowled at her. Of course, that was probably a fair warning. I'd hit a lot of people in this bar.

I glanced at the time. Where the hell were my brothers?

"Something's gotta give," one of the old-timers said, his voice rising. "We can't keep living like this."

"Wendell ain't lyin'."

"God's honest truth."

"I ain't built for this."

"Well, what are we gonna do about it?" Wendell asked.

Old Jefferson Waverly stood. I had no idea how old he was, but his back was still straight, even if his flannel hung off his now-thin frame. "We take a stand."

I was bored enough to want to know what they were talking about. "Take a stand about what?"

"Our women," Marvin Lloyd said, shoving a finger in the air like a politician making a speech. "We ain't takin' this no more."

I shifted the toothpick to the other side of my mouth. "What'd y'all's wives do now?"

"We ain't getting a moment's peace," Marvin said. "It's nothing but lovemaking, every single day. Why, I've had my willy wet more in the last couple of weeks than I have in the last twenty years."

Pulling the toothpick out of my mouth, I tried not to gag. "Jesus. Sorry I asked."

"A young'un like you wouldn't understand," Old Jefferson said, shaking his head. "I don't know how they expect us to keep up with their raging appetites."

"Are y'all cracked? I know y'all's wives. You're telling me they're chasing y'all around for—" I stopped before I said it.

"For the sex," Marvin hissed out in a loud whisper.

I had no idea what was going on with the elderly of Bootleg, but I decided I did *not* want to know more. "Good luck with that," I said, turning my back on them.

They kept up their griping. Made a shudder run down

my back. Luckily for me, the door opened, and my brothers finally walked in.

"What took y'all so long?"

Bowie started cuffing the sleeves of his button-down shirt. "I had a meeting. You know, the job I have with a schedule I have to keep."

Jameson didn't offer a reason for being late. He slid onto the stool next to me and rubbed his eyes.

"What's wrong with you?" I asked.

"Tired."

Jonah didn't look much better. Which was odd, because he was usually the healthy, energetic one. But he was sporting some dark circles under his eyes.

Come to think of it, Bowie didn't look so hot, either.

"Did y'all get drunk last night?" I asked. "You look like hell."

They all glanced at each other, a mix of surprise and confusion crossing their faces.

Bowie pinched the bridge of his nose. "I don't know about these guys, but it's Cassidy. She's been wearing me out."

"You too?" Jonah asked, and Bowie's face snapped to his. "I mean, that sucks."

They both looked at Jameson.

"I ain't saying shit," he said.

"Wait, is this some kind of weird Bootleg thing I don't know about?" Jonah asked. "But why would Shelby be in on it? She's not from here."

"What the fuck are y'all talking about?" I asked. "I have important business."

Bowie glanced around, like he was worried about who might overhear. But none of the Dirt Hogs behind us could hear worth a damn. "Cassidy's sex drive has been through the roof lately. She wants it multiple times a day. At first, I thought I'd won the damn lottery. But now I'm fucking exhausted."

"It is some weird Bootleg thing," Jonah said, his eyes wide. "Shelby's the same. She can't get enough."

"Really?" Bowie asked.

"Leah Mae, too," Jameson grumbled, pulling down the bill of his cap. "Truth be told, I didn't know a man could come that many times in a single week."

"Wait, wasn't George complaining about the same thing?" Jonah asked.

Devlin pushed the door open and came in, looking rumpled. His dark circles rivaled Jonah's.

"Scarlett too?" Jameson asked.

"Insatiable sex drive?" Jonah added.

Devlin took a seat at the bar, his eyebrows knitting together. "How do you know that?"

"No one's watching y'all," Bowie said, scowling. "We're in the same boat. Seems it's all of 'em."

"You bunch of pansy-asses," I said. "Y'all show up late, then you want to sit around and bitch about getting too much sex?"

"Clearly you're either not sleeping with Maya, or whatever's happening to the rest of our girls ain't hit her yet," Bowie said. "Trust me, Gibs. You have no idea."

People sometimes said Bootleg was a strange place, and I usually disagreed. I'd lived here my whole life—couldn't quite imagine living anywhere else—so our shenanigans generally seemed normal. But this? My brothers, and the Dirt Hogs, all talking about their women suddenly running them ragged with out-of-control sex drives? That was fucking weird.

"Maybe it's something in the water," Bowie said.

I gave the water Nicolette had given me the side-eye. "Hey Nic, you back there?"

Nicolette poked her head out of the kitchen. "What?"

"You been putting something in the drinks that makes women horny?"

"Good lord, Gibson," Bowie said. "Shut your damn mouth."

"But has she, though?" Jameson asked, lifting his head.

Nicolette looked at me like I'd just told her she should stop serving blackberry moonshine. "No. I don't think there is such a thing."

Bowie scrubbed his hands up and down his face. "Okay, Gibs. Why are we here? I need to get home and see if I can catch a nap before Cass gets off work."

It was my turn to glance around, but the Dirt Hogs had all fallen asleep in their chairs. Old Jefferson let out a quiet snore.

Still, I lowered my voice. "I found the lab technician."

That got their attention. Jameson sat up, Devlin leaned forward, and Bowie and Jonah both asked, "What?" at the same time.

"The guy who matched the dental records," I said. "Someone paid him to fake the results."

"The judge?" Bowie asked.

"Not directly. But it was the guy who showed up in town, asking me questions. The one *she* said worked for the judge." I still didn't want to say her name out loud in public.

"Holy shit," Jonah said.

"Do you have proof?" Devlin asked. "Will he talk?"

"Oh, he'll talk." I stuck the toothpick back in my mouth.

Devlin narrowed his eyes at me. "Gibson, you can't—"

The door opened again, spilling sunlight into the dim bar. Cassidy pulled off her aviators, looking mighty official in her uniform. I figured it didn't matter if she was dressed for work. She was a cop either way, so I wasn't going to worry about whether she'd get too official on me. Scarlett wore a Bodine Home Services t-shirt knotted at the waist. Her jeans were dirty at the knees and she still wore her tool belt.

Both girls made beelines for their significant others. Cassidy draped her arms around Bowie's shoulders and whispered something in his ear. He patted her hand, looking like he might be willing to chew his own arm off to get away. Scarlett was... Scarlett, which meant she lacked subtlety.

"Hey, baby," she said, sidling up to Devlin and putting her hand in his lap. I couldn't see what she was doing, and I didn't want to know.

"For fuck's sake, y'all," I said. "Can we focus? I got the forensics guy."

Cassidy stood up straight, suddenly all business. All cop. "What did you say?"

I repeated what I'd just told my brothers. Scarlett didn't stop pawing at Devlin.

"He'll talk?" Cassidy asked, eying me warily. "What'd you do to him?"

I pushed the toothpick around my mouth again. "We just had a conversation."

"Uh-huh." Cass crossed her arms.

"He's fine," Scarlett said. "We made him very comfortable at the Red House last night."

Cassidy's eyes moved from me to Scarlett, then back again. "You knew about this? Please tell me you didn't kidnap the lab technician."

"I didn't kidnap the lab technician."

"Well..." Scarlett said, drawing out the word.

I shot her a glare. "It ain't kidnapping if he comes willingly."

"Oh my god," Cassidy said. "What is wrong with you two? You can't kidnap someone and hold them hostage."

I rolled my eyes. "He ain't a hostage, Cass. And Scarlett wasn't even there."

"Did he come here of his own accord?" she asked.

"Mostly."

Her eyes went icy and I knew I was skirting the edge of serious trouble. Cass was scary when she went cold like that. "Mostly? Gibson Bodine, if you make me arrest you for abduction and unlawful imprisonment, I swear to god—"

"Calm down, Cass," Scarlett said, interrupting her tirade. "I talked to him. Gibs didn't lay a finger on him. Probably gave him a good scare, but by the time they got to town late last night, he was on our side. We're hiding him from you know who."

"You know who?" Cassidy asked. "What is this, Harry Potter?"

"Well, I ain't saying it right here," Scarlett said. "Just like I ain't saying the other thing."

I put a hand up. I didn't need those two getting in an argument about what we could and couldn't say in public. One of them was liable to say Callie's name by accident. Empty bar or not, I didn't want to do anything to risk her safety. "Okay, we get it. We still have to keep this quiet. This kid will tell the truth, especially if your dad can get him some kind of immunity or something. Keep him out of trouble for taking the bribe."

"Poor guy is pretty damn scared," Scarlett said with a laugh. Her face got serious. "Dev, maybe I should bake him some cookies."

"Don't cook," we all said in unison.

Scarlett glared at me, like I was the only one who'd said it. "Fine. I'll buy some. But just because he's an almost-hostage doesn't mean I can't be neighborly."

Cassidy closed her eyes in exasperation. "Don't call him an almost-hostage, Scar."

"Guest, then," Scarlett said. "I thought you'd be a lot more excited. This is a big break in the case."

"Possibly, but if y'all do something illegal, I don't care how big of a break it is, it won't help us," Cassidy said.

"This will help us because the kid's gonna talk," I said, my voice rising. I was tired of going round and round about this. "He told me the truth, and he'll tell the sheriff. With his statement, maybe your dad can finally get the attention of the feds. Get someone on this case who can take the fucker down."

"I'll talk to Dad," Cassidy said. "But I don't know if it'll be enough if the judge isn't the one who bribed him."

"I thought we weren't saying who it was out loud," Scarlett said.

"Shut up, Scar," I snapped. "Maybe the judge didn't, but the guy who did works for him."

"Can you prove that?" she asked and kept talking before I could argue. "Gibson, I know. I want to take that sorry son of a bitch down as much as anyone."

"Do you?" I asked, my temper a thin twig ready to snap at the slightest pressure. "Because all I'm hearing from you is a lot of shit about what we can't do and what won't work. And here I am, driving to fucking New York because law enforcement can't even do its damn job."

Bowie stood. "Watch it, Gibs."

"No, fuck that. We know the truth, and that piece of shit is going to get away with it. You know what's worse? She can't even live her life. What would y'all do if you had to pack up and leave, huh? Where would you go? What would you do when life got hard and you needed your family and friends around to make it fucking bearable, but you couldn't go home?"

I stopped shouting and the bar went silent except for the soft snores of the Dirt Hogs. Clenching my hands into fists, I looked down at the floor. My knuckles ached with the desire to hit something. I wanted the pain of it reverberating up my arm. I wanted to taste blood. But I wasn't about to haul off and sucker-punch one of my brothers. Even I wasn't that much of a dick.

"We're trying to help, Gibs," Cassidy said, her voice quiet.

"It ain't enough," I ground out through my teeth. "If she has to run again, I'm going with her. You hear me? She goes, I go. I just want y'all to know that."

Without waiting for anyone to reply, I stomped out the door.

29

MAYA

I stared at the blank page in my journal. There were songs inside me, trying to get out. I could feel it. How many times had I coaxed the words or melodies out of someone else when they were doing this very thing? A few questions, a little conversation, sometimes a glass of whiskey or a bottle of wine, and they'd push aside whatever it was that blocked them. Their creativity would break free, and they'd find a way to work through whatever had been holding them back.

So why couldn't I do the same for myself?

I'd tried. I'd used my own tricks on myself. Written down the questions I might have asked, had I been talking to a client. Tried to answer them. I'd meditated on it, done juice cleanses, and used crystals to realign my energy. I'd taught other people to crochet because I'd learned to do it myself, hoping busy hands would help free my mind.

Nothing worked. The words never came out right.

The fact that my creativity had felt blocked before I'd

come back to Bootleg Springs made sense now. Callie had been locked up too tight. I knew there were things in my past that needed to come out. Pain I needed to face. The logical part of me—the Maya part—understood that.

But there was something back there I couldn't reach. Something in that box in my mind. Even here, in the safe comfort of Gibson's house, I shrank back from it. Flinching like there was a demon inside with claws and sharp teeth. If I let it out, it would rip me to shreds.

I heard the rumble of Gibson's truck outside, so I shut the journal, shaking off the unsettling images. Cash jumped up and ran for the door, his tail wagging.

Gibs had gone to talk to his brothers about Darren Covington. So far, we'd only told Scarlett, because we'd needed a place for him to stay last night. She'd been more than willing to put him up in one of her cabins for the time being.

Leaving him there alone did mean he was a flight risk. But I didn't think he'd go anywhere. At first, it had been Gibson's intimidation that had swayed him into coming with us. But I'd talked to him on the long drive back to Bootleg. I hadn't told him who I was—not yet—but I'd told him enough to make him realize he'd gotten into bed with some very bad people. And he seemed to be too worried about his own hide to question who I might be.

He was foolish—he'd taken a large bribe and blown through most of it already—but he wasn't completely stupid. He knew the sort of people willing to bribe a lab tech to falsely identify a body were not upstanding citizens of the law. He wanted a way out.

I'd told him we couldn't promise him anything. But if he helped us, we'd do what we could.

The door burst open and Gibson barreled his way in,

like a hot wind blowing off desert sand. Without looking at me, he stalked into the kitchen and threw open the refrigerator, only to slam it again a few seconds later. Cash ran around his feet, but Gibson ignored him.

"What's wrong?" I asked.

"Nothing."

Rage was coming off him like sparks, crackling in the air. I got up but kept distance between us, like I was approaching a wounded animal in the wild. Cash seemed to sense trouble. He backed up and sat.

"What happened?" I asked, my voice calm but not overly soothing. I didn't want him to think I was trying to calm him down. "Did Darren leave?"

"No."

"Then what—"

"It ain't enough. We have the guy who told the goddamn world that body was you, and they're saying it might not be enough. What the fuck do we have to do?"

"I don't know. We keep looking. Keep digging."

"And then what?" He spun around. "That bastard has been getting away with shit for years. Decades, even. The truth doesn't matter, we both know that. That's why you ran. Because even back then, you knew it was fucking pointless."

"I ran because I was a terrified child."

He grunted something I couldn't make out and stalked past me, clenching his fists. His heavy footsteps pounded against the floor and a few seconds later, the back door slammed shut.

I glanced at Cash and his head tilted to the side. "Yeah, Daddy's upset. It's okay, buddy. Just go lie down. I'll talk to him."

Cash was either the smartest dog in the universe, or he just wanted to get back to his nap. He trotted over to his bed and lay down. I pushed the sleeves of my flannel shirt up to my elbows and followed Gibson.

He stood with his hands on the porch railing, his back to me. His shoulders were bunched up tight and I could practically see the anger seeping from his pores.

"So we give up, is that it?" I was done with this temper tantrum. "One thing doesn't go the way we thought it would and it's over?"

He didn't turn around and his voice was dangerously low. "That's not what I said."

"Maybe not, but that's what I'm hearing in everything you aren't saying. I know you're frustrated. I know you're scared." I paused, giving him an opportunity to argue with that, but he didn't. "I am, too. But we knew the sheriff wasn't going to issue an arrest warrant based on Darren's statement. It's just the first step."

"I fucking know that," he shouted over his shoulder.

I crossed my arms. "You don't have to yell, I'm standing right here."

With a roar that made me take a step backward, he balled his fist and slammed it against the wooden beam. His knuckles came up bloody.

"What are you trying to do?" I asked, my tone of voice still not changing. "Scare me? Make me leave you alone? Or are you just so mad you don't even know?"

He whipped around and if human eyes could glow red, his would have. His jaw was tight, the cords standing out in his neck. "Get the fuck out."

I didn't move. Didn't take my eyes off him. He was going to apologize for that later, but right now, he wasn't going to ruffle me. Had it been any other man in the world, I probably would have backed off, just in case he snapped and I'd underestimated what he was capable of. I wasn't stupid. He was a lot stronger than me, especially with all that adrenaline coursing through his veins.

But I wasn't backing down. Not from Gibson Bodine. Because even though he was out of control with rage, I still trusted him.

"You need to be real careful what you say to me right now, Gibson Bodine."

"Or what?"

"Or you're going to have to live with what happens next."

He put his back to me again, his hands gripping the railing. Blood ran down his fingers, but I doubted he could feel it yet.

"Just leave me the fuck alone."

I sighed. "What are you even mad about? Did something happen that you're not telling me?"

"No."

"Then what?" I said, finally raising my voice. "What has you so out of control you're shouting at me and telling me to leave?"

"I don't know," he barked and suddenly his shoulders dropped, his aggressive posture softening. He looked down at his hand, spreading his fingers, as if he'd just realized he'd hurt himself.

"Why are you mad?" I asked again, softly this time.

He stood there for a long moment, breathing hard. Leaning against the railing, his back to me. When he finally spoke, his voice was a normal volume. "Because I spent thirteen years thinking you were dead. Because my father knew the truth. Because he was a shit father to us, but for some reason he decided to be your goddamn hero."

I stayed quiet, waiting. I knew he wasn't finished.

"Don't get me wrong, if he was going to do one good thing in his life, I'm glad it was saving you. It's hard to feel anything good for that man, but I'm grateful he helped you. I just don't understand why. Why did he go so far out of his way to help a girl he barely knew when he couldn't even parent his own kids worth a damn?"

I stared at his back, my heart breaking for him. He didn't know. But how could he? I kept avoiding the memories of that night, assuming everyone understood what had happened well enough that I didn't need to spell it out. His father had never told him the truth, and neither had I.

"He did it to protect you, Gibs."

He looked at me over his shoulder, a deep furrow in his brow. "What?"

I took a deep breath, reaching into the box in my mind. Drawing out the memory. This part was clear, the details sharp even after thirteen years.

"When he found me on the side of the road, I was heading to your place. I was running to you." I balled my hands into fists to keep them from shaking. I felt myself teetering between Callie and Maya again. "When he stopped, I told him where I was going. I asked him to take me to you. He said no."

"Why?"

"He said he was afraid of what you'd do if you saw me like that. He told me he was sorry, but he couldn't let you do something stupid and go to prison for the rest of your life. That's why he helped me. Why he kept me hidden and got me out of town in secret."

"I don't believe that," he said, but there was a quaver in his voice. He turned to face me. "He didn't take your secret to his grave because of me. He walked by your missing-persons posters every goddamn day, and he knew you were alive. He was hearing from you with those damn postcards. He didn't keep his mouth shut for me. He helped a teenage girl run away and he didn't want to get in trouble for it."

"He kept my secret for so long for many reasons, Gibs. Yeah, maybe one of them was to keep out of trouble. And he understood that my father was dangerous. After your mom died... That had to have kept him quiet, too."

He shook his head and glanced away. "That's what Jenny said. He told her it wasn't an accident, but she didn't know whether to believe him."

"See, he was protecting his family. And I'm telling you, right here and now, the reason he helped me in the first place was you. That was why he put me in his truck and hid me in that shack for the night. And why he convinced your mama to come out with bandages and blankets. Why he drove me all the way to New York in secret while the whole town was looking for me. A little piece of it was to help a girl in trouble. But really, he did all that for you. He did it to protect his son."

Gibson's expression changed, his anger crumbling to pieces. His stormy eyes revealed the depth of his pain. A boyish innocence and desire for love long since crushed.

"He hated me." There was no more rage in his voice. Only hurt. "He blamed me for his life not being what he wanted. He told me I was nothing."

Tears welled up in my eyes. His painful honesty was hard to hear. It made me ache for him and dredged up shadows of my own childhood trauma. "It's awful that he treated you that way. But I don't think he hated you. I think he hated himself, and he wrongly took it out on you. I wish he hadn't, Gibs. I wish he'd have been a good father to you. But I think there's a piece of his truth in what he did for me. Deep down, he loved you."

Gibson took three quick steps and grabbed me, hauling

me roughly against him. His legs buckled and we both collapsed to our knees. I wrapped my arms around his shoulders while he buried his face against my neck. His breathing was ragged, and he didn't say a word, so I just held him. Closed my eyes and gently rubbed his upper back.

His muscular arms tightened, his hands fisting the back of my shirt. Tears streamed down my cheeks as I felt his pain with him. Let it roll through me like a summer rain. I rested my face against his head, wishing he'd had better. Wishing we'd both had better.

"Why are you still here?" he asked, his voice muffled.

I sniffed. "What are you talking about?"

"I'm no good, Callie. I don't deserve you."

"Why, because you lost your temper and snapped at me?" I asked. "Gibs, I know the difference between someone who's lashing out and someone who truly wants to hurt me. Don't get me wrong, I'm not going to let you get away with it. You keep yelling at me like that and I *will* get the fuck out."

He pulled back enough to look me in the eyes. "I'm shit at apologies. It ain't how Bodines do things. But... I'm sorry. I didn't mean that."

I touched his face, feeling his rough stubble beneath my hand. "Apology accepted."

He didn't break eye contact, the raw vulnerability in his eyes making tears well up in mine all over again. "I love you."

A tear broke free, leaving another hot trail down my cheek. "I love you, too."

And I knew, in that moment, that somehow we were going to be okay.

30

MAYA

For a place that was supposed to be quiet, the Bootleg Springs library was hopping. The hum of conversation filled the air. Not exactly outside-voice volume, but much louder than the usual hushed whispers in a place like this.

I went inside with my big handbag slung over my shoulder. The smell of food mixed with the scents of paper, leather, and lemon furniture polish. The library wasn't large, but it was cozy, with a neat front counter, rows of shelves, and natural light from high windows.

I'd received no fewer than six invitations to June's book club. Nine, if you counted the three times I'd been invited to the last meeting. I'd only just started the current book, but everyone—including June—had assured me I was still welcome.

Gibson and I had paid Darren a visit earlier today, bringing him a few groceries and making sure he was comfortable—and still willing to be cooperative. He'd gone from scared, to reluctant participant in our strange—and as yet unfinished—plan, to downright cheerful.

No one in town knew he had any connection to the Callie Kendall case. To them, he was just a tourist named Darren. He'd told his family and friends he was doing a little traveling, and proceeded to soak up all Bootleg Springs had to offer. As far as he was concerned, for now he was getting a free vacation.

I wasn't sure how I felt about that, considering what he'd done. But at least he was being cooperative. And we didn't have to try to hold him forcibly. Cassidy and her father were especially glad about that.

Pausing near the front, I gazed at the two long tables set up in an open space near the fiction section. They were covered with food, potluck style. Casseroles, jello molds, baskets of muffins and buttermilk biscuits, fried chicken, at least four different pies, and numerous other dishes, baskets, and containers crowded together along the rectangular surfaces. It was an enormous amount of food, but the library was packed with people.

It looked like half the female residents of Bootleg Springs had turned out for June's book club. Many wore matching t-shirts that said *Book Babes* on the front. I saw everyone from Carolina Rae Carwell—who'd been claiming to be sixty years old since before I had disappeared—to Lula, the drop-dead-gorgeous owner of the Bootleg Springs Spa.

There were young women in sundresses or flannels and cut-offs, and a little cluster of new moms who'd worn heels and lipstick, like they were living it up on a rare night out. Women whose grown daughters were here with them, and a circle of white-haired women with crepe-paper skin, several of whom had their knitting out.

Jenny Leland was here, who for so many years had been my one last tenuous—almost anonymous—tie to this place. To the good parts of my past. She stood smiling and talking with Nadine Tucker and Betsy Larkin, Leah Mae's stepmom.

And among the large group, the women who'd scooped me up into their lives without question. Scarlett, Cassidy, June, and Leah Mae—girls I'd known when we were young. Girls I'd spent summers with—long days of running around town, piling into booths at Moonshine to share milkshakes, giggling about boys, swimming in the lake. And Shelby, who in the short time we'd known each other had treated me like we were long-lost friends.

It was like looking at the intersection of my past and my future, all in one place. A past I'd been struggling to outrun, and a future that, until recently, hadn't seemed possible.

With a deep breath, I let the flurry of emotions pass through me. One feeling settled like a gentle mist. Contentment. I didn't feel anxious or antsy, wondering where I was going next. Despite the fact that I was closer to danger than I'd been in years—in terms of physical proximity—I wasn't compelled to constantly look over my shoulder.

I'd developed habits as Maya that I'd barely noticed. Watching over my shoulder. Checking and double-checking locks. Wiping down surfaces to get rid of fingerprints. I'd willfully ignored them, telling myself they weren't out of the ordinary. Trying to convince myself that I was fine. I'd moved on.

But here, in this funny little town that was famous for not letting go of the past, I felt some of those habits slipping away. Or easing their hold on me, at the very least. I didn't look over my shoulder as often because I knew there were other people around who had my back. I'd stopped wiping down the booth at Moonshine or the table at Yee Haw Yarn and Coffee before I left. I still checked locks, but not as frequently.

And there was no doubt in my mind those things meant something.

"There you are," Jenny said, her gaze landing on me. She wore a pretty floral blouse and capri length pants. "I was hoping we'd see you here."

I hugged her, enjoying her motherly embrace. "Looks like I've been missing out. There are so many people."

"Fun, isn't it? I've only been one other time, but now I'm hooked. Oh, and the books are good too." She winked. "There's more than enough food. Feel free to dish up. And Nadine says to make sure we all pack up at least one full plate for our men before we go. They need to keep up their strength."

I took a plate and wandered down one side of the tables, adding a few things that looked good. If I tried even half of what was here, I'd be too stuffed to breathe. But I did make sure to grab a good-sized piece of Carolina Rae's cornbread. I remembered it from before, and it was famous in four counties for a reason.

Millie Waggle approached, in a blue calico dress with a white collar that closed at her throat. She wore a name tag that read *Hi, My Name Is*, and she'd written *Millie Waggle* in perfect cursive. She was the only one with a nametag. "Hi, Maya. It's awful nice to see you."

I smiled at her. "Thanks. You have to tell me what you brought tonight so I make sure to get at least two."

"Lemon bars and blueberry muffins," she said, beaming with pride. "I thought about baking something with chocolate, but I feel like I've been getting too predictable lately."

"Have you ever thought about opening a bakery?" Millie

Waggle's baked goods could turn the staunchest low-carb dieter back to the dark side of sugar and flour.

"Oh, I don't know." Her cheeks took on a hint of pink. "It's just something I do for fun."

"That's nice too. I know everyone enjoys your baking."

"Thank you kindly. Can I just say, I like your hair? And... well... it's just real good to see you again."

"Thanks." My smile faded and I busied myself reaching for a blueberry muffin. The way she'd said that... Did she know who I was?

Looking up, I noticed a handful of the women watching me. A few leaned together and spoke quietly. I couldn't be sure that they were talking about me—or that, if they were, it was because they knew the truth. But I had a feeling my identity was on the verge of coming out. These people were smart and observant. And their memories were sharp. The novelty of Gibson having a woman in his life had been distraction enough for a little while. But now they were starting to see me, and more than a few probably guessed who I was.

And yet, if they did know, they were keeping it quiet.

I decided the chance of an unexpected Callie Kendall reveal at tonight's book club was unlikely. I'd discuss it with Gibson, but we needed to come forward to the rest of the town with the truth sooner rather than later.

"Everybody, direct your attention here." June gestured for people to be quiet. Her dark blond hair was pulled back in a simple ponytail and she had an extra helping of summer freckles scattered across her nose and cheeks. Her *Book Babes* t-shirt was white with blue lettering. "Thank you. Since our group is increasing in size, it has become necessary to dichotomize into separate sub-groups. I've created a spreadsheet detailing the members of each. You've been separated by a process of random number generation that allowed for the greatest chance of demographic diversity within each smaller classification."

The room went silent, eyes darting around.

George's voice broke the silence. "She means she divided y'all up into smaller groups because there's a lot of you." The lone man in the room—at least that I could see—sat away from the gathered women. He had an ankle crossed over one knee, his large frame dwarfing a rickety folding chair.

"Precisely," June said with a satisfied nod. "If you'll just refer to page three of your handouts, we can begin rear-ranging into the aforementioned groupings."

Another silence followed her instructions, only broken by the rustling of paper as some of the book clubbers flipped through a stapled packet.

George didn't look up from the magazine in his lap. "June Bug, maybe everyone can just break up into groups on their own. Might be a touch easier."

"That's also acceptable," June said.

"Y'all, just sit with who you want so you can discuss the book," George said. He glanced up, meeting June's eyes, and his face broke into a wide smile. She beamed back at him.

The noise level rose again as the ladies all gathered purses, tote bags, and paper plates piled with food, and moved their chairs into smaller circles. I walked over to Shelby, who gave me a quick hug hello. We tucked in with a group that included Cassidy, Scarlett, EmmaLeigh—who also eyed me like she knew a secret—and Dixie Miller, a white-haired woman with clear blue eyes and a lap full of her knitting.

It occurred to me as I watched all the ladies settle in that there was a distinct lack of Misty Lynn Prosser in this room.

Of course, it was a book club. That sounded like Misty Lynn repellent to me.

Nadine paused by our circle, met Cassidy's eyes, and gave her a little smile. Then she dragged her chair to another group nearby. Looking around, it seemed like none of the ladies with grown daughters in attendance were sitting with them. Maybe they were just trying to sit with people they didn't see as often—a nod to June's attempt at randomization.

"Well, y'all, I don't even know where to begin with this one," Scarlett said. "It was even better than the last book. Do y'all agree?"

Heads bobbed with enthusiastic nods.

"I was particularly interested in the shenanigans on the couch," Scarlett continued. "Did y'all find that difficult to picture, or was it just me?"

"I actually found the description quite helpful," Cassidy said. "And by god, once you get it right, it's worth it."

"Is it?" Shelby asked, leaning forward. "I wasn't sure, but maybe we should give it a go."

"Are you kidding?" Cassidy asked. "Jonah was basically made for that sort of thing. Trust me. Try it."

"Ladies, that wasn't even my favorite part," EmmaLeigh said. "I was all aflutter at the end when he met her out on that balcony. There were all those people down below, but they just..."

A chorus of *ooh*s and *ahh*s went around the circle.

"For me, it's not so much about the way the scenes play out," Cassidy said. "Because let's be honest, a lot of it is more than any of us would really indulge in."

Heads nodded in agreement.

"But there's a freedom in it," she continued. "I think that's what I'm enjoying the most."

I leaned down, reaching into my bag to dig out my Kindle.

"You know what I really appreciate," Dixie said, glancing up from her knitting. "I feel like I've been able to connect with Clyde in ways we haven't in years."

"That's so beautiful," EmmaLeigh said.

"It is," Dixie said, her expression going wistful. "Here I thought my lady parts had all but dried up. They just needed a little spark to wake 'em up again."

"Good for you," Cassidy said.

"Get it, girl," Scarlett said with a grin.

"You're never too old to rev up your engine," Dixie said, pointing around the circle with one of her knitting needles. "Don't forget that."

"I won't," Scarlett said, leaning back in her chair. "I plan on having orgasms until the day I die."

"Use it or lose it," Dixie said. "Although take it from me, if you lose it, you can still bring her back to life. Clyde and I ain't what we used to be, but some old-fashioned horizontal refreshment is still plum good. Even at our age."

I blinked a few times, still bent over with my arm in my bottomless bag. What on earth were they talking about? I sat up and leaned closer to Shelby.

"I thought this was a book club," I whispered.

"It is," she whispered back.

"Then why does it sound like Dixie Miller is talking about sex?"

"Because she is," Shelby said, as if that was what all seventy-plus-year-old women talked about at book clubs.

"Why?"

"Haven't you read the book?" she asked.

"Just the beginning. Everyone said I should come anyway, but I'm lost."

"Oh," Shelby said, like it all made sense to her now. "Skip to chapter six."

I dug around in my bag again until I found my Kindle, then swiped through the pages to chapter six. The rest of the women continued their conversation—EmmaLeigh started in on a list of ten ways to get in a quickie when you're pressed for time—and I started reading.

My eyes slid across the page, a scene that began with the two main characters chatting over dinner in a fancy restaurant. Their conversation quickly turned seductive, then became downright dirty. He leaned over the table and described a long list of things he planned on doing to her as soon as he had the chance. Just reading the dialogue made my heart pump.

The female character got up and made her way to the ladies' room. A minute later, her date joined her. I tracked the words faster now, the scene getting intense. Clothes being taken off, piece by piece, each article exposing new areas of skin to be touched and kissed. Low murmurs and sexy growls, neither of them seeming to care that they could be caught at any moment.

I kept reading, feeling my cheeks flush and everything below the waist tingle. The couple in the book started having sex. Their positioning seemed unlikely, if not impossible, but it was written so convincingly, I was transported to that posh bathroom with marble tile and wide mirrors. I could see it all. The way he maneuvered her body into previously unknown positions that allowed him to drive his abnormally large penis deep inside her. Her blissful pleasure as he gave her the most amazing, intense, and all-encompassing orgasm of her life.

And it didn't end there. A waitress opened the door, but the salacious couple didn't stop. Despite being seen, and the startled waitress staying to watch, they continued their breathtaking foray into sexual exploration.

In real life, I had no desire for someone to watch me have sex. But I was captivated by this riveting scene in which two people overcome with sexual desire threw off their inhibitions and participated in a symphony of dirty talk, and even dirtier actions, resulting in multiple orgasms— including a masturbatory climax for the watching waitress.

I'd spent my adult life working in the music industry. I'd toured with rock stars. I'd walked in on more than my fair share of people having sex. Sometimes in odd places, or with more than two participants. But I'd never seen—or done—anything like what I'd just read.

Letting out a long breath, I closed the book. I was warm, the pressure between my legs making me want to squirm in my chair.

The discussion continued, and it turned out the book had a lot more than vibrantly-written erotic sex. The plot sounded engaging, and everyone talked about how much they swooned over the romantic ending. The epilogue was a favorite, apparently including some extremely arousing sexual exploits on a couch, which the ladies in my circle agreed were worth trying at least once. Except Dixie—she and Clyde preferred to keep it basic so neither of them broke a hip.

Nadine stood and called for everyone's attention again. "Ladies, we're almost out of time. Before y'all go, don't forget we have a recipe-sharing circle online with plenty of libido-enhancing meals and ingredients. EmmaLeigh was kind enough to add her write-up on five ways to get your man aroused when he's tired. And I think we can all agree that Scarlett's contribution last week on the topic of oral activities was enlightening, so we've put a short summary there for you as well."

June rose from her seat. "The next book is already posted on the website, and is available in both ebook and paperback formats. Piper has once again ordered extra copies from neighboring libraries to meet the demand. And if you'd like to read similar books by comparable authors, there's a list for your reference. Any questions?"

Dolores, an elderly woman with a wispy gray bun, raised her hand.

"No, Dolores, you cannot spike Murray's food with extra Viagra," Nadine said before the woman could speak.

Dolores lowered her arm with a scowl.

"Thank you for attending," June said.

"And enjoy those orgasms," someone said from the back.

Her exclamation was met with whoops and hollers around the room.

"It's hot, right?" Shelby asked, pointing at my Kindle.

I nodded, still feeling a little shell-shocked. "I had no idea."

"Read the rest and you'll be hooked," she said with a little grin. "Just plan on Gibson being overwhelmed by your enthusiasm at first. It happens to all of them. Jonah adjusted and now..." She sighed heavily, fanning herself. "So amazing. You'll both be very happy. Trust me."

I helped the women clean up and, at Nadine's urging, packed a plate full of food to bring back to Gibson. George put away chairs and tables, casting adoring looks at June. They sure seemed happy. In fact, all the women in attendance had smiles on their faces.

They looked good. Vibrant and alive, even the older ladies. I wondered if it was the female bonding over a naughty book, or the extra sex they were having with the men in their lives. Maybe it was a bit of both.

Regardless, I needed to get back to Gibson's. The throbbing between my legs had only grown, and I couldn't stop thinking about the scene in that book. The things he'd done to her. I wasn't sure half of them were possible, but I was going to make Gibson a very happy man tonight while we gave a few of them a try.

31

GIBSON

a bunch of trucks were parked around the perimeter of the softball field, bathing it in light. Necessary for a night game when your field didn't have fancy lighting. It did mean there were about a dozen places where the light blinded the players if they glanced in the wrong direction. But they'd also be guzzling moonshine in between innings, so a few blind spots weren't going to make much difference.

The school buses were already lined up, waiting to take people—players and spectators alike—home after the game. Here in Bootleg, we took our drinking seriously, but we weren't stupid. Cars and trucks stayed parked at the field overnight, and by the end of Wasted Wednesday—when everyone tried to recover from the town-wide hangover—the now-sober townsfolk would wander back to get their vehicles and drive them home.

The moonshine concession stands were doing big business and the bleachers were full of Bootleg residents. They scarfed down hot dogs and baskets of greasy fries, and just about everyone of age had a cup of moonshine in their hand.

Except me, of course. I didn't drink.

Mostly that was because of my dad. He drank, so I didn't. Although it wasn't as simple as a stubborn attempt to turn myself in the opposite direction of everything he'd ever done. I worked with my hands, much like he had. He'd been more handyman than craftsman, but there was a similarity to our trades. That hadn't swayed me from my profession. I sang and played guitar. I'd gotten that from him, too.

I didn't drink because it felt like too big a risk to take. I'd had alcohol before. I'd been everything from tipsy to shit-faced, out-cold, drunk off my ass. The problem was, I liked it too much. It was a guaranteed escape. Felt good to check out and stumble around without a care in the world, my head swimming in liquor. I knew what I'd find at the end of that road, and I'd made a conscious choice to take a different one.

We were playing the Gableton Miners tonight. Their shirts featured a cartoon man covered in coal dust, holding a shovel like a baseball bat. They wore headlamps over their caps, adding to the light show on the field.

Opal warmed up with a few practice swings while Buck and Nash stretched their shoulders. Bowie looked right at home with a mitt dangling from his hand. Baseball had always been his game. The guy was good, even when he was three sheets to the wind in the seventh.

Jameson was nearby, being all kissyface with Leah Mae. I thought about barking at him to get his head in the game —it's what I usually did—but kept my mouth shut. It was weird, but I didn't mind seeing my brother loving on his girl so much these days.

Scarlett walked toward the dugout, a half-empty mason

jar of moonshine in her hand, her long ponytail sticking out the back of her Cock Spurs hat. Someone in the stands shouted her name, and she raised her moonshine in greeting, a big-ass smile on her face.

I took a deep breath, a sense of resignation stealing over me. I wanted to have this conversation with her like I wanted a kick to the teeth. But it needed to happen. And although my sister could hold her alcohol like nobody's business, it'd be better if she was completely sober. That was probably her first drink, so now was the time.

I flexed my busted hand, feeling the scabs pull. I hadn't broken anything when I'd punched the beam, but I'd bloodied my knuckles a bit. With a sigh, I walked over to stand beside her—faced the field, rather than looking at her straight on. "Hey."

"Hey, yourself," she said. "Where's Maya?"

Her question poked at the big knot of feelings in my chest. Not because there was anything wrong with Callie. She was over by the concession stands with Cash. But it was an in-my-face reminder of who Scarlett really was. She had my back. Always. Even when I didn't deserve it.

"She's getting a hot dog."

"Okay."

She didn't say anything else. Just stood next to me. She knew I was fixin' to say something. I could tell by the way she waited, doing me the courtesy of not forcing me to make eye contact with her.

"You might have been right about some things," I said, finally. "I'm not going to say he was a good dad, because he wasn't. But you weren't totally wrong about him."

"No shit, Sherlock."

"And maybe..." I paused, clearing my throat. We Bodines were terrible at apologies, especially me and Scarlett.

"Maybe I shouldn't have been so hard on you about it. Loyalty is one of your best qualities."

"Aw, Gibson." She threw herself at me, sloshing moonshine all over, and wrapped her arms around me.

I grumbled and squeezed her back.

"You're a good man, Gibson Bodine," she said. "I'm glad you're my brother."

"Yeah, you're all right too." I pried her arms off me and pushed her back a step. "Go get warmed up. We have a game to win."

"Sure thing, Coach." She punched me in the arm before walking away, her ponytail swinging.

Huh. I felt lighter. Like a bit of the weight I'd carried for so long had just lifted.

I went back to the dugout to get my team ready for the game and spotted Darren in the stands. The bribe-taking lab tech hadn't bolted on us. It helped that he was staying free of charge in one of Scarlett's rentals. Sheriff Tucker had interviewed him—twice—and he'd been true to his word. Told him everything. At this point, we were keeping him here in Bootleg more for his protection than for his cooperation.

Once the investigation against the judge finally broke open, things were liable to get dicey. We'd all rest easier when he was behind bars. But we had one shot at him. As much as the wait stretched my patience, like a stringy piece of Misty Lynn's gum, I knew the sheriff was right to hold out until the case against him was rock solid.

I did a double-take. Speaking of that nicotine-gum-chewing shrew, Misty Lynn was currently seated next to Darren, arching her back to shove her fake boobs at him. The lopsided grin on his face told me she had him fooled. I rolled my eyes. We'd have to pull him aside and give him a warning. I didn't much like Darren, but I still wouldn't wish Misty Lynn on him.

"Okay, players, let's get warmed up." I clapped my hands together a few times. Coaching the Cock Spurs was mostly a matter of herding the players as they got progressively more drunk, then getting them on the school bus so they made it home. It was a pretty good time.

I had to shout at George twice to stop trying to grab June over at home plate—she was our umpire—and get his ass over here to warm up. That, and guzzle an extra-large jar of moonshine. Getting George sloppy drunk early was our concession to having a former professional athlete on our team.

Jonah joined us after kissing his girl, Shelby, and sending her up to the stands.

"You gonna show us all that muscle is good for something tonight?" I asked. "Or is it just to look pretty?"

He shook his head, smiling. "At least I don't look like a big, angry lumberjack."

Bowie glanced back, raising an eyebrow, his eyes darting between us.

"The shitty thing is, I can't even insult your face," I said. "Because we look too fuckin' much alike."

Jonah shrugged. "What are you gonna do? We're Bodines. We make this look good."

"That we do, brother." I gave him a friendly slap on the back. "That we do."

Bowie was still watching, but I ignored him, my attention suddenly fixed on the beautiful girl with crazy hair strolling our direction. My blue flannel was tied in a knot at her waist, emphasizing her curves, and her denim shorts gave me an eyeful of her tanned thighs. She had a hot dog in one hand, Cash's leash in the other.

I didn't need an ounce of moonshine. I was drunk in love with that girl.

She came around the outside of the rusty chain-link fence. Cash jumped up, his paws sticking through the gaps, his tail wagging.

"Is that Daddy?" Callie asked, grinning down at our dog. "Good boy, say hi to Daddy."

I crouched in front of Cash and stuck my fingers through the fence to pet his head. He was too excited to hold still, licking my hands, and the fence with them.

"Hey, buddy." He finally stopped flailing his head around long enough for me to rub between his ears a little. "You being a good boy and watching out for our girl?"

"You bet he is," she said. "We also discovered he loves hot dogs, especially when they're snatched out of Wade Zirkel's hand."

"You are a good boy."

She laughed, and cliché as it was, the sound was music to my ears. I stood and held onto the fence, leaning forward to kiss her through one of the gaps.

Someone behind me whistled, but I didn't care. Callie's lips were soft and she treated me to a little swipe of her tongue.

"Get a room," Jameson called out.

I twisted my arm around to flip him the bird, but I was smiling against Callie's mouth while I did it.

Reluctantly, I pulled away. From the corner of my eye, I saw Misty Lynn glaring daggers at Callie while Darren seemed to be trying to draw her attention back to him. Whatever. She wasn't my problem.

"I brought this for you," Callie said, pushing the hot dog through the fence. "Thought you might be hungry."

Funny how such a little thing could punch me in the

feelings like that. But the thoughtfulness of my girl bringing me a hot dog before the game made me really fucking happy.

"Thanks, honey."

She tilted her chin up and I leaned in to kiss her again. "I'm going to go sit with Shelby. Good luck, Coach."

"Have fun."

I leaned against the fence with the hot dog in my hand, watching her go. Admiring the sway of her hips. The roundness of her backside. I was gonna nibble on that ass later.

"Gibs, quit ogling," Bowie said. "You look like a lovesick puppy over there."

Well, he wasn't wrong.

I walked back to the dugout and ate half the hot dog in one bite.

Bowie smirked at me.

"What?" I asked, my mouth full of food.

"You got rust in your beard."

I just shrugged and kept chewing. "Worth it."

The game got going, the moonshine flowed, and like usual, we were ahead by the fifth inning stretch. The Miners were stumbling over their shoes and dropping catches. One particularly drunk player chased a guy around the field with the ball in her hand, trying to get her own teammate out.

Truth was, a bunch of Bootleggers had founded the West Virginia Moonshine Softball League. They'd been the ones to add the moonshine drinking rule, knowing it usually gave our town the advantage. No one could handle their liquor like a Bootlegger could.

Jameson caught a pop fly from flat on his back in the bottom of the fifth, earning him a chorus of cheers from the hometown crowd. Scarlett was her usual badass self, scoring a run in the sixth and sending Opal home on her next at-bat. George had been responsible for our first two scores. And now, even though he could barely stand up straight after all the moonshine, he kept earning his keep, using his long reach to tag a Miner out at third base in the eighth. Then he doubled over, laughing hysterically, like it was the funniest thing he'd ever done.

But like a drunk Scarlett after a big meal at Moonshine, the Miners rallied in the top of the ninth. I shouted instructions to the team and squinted, looking across at the Miners' dugout for a covert coffee maker or stash of energy drinks.

Two runs later, we were all tied up. Bernie O'Dell's voice on the loudspeaker announcing the score sent a hush through the otherwise rowdy crowd.

"Shit," I muttered. I cast a glance into the stands, finding Callie. She sat next to Shelby with Cash in her lap. Someone had given her a Cock Spurs cap and her colorful hair hung around her shoulders. Damn, she was adorable.

Blowing out a breath, I turned my attention back to the game. Bowie was still on the pitcher's mound, but he was swaying like he might not make it through the inning.

"Come on, Bow," I shouted. "Bodine up."

Like I'd just yelled a sobriety-inducing battle cry, Bowie straightened, getting his legs under him. He wound up for the pitch, looking steady and focused. Opal signaled behind the batter. We just needed one more out, then we'd have a chance to win.

If any of my players were still capable of hitting.

Bowie's pitch flew straight, smacking into Opal's mitt with a puff of dust.

"Strike," June yelled.

The crowd cheered but quickly quieted again. Bowie dug his toe in the dirt, rolling the ball in his hand. After another signal from Opal, he nodded. Wound up. Let loose.

I heard the smack of the ball hitting leather. The Miner stumbled, the force of his swing almost pulling him over. The crowd cheered again. Bowie didn't acknowledge it. He was in the zone.

"Strike."

A hush settled over the field. One more out was all we needed. Half the Miners had passed out in their dugout, but they had just enough conscious players to finish out the game. And the score was still tied.

There was a rustle of air as everyone present took—and held—a collective breath.

Bowie's pitch flew dead center over the plate. The Miner swung and for a second, it looked like he'd connect.

His bat came within a kitten's whisker of skimming the top of the ball. Opal caught the pitch, the Miner spun around in a circle, and June yelled the final, "Strike."

I blew out the breath I'd been holding. Bowie took off his hat and waved at the crowd as they cheered him in. Cassidy ran out and jumped on him, throwing her arms around his neck and her legs around his waist. They toppled to the dirt together, laughing to even louder whoops and hollers from the crowd.

But it wasn't over yet. Bottom of the ninth and Jonah was up to bat.

He chugged water, then wiped his mouth with the back of his hand.

"Go get 'em, brother," I said.

The Miners took the field and their unnaturally liquor-tolerant pitcher stood on the mound. The girl didn't even look tipsy. It was like she was Gableton's version of Scarlett.

Jonah's Cock Spurs shirt was snug around his muscled arms. He held the bat up, his eyes on the pitcher, stance firm.

The first pitch flew in, sailing past Jonah's bat.

"Strike."

"Shit," I mumbled.

Jonah readjusted his footing and got into position, the end of the bat wobbling in a tight circle over his shoulder.

Second pitch and Jonah swung hard, his body twisting. The ball hit the catcher's mitt with a thump.

"Strike."

Growling, I clenched my teeth. "Come on, Jonah!"

The chant started low while the pitcher took her time setting up. It rose behind me, the word rippling through the crowd, gaining strength and volume.

"Jo-nah! Jo-nah! Jo-nah!"

Feet stomped against the bleachers, hands clapped in time with the syllables of his name. Scarlett and Opal joined in beside me, cheering for him.

Jonah's hands gripped the bat hard, and he narrowed his eyes. The crowd kept chanting as the pitcher wound up and released.

A sudden silence filled the air as everyone stopped cheering and watched the ball fly toward home plate. Jonah swung and his bat connected with a metallic crack of aluminum.

The ball flew into the dark night sky, almost disappearing against the starry backdrop. I watched the arc, trying to judge the distance. Their outfielders tracked its path, backing up fast. One stumbled and hit the grass, rolling onto his stomach. The other kept his feet, running backward, his face tilted up, gloved hand ready to make the catch.

The ball kept right on going.

The outfielder backed into one of the moonshine stands as the ball sailed over his head. It came down with a hard thunk in what looked like the bed of Rhett Ginsler's pickup truck.

"Home run," June yelled.

The crowd went crazy. Jonah dropped the bat and jogged the bases, a contented smile on his face. All the Cock Spurs who weren't too drunk to walk rushed out to meet him at home plate, shouting and jumping. George and Nash tried to hoist him up on their shoulders, but they were too unsteady after all the moonshine. They crumpled into a heap with Jonah laughing on top.

For a second, Jonah's eyes met mine. I gave him a proud chin tip.

"Gibs." Devlin jogged up beside me and his expression wiped the smile from my face. Something was wrong.

My eyes darted to Callie, but she was fine—still in the stands with Shelby. She had her arms around Cash, like she was trying to keep him from scrambling away.

"What's wrong?" I asked.

"Lee Williams," he said, and my blood instantly ran cold. "He's here. I ran to my car to get Scarlett's hoodie and I saw him."

"You sure? You sober?"

"Stone-cold sober. Never doing that again. And yes, I'm sure. I wouldn't raise the alarm if I wasn't."

"Keep it quiet," I said. "I don't want a scene. I'll get Maya out of here. I saw Darren in the stands. He still here?"

"I don't think so, but I'll check."

"Thanks, Dev. Make sure everyone gets on the buses to go home. And don't tell Scarlett until morning. She'll just want to go after him."

"Agreed."

Without another word, I raced around the fence to the bleachers, dodging through my neighbors. Callie was at the bottom, wrestling with Cash, who was trying to break free of his leash to get to me.

"We gotta go." I grabbed the leash from her and took her elbow to spin her around. "Now."

"What's going on?"

"Devlin spotted Lee Williams."

She didn't reply. I kept hold of her arm and led her around the bleachers. Despite my desire to get her the fuck out of here, I didn't run. Didn't want to call too much attention.

We walked to the edge of the field where I'd parked my truck. I opened her side first, casting a glance around to see if anyone had followed while she climbed in with Cash. It was too damn dark. I couldn't see a thing.

The crowd had congregated on the field to celebrate. No one seemed to have noticed us leave. That was good. I went around and hopped in, slamming the door shut.

"Get down," I said. "Just in case."

Callie ducked down, leaning toward the center to stay out of sight. Cash seemed to sense things were serious. He hunkered down on the seat with her.

We high-tailed it out of there as fast as I dared, heading out of town. My eyes darted between the road and my rear-view mirror. No one followed that I could see, unless they were trailing pretty far back and weren't using their headlights.

As soon as we were past the edge of town, I gunned it, tearing up the road to my house. I took the corners fast, leaning hard. If someone was behind us, I wanted to get to my private drive before they could see me turn. Then they'd drive right by and end up in the middle of nowhere.

"Hold on," I said, my turn coming up. I cut my lights and downshifted instead of braking, flying around the corner just shy of fast enough to flip us over. Callie braced herself against the cab, one arm holding Cash around his middle.

The tires spat gravel at the surrounding trees. I didn't slow down until my house was in sight. I pulled to a stop and we got out, rushing into the house. Cash jumped with excitement, like we were playing an energetic game. Callie and I both planted our hands on the front door and slammed it closed.

I threw the lock and she covered it with her palm. We were both breathing hard and my heart felt like it was stuck in my throat.

"Fuck," I muttered. "I'm sorry if I overreacted, but I don't want to take any chances."

She turned around and put her back to the door, leaning her head against it. "It's okay. We're safe here either way."

My phone buzzed so I pulled it out of my pocket.

Devlin: *Second sighting. Leah Mae saw him getting a cup of moonshine.*

Me: *Where is he now?*

Devlin: *I'm checking. Darren's already back at the Red House.*

I glanced up at Callie. "Definitely him. Leah Mae confirmed it. Devlin's trying to find him."

She nodded. Cash jumped up, front paws on my legs.

"Come here, buddy," she said and took him to the couch. She sat with her legs tucked beneath her, Cash in her lap.

Devlin: *Spotted him heading to his car.*

Shit. I couldn't ask Dev to follow him. He needed to do my job and get everyone's drunk asses on the buses. Not to mention watch out for Scarlett and get her home. But at least we knew the asshole hadn't followed us out here.

Me: *We made it home. Safe for tonight.*

Devlin: *Good. We're fine out here. I've got it handled.*

Me: *Thanks, man.*

Damn, it was good to have family.

"We need to tell Bootleg the truth." Callie's voice made me look up.

"Uh, no." I put my phone down. "We need to keep your secret now more than ever."

I could tell by the set of her jaw that she wasn't letting this go. "People are starting to figure it out. I see it in the way they look at me. Do we want this blowing up in our face and turning into a town-wide spectacle? Right now, we can still control the information and deal with the uproar."

Crossing my arms, I chewed on that for a second. She had a point.

"Plus we need to warn everyone about Lee Williams. He's dangerous. We can't sit on that knowledge if it puts our neighbors at risk."

"Coming forward puts you at risk."

"I know, but we have to. It's the right thing to do, Gibs. We can talk to Sheriff Tucker first, but I really think we have to. It's time."

There was a lot about this I didn't like. It was my job to protect her. Could I keep her safe if news of who she was carried all through Bootleg? I'd been hoping the Kendalls wouldn't have to know she was here until the authorities knocked on their door to make an arrest.

But then again, if Bootleg knew, I'd have an entire town full of people watching out for her. Keeping their eye on Lee Williams. Usually, I didn't like to rely on other people. That opened you up to disappointment. But maybe I wasn't giving my town enough credit.

"All right," I said. "I'll call Harlan. Then Nadine. We need a secret town meeting."

32

GIBSON

*O*ld Jefferson Waverly's barn was packed to the rafters with Bootleg Springs residents, most of them still nursing hangovers after last night's Cock Spurs win. Wasted Wednesday had been interrupted by the call for a secret town meeting, the chain of communication kicked off by Nadine Tucker. We'd given them until six in the evening to recover, and true to form, everyone had turned out.

I sat on a crate up front, my back knotted with tension. Callie was tucked under my arm, her legs pulled in, like she was trying to disappear into me. We'd left Cash at home. There was enough to worry about without having our attention divided.

Callie and I had stayed home all day, relying on my family to be our eyes and ears in town. Lee Williams was definitely here. June had discovered that he'd taken a room in the shabby Bootleg Springs Motor Inn just on the outside edge of town. Jonah and Shelby had spotted him at Moonshine Diner around noon, having lunch. Leah Mae and Jameson had kept eyes on him while he wandered around downtown, acting like he was just another tourist. Everyone else had been on high alert, watching.

After that, our little team of Bodine-Tucker-Thompson-McAllister spies had lost track of him. Callie and I had spent a tense hour not knowing where he'd gone. Had he left town? Not knowing why he was here, or whether he knew about Callie, made it worse. There was no way he'd come back to Bootleg just for a visit. But without knowing why he was here, I didn't know how worried we needed to be.

He'd turned up later, driving in from the other side of town. I had a feeling he'd been exploring the area.

It stood to reason he didn't know Callie was here, and that the Kendalls didn't know either. My family and I all had our ears open to the town gossip. Not a single person had been heard whispering that Maya was Callie. That Callie Kendall was back in town.

I figured Callie was right and a few people had figured it out. Or at least they had strong suspicions. But if they did, they weren't talking about it yet. Not where anyone could hear them.

More lawn chairs scraped over the floor and people took their seats. My heart thumped, adrenaline making me jittery. I wanted to scoop Callie into my lap and hide her from everyone. Coming forward with the truth meant it was only a matter of time before the world knew she was here. The more people who knew a secret, the harder it was to keep. And we were about to share our secret with an entire damn town.

My family sat up front with us. Devlin, resting his elbows on his knees with Scarlett by his side. Bowie and Cassidy, hands intertwined. This might have been the first secret town meeting Cass had actually been invited to. We tended to hold these when we needed to do something just outside the law.

Jameson and Leah Mae sat beside Jonah and Shelby. Jenny was on Callie's right, with Jimmy Bob Prosser on the other side of her. George took up space for two, as did his father. George and Shelby's mom sat with them, as did June and Nadine. Harlan, too. Hell, it might have been Harlan's first secret town meeting as well.

It felt good to have them all here, sitting together. We weren't all related by blood. Some hadn't been here that long. But I felt the force of their support. We were a united front, here for a purpose.

Mayor Auggie Hornsbladt, dressed as usual in denim overalls and a cowboy hat, climbed onto a milk crate up front and spoke into a wireless mic. "Let's call this meeting to order. Quiet down, now."

The hum of chatter faded as people turned their attention to the mayor.

His eyes flicked to mine. Twenty minutes ago, we'd had an impromptu meeting with the mayor in a secluded corner of the barn while my brothers, George, and Devlin stood around acting casual, blocking people's views. He'd gone white as a sheet, then teared up a bit and crushed Callie in a bear hug. We'd filled him in on the basics and she'd happily produced the DNA results that verified her identity. That had been easy to get. Apparently, June had a guy. I had no idea why June would *have a guy* who did DNA testing, but I appreciated it nonetheless.

"Y'all, the purpose of this meeting is something that we've been waiting a long time for. Thirteen years ago, we lost one of our own. Callie Kendall disappeared on a July evening, gone without a trace. And for most of those thirteen years, we didn't know the truth about what happened to her."

Murmurs ran through the crowd.

"Recently, we got the terrible news that her remains had been found and identified," Mayor Auggie continued. "It was over. We didn't know the how or the why, but we knew her fate. Or so we thought."

The murmurs grew stronger, a hum of discontent and curiosity filling the air.

Mayor Auggie held up a hand for quiet. "I have the very special honor and pleasure of bringing you this announcement. Callie Kendall is alive and well. And she's here with us tonight."

The barn erupted with noise. Voices, questions, people shooting out of their chairs, knocking them over.

"I knew she wasn't dead!"

"Where is she?"

"Can we see her?"

"I don't believe that for a second."

"Is this a joke, because it ain't funny."

"What if it's another fake?"

"Do her parents know?"

That last question made me whip around in alarm. Callie rubbed a soothing hand on my chest and Jenny reached across to give my leg a squeeze.

"It's all right," Jenny said. I wasn't sure if she was talking to me or Callie. Maybe both of us.

"Now, now, let's all settle down," Mayor Auggie said, holding his hand up. "Settle down, now. We'll answer your questions, but y'all gotta be quiet."

George glanced around at the increasingly noisy crowd. He stood, unfolding from his spot on a crate to his full and rather impressive height. "Quiet please," he bellowed. His voice echoed off the ceiling and the audience went silent. With a nod at the mayor, he sat down.

"Thank you, George," Mayor Auggie said. "First, let me address your concerns about her being another pretender. We have confirmed, with scientific evidence, that she is in fact Callie Kendall. There's no question about it, folks. She's real and she's back."

He paused and let that settle over the audience.

Millie Waggle was up front, sitting across the aisle from us. She caught my eye and gave me a subtle nod. I had a feeling she was one who'd already figured it out.

"Callie, sweetheart, would you please join me up front?" Mayor Auggie said, his voice gentle. He held out a hand to her.

My heart stood still as she emerged from under my protective arm. She seemed to move in slow motion, separating from me, rising to her feet. I could almost see the Maya façade fall away, the adopted identity dissolving into the air, leaving her raw, exposed. Real. The Callie I remembered. The Callie we'd all known.

Gasps and murmurs greeted her as she turned to face Bootleg Springs. Mayor Auggie handed her the microphone and gave her a reassuring pat on the shoulder.

She took the mic and met my eyes. I could see her fear. It made me want to scoop her up and carry her out of here. But she took a deep breath and began.

"Many of you know me as Maya Davis. And that name wasn't a lie. I've been Maya for the last thirteen years, since I left Bootleg Springs. But I am Callie Kendall."

She shifted, re-gripping the mic, while the audience murmured again. I nodded to her. She could do this.

"I ran away and disappeared because I was afraid for my life. I'd been abused at home from the time I was young.

The night of my disappearance—" She closed her eyes and a tear trailed down her cheek. It took her a second, but she opened them again. "I was badly injured, trying to get away. Jonah Bodine Sr. found and helped me. He obviously didn't murder me, or hit me with his car. He found a bleeding, terrified girl on the side of the road and he helped me get to safety.

"I went to a little town in upstate New York where a wonderful family took me in. They loved me and cared for me and helped me heal. When I became an adult, I went out and lived my life. I did my best to move on from my past. I wasn't Callie Kendall anymore. I was Maya Davis."

"Why didn't you tell anyone?" someone asked from the back.

"Fear," she said. "I was afraid for my life if my parents ever found me. It hurt me terribly to leave all the good things in my life behind. All the friends and people I cared about." Her eyes landed on me. "But I didn't have a choice. I want you all to know I'm so sorry you hurt for me for so long. And I'm sorry I didn't tell everyone the truth about who I am when I first came back."

"What kinda danger are we talkin'?"

"Are you saying the judge hurt you?"

"Why are you here now?"

The questions were coming from every direction. I wanted to turn around and tell them all to shut the fuck up and let her talk.

"Yes, Judge Kendall..." She trailed off again and swallowed hard. "The judge is a dangerous man. And he has a lot to lose if I reappear. He wants me to stay missing. Stay dead. He had a man who works for him bribe a lab tech into faking the forensics report on the remains of that girl in New York to say it was me. And that's not the worst of it. He has a long history of using coercion, threats, bribery, and even violence to get what he wants and maintain his power.

"When I was a girl, I hid the truth from everyone. No one knew what was happening to me. Now, I'm back to face my past. I'm here to clear Jonah Bodine's name. And to find a way to bring the real wrongdoers to justice."

That was met with a round of applause. My family and I glanced around, meeting each other's eyes. This was the Bootleg who'd raised us.

"What about Gibson?" someone shouted. "Did he know where you were?"

"No. Jonah and Connie kept my secret, even from their children. And they didn't do it just for my safety. They did it to protect their family, and their town. They understood that it would put a lot of people in danger if the truth got out."

"Gibs, why did you have her picture?"

"Were you running around with her when she was sixteen?"

"Gibson Bodine, how dare you?"

"Weren't you twenty-five?"

I ground my teeth together and clenched my fists.

"Gibson Bodine was my friend," Callie said, her voice suddenly clear and strong. "He was twenty, and I was sixteen, but we were *just friends*. Gibson was respectful and kind. He gave me his friendship without any strings or expectations. He never acted inappropriately, even though we were alone so much, he certainly could have. I trusted him more than I trusted anyone in the world. I still do. And y'all should be ashamed of yourself for assuming the worst of him. Gibson Bodine is a good man. He's the best man I know."

I stared at her, my eyes wide. My throat was thick and it felt like my heart might have gotten stuck in my ribs.

"I'm going on thirty now, and I'm plenty old enough to say I love him. I loved him as a friend when I was young, and I love him as so much more now. I'm the luckiest person in the world to be Gibson Bodine's girl."

A ripple went through the audience, some people reacting to Callie's speech with *oohs* and *ahhs*. Others with phrases like, *how sweet*, and *they're just precious*, and *bless my soul, this is so much to take in*.

I rose from my chair and went up to the front. They didn't need every detail of her painful past. It hurt her to remember it—even more to speak of it—and she'd told them enough. And I didn't want them getting sidetracked looking for the juicy details of our current relationship. Right now, we needed to deal with the threat in our town.

She handed me the mic and I paused, captivated by her beautiful face. The tip of her tongue darted into the notch in her lip—she did that when she was nervous—so I took her hand before turning to address the town.

"Callie came forward today because we need y'all's help. Just so we're clear, the judge is the bad guy. We got that?"

People spoke in low voices to their neighbors, but they nodded.

"We need to come together as a town to protect our girl. That means, for now, she ain't Callie to anyone outside this room. She's still Maya. Understood?"

More nods. They were with us.

"Sheriff Tucker is working on things from a law enforcement standpoint. There's still evidence to gather to make a case against the judge."

There were sudden calls for Bootleg Justice from several parts of the barn.

"I know. Believe me, I'd love nothing more than to get my hands on that sorry son of a bitch. But this goes beyond

Bootleg. And it calls for the kind of justice that ends with him in prison, where he can't hurt anyone again."

Shouts of agreement filled the air and several people raised their fists.

"We have reason to believe a low-down, dirty scum who works for the judge is in town right now."

This time there were boos and voices bordering on outrage.

"It ain't yet clear why he's here, and we need solid evidence to tie him to the judge. So no one take this into your own hands. This ain't a situation for Bootleg Justice, either. But it's important he doesn't find out that she's Callie."

"We've got this, Gibs."

"You can count on us."

"Callie who?"

"Never even heard of her."

I nodded, squeezing Callie's hand again. "We're asking a lot of y'all. And it means a lot that you'll stand by us."

My brothers rose from their chairs—Bowie, followed by Jonah and Jameson—to nod gratefully at the people around us. Scarlett looked teary when she stood.

This was us. My family. My people. And holy shit if it hadn't taken Callie Kendall coming back from the dead to make me see it. Make me realize what I had.

"Are y'all gettin' hitched?" a woman asked from somewhere in the middle. Might have been Clarabell.

"Callie, are you here to stay?"

"Are you gonna marry Gibson Bodine?"

"I can arrange the flowers."

"We should have it at the park."

"Do y'all still have the trellis from Bowie and Cassidy's wedding?"

"What kinda cake do y'all need?"

Callie laughed, touching her fingers to her lips. And what the hell, I laughed too.

"Y'all are getting a bit ahead of yourselves," I said into the mic. But I cast a quick wink at Callie. "Let's just get through the current crisis."

Sheriff Tucker and Nadine stepped up and took the mic. Callie and I went back to our seats while Harlan gave them a few more details—a description of Lee Williams so they knew who to look out for, and more reminders to stay out of it and let law enforcement do their job. Nadine gave everyone ideas for what to do if they spotted trouble.

Afterward, almost everyone present lined up to say hello to Callie. It was like the longest receiving line I'd ever seen. They gave her hugs, patted her hands, told her how much they'd missed her. There were exclamations of how pretty she'd grown, what a nice young woman she'd become. There was hardly a dry eye in the place as the surprise of the truth settled into acceptance and relief.

Callie Kendall was home.

33

MAYA

I couldn't remember ever being so exhausted in my entire life. I sagged against Gibson while he unlocked the front door. My legs were heavy and my arms hung loose at my sides because I didn't have the energy to lift them.

Telling the town the truth about me had been the right call. I felt it deep in my soul. The way they'd responded, rallying around us like that, made my heart so full I thought my chest might burst. And all their tearful greetings, hugs, cheek kisses, and enthusiastic suggestions for engagement and wedding ideas had made me feel like I belonged to them.

But really, I always had.

Cash was excited to see us, as usual. We let him inside, and gave him some love and a toy filled with peanut butter. He plopped on the floor, happy as a dog could be.

"Come here," Gibson said. He stood near the short

hallway and reached out to draw me closer. Tucked my hair behind one ear. "I'm so proud of you."

"Thanks. I feel good about what we did tonight."

"Me too." He leaned down and captured my lips with his.

I slid my hands up his chest, melting into his kiss. His hands sat at my waist and his grip tightened when I brushed his lips with my tongue.

A tingling energy pulsed through my body. A moment ago, I'd been so worn out, all I'd wanted was sleep. But Gibson's sensual kiss was waking me up, all my nerve endings singing.

The low rumble in his chest made me smile against his lips. I nipped him gently with my teeth. "I love it when you kiss me like that."

"Honey, I've got something on my mind. You wanna hear about it?"

"Tell me."

His rough jaw brushed the side of my face and he put his mouth next to my ear. "I'm gonna take those clothes off you, real slow. Then I'll get you on the bed and bury my face between your legs. And I'm gonna lick that pretty pussy until you come in my mouth."

I trembled and my voice was breathy. "Yeah?"

"Uh-huh. I'll lick you until you beg me to stop. Then I'm gonna turn you over, get you on your knees. And I'm gonna hold those hips and fuck that wet pussy from behind. Maybe smack that ass a few times while I do it. You opposed to a little spanking while I fuck you?"

"No," I breathed. "Not if it's you."

"I won't hurt you, honey," he growled in my ear. His hand slid down to cup my ass and he squeezed. "I just wanna get a little dirty with you."

My eyes rolled back. I was already so turned on, he wasn't going to have to work very hard to get me to come. "I love it when you get dirty with me."

He kissed me again, rough this time. I slid my hand down to grab his erection through his pants. He grunted, squeezing my ass cheek harder.

"Bedroom," he said against my mouth.

Without breaking the kiss, he led me down the hall, walking backward, and I shut the bedroom door behind us. His tongue darted in and out of my mouth a few times, mimicking what he'd promised to do between my legs. Giggling, I unfastened his jeans and shoved my hands inside, wrapping my fingers around his cock.

He grunted again. "Fuck."

I was messing up his little plan, but I didn't care. While he kept kissing me, I worked his cock out of his pants. Teased the tip with my fingertips. I took him by the shaft and pumped it a few times, enjoying the way he growled. The way his hips jerked, like he couldn't help himself.

With my other hand, I shoved his pants lower so I had better access. We both looked down at his thick erection, standing straight up. I stroked it, up and down the shaft, watching as beads of moisture collected on the tip.

I liked where this was going. Me, in control of his pleasure. Making him come was such a rush. He watched with rapt attention while I slowly lowered to my knees in front of him.

With my hand firmly around the base of his cock, I slid my tongue slowly up his length. "Mind if I do this first?"

"Darlin', I ain't sayin' no." He took off his shirt and tossed it on the floor.

I grinned up at him. "Didn't think so."

He shuddered as I slid the tip in my mouth. I started

slow, getting him nice and slick. His fingers twined through my hair, his grip gentle.

Every low growl made me want to take in more. His cock slid in and out of my mouth, and his hips started to jerk. His gaze stayed locked on me as I sucked his cock, his eyes glassy.

"Fuck, that feels so good."

He massaged my head, groaning as I worked his dick in and out of my mouth. His enjoyment made my spine tingle and the pressure between my legs increase. I loved that I could do this to him. I moved faster. I didn't always finish him with my mouth, but tonight I was going to.

His grip on my hair tightened and his hips thrust faster. "God, you're fucking sexy," he ground out through gritted teeth.

I purred my own enjoyment as I felt his dick pulse. He was close. His brow furrowed and he started breathing harder, grunting every time I plunged down.

"You want me to come like this?" he asked, almost breathless, and loosened his grip on my hair.

In answer, I took him as deep as I could. He grunted hard and fisted my hair.

And I felt him unleash.

He drew his cock in and out of my mouth with quick thrusts. Never hard enough to hurt me, but enough that his girth thickened and a low growl rumbled in his throat. His eyes rolled back as he started to come, the thick spurts hitting the back of my throat. His cock pulsed between my lips and his deep grunts and ragged breaths were so sexy I couldn't get enough.

I swallowed quickly and let his cock slip out of my mouth. He staggered backward, his pants around his ankles, and blinked hard.

"Holy fuck."

I brushed my hair back from my face and stood. "You like that?"

"Oh my god." He blinked again, like he was dumbstruck, then his icy blue eyes fixed on me. "Get the fuck over here."

I giggled while he manhandled me onto the bed. He kissed my mouth, then down my neck. Nibbled on my collarbone. His hand slid beneath my shirt to splay across my ribs, just below my bra.

We'd already decided we didn't need condoms. We both knew we were clean, and I was on birth control. It was nice not to have to worry about them anymore.

He kicked his pants the rest of the way off, then went to work on my clothes. He'd said he'd undress me slow, but he hadn't said he'd be soft. He grabbed my shirt in his fist and pulled, jerking it up over my face. With my view obscured, he dragged his teeth over my nipple through the lacy fabric of my bra.

With rough hands, he pulled my shirt over my head, then pinned my arms down. He sucked on my neck, then kissed his way down to my chest. He nuzzled between my boobs, kissing and licking his way from one nipple to the other.

He let go of my arms to unfasten my jeans, then yanked them down my legs. Flipping me over, he unclasped my bra. I pushed myself up onto my elbows and let it fall down my arms.

His hand slipped beneath my panties and I arched my back, lifting my hips and sticking my ass in the air so he could take them off. His mouth followed his hand, kissing down my back, across my ass cheek, over the back of my thigh.

Finally, he had me undressed. He flipped me back over

and settled between my thighs, draping my legs over his broad shoulders.

"Mm," he hummed. "I love this pussy. So fucking pretty. So good."

I lay back on the pillow and enjoyed the feel of his tongue making lazy laps around my clit. Up my soft folds. It was rough and wet and warm, and next to his cock when he fucked me hard, it was the best thing I'd ever felt.

He was no quieter licking me than he had been when I'd sucked his dick. He groaned, lapping at me with enthusiasm. Pushing my thighs back, he sucked on my clit, moaning like he couldn't get enough.

Heat and tension built so fast, it took my breath away. I moved with him, rolling my hips, grinding myself against his mouth. He slipped a finger inside me and I moaned, the extra pressure so good.

His tongue was relentless. I writhed against the sheets, running my fingers through his hair. He didn't let up. A second finger slid inside, and my silky inner muscles trembled.

"Don't stop that," I breathed.

I was so close, my pussy hot and clenching around his fingers. He growled again and the vibration sent me over the edge. Leaning my head back, I rode out my orgasm, the pulses rippling through me in waves.

He still didn't stop, and my climax stretched out until I couldn't take it anymore.

"Stop," I begged, starting to giggle again. "Stop, oh god, Gibson."

His face lifted, his mouth wet, and he grinned. "Told you you'd beg me to stop."

My legs fell to the sides and my arms flopped onto the bed. "That was amazing."

"Good. But I'm not finished with you. On your knees, beautiful."

I smiled back at him. Gladly. I still wanted to feel his cock inside me.

He muscled me onto my tummy, then grabbed my hips to lift my ass into the air. I braced myself on my forearms and looked back at him over my shoulder.

Caressing my skin, he looked me over. "So beautiful. God, I love you."

"I love you, too. Now get busy fucking me."

Biting his bottom lip, he took his dick in his hand and stroked a few times.

"Keep going," I said. I wanted to watch him make himself hard.

He stroked a little faster and his cock quickly hardened. His abs flexed and he squeezed my ass with his other hand.

"You like that, baby?" he asked, still stroking himself.

"Yeah," I breathed. "That's so hot."

"How about this?" He slid his hand to the base of his shaft and scooted closer to me. Then he rubbed the tip up and down my slit.

I moaned at the feel of him rubbing himself all over me. "That's good."

Focusing the tip right over my clit, he rubbed it up and down fast. "Holy fuck, this looks good."

Pressure built again as he teased my clit with his cock. I rocked my hips back, seeking more. The friction was good, but I needed to feel him filling me.

"Gibson," I whimpered.

"Yeah, baby?"

"Gibson, please."

"You want this?"

I looked over my shoulder and he stroked his cock again.

Fast, this time, like he was serious. His abs were tight, his chest glistening with sweat. He groaned, his jaw clenched, as he rubbed his hard length, his fist moving up and down his thick shaft.

"You better put that cock inside me," I said.

"Yeah?" he asked, still stroking hard.

I rocked backward. "Now, Gibs."

Grabbing my hips, he shoved his cock into my soaking wet pussy. I cried out at the sudden pressure—the agonizingly sweet feeling of his thickness inside me. Two hard thrusts and my inner muscles danced, vibrating with tension.

He smacked my ass check with a sharp crack. I arched harder, the sting of it driving me crazy. One more smack and I laughed. Safe in Gibson's bedroom, I was uninhibited and free. I loved the way he made me feel deliciously dirty in all the best ways.

"I'm gonna come so hard in you, baby," he growled. "This pussy feels fucking amazing."

His grip on my hips tightened and he thrust harder. I fisted the sheets, breathing hard, relishing the way he fucked me like this. Like I could take it. He didn't treat me like I was broken. He loved me like I was whole and strong enough to handle him.

I loved it.

The heady rush of a second orgasm hit me like fireworks. He grunted hard and drove in deep while my pussy pulsed around him. I felt his cock throb as he emptied himself into me. Groaning, thrusting hard, both of us lost in this moment. In each other. In the intense physical expression of everything we felt.

When he finished, he slipped out and let go of my hips. I collapsed onto the bed, breathing hard.

"I don't think I can move," I said, my face in the sheets.

He toppled over next to me and slid his hand around my waist. Hauled me against him. "Then just stay right here, love."

We lay together, completely spent, catching our breath. His sweat mingled with mine and he peppered my ear and neck with gentle kisses.

It was everything I needed. He was everything I needed. I was sated, content, and so in love.

34

MAYA

*S*aturday afternoon, we sat out on the back porch steps, side by side. Gibson idly tossed a ball for Cash—his fenced-in area was working out great—and listened to the birds sing.

Without a pressing need to go anywhere, we'd spent the day at home. We didn't know what we were going to do if Lee Williams stuck around, or if he started poking around enough to come out here. For now, he had an entire town watching his every move, and he had no idea they were doing it.

Gibson's phone buzzed and he gave it the side eye for a moment before checking.

"Huh. Henrietta's got something trapped in her cabin again."

"Henrietta? The woman who doesn't speak?"

He nodded and stood. "She says it's a bear, but it's probably just an angry raccoon. I should hike up there and help her get rid of it."

I blinked at him a few times. "I have so many questions right now."

His mouth curled in that slow, sexy grin that turned my insides to liquid. "Do you want to come out with me? It's a bit of a hike, but nothing you can't handle."

"Yeah, that sounds great."

Gibson suggested I put on long pants to keep my legs from getting scratched, so I changed into jeans. A bank of clouds had rolled in, dimming the sunshine, and there was a crispness to the air. Fall was descending on the West Virginia mountains.

With a very excited Cash on his leash, we struck out into the woods. Gibson had a backpack stuffed full, although I wasn't sure what he'd put in it. The land rose steadily, and we had to pick our way through the underbrush, eventually coming to a more defined trail. Cash scrambled over logs and rocks, his tail wagging. He seemed to be enjoying our little adventure.

"I take it you've been out here before."

"Couple times," he said. "She got real sick once—the flu, I think—so I brought her a supply of canned soup and some Tylenol to get her fever down. And last year she had a raccoon problem."

"Do you know anything about her? Why she lives out here?"

"Nope."

I grabbed a branch and used it to balance as I pulled myself up a particularly steep incline. "But aren't you curious about her?"

"A bit. But it's her life. She should be able to live it how she wants without people bothering her about it. Besides, if she wanted me to know more, she'd tell me."

"But she doesn't talk."

"She communicates just fine."

We continued in silence for a while. It was a tough hike. Yoga kept me strong and flexible, but this was something else. Just when I thought I might have stop and rest—my legs were burning—the land leveled off. The trees were thick and the cool air felt good.

There was something about the way Gibson navigated the woods with such ease. A big, bearded man in a flannel and jeans, with his strong, calloused hands.

I indulged in a brief daydream. Gibson and me, taking to the woods to disappear. Building a shelter, living off the land. Watching him chop wood. Cozying up in front of a fire to keep warm.

The reality of living in the wilderness wouldn't be nearly as romantic. But it was still fun to imagine Gibson as a mountain man, taking care of me in the forest.

It made me wonder what would have happened if I'd made it to his apartment that night, instead of being picked up by his father.

"It's just up here," he said.

We emerged into a small clearing with a weathered cabin in the center. The wood was gray with age, but the boards were straight. It had a small porch at ground level and one old window that I could see, with remnants of chipping paint on the frame.

Henrietta sat on the porch, her thin legs bent, her back against the door. She had long, graying hair that hung around her shoulders. Her clothes were worn but her sneakers looked new.

"Having some trouble?" Gibson asked.

She nodded and jerked her thumb behind her. As if on cue, there was a crash inside the cabin. Cash barked.

"Another angry raccoon?" he asked.

She shook her head hard, making her hair whip around her face, then held up an arm to indicate height.

"Bigger than an angry raccoon?" he asked.

She nodded, just as vehemently.

"That's why you think it's a bear?"

She nodded again, her brown eyes wide.

I grabbed Gibson's arm. "You can't go in there if it's a bear."

He laid his hand over mine and turned to speak quietly. "It ain't a bear. Henrietta's not afraid of much, but for some reason, she's terrified of raccoons. Makes her exaggerate."

There was another crash inside the cabin. I still didn't like this. "Even if it's a raccoon, that doesn't sound good. What about rabies?"

"I've been vaccinated."

Cash barked again, the leash going taut in Gibson's hand.

Henrietta's eyes fell on me, like she'd noticed me for the first time. Using the door handle to help her stand, she rose on skinny legs. I stood still, mesmerized by her intense gaze. She had deep lines in her forehead and around her eyes. She took slow steps forward, scrutinizing me.

Gibson placed a hand on the small of my back. "This is my friend, Callie. You remember Callie?"

She touched her hand to her chest, still staring at me, then nodded slowly.

"She was gone for a long time, but she found her way back," Gibson said.

Her face broke into a wide smile. She stopped in front of me and took one of my hands in hers. Her skin was somehow soft and calloused at the same time, her finger-nails short and clean. She held my hand up, laying her other hand on top of mine. Her eyes still didn't leave my face and she nodded, squeezing my hand.

"Hi, Henrietta."

"I was glad to see her, too," Gibson said.

Another crash in the cabin reminded us why we were out here. I took Cash's leash while Gibson dropped his backpack and opened it, pulling out a pair of thick leather gloves, a baggie of dog food, and a big green tarp.

"Okay, Henrietta," he said, fitting his hands into the gloves. "You stay out here with Callie and Cash. I'll get your bear."

Henrietta and I backed up a few steps. Cash barked again but didn't seem interested in following Gibson into the cabin. He stayed near my legs.

"Be careful," I said.

Gibson just grunted. He paused at the door, his hand on the handle, took a deep breath, and went inside.

Henrietta clasped my hand. We waited, staring at the cabin. For a long moment, all was quiet. I couldn't decide if that was a good sign. What if Gibs was wrong and there really was a bear inside? Or what if the raccoon bit or scratched him? Had he been serious about already having a rabies vaccine?

Sudden crashes and clatters rang out from inside, making me jump. Seconds later, the door flew open and Gibson barreled out, the tarp bundled up in his arms. Whatever was inside growled, and the tarp shook.

Gibson's face was calm, his jaw set. With his arms around the violently thrashing tarp, he jogged into the trees, disappearing from sight.

Henrietta let out a sigh and let go of my hand, as if the worst was over. My heart raced and I held Cash's leash to keep him from following Gibson into the trees. Quiet settled over the forest and Henrietta went into her cabin, leaving the door open.

It felt like ages before Gibson emerged, walking through the woods like he hadn't just wrestled a wild animal. He had the tarp slung over his arm, obviously no longer filled with a raging raccoon—or whatever it had been.

"Are you okay?" I ran to him, Cash leading the way. I expected to see scratches and bites. Maybe blood. But he seemed fine.

"Of course. Fucker was pissed, though. I can see why she was scared. That was one of the biggest raccoons I've ever seen."

"How did you catch it?"

"Suckered him onto the tarp with some dog food, then wrapped him up." He crouched down to give Cash some attention, rubbing his head and letting him lick his face a few times. "Works every time."

"You're something else, Gibson Bodine."

He glanced up at me and grinned.

"Should we go talk to Henrietta?" I asked.

"Yeah. We'll leave Cash out here. It's a bit cramped inside."

I helped him stuff the tarp in the backpack. Then we tied Cash up on the porch. Gibson fished in his pocket and handed him a dog treat.

He rapped his knuckles on the open door. "Everything all right now?"

Henrietta was busy cleaning up the mess the raccoon had left. She set a small wooden sculpture on a rough wood shelf, then nodded and gestured for us to come inside.

It was like walking into an antique store, only far more fascinating. Bits of broken CDs hung on strings, glinting in the light as they twirled. The walls were covered with a dizzying arrangement of items. Faded signs, pieces of rusty metal, old license plates. There were oddly shaped sticks, shelves full of rocks, baskets overflowing with odds and ends, and something that looked like it might be a piece of broken road cone. She'd arranged everything in such a way that it was strangely beautiful.

An old-fashioned ceramic sink that looked like it weighed about five hundred pounds sat on a sturdy cabinet, the dark stain faded.

"Does she have a well?"

"Yep," Gibson said. "I don't think she's the first person to live up here, but I don't know who built it."

There was an interior door, open a crack, and a curtained area at the back. She had shelves with food and supplies from a store. Herbs hung from the ceiling above the sink and she had almost an entire wall of shelves holding mason jars. Red ones looked like they might have jam or berry preserves. Others had dried meat and various things I couldn't place. A wood stove appeared to provide both heat and a cooking surface.

Gibson dug in the front pocket of his backpack and handed her a cell phone. "Fully charged, and no crack in the screen."

She took the phone and held it to her chest, smiling at Gibson. With a nod, she carefully put it on a shelf, patting it as if to say she'd take care of it.

I didn't see any lights or outlets. "Does she have power?"

"No, but I got her a few spare batteries that charge it. When she comes into town, she charges everything up at the library. Or sometimes she just comes to my place and swaps out a dead battery for a full one."

"Wow. I guess you guys have a good system."

He shrugged, like it wasn't a big deal. "It's mostly for

emergencies. I doubt she keeps it on most of the time. But it has GPS, so if she got in real trouble, she could call for help and a rescue crew could get out here."

"Or if she has a bear in her cabin, she can let you know."

He grinned. "Exactly."

Henrietta worked quietly, righting her belongings. Picking things up off the floor and finding places for them on her many shelves.

"Can we help?" I asked.

She nodded, so Gibson and I picked up what we could. She directed us with silent gestures, ensuring we put things where she wanted them.

"You have quite the interesting collection." I righted a little wooden sign that had toppled over. The paint was faded almost to nothing, but I could see the faint outline of the words *ice cream*.

She beamed with pride, clasping her hands and looking around.

There was a beat-up Virginia license plate next to the ice cream sign. I brushed my fingers across the bent metal, and it felt like a bolt of electricity shot through my body. Gasping, I jerked my hand away.

"You all right?" Gibson asked. "Did you touch something sharp?"

"No." I stared at the license plate, unable to look away. The frame was warped, but still intact. White scratches marred the surface, but I could read it. Richmond Music and Dance Academy.

The box in my mind exploded, as if a bomb had gone off inside, blowing the lid off its hinges. I clutched my chest, gasping for air. I couldn't breathe.

"Callie, what's wrong?"

My arms burned, as if new slices oozed blood. As if I was

sixteen all over again, with razor cuts in my skin. Shoving my sleeves up, I stared at my arms. The scars were still covered in tattoos. No blood. No new wounds.

But I knew. I remembered. Those old memories that had been shrouded with hazy darkness suddenly broke free, clear and terrifying. The last piece of Callie's life—the piece I'd buried so deep it could never hurt me again—came ripping to the surface.

"It was her."

"Honey, what's going on?" Gibson was there, his hands on the sides of my face, his brow furrowed with concern.

"My mom had a license plate like that," I said, my voice shaky and weak. "I took music lessons there and they gave us those frames. She put it on her car. It was prestigious. I had to audition to get in. She wanted everyone to know."

He brushed my hair back from my face. "You don't have to—"

"Yes, I do." I held his arms, drawing strength from his touch. I kept my eyes down, remembering.

35

CALLIE

Thirteen years ago

A droplet of sweat trickled down my back as I walked down my driveway. I'd been at the lake all day, but that wasn't why I was sweating now. I didn't know what was wrong, really. I wasn't coming home late. I hadn't done anything that I wasn't allowed to do.

Today, that is. Yesterday was another story. But my parents didn't know about that.

I tugged at the sleeves of my red cardigan—a reflexive gesture. They were already down. It was amazing how quickly I could go from feeling relaxed and carefree— hanging out with all the Bootleg Springs kids—to anxious and afraid. This was my home—my summer home, at least. The sight of it shouldn't have made my stomach knot with fear. But I couldn't remember a time when I'd felt safe at home.

Taking a deep breath, I went inside.

I closed the door hard enough that it would make a sound without slamming it. It was a delicate balance—make sure they knew I was home, but avoid calling too much attention to myself.

Luck seemed to be in my corner this evening. Dad was in his study, but Mom was nowhere to be seen. He looked up as I walked by, giving me a brief nod. Even seated, my father was an imposing figure. His hair was going white, but his shoulders were square, his posture rigid. He was authority personified.

The tightness in my back eased as I went upstairs to my room and softly closed the door behind me. The lavender floral bedspread had ruffles around the edges, and a pile of decorative pillows were placed with precision. The walls were painted lavender to match, the furniture all white-washed beige.

Most girls I knew had posters of bands or celebrities papering their bedrooms. Not me. I had colorful framed prints of flowers and ducklings. It looked like a ten-year-old lived in this room, not a sixteen-year-old girl with only two years until adulthood.

Until freedom.

Although I was itching to put on my headphones and lose myself in music—pretend I was anywhere but here—I couldn't risk it before dinner. I might miss my summons to the family table.

Instead, I sat on my bed and took out my journal. Flipped through the pages. I didn't keep a diary. My parents would never have let me record the truth on paper. Not even in a diary that no one else would see.

So I wrote songs. Deep inside the words penned on

these pages was my truth. And maybe someday, I'd be brave enough to share it.

I traced my fingers over the newest page. A song I'd written late last night after the biggest act of rebellion I'd ever committed.

I was allowed out of the house—for now, at least. My parents dangled the possibility of house-arrest over my head constantly. I was to stay in town, never enter someone's house, and be home for dinner. I followed those rules, each and every day.

Except yesterday. I hadn't gone inside anyone's home. I'd been back before dinner. But I'd left town. Worse, I'd left town with Gibson Bodine.

It had been such a risk, but when he'd said there was an outdoor music festival in Perrinville, I hadn't been able to resist. I'd wanted to jump up and hug him, but Gibson wasn't a hugger. And it would have been weird, anyway. Gibs and I weren't like that. He was my friend. Probably the best friend I'd ever had. But not someone I'd hug.

When he'd asked if I wanted to go to Perrinville to see the festival, I'd taken the leap and said yes. He'd met me outside town so no one would see us leave.

It had been the best day of my entire life. I closed my eyes, breathing in the memories. The sights. The sounds. I'd never heard music like that live before. It had filled my soul. Soothed every ache and wound I carried. For a little while, I hadn't been Callie Kendall, obedient daughter. I'd been someone else. Someone free.

I was desperate for that. For freedom. I had two more years, but sometimes I wasn't sure if I could make it.

"Callie." My mother's voice carried up the stairs. "Dinner."

Her sweet tone set me on edge. Sixteen years of this, and I couldn't tell when she was faking. Sometimes that soft call meant she was in a good mood, and I'd have a peaceful evening.

Other times, it masked her displeasure, lulling me into a false sense of security. I'd let my guard down, thinking all was well, only to be blindsided by her cold anger for some perceived transgression.

I hurried downstairs, not wanting to give either of them a reason to be angry tonight. Mom was in the kitchen, pulling a roast with potatoes out of the oven.

"Set the table," she said without turning to look at me. She wore a silk blouse with an apron tied around her waist, and her hair was pulled back in a bun.

"Yes, ma'am."

Keeping my eyes down like a good girl, I took the plates and silverware to the table. Set them neatly atop the beige lace place mats.

Mom brought the serving dishes to the table and I poured ice water for the three of us. Dad emerged from his study, his face cold and serious.

Worry ate at me, making my stomach hurt. I took my place at the dinner table and gently unfolded my napkin in my lap. My parents engaged in meaningless small talk while we dished up our food. I didn't mind. Shallow conversations about the weather were preferable to Dad talking about work. I already knew far more than I wanted to about the things my father did.

My fork dangled from my fingers while I picked at my food. It was hard to eat. My parents behaved as if I wasn't there—a good sign—but there was an electric tension in the air. It rippled through me, making my back knot up tight and my throat go dry. Was it my imagination? Or was she about to—

"Callie."

My gaze lifted to hers and my blood turned to ice. She had the eyes of a corpse, flat and unfeeling.

"Callie, I addressed you."

"Yes, ma'am?"

She put her fork down. "We have something to discuss."

My heart beat wildly and another trickle of sweat ran down my spine. "What?"

"Where were you yesterday?"

I felt suddenly paralyzed, as if my brain and body had ceased to be connected. Did she know? Was she testing me to see if I'd lie? Or was this a drill? A means of ensuring I remembered that they could take away what little freedom I had in the blink of an eye?

Maybe I'd start with where I'd been in the morning. Not a lie, but not the entire truth, either. "I took a walk on the beach."

"Don't lie to me," she snapped.

I shook my head, looking away, gluing my eyes to my plate. "No. I really did. I went to the lake and took a walk."

"Do you mean to tell me that you spent the entire day walking around the lake?"

"Well, no. I mean, no, ma'am."

"I know you left town, Callie Dawn."

I tried not to visibly flinch at the use of my first and middle name. Panic swept through me, twisting my stomach and making my palms sweat. She knew. Oh god, she knew.

"Yes, ma'am," I said, my voice barely above a whisper.

Dad looked up as if only just now taking an interest in the conversation.

"This is your chance to come clean," she said. "All I'm asking for is the truth."

"I didn't go far. Just to Perrinville."

"You know the rules, Callie. You left town without our permission."

My eyes still downcast, I nodded.

"Who were you with?" Dad asked.

The lie slipped off my tongue so fast, it was as if someone else was speaking. "Some other summertimers. High school kids. A group of them were going, so I tagged along."

"This is unacceptable," Mom said. "What makes you think I'll tolerate this level of disobedience? You're not allowed to leave town, especially not with some ragtag group of miscreants."

I nodded like a good girl. The way her voice kept rising should have had me terrified, but all I could feel was relief. She didn't know I'd gone with Gibson. And I realized something: I'd face her at her worst to protect my friend from my parents. I'd never tell them.

"Do you hear me, Callie?" She slammed her hand on the table. "Your father and I will not be disrespected like this."

I desperately wanted to ask how they knew I'd left town, but I knew better than to ask questions when she was like this. "Yes, ma'am."

"This is the problem with kids these days," she said, and I didn't know if she was speaking to me, or my father. "You let them out of your sight and it breeds nothing but rebellion."

She stood and clamped her hand on my arm, her grip unnaturally strong. I didn't resist her pull as she dragged me into the kitchen, dread making me want to vomit.

Dad didn't get up. He never watched her punish me.

"I'm doing this for your own good, Callie." The lack of emotion in my mother's voice was chilling. She stopped at the counter next to the sink and pulled my arm onto the cold marble, my palm facing up. "I can't allow disobedience to fester inside you. It'll ruin you if I let it."

My lower lip trembled, but I swallowed back the tears. She dragged the sleeve of my sweater up to my elbow, baring my forearm. My skin was marred by a few fresh scabs on top of older scars—a crisscross pattern of horizontal slices.

When I was little, it had just been bruises. By the time I was twelve, she'd started drawing blood.

She held my arm down against the cool granite counter-top. "Look at this. Look at what a horrible girl you are."

I didn't want to look. I hated seeing my arms. But I didn't dare disobey.

"Pain is the price you pay." She opened a drawer and took out a box cutter. *The* box cutter. "It's the only way, Callie Dawn. You keep making me do this."

I sucked in a quick breath and held it as she lowered the blade to my arm. The point bit into my skin and I squeezed my eyes shut.

"When will you learn?" She drew the blade across my arm, leaving a hot trail of burning pain. "When will you stop disobeying us?" Another line of fire on my skin, close to the first. "When will you stop making me do this?"

Cracking my eyes open, I tried not to flinch at the blood. It seeped from the wounds she'd inflicted, dark red droplets trailing down to the counter. Dad would come in later and clean everything with bleach. He wouldn't stop her, but he always cleaned up her messes. He knew her punishments kept me silent—kept me from telling people what I knew about him.

My arm was on fire, but she held it in place. If I moved, she'd keep going. Maybe start on my other arm. But if I held very still, kept quiet like a good girl, maybe she'd stop. Maybe tonight I'd only get three.

Another slice, closer to the inside of my elbow. I shuddered, choking back a sob. That one was deep. She hated it when I cried, so I held it in, desperate for this to be over.

"You're a stupid child," she said. "Anyone else would have learned by now. I hate that you force me to do this, Callie. Apologize."

"I'm sorry," I whispered.

"I can't hear you. Apologize for your disobedience."

"I'm sorry I disobeyed. I won't do it again. I'll be good, I promise."

She let go and I fumbled for a paper towel. Dad would burn it later. I held it over my latest wounds and clutched my arm to my chest, my eyes on the floor.

My heart raced. Was she finished? Would she let me go? I risked a look. She stood with the razor still in her hand, staring at me, her eyes cold and dead.

"Give me your other arm."

I didn't move. For the first time in my life, I didn't jump to do what she said. Pain and fear swirled like a tempest and a voice in my head screamed at me to obey. Be a good girl. If I did what she said, maybe it would be over soon.

"Callie Dawn."

Something inside me snapped. I could feel it break, the cracks snaking out like broken glass.

"No."

She stared at me for a beat, shock plain on her face. "Excuse me?"

Never in my life had I refused my mother. But now that I had—now that I'd uttered that one forbidden word—I felt heat rise from deep inside. I was sick of living in fear. Sick of subjecting myself to her pointless torture. Because no matter how hard she'd tried, she'd never broken me. She'd never convinced me she was right.

She was insane.

"I said no." I held my wounded arm tight against my chest. "You're not going to hurt me again."

She shook her head, her dead eyes never leaving mine. "Just this once, I will repeat myself. Give me your other arm."

"No."

Her jaw clenched and one eye twitched. My heart beat furiously, the urge to run almost overwhelming.

Without a word, she surged forward and backhanded me across the face. Pain erupted across my cheek, the shock of it crushing the air from my lungs. I turned, trying to shield myself from her next attack.

"Mom, stop."

A heartbeat later, her next blow came. Something hard cracked across my shoulder. A book, maybe. One of the heavy cookbooks she kept on the counter. I ducked to avoid her, but she hit me again and again, each smack harder than the last. I could feel the bruises already blooming across my back.

"Stop," I screamed.

I risked a glance at her and realized my mistake, but it was too late. She swung the book right at my face and it smashed into my nose with an audible crunch.

The pain was blinding but somehow I didn't crumple to the floor. Staying hunched over so she couldn't get to my face again, I bolted from the kitchen.

Steady footsteps followed me, her pace unhurried. Before I could reach the front door, she grabbed a handful of my hair, yanking me backward.

I screamed, kicking and flailing. Fighting back for the first time in my life. How was she so freakishly strong?

And why was she so silent?

I shrieked, trying to duck away. She let go of my hair and I covered my head. She didn't say a word. Twisting, I hit back, scoring an open-handed slap to her face. She staggered back a step. Rage burned in her eyes, searing away the deadness. Sheer hatred twisted her features.

"How dare you," she snarled.

Her attack was so fast, I barely saw it coming. I tried to turn away, but she lashed out and the box cutter sliced my face. I screamed, clutching my cheek, the pain searing.

"You will be a good girl. I will *make you* be good."

"Imogen." Dad's voice was hard, and my mother stopped, her hand with the box cutter raised. "Enough."

I crumpled to the ground, gasping for breath. What had happened? He never stopped her.

"Callie, go to your room," he said.

I was bleeding and could barely see, but I scrambled to my feet. Anything to get away. I rushed upstairs to my room and shut the door behind me.

I was too afraid to look in the mirror, but I could feel the long, jagged cut running from my cheekbone to my upper lip. My nose throbbed. I couldn't get my fingers anywhere near it without fresh waves of nauseating pain ripping through me.

But in that moment, standing in a bedroom I hated, dripping blood onto the floor, I decided I was leaving.

I wasn't going to wait for my father to come upstairs and tell me why she'd done it. Explain how important it was for a man like him to have an obedient daughter. That she did it for the good of our family, and if only I'd be a good girl, she could finally stop.

No. She was crazy. And I wasn't going to live like this anymore.

I had no idea where this newfound courage had come from. Maybe I was finally going nuts. But it chased away the blinding pain just enough that I quietly opened my bedroom door and peeked out. One of my eyes was swelling shut, so I turned my head to get a better look. I didn't see my parents.

Maybe I could have waited until they were asleep. But my heart swelled with resolve and I knew I had to go now, or I might never feel this brave again.

Tiptoeing as softly as I could—I didn't have shoes on—I crept downstairs. Voices came from Dad's study. It was now or never.

With my heart racing so fast I wondered if it might burst, I silently padded to the back door. It opened without a sound. Risking one last glance behind me—no sign of my parents—I went outside and shut the door.

And then I ran.

My bare feet tore over the cobblestone patio. Then dirt and bark. Grass. I ran harder than I'd ever run in my life, sprinting for the woods near our house.

I didn't slow down until I was surrounded by trees. My arm was bleeding worse than I'd realized and my entire face felt like it was on fire. I slowed so I wouldn't trip; it was too dark to see much. Luckily I knew these woods well. Veering toward the road, I jogged as fast as I dared, only one thought in my mind.

Gibson.

He'd help me. I knew he would. Most people were afraid of my father—and rightly so—but Gibson wasn't scared of anything. He'd find me a place to hide. Help me figure out where to go. Because I wasn't going back.

I couldn't turn them in. They'd kill me if I did. Dad might balk at killing his own daughter, but not enough to stop my mother from doing it. And she'd do anything to protect their perfect image. Protect their power.

Gibson. He'd help me.

Before I reached the road, my feet were cut and scraped, and I could barely see out of my left eye. Gingerly, I touched my nose. Blinding pain almost made me drop to my knees. It hurt to breathe. Hurt to move. But still I kept going.

The trees parted and I stepped out onto the shoulder of the road. I was right on the edge of town; Gibson's place wasn't far. I'd never been there, but I knew where he lived.

I limped along the road, the pain in my face making my eyes water and my stomach churn. It was getting worse by the second. I had to get off the street before my parents started looking for me. Just a little bit farther. One foot in front of the other. I could make it.

The sound of a car behind me sent my heart into over-drive. *Oh god, please don't be them. Please.* It slowed, pulling over to the side behind me.

"No," I whimpered. I wanted to run, but my feet were scraped raw. My knees buckled and I crumpled to the ground.

"Hey there, are you all right?"

I took a shuddering breath. That wasn't my father's voice.

Shaking with shock and pain, I glanced over my shoulder. A man stood just outside his truck, looking at me from around the open driver's side door.

I knew him. Jonah Bodine. Gibson's father.

A second later, he was there, kneeling beside me. "Oh my god. What happened to you? Did you get hit by a car?"

I looked up at him with my one working eye. My sliced

lip made it hard to speak, my voice coming out in a croak. "Gibson."

"What?"

"Need to get to Gibson. Help."

"Did he... he didn't do this to you, did he?"

I shook my head.

"You're Callie Kendall," he breathed. "The judge's daughter."

I nodded.

"Sweetheart, you're bleeding. My god, your arm."

My face had to look a mess, but blood was flowing freely from my arm. Jonah yanked his shirt off and quickly tied it on, gently pressing the fabric to soak up the blood.

"Do you want to go home, or the hospital?"

I shook my head, crying out at the pain it caused. "No."

"Who did this to you?"

I looked down. I couldn't tell. They were too dangerous. They'd kill me.

"All right, you don't have to say. Not now."

"Please." I reached out and grabbed his arm, pleading for all I was worth. "No hospital. No police. Please, take me to Gibson. I need his help."

He stared at me for a long moment, a deep groove between his eyes. I could smell the faint hint of beer on his breath, but he didn't seem drunk. His eyes were crystal clear.

"Are you and Gibson..." He trailed off, but I knew what he meant.

"No. Friends."

Finally, as if coming to a decision, he shook his head. "No. If you go to Gibs, there's no telling what he'll do. Look, I'll help you, okay? But don't get him mixed up in this. You're trying to get away, is that it?"

I nodded. "Can't go back."

"No," he said again. "No, you can't. All right. We'll figure something out. Come on, let's get off the road."

He cast a wary glance around, then stood and gently helped me to my feet. I couldn't stop shaking. He got me into his truck and dug through the glove box for some napkins. I pressed the coarse paper to my face, careful not to touch my nose.

He went around to the driver's side and got in. Muttering about ice and bandages, and something that sounded like *Gibs would kill him*, he started his truck and pulled out onto the street.

36

MAYA

"*M*y dad didn't hurt me, Gibson. He never touched me. He just cleaned up the messes afterward." I still held his arms and tears ran down my face.

"Jesus, Callie," he whispered.

"It was her. I couldn't remember. After I ran away, people always assumed it was my father. I got to Blue Moon with a nose that was smashed to pieces and deep cut on my face. I had bruises on my back and my arm was sliced to ribbons. People thought it must have been him, and I never corrected them. I had to get it all out of my head. It was torturing me. Her face. Her voice. Her dead eyes."

I stopped, a sob choking off my words. Gibson gently drew me into his arms. Held me against his chest and stroked my hair. I was having a breakdown in poor Henrietta's cabin, but I couldn't stop. The dam had finally broken.

"She was always cold, but it started when I was eight." My voice was muffled in his chest. "I overheard things I shouldn't have. Illegal things my dad was doing. She said she had to for my own good. She had to make me obedient so I'd never tell anyone about him."

"Oh my god."

"It got worse when I was older. She started slicing my arms. Drawing blood. She made it look like I was hurting myself. She told her friends I was troubled. Made me see a psychologist. She'd hurt me before each session to remind me not to tell them anything. She'd whisper in my ear that I was a terrible girl and if she had to, she'd cut too deep and let me bleed."

"Fuck, Callie." Gibson's voice was strangled.

"And he never stopped her. He knew what she was doing to me and he didn't stop her. Just went behind her with bleach and kept the cabinet stocked with bandages so he could hide what she did. He justified it, telling me it was necessary."

Gibson held me in his strong arms, stroking my hair. Neither of us said anything. I felt sick and exhausted, like I had poison in my veins. The taint of it clung to me, the terrible memories so hard to face.

But just when I thought I might crumble beneath the weight of the horror threatening to crush me, I breathed in Gibson's scent. Felt his hand slowly rubbing my back. His cheek resting against my head. I sank into him, the raw power of his love like a cleansing shower. It washed away the worst of the poison. Reminded me I wasn't that girl anymore. That it had never been my fault.

His strength fed mine. The power I'd always had inside of me. The courage that had allowed me to live a life after being so brutally abused. I wasn't a victim anymore. And I wasn't going to allow my mother to continue harming me all these years later.

Closing my eyes, I wrapped my arms around Gibson's

waist and faced the truth. Owned it. And decided not to let it break me.

I pulled away, feeling shaky, but whole. "Thank you."

"For what?" He had tears in his eyes.

"For loving me."

He leaned his forehead against mine. "I'll always love you. Honey, are you serious about this? Are you okay?"

"Yes. I couldn't remember. I'd locked it all away. But I'm sure of this, Gibson. I can see it now. It was my mother who hurt me."

The license plate still bothered me. Not that it was from Virginia. Plenty of Virginia drivers must go through this area. One of them losing a license plate—probably in an accident—wasn't unusual. But why would it have that frame? The one my mother had used to project the image of the proud parent with an accomplished child?

"Henrietta, do you remember where you found the things in your collection?"

She nodded an enthusiastic yes.

"All of them?"

She nodded again. It was clear her collection was important to her.

"Can you please tell me where you found this?" I pointed to the license plate, afraid to touch it again.

She held up a finger, gesturing for us to wait. From a cabinet, she produced a rolled-up piece of paper. Gibson helped her spread it out on the floor. It was an old map of Bootleg Springs and the surrounding mountains.

We crowded around it and she touched her finger to the spot marked *Bootleg Springs*.

"Did you find it in town?" Gibson asked.

She shook her head, then traced her finger along one of the roads leading out of town. Tilting her head, she studied the map for a few seconds, as if making sure. Then she stopped her trace and tapped her finger a few times.

"There?" Gibson shifted so he could look more closely. "That's Mountain Road. That's where my…"

Henrietta nodded, grabbing the license plate, then took down a basket. She placed the license plate on the map and covered it with rocks, sticks, and pinecones from the basket.

"It was buried when you found it," he said.

Another nod.

Gibson stared at the license plate like it might burst into flames. "That might be why no one else did. Henrietta, when did you find this? Recently?"

She shook her head and scrunched up her face, her eyes narrowing, as if she was thinking hard. Finally, she held up both hands, splaying her fingers. Then closed them and held up two.

"Twelve. Do you mean twelve years?"

One sharp nod.

I met his eyes, but neither of us spoke. We didn't have to. His mother had died in an accident on Mountain Road twelve years ago. An accident that might not have been an accident.

This wasn't a coincidence. This was proof. My parents—probably my mother—had killed Connie Bodine.

37

GIBSON

*C*allie's revelation left me reeling.

We packed up the license plate and brought it back to my place. She changed out of her jeans and curled up on the couch with Cash.

"You should take it to the sheriff," she said, running her hand over Cash's soft fur.

"How are you so calm?" I asked. She'd just dredged up those godawful memories, but I was the one pacing around the room.

"I feel clear," she said. "It was like cleaning poison from a wound. It hurt, but now that it's over, I think I can finally finish healing."

I knelt in front of her and touched her face. "You're amazing. Do you know that?"

Her smile soothed some of the rage boiling inside me. "Thanks. So are you."

I grumbled something incoherent as I stood. "All right,

I'll go see the sheriff. You sure you're okay? Do you want me to call Shelby or Leah Mae or Scarlett or something?"

"I have Cash to keep me company. I'll be fine. I think I need a little time."

Cash's ears twitched and he opened his eye.

"Good boy. Take care of our girl."

I was glad Callie was handling things so well. I was proud of her for being strong enough to face her past.

Me, on the other hand—I was fucking done with the whole thing.

I was sick of waiting. Sick of being told we didn't have enough evidence to put these monsters away. There wasn't long until the judge's confirmation hearing. I wasn't going to sit around and hope there was enough paint on the license plate to get a match. Or that someone else would find a way to prove Lee Williams worked for the judge. The fucker was wandering around my town, making my girl afraid to go out.

It was getting on toward dinner, but I found Sheriff Tucker still at the station. Bex brought me back to his office.

"Gibson," he said, looking up from a stack of paperwork on his desk. "What can I do for you?"

He raised an eyebrow when I lowered myself into the chair on the other side of his desk. I pulled the license plate out of my bag. He moved his papers aside so I could set it in front of him.

"What's this?"

"I think that when you run that plate, you'll find it belonged to Mrs. Kendall. Twelve years ago."

His eyes widened slightly, and he smoothed his mustache a few times while he studied the plate.

"All right, Gibson. I'm listening."

I told him everything, and the more I talked, the more

shaken up he looked. His jaw hitched and I could see the fury in his eyes—anger that matched mine. It burned like a bed of coals in my gut.

When I finished, he was quiet for a few minutes. He nodded his head silently a few times, like he was digesting everything.

"Damn," he said, finally. The sheriff had always been a man of few words, and he didn't need to say anything more. I understood. Felt the same way.

"Yep."

He shifted the license plate and clicked his mouse a few times. Typed something on his keyboard.

"You're right, Gibs. This plate was from a blue Audi A6, registered to an Imogen Kendall."

"Did you say blue?"

He met my eyes. "I did."

"Cass found blue scratches on Mom's car."

"She did."

I felt like I was about to pop out of the chair like a jack-in-the-box, but Sheriff Tucker put up a hand.

"Easy, Gibs. We'll have to see if forensics can match the paint. How's Callie handling it? Is she okay?"

"Yeah, she's all right. Said she feels better now that she can remember. Like cleaning poison out of a wound." I shook my leg, unable to keep still. "So what do we do now? More tests? More waiting?"

He tipped his fingers together. "Well, I've got an entire town full of amateur surveillance detectives keeping tabs on Lee Williams' every move. Seems he's settled into a routine. Breakfast at Moonshine. A drive around town, circling past the vacation rentals and the Kendalls' house. Sometimes trips to the Pop In or Shop 'n Buy. He's wandered into Build-

A-Shine a few times. Browsed the other stores. Sits in Yee Haw Yarn and Coffee or down at the lake with a cup of joe. Then a drink or two at the Lookout each night."

"What in the hell is he doing?"

"Watching. Chatting up the locals. My guess is, he's listening for any mention of Callie Kendall." One corner of his mouth lifted in a subtle smile.

"But Bootleg ain't talking about Callie Kendall, are they?"

"No, they're not. Tongues are waggin' about the big new tires Trent McCulty put on his pickup and whether they're making up for a deficiency elsewhere. Whether Old Jefferson Waverly's going to build a new barn on his land. Who got into Bex's garden shed and ran off with her favorite set of pruning shears. Or who's gonna play matchmaker for Mona Lisa McNugget and get a town rooster."

"It still won't keep the truth from that jackass forever."

"No, it won't." He smoothed his mustache again. "Would be real interesting if some motivated individuals could get Lee Williams to sing like a canary, wouldn't it?"

I stopped shaking my leg. "Sure would."

"Interesting that he stops for a drink at the Lookout every night, too."

My eyes narrowed. "Sure is."

"Thanks for bringing this in." He moved the license plate aside and shifted the stack of paperwork.

I stood and went to the door, my mind already racing. Making a plan.

"Gibs."

"Yeah." I glanced at him over my shoulder.

He didn't say anything. Just held my eyes for a few seconds. I nodded. It wouldn't do any of us a bit of good if I pounded the guy's face into the dirt. We needed Lee Williams locked in a cell, not me.

But it was time to handle this Bootleg style.

38

GIBSON

*N*ext day, I went to work making preparations. Then I called my brothers and George, and told them to meet me at the Lookout before the evening rush.

"I can already tell I'm not gonna like this." Bowie kicked out a chair at the table I'd chosen in the back corner of the bar.

Jameson, Jonah, George, and Devlin were already here, barely drinking the beers they'd ordered. I had a basket of fries I had no plans on eating. They were just to give Nicolette some business while I took up one of her tables.

Callie had shared her newly-remembered details with Shelby. I appreciated how well Shelby had talked her through it, gently asking questions and helping her work out what she knew. Cassidy had sat in on it, eventually taking down an official statement. It had been hard to watch Callie go through that—recalling all those horrible things— but I'd been so damn proud of her.

Shelby and Cassidy had done the job of filling in the rest

of my family. So the dark looks on my brothers' faces were no surprise.

"This ain't a get-away-from-it-all trip to the bar, is it?" Jameson asked.

"Nope. Tonight we're on a mission. We're gonna get the truth out of that Lee Williams asshole."

I probably could have handled this thing myself—with Nicolette's help, of course—but I wanted my brothers here as backup.

"Oh boy," Devlin muttered and took a swig of beer.

"How do you plan on doing that?" Bowie asked. "You gonna chat him up at the bar?"

"In a manner of speaking, yeah. We're gonna bring out the big guns."

Jameson and Bowie shared a look.

"You don't mean..." The corner of Bowie's mouth ticked, like he was trying not to smile.

I crossed my arms and nodded. "Moonshine truth serum."

Jameson didn't hide his grin. "Oh, shit. You got Sonny to give you some?"

"Of course he did. I told him what it's for."

"What's moonshine truth serum?" Jonah asked.

"I'm glad you don't know either, because I was just about to ask the same thing," George said.

Bowie let out a short chuckle. "Sonny Fullson has a very special moonshine concoction. The recipe is a closely guarded secret."

"The world couldn't handle it," Jameson said. "It's important to keep it under wraps."

"Are you saying it makes people tell the truth?" Devlin asked, clearly skeptical.

"Is it anything like that stuff you fed me before you shot me into the lake?" George asked, wincing.

"Nah, that was just the peach cobbler brew," I said. "Moonshine truth serum is different. It opens people right up. They'll talk your ear off and tell you every secret they've ever kept."

"Do you remember when Nash took a shot of it by mistake?" Jameson asked.

"Who knew the big guy's favorite hobby was quilting," Bowie said.

"Or that he was the one who broke Mrs. Morganstern's upstairs window with a baseball in junior high," Jameson said.

"How is this supposed to work?" Devlin asked. "Because right now I'm picturing you tying him to a chair and forcing liquor down his throat."

"That's why you wanted me here, isn't it?" George asked, leaning away from the table like he was about to get up and leave. "You want me to hold him down."

I shrugged. "It shouldn't come to that. Nicolette'll serve it to him. Don't y'all remember? It's Moonshine Day, the best unofficial holiday of the year. Shots of moonshine on the house for everyone."

"That could definitely be a real thing," Jonah said.

"It is, but it ain't until October," Jameson replied.

"Do you think he'll notice what we're doing?" George asked. "Get suspicious?"

"The thing about moonshine truth serum, it hits you fast," I said. "Makes you go all woozy for a minute. He'll be busy trying to figure out why his eyes won't focus, and then he'll feel great."

"Nicolette on board?" Jameson asked.

I gave him the side-eye. "Do you even need to ask?"

"Guess not." Jameson raised his beer to Nicolette, who stood behind the bar. She gave him a solemn nod.

"What do you need us to do?" Bowie asked.

"Backup mostly, in case this goes south," I said.

"All right," Bowie said. "Let's do this."

Customers trickled in and we spread out, filling them in on the plan. We didn't want any accidental bar brawls or other interruptions tonight.

Then, all we could do was wait.

I sat with Jameson at the table in back, bouncing my leg, unable to keep still. Bowie, Dev, and Jonah nursed beers at the bar, making sure to leave a few stools open. George stayed farther back. Music played in the background and the mood in here was subdued. Tense.

My edges felt sharp, but I was focused. I knew I couldn't let my temper get the best of me tonight. Flying off the handle and breaking the guy's face wasn't going to get us the answers we needed.

I'd keep my shit together for Callie. I could do it for her.

Finally, Lee Williams wandered in, crooked nose and all. Took a seat at the bar, just like we'd hoped. His clothes were plain—a shirt and brown pants—and I didn't see a bulge at his waistband. Hopefully he wasn't packing heat tonight.

I waited to give Nicolette the signal. Let him order a beer and sit with it for a while. Didn't want to make him suspicious before we'd had a chance to get the moonshine down his throat.

Jameson met my eyes and we nodded to each other. It was time. I caught Nicolette's attention and gave her a nod.

"Hey, y'all." She lined up shot glasses and started pouring. Damn, I hoped she'd keep them straight and give Lee Williams the right one. "You know what today is—Moonshine Day! That means shots of the Lookout's finest, on the house."

Cheers rose up from the patrons and her customers went to the bar to collect their shots.

Nicolette pushed a shot glass at Lee. I held my breath, too far away to hear if he said anything to her. People around him downed their shots and set their glasses on the bar, thanking Nicolette.

Come on, you piece of shit. Drink it.

He lifted the shot glass to Nicolette, then tossed it back in one swallow. And then, badass bartender that she was, she grinned and poured him another. He drank that one, too.

Jameson twitched.

"Wait for it," I said, my voice low, eyes locked on Lee.

Nicolette started cleaning up the shot glasses. Bowie took up a spot at the end of the bar, leaning against it like he didn't have a care in the world. Jonah and Devlin went back to their stools, looking tense.

Lee tilted to the side, almost falling off his stool. Bracing himself on the bar, he struggled to keep his seat. He straightened, but shook his head and started rubbing his eyes.

"Now," I said quietly.

I stood and wandered to the bar, taking the empty stool next to Lee. Jameson hung back, ready to detour anyone who might try to get too close. Jonah and Devlin were on Lee's other side, and Nicolette kept on with what she was doing.

Nothing unusual here.

"Holy shit," Lee muttered, still trying to shake off the initial dizzying rush of the moonshine.

I leaned forward, elbows on the bar, keeping my face forward. "Potent stuff."

"Jesus fuck," he said. "What the hell was that?"

"Bootleg moonshine ain't for the weak," I said.

He glanced at me, blinking hard like he was trying to focus. Between the dim lighting and the quick dose of moonshine, he didn't seem to recognize me. Yet. "Guess so."

"Seems like you're new around here. What do you think of Bootleg?" I needed to get him answering questions so I could be sure it was working.

"Small town shithole, basically."

He might have said that without the truth serum. I couldn't be sure. "Is it, now? I take it you're a city boy?"

"Oh yeah. Born and raised in Baltimore. Wound up in Virginia, but Richmond isn't bad. Always wanted to live in New York City, though."

I suppressed a grin. It was working, all right.

"You know what I hate about small towns?" He turned toward me, resting one arm on the bar, and his voice was nothing but friendly. Part of the magic of Sonny's moonshine was what it did for a person's mood. Made them feel great. And extremely chatty. "There's nothing to do. I'm stuck out here, bored off my ass."

"That's a damn shame," I said. "What are you stuck here for?"

"A job. It's a dead end, if you ask me. But my boss is fucking paranoid."

"Huh. Paranoid about what?"

"Oh man, it's a good story." His speech slurred a little and he jabbed a finger toward me.

"I'm always up for a good story," I said, trying to seem like a friendly listener without looking at him straight on.

"This guy I work for, he's a big shot, right? Dirty fucker, but he keeps his hands squeaky clean. I mean, he's good. Even kept me out of prison all these years. Anyway, some twelve or thirteen years ago, his teenage daughter goes missing. Shady shit, let me tell you. He had me searching for her, but he called me off after a while. Didn't say a word to me about it for, I don't know, ten years? I always figured she was dead."

I resisted the urge to clench my fists and made a noncommittal noise. Nicolette kept acting like she was working.

"Anyway, about a year ago, the kid's case gets reopened. New evidence or some shit. So he sends me out to look for her again. I come up with nothing, and he's pissed. This guy's so twisted he wants his own kid dead."

Stay calm, Gibson. Stay calm. "Shit. He wanted you to take her out?"

"Yep. Wouldn't be my first hit, but I don't like it. She's not a kid anymore, but still. What kind of guy does that?"

"Good question. But why would he want her dead?"

He shrugged, hiccupping. "Don't know. My guess is, she knew something and they don't want her around to tell."

"You were right, it's a damn good story. Did you ever find her?"

"No, and here's the real rub. I made everything a hell of a lot easier for him and he still sends me out to this crappy town. She's officially dead, we have the forensics report to prove it. Fake report, but no one's going to question it. Even if she did turn up, who would believe her? Some chick already burned that bridge when she claimed to be her."

"You're shitting me."

"Don't you follow the news out here?" he asked. "I guess if it doesn't involve someone driving a tractor into a fence or a chicken taking a shit in someone's roses, you people don't pay attention."

God, this fucking guy. "Guess not. What happened?"

He proceeded to tell me all about Abbie Gilbert. How

she'd turned up at a hospital, claiming to be his boss's missing daughter—he still hadn't said anyone's name—and how his boss had gone out to see who she was. Brought her home and told the media his daughter had been found.

"Did he know it wasn't her?" I asked. "I mean, a guy would have to know his own daughter."

"Oh, he knew. I think it was his wife's idea to use her. They figured this would close the case for them. They were getting sick of these damn investigators poking their noses everywhere."

"Smart move," I said. "So what'd they do? Pay her off to keep up the lie?"

"That's exactly what they did." Swaying on his stool, he poked my shoulder. "Paid her a solid chunk of change and set her up out in Philly. I took her out there, myself. Dumb girl thought she'd won the lottery."

"What happened to her?"

"This is good, too," he said, practically laughing. "So someone outs her, right? Gets their hands on a DNA sample —don't ask me how, because I don't know—and makes her come clean. So she loses her fancy apartment and the allowance they were giving her. Guess she wasn't happy because she came back and tried to blackmail them. Said she'd go to the media and tell the truth about their agreement. I'm sure you can guess how that ended."

"Tell me."

He made a slicing motion across his throat.

"Damn," I said. "You have to do it?"

"I hired a guy," he said. "It cost me a little extra, but I don't like killing girls if I don't have to."

I stopped myself from saying that hiring someone to kill a girl wasn't any different than doing it yourself. But we were so close. I just had to hold it together a little longer.

"I don't know, man. This all sounds like a bunch of made up bullshit to me."

"All true," he said, putting a hand on his chest and hiccupping again. "Swear it on my mother's grave. So anyway, my boss keeps getting more and more paranoid, right? I really think he might be going off the deep end. Then he finds out some former social worker's been trying to dig up stuff on his daughter. Guess who got saddled with that problem?"

"You?" Holy shit, he was going to tell me about Shelby's kidnapping.

"Damn straight it was me. But, hey, the boss man pays me good money to take care of shit like this for him."

"What'd you do?"

"It was almost too easy. I found out who she was and did some research. She had some guy stalking her a while back. He was perfect. Legitimately crazy. So I tracked him down and gave him some rather specific information about her whereabouts. It was like throwing a dog a stick. He couldn't help himself."

"Did it work?"

He hiccupped again. "Well enough. She backed off. But then it got worse again. Some local guy got hauled in for questioning about the daughter. So the boss man sends me out here to find out why. The guy's nobody, just some redneck carpenter who had an old picture of her. It was a total dead end, just like the rest of her case. I keep trying to tell him he's in the clear. We have science on our side, for fuck's sake. The dumbass lab tech was easy as shit to buy off. And after thirteen years, or however long it's been, his daughter isn't going to turn up."

"Sure doesn't seem like it," I said. "But what does all this have to do with you being stuck out here, bored off your ass?"

He rolled his eyes and reached for the full beer Nicolette had quietly set in front of him. "He's convinced something is going down in this little backwoods town. Sent me out here to fill him in on all the gossip in case her name starts being mentioned again—you know, more than usual. Like maybe somebody knows something. I shouldn't complain too much, though. The drinks are good, and the women aren't bad, either."

"A man's gotta do something to pass the time."

"Damn straight." He took a swig of beer, sloshing some in his lap. He didn't seem to notice. "I hooked up with a sweet piece of ass last night. Dumb as a box of rocks, but who cares, right?"

I risked a quick glance over my shoulder. Jameson was watching, wide-eyed. We were thinking the same thing.

"No shit? Who was she?"

He barely got the mug back on the bar. "Does it matter? She had two names. Missy something? No, that wasn't it. Misty? That's it. Misty Lynn. Crooked fake tits. Hard as concrete. She wasn't a bad lay, but afterward she wouldn't shut the hell up. Kept whining about her ex-boyfriend."

My back and shoulders knotted with tension. "Huh."

He shook with a sloppy, drunken laugh. "Get this. She said her ex-boyfriend's new girlfriend is my boss's fucking missing daughter, Callie Kendall. Swear to god, this town is obsessed with that girl. As if she'd be back here, dating some redneck, and the whole world wouldn't know. Like I said, my little side job last night wasn't blessed with much upstairs."

"You pass that on to your boss?" I asked, trying hard to

keep the alarm out of my voice. "I mean, obviously it ain't true. Probably best to keep the rumors out of it."

"Nah, I told him. If he got wind that I'd heard something and hadn't let him know? He's so on edge lately, he'd probably put a hit out on me."

It ate up every scrap of willpower I had not to wrap my hands around this fucker's neck and choke him out. I couldn't even think about Misty Lynn. Damn her. A red haze tinged my vision and fire seared through my veins.

Jameson casually sat on the stool on my other side and whispered, "Easy."

Nicolette slid another shot glass across the bar. "Looks like you could use another."

"You know, I'm liking this town more and more," he said, grinning at her. He tossed the shot back and winced.

I waited while his eyes crossed, and he held the bar like he couldn't stay upright. The rush seemed to pass, and he shook his head.

"Goddamn, this shit is strong."

I ground my teeth together, my nostrils flaring. Took a breath before I trusted myself to speak.

"Must be tough working for a guy like that," I said. "He has you do his dirty work and you gotta worry about whether he'll get rid of you someday?"

"I'm not too concerned. I have so much dirt on this guy, I could bury him under a mountain of it. See, I'm not stupid. I have insurance."

"What sort of insurance?"

"Recordings. Log books. I keep track of everything."

After three shots, I wasn't worried about whether he recognized me. He'd talk no matter what. He wouldn't be able to help himself.

Turning on my stool, I looked him straight in the eyes. "Where do you keep all that insurance?"

He regarded me through droopy eyelids, his jaw going slack. "Wait. I know you. You're that guy. The one with the photo of her."

"Yep. But where's the insurance? You keep it locked up somewhere?"

He laughed again, his shoulder shaking with a drunken giggle. "It's all at home. I have a file cabinet with a lock."

"Good place for it." I glanced at Nicolette. "You been getting all this?"

She smiled and pulled my cell phone from beneath the bar. Set it on top. "Every incriminating word."

Lee gaped at the phone, his mouth hanging open. Then he swiveled his head to look at me. "What's goin' on?"

"Just for shits and giggles, what's your boss's name?" I'd gotten enough out of him, but I wanted to see if I could get him to say it.

He closed his mouth, narrowing his eyes at me, like the gears in his drunken brain were slowly turning. "His name? You're recording me, aren't you?"

"Yup. And West Virginia is a one-party state. I can legally record you without your knowledge. But really, who do you work for? You know you want to tell me."

He hiccupped and laughed at the same time. "Judge Henry Kendall. He's the boss man. Did I tell you he's a shady fucker? Knows how to keep his hands clean, though."

"I imagine he does." I grabbed the phone and tapped the screen to stop recording and make sure it saved. Then I held it up. "You're too shitfaced to understand what just happened. But when you wake up in a jail cell in the morning, I want you to remember two things. One, you told us everything we need to know to put that piece of shit judge away for good. And two, if you slept with Misty Lynn Prosser, I suggest you get yourself tested for just about everything under the sun."

Nicolette held up another cell phone. "Used both, so there's a backup."

"Thanks, Nicolette," I said. "I owe you big for this."

"Just doing my part."

I got up and nudged the swaying Lee. "Where's the judge now?"

He burped. "Not sure. He was in Washington. Congressional hearing soon."

"Is he coming out here? When you told him Misty Lynn said Callie Kendall is in Bootleg, did he say he was coming?"

"Don't know. He wasn't happy about it, I can tell you that. Did I tell you he kept me out of prison? Dirty fucker, but he knows how to keep his hands clean. That's my job."

"Fuck," I muttered. "Hey Bow, can y'all get this guy out of here? Take my phone with you and give it to the sheriff."

George came up behind Bowie and cracked his knuckles. They wouldn't have any trouble lifting him into someone's car.

"We got it," Bowie said. "Where you going?"

"I gotta get back. If the Kendalls might be coming..."

"Shit," Jameson said.

"Exactly. Get this fucker in a jail cell."

I left Lee Williams in the capable hands of George and my brothers and took off to find Callie. She was with my sister tonight. Hardly a person alive I trusted more than Scarlett Rose.

I'd gotten everything out of him. Sonny Fullson was some kind of goddamn genius. So I should have been relieved. Breathing easier.

But I wasn't. The Kendalls knew. Lee hadn't believed

Misty Lynn, but the judge and his psycho wife would. They knew their daughter was here, in Bootleg Springs. And I had a very strong feeling they were about to show up, looking for her.

Or looking to get rid of her for good.

39

MAYA

*G*ibson was up to something. I didn't know what, but it was obvious. He'd spent a full ten minutes texting earlier today. That was the equivalent of a half-day of conversation for Gibs. Then he'd left me at his house with Scarlett while he went out.

He'd barely let me out of his sight since the Cock Spurs game. The only place I'd gone in the last week had been Henrietta's cabin. Since then, I'd been hiding out at Gibson's, usually with the doors locked and the windows covered.

Scarlett had turned up with snacks, and we'd gotten comfortable on the couch, Cash happily napping between us. She'd spent the last hour trying to pry sordid rock-star stories out of me. She was a Bootlegger. Gossip-hunting was in her blood.

"I'm bored," she said, crumpling up a food wrapper. "I don't mean I'm bored talkin' to you, I just mean being here makes me bored. I feel like getting out."

For the first time since arriving, I was starting to feel a little stir crazy myself. "I could stand a few hours of different scenery. But I don't think I should go into town."

"I completely agree." She sat up and started typing on her phone.

"What are you thinking?"

"We'll bring the party to us. Outside, not in here. Gibs has plenty of space. We'll get a good bonfire going, turn on some music. It'll be fun. And totally safe."

Gibson wasn't going to like Scarlett throwing a bonfire at his house. But I'd be able to make him feel better about it. If he got mad, I'd just take him inside and take off my clothes. That was a win for both of us.

"Let's do it."

Scarlett put the word out and it didn't take long for people to start showing up. Cars and trucks—everything from Millie Waggle's compact sedan to Rocky Tobias's souped-up pickup—rumbled down the long drive. We picked a clear spot away from the house for a makeshift fire pit. Hauled in some wood and got the blaze going. It wasn't a big fire, like the ones on Scarlett's beach. But it was cozy.

More people arrived, someone turned on music, drinks were passed around. Cash happily darted around people's legs, his tail wagging. Scarlett Bodine could go from zero to full-fledged bonfire party in no time flat.

The sound of the crackling fire, tinny country music coming from a dashboard stereo, and good-natured conversations filled the air. Sparks danced in the darkening sky. I hugged one of Gibson's flannel shirts around me. Fall had arrived in Bootleg. The leaves were turning, and the air had a bite to it.

Scarlett wandered over with two beers and handed me one. "Better?"

"Better. Thanks. I don't feel like I'm in the witness protection program anymore."

"Now, why didn't anyone think of that?"

I glanced at her. "Think of what?"

"There were all sorts of theories about what'd happened to you. Different factions, if you will. But I don't remember anyone coming up with *she's gone into the witness protection program*."

"I guess that would have been close."

"This is all gonna turn out fine. You know that, right?"

The beer bottle dangled from my hand. "I hope so."

"You keep right on hoping, but I'm here to tell you, it will. Gibson ain't gonna stop until he makes sure no one can ever hurt you again. He's a Bodine. We're not quitters."

"You're stubborn is what y'all are."

She laughed. "You ain't wrong. Sometimes it's our best quality."

"Speaking of Bodines, where are the rest of them? And where's Devlin tonight?"

"With Gibs." She took a swig of beer.

"Scarlett," I said, my voice stern. "What are they doing?"

"I have no idea what you're referring to."

"He said he had things to do and left before I could ask questions. What's going on?"

She patted my arm. "Trust me. Everything is gonna be fine."

"Oh god, he's going after Lee Williams, isn't he? Why'd you let him do that? That man has killed people."

"And I'm telling you, there's no need to worry. They have it handled."

"He picked you to babysit me because he knew you wouldn't let me leave, didn't he?"

She paused with her beer halfway to her mouth and grinned. "Maybe."

"What'll you do if I try?"

"I have options," she said with a shrug. "He told me you're not to leave his property under any circumstances. And I intend to keep my word."

I sighed, then took a long pull of beer. Gibson had been right to get his sister to keep me here. Going toe to toe with Scarlett Bodine wasn't something I had any interest in experiencing. I decided I'd trust her and stay—for now. "Tell you what, I'll go easy on you. I won't even try to run."

"I think that's smart." She winked at me and we both smiled.

I stepped closer to the warmth of the fire. Cash seemed to be enjoying it. He rolled onto his back, his stocky legs sticking in the air.

A slow song came on and a few couples paired off to dance. Another car rumbled down the driveway and parked, four people pouring out. I couldn't see who they were from here, but none of them were Gibson. It was hard not to worry about what he was up to. Maybe if his brothers were with him, that meant he'd be all right. Cassidy wasn't here either. Did that mean they were involving the law? That was a comforting thought.

Apart from my concern for what kind of trouble Gibson might be getting himself into, I felt calm. The box in my mind wasn't just empty—it was gone. I'd released all the horrible things inside. And I'd survived.

My parents hadn't broken me when I was a child. And the trauma they'd inflicted wasn't going to break me now. I still felt fear. The idea that they were out there, and quite possibly wanted me dead, was terrifying. I knew I'd never be completely safe until they were both behind bars. But my two halves had become whole.

I wasn't Callie anymore—not the Callie of thirteen years ago, at least. I wasn't Maya, either. I was both. I was a girl who'd been abused. A woman who'd built a new life. The demons of my past no longer festered in my mind. I'd faced the worst of them and come out on the other side.

I'd survived.

"Oh, hell no. What is *she* doing here?" Scarlett said. She widened her stance and crossed her arms. "I did *not* invite skankzilla."

Misty Lynn stood on the other side of the fire, holding a lit cigarette between two fingers. Her teased-out hair looked like it had been hair-sprayed into granite, and despite the chill in the air, she wore a bright yellow halter top and denim miniskirt.

"Bless your heart, Misty Lynn," Scarlett said. "Did you have to give up your nicotine patches while you finished your chlamydia meds?"

Misty Lynn made a dramatic show of rolling her eyes. She walked around the fire and stood in front of Scarlett. Took a long drag from her cigarette and blew the smoke in Scarlett's face.

Scarlett waved her hand in front of her. "Get your cancer stick out of here. And I swear to all that's holy, if you leave a single cigarette butt on my brother's property, I'll give you a missing tooth to go with that crooked nose."

"Shut your damn mouth. It's bad enough your daddy's old whore is trying to sink her claws into my dad. I don't need you mouthing off at me too."

I dropped my beer and threw my arms around Scarlett's middle, dragging her out of arm's reach before she gouged Misty Lynn's eyes out.

"Don't you dare talk about Jenny like that, you dirty home-wrecker."

"Go home, Misty Lynn," I said. "You're just out here trying to make trouble and we don't need any more of that."

Misty Lynn stuck a hand on her hip and took another drag from her cigarette. "You ain't special, you know. You probably think you are because the stupid people in this stupid town kept your posters up for so long. But they were wrong about you. You're not the town sweetheart. You're a filthy liar."

Scarlett squirmed against my grasp. I was going to lose her. "Can I get a little help, here?"

Nash jogged over, his thick arms like tree trunks stuffed in flannel. He eyed us warily.

"Come on, Nash, just hold on to her for a minute," I said.

"I'm gonna kill her," Scarlett snarled.

"Crap on a cracker," Nash muttered, getting his arms around her so I could extricate myself. "Scarlett, don't blame me for this."

"Let go of me, Nash. It's about time someone served up some Bootleg Justice on that lying, cheating, piece of bleached-out fake-boobed garbage."

"Go home, Misty Lynn," I said again.

She tried to flick her cigarette toward me, but it wound up flying into the fire.

"You think you can just waltz back into town, with your ugly purple hair, wearing the same dress every other day. Do you even own another one?"

"This from the girl who's been wearing the same tube tops and ratty leggings since seventh grade," Scarlett said.

Misty Lynn wasn't paying attention to Scarlett, and I had a feeling trading insults with Gibson's sister wasn't why she'd come out here.

"Gibson doesn't know what's good for him," she said, her eyes on me.

"You think that's you?" I asked.

"Better than you," she said. "At least I didn't trick a whole town into believing I'm someone else."

Why was I even having this conversation? "What's your point?"

Something in her expression changed, her heavily mascaraed eyes narrowing, the corner of her mouth tilting upward. It was like she could sense she wasn't getting to me and had just thought of a new angle.

"I had him first, you know."

"Had him?" I asked. "What you did was fake your way into his life for a very short time when he was too young and dumb to see you for what you are. And then you cheated on him after his mother died. Instead of holding onto him and loving him through one of the worst times of his life, you kicked him when he was down. I don't know if you're trying to make me jealous, but it won't work. There's nothing to be jealous of."

Misty Lynn crossed her arms, but I turned toward the sound of tires tearing down the long drive. Gibson's truck spat gravel as he slammed on the brakes. He hopped out and ran toward us, rushing straight toward me.

"Gibs, don't be mad," Scarlett said, shrugging out of Nash's grip. "We just wanted something fun to do while we—"

"I ain't mad at you, Scar," he said, his eyes on me. "I need to talk to you. Now."

"Where's everyone else?" Scarlett asked.

"Goin' to see the sheriff. Get everyone out of here. This ain't the time." His gaze swung around and landed on Misty Lynn.

I'd seen Gibson angry. I'd seen him so far gone with rage he'd bloodied his own knuckles. But I'd never seen his face like this.

"Get her off my property," he growled.

"You ain't still mad about the wallet thing, are you?" Misty Lynn asked.

He stared her down, fists clenched, and I had no idea how Misty Lynn wasn't wilting under the intensity of his gaze. I'd never been afraid of Gibson, but if I'd been in her shoes, I would have been.

Maybe she was just too stupid to realize how close he was to snapping.

"Go," I said. "Party's over anyway."

"This is on you," Gibson said, his voice low and dangerous. "If they fucking hurt her, it's on you."

I gently touched his arm. "Gibs, what are you talking about?"

"She squealed on us."

"What?"

"She went back to Lee's motel with him last night. Told him who you are. Used your real name."

Everything seemed to move in slow motion. I was vaguely aware of Scarlett's screeching war cry. Nash's grunt as he grabbed her around the waist. Misty Lynn's crispy hair backlit by the fire.

But all I could feel was rage. A hot surge of anger so deep and so potent, I didn't even try to fight it.

I went supernova.

With two fast steps, I was on her, my arm already cocked, my fist closed. I swung from my hip, twisting at the waist, channeling every bit of strength I had through my arm and into my hand. My punch connected with the back of her jaw, just below the ear. I felt no pain. Just the satisfying collision of my knuckles smashing into her face.

She spun with the force of my blow and it looked like her legs instantly turned to jelly. She crumpled to the ground in a heap.

40

GIBSON

*M*isty Lynn didn't move. Her legs buckled and she dropped to the dirt, out cold.

Caught between shock and pride, I stared at Callie. She'd just knocked out Misty Lynn with one swing. A second ago, I'd been so mad I couldn't see straight. I didn't hit women, but I'd been an inch away from hauling Misty Lynn bodily off my property. And then Callie had laid her out.

"Holy shit," I said in awe.

"Ow." Callie winced, clutching her hand to her chest. "Crap, that hurt."

That jerked me out of my stupor. Ignoring the cheers that rose up around the fire, I led Callie toward the house. Scarlett followed close behind, with Cash right on her heels. We got inside and I shut and locked the door behind us.

"Oh my god, I'm a tiny bit in love with you right now," Scarlett said. She went for the freezer to get ice.

Callie kept her hand cradled against her chest. "I can't believe I just did that. I've never punched anyone before."

"That had to have felt good." Scarlett cracked the tray to loosen the ice cubes. "Did you see the way she collapsed? She was out before she hit the ground."

"Yeah, it did feel good, actually," Callie said with a weak smile. Cash sat right at her feet, looking up at her like he was worried.

I gently took Callie's hand and turned it palm down so I could see the damage. Not too much swelling, which was a good sign. "Can you move it?"

She wiggled her fingers. "It hurts, but I don't think I broke anything."

Scarlett handed me a bag of ice and a paper towel. I took Callie to the couch and held her hand, carefully laying the ice on top. Cash jumped up and put his head in her lap.

"Thank you," she said, absently petting Cash with her good hand.

"Remind me not to get on your bad side."

She laughed. "Yeah, you better not mess with me."

"Damn, I wish someone had been recording that," Scarlett said, flopping down into a chair. "I'd watch it every morning just to put me in a good mood."

"Do you think she's okay?" I glanced toward the curtained front window.

"Someone'll drag her dumb ass home," Scarlett said. "If you loosened a few teeth, that's her problem. She deserves worse."

Callie met my eyes. "Where were you?"

Still holding the ice on her hand, I told her everything. About the moonshine truth serum. All the things Lee had said. We had it all, the truth about everything. It was more than enough to get the FBI involved, I was sure of it.

"That worked as well as expected," Scarlett said. "Well done, Gibs."

"Where's he now?" Callie asked.

"Probably sleeping off the moonshine in a jail cell by now. He's in for one hell of a hangover when he wakes up."

"Yep," Scarlett said. "Dev just texted and said the package has been delivered. They're all on their way here."

"Good."

"So what happens now?" Scarlett asked. "When do all the black unmarked cars roll up to the Kendalls' place, wherever the heck they are, and haul them off to prison?"

"Not soon enough for me," I said. "The sheriff is gonna do everything he can to get the FBI in on this. But I don't know how long it's going to take."

"Which means what?" Scarlett asked. "A day? A week? More?"

Damn, this was frustrating. "I don't know. We can ask Harlan what he thinks tomorrow."

"Too long," Callie said. "Because the Kendalls know I'm here."

"Maybe they'll leave it be until after the hearing," Scarlett said, her voice lilting slightly, as if she was trying to sound hopeful.

Callie stared ahead of her, like she was seeing through the wall. "I think they'll come."

I didn't want to make her feel worse, but I did too. Lee had said the judge was acting paranoid. Going off the deep end. If the judge was a reasonable man who felt in control of his fate, he'd probably leave his lackey to keep an eye on things here and focus on all the politics. Rubbing elbows with senators or whatever he was doing.

But I didn't think the judge was a reasonable man who felt in control of his fate. I'd have put money on him being a man who'd spent the first twelve years of his daughter's disappearance with fear in the back of his head. Fear that she'd turn up and tell the world what he and his wife had done to her. A man who'd spent the last year, since her sweater had been found, constantly trying to put out fires. Trying to keep them from burning down his whole life.

And now the thing he feared most was on the cusp of coming true. Callie was back in Bootleg Springs.

"We need to go to the press," Callie and I said at the same time.

She laughed. "What? I was ready to argue with you."

"You're right," I said. "It's time. If the Kendalls come to Bootleg Springs, it'll be because they're afraid you're going to go public and ruin them. So let's fucking do that."

"Okay. We go to the press."

My family started showing up, one couple after another. There wasn't much more to talk about. They all agreed we were probably right to go public, even Cass—and I assured her we'd run it by Harlan. And Jayme. But at this point, it seemed inevitable.

"Well, we can sit in here and feel glum, or we can go out and enjoy the fire," Scarlett said. "I vote fire."

Everyone agreed, and we poured out of my cabin into the cool night. The fire had burned down, but we got it going again. And for a little while, it kinda felt like everything was fine. Like maybe we were just out here, doing what Bootleggers did. Enjoying an evening with friends and family beneath the stars.

Callie stared into the fire, her forehead creased with worry. I wandered over to her and brushed the hair back from her face.

"What's wrong?"

She looked past me. "I just keep wondering what would

have happened if I hadn't come back here. I brought all this trouble on everyone."

"Honey, what are you talkin' about?"

She took a deep breath. "What if it doesn't work? What if people don't believe me? Or they can't use the evidence they find for some reason? My father's been getting away with everything for so long. He'll have contingency plans or... I don't know, something. Then what? I'll never be safe, and neither will you or your family or this town. What if everything goes wrong and we look back and realize your life would have been so much better if I'd just stayed away? If Callie Kendall had stayed dead."

I took her face in my hands. "Don't you ever say that, you hear? Nothing would have been right if you hadn't come back. If this goes to shit, we'll figure it out."

Her lips turned up in a weak smile.

I kissed her forehead.

"Besides, my life was boring as hell before you showed up."

"Yeah?"

I gave her a little grin. "I think the highlight was when we found out Devlin got Scarlett's name tattooed on his ass and the artist spelled it wrong."

"I regret everything about that, especially telling you assholes," Devlin said.

"How could you regret everything about your cute little butt tattoo?" Scarlett asked. "It says my name on a rose."

"Oh god, there's a flower too?" Bowie asked. "That's more information about Devlin's ass than any of us needed."

Devlin pointed at me with his beer. "Gibson brought it up."

"You're the one who lost the bet," Scarlett said, crossing her arms. "It ain't right for you to complain about it now."

394 CLAIRE KINGSLEY & LUCY SCORE

Callie laughed. "Who'd you lose a bet to?"

Scarlett grinned, looking proud. "Me, of course."

"Can we stop talking about my ass, please?" Devlin asked.

"If you're going to have to live with your future wife's name permanently misspelled on your body, at least it's on your posterior," June said. "Very few people will see it."

"Until we pants you next time we're all at the rusty reef," Jameson said.

"You're all assholes," Devlin said, but he was trying to hide a grin.

He knew my brothers were fucking with him. Mostly.

Best of all, Callie was perking up.

"Is her name really spelled wrong?" she asked.

"Yeah," Devlin said with a roll of his eyes. "The guy spelled it with an i-t-t, not e-t-t."

Scarlett went for his waistband. "Here, look—"

"Don't take my pants off," Devlin said with a hearty laugh, twisting so she couldn't drop his drawers.

"I was just going to show her that it isn't really that bad. At first glance, you can't even tell. And the rose is real pretty."

Callie covered her mouth to stifle a laugh. "That's okay, I don't need to see it. I was just going to tell you, I know a tattoo artist who does incredible work. I bet he could fix it for you. He's up in Blue Moon, but it would be worth the drive."

"Thanks, May—I mean, Callie," Devlin said. "I guess we can call you by your real name now."

She smiled. "Yeah. It feels good. Like I can be me again. Although that reminds me, I have no idea how I'm going to explain this to my boss."

"You should invite him out here to visit," Scarlett said. "Introduce him around town. I bet it'll help clear things up."

"She makes a good point," Cassidy said. "Bootleg Springs is a place that needs to be experienced to be understood."

"That's actually a good idea. I know he'd love to meet you." She poked my chest.

"He won't try to talk me into some record deal, will he?"

Callie ran her hand down my chest. "He might nudge you a little, but he won't push hard. He's a man who knows how to take no for an answer and not let it hurt his ego."

"I hate him less already."

She laughed and I pulled her against me. Wrapped my arms around her. I kissed the top of her head and held her close.

"I don't care what happens, I wouldn't trade this for anything," I said quietly. "Before you, my life wasn't much. Now I have everything. And you can be damn sure I'm gonna fight to keep it."

Slipping her arms around my waist, she rested her head against my chest and took a deep breath. "I love you so much, Gibson Bodine."

"I love you too, Callie. Everything's gonna turn out okay. I promise."

41

MAYA

*T*he mood in the Brunch Club was serious, despite the stack of bacon and egg pastries on the table. I sat near the back with a wall of men blocking my view of most of the cute little restaurant. George, Devlin, Jameson, Jonah, Bowie, Buck, Sonny Fullson, Nash, and Jimmy Bob Prosser all stood in a curved row, partially surrounding my table while we waited for my press conference.

Jenny sat with me, alternately giving my hand, then Gibson's, reassuring squeezes. Like she couldn't help momming on us both. I appreciated it. And the sweetest thing was, I could tell Gibson did, too. He didn't let many people touch him—other than me and our dog—but he let her. He didn't pull away or glare at her, or cross his arms so she couldn't reach his hand. He left it sitting out, like he was inviting her to keep loving on him a little.

It made me love both of them even more.

The Bodine's family lawyer, Jayme, tapped the toe of her stiletto. She stood with arms crossed, her attention on her phone. She was sleek and intimidating in her black pantsuit. Although she wasn't here for me—she was here as legal representation for the Bodines—her mildly threatening presence was oddly comforting. At least she was on our side.

The media turnout wasn't big, but we hadn't expected it to be. The way Bootleg had fooled so many bloggers and journalists last winter made a lot of them reluctant to come back, especially for anything related to the Callie Kendall story.

And Sheriff Tucker had been adamant about not leaking too much information, even in an effort to get more reporters to come. He wasn't sure about going to the press at all. Said he'd rather we wait until the FBI had a chance to review the evidence and arrest the Kendalls.

He didn't know my parents like I did. They were coming. I could feel it, as if the fall winds carried the stench of their evil all the way to West Virginia.

If I told the world who I was—if people knew and word started to spread—at least they wouldn't be able to have me killed and sweep my death under the rug. I needed more than the people of Bootleg Springs to know I was alive.

And I had no doubt they wanted me gone. I'd always known. From the moment I'd walked out the door and run away from home, I'd known what it meant.

I just had to hope the FBI would move in on them soon. And that the case would stick and they'd both go to prison. Hopefully forever.

For now, I told myself we didn't need a lot of journalists here. Once I made my public statement, and we showed my DNA results proving who I was, word would spread. We'd help it along. Leah Mae was already poised to post the story in a hundred different places online. She had bloggers on standby all over the country, waiting for the big news out of Bootleg Springs.

The door opened, but I couldn't see past the wall of Bootleg men.

"Y'all about ready?" It was Scarlett's voice.

Jenny reached over and squeezed Gibson's hand again, then mine. "You're going to do great."

"Thanks, Jenny," I said. "For everything."

The men parted like an automatic door. Gibson shadowed me as I walked outside, his imposing presence palpable behind me. I clutched a stack of index cards with what I wanted to say written on them. I didn't want to let my nerves get the best of me and forget everything in the face of the crowd.

Because a crowd there was. It looked like all of Bootleg Springs had come to Gin Rickey Park, gathering in front of the makeshift podium Mayor Auggie had erected this morning. The wooden platform was slightly more official-looking than the crate in Old Jefferson Waverly's barn. Speakers had been set up and a microphone was ready on a metal stand.

My stomach fluttered, and not in the good way. Those nervous butterflies flapped their wings so hard they whipped up a tornado in my belly. Suddenly that breakfast Shelby had talked me into eating this morning seemed like it might have been a terrible mistake.

Gibson's gentle touch on my back instantly calmed the storm. I realized I'd stopped walking.

"You're gonna be just fine," he said quietly into my ear. His low voice washed over me like cool water on a hot summer day. "I'll be with you the whole time."

"Thank you," I whispered. Took a deep breath. And kept walking.

The crowd hushed as I made my way to the podium.

Mayor Auggie and Sheriff Tucker stepped up behind the microphone. A knot of journalists stood in front. Everyone from the editor of the Bootleg Springs Gazette and a reporter from the local news station—complete with a camera guy—to a handful of journalists and bloggers with nothing but cell phones. Behind them, most of Bootleg Springs.

I waited behind the podium with Gibson. Next to him stood his family. Scarlett and Devlin, Jonah and Shelby, Jameson and Leah Mae, and Bowie with a uniformed Cassidy. A united front. Jayme bookended them on the other side, her fierce gaze scanning the crowd.

George stood with June, his parents, and Nadine Tucker. They were up front, but off to the side, as were Jenny and Jimmy Bob. Seeing their friendly faces was comforting.

Mayor Auggie stepped up to the mic. With a fist to his mouth, he turned and cleared his throat before beginning. "Thank y'all for coming. We have important news to share today. Without any ado, I'll turn things over to Sheriff Harlan Tucker."

My eyes scanned the crowd. Lee Williams was safely locked up in the Bootleg Springs jail. But I hadn't heard a word about the Kendalls. Gibson's family had taken turns driving by their house on Speakeasy Drive this morning, but the driveway had remained empty. No one had seen them pull into town.

Even if they'd arrived, they couldn't have been among the faces of Bootleg Springs. The town would have gone into an uproar. But I couldn't help looking for them, fear knotting my belly.

Maybe I'd never have to see them. Maybe they'd stay in Washington and be arrested there. They'd go to trial and there would be so much evidence against them, my statement would be enough. I wouldn't have to testify. I wouldn't have to look at my mother's cold, dead eyes ever again.

Gibson squeezed my shoulder, jerking me back to reality. Harlan was about to speak.

"It's my pleasure to bring you this announcement," he said, his voice steady. "There has been a significant development in the case of Callie Kendall. Thirteen years ago, she went missing from our town. Recently, it was reported that her body had been identified. I'm here to tell you, that report is false. Callie Kendall is not dead. She's alive and well and she'd be happy to tell you so herself."

Instead of the surprised gasps of the secret town meeting, the residents of Bootleg cheered. Applause rose from the crowd. People whooped and hollered. Shrill whistles rang through the air. It made my breath catch in my throat. I loved these people so much, I didn't know what to do with myself.

Most of the journalists turned, pointing cameras and cell phones behind them, recording the town's reaction.

Gibson took my hand and gave it a tight squeeze, then let go. I stepped up to the mic on the podium.

"Thank you," I said, my voice projecting through the big speakers. "My name is Callie Kendall."

Cheers erupted again and I had to stop until the whooping, hollering, and whistling died down.

"I disappeared from Bootleg Springs thirteen years ago. I'm sure your first question is whether I can prove it. After all, there's a forensics report that says I'm dead. And a woman already tried to claim she was me. I can assure you, I'm the real Callie Kendall."

Sheriff Tucker handed me the DNA report and I held it up.

"This is DNA evidence proving my identity. I've had it

verified and notarized. Copies will be made available. But this is irrefutable proof that I am who I say I am."

I had the attention of the journalists now. None of this was news to the Bootleg crowd, but they still listened with rapt attention. Sheriff Tucker took the DNA report and I adjusted the index cards.

"Thirteen years ago, I ran away from home. My parents, Judge Henry Kendall and Imogen Kendall, were abusing me. I still bear the scars of their abuse." I touched my face, calling attention to the scar on my cheek. "I left in fear for my life. Jonah Bodine Sr. and his wife Connie helped me that night.

"Mr. Bodine has been wrongfully accused of kidnapping, harming, or even murdering me. I would like to set the record straight, once and for all, that Mr. Bodine did none of those things. He and his wife were heroes to me. They saved a terrified, wounded child and risked themselves to get her to safety. For that, I will always be grateful."

Another cheer rose up from the crowd, people shouting Jonah and Connie's names. I glanced over my shoulder at Gibson and his family. Emotion shone on all their faces. Gibson met my eyes and nodded.

I turned back to the mic. "I was taken somewhere safe where kind people cared for me and helped me heal. I grew into adulthood and struck out on my own, with a new name. And until recently, I thought I'd left everything about my life as Callie behind.

"I was traveling out of the country for my job when my missing-persons case was reopened last year. It wasn't until recently that I became aware of all the new developments. I stayed hidden for all those years to protect myself. But I can't hide any longer. Too much is at stake. There are many parts of this that I can't comment on because they're a part of a larger ongoing investigation. Justice still needs to be served. But I'm here today to share the truth. My name is Callie Kendall, and I'm very much alive. Thank you."

The town cheered again as I stepped away from the mic. Sheriff Tucker took my place, giving me a proud smile.

The journalists swarmed toward the podium, everyone suddenly very interested in this story. Hands shot in the air and many shouted questions.

"I'm afraid we can't answer any more questions due to the sensitive nature of this investigation," Sheriff Tucker said. "But thank y'all for being here."

"Let's go," Jayme said, her voice sharp. She motioned for us to follow.

She'd insisted we have an exit plan, and she'd been right. Journalists were already trying to get past Sheriff Tucker and his deputies. Jimmy Bob and George casually strode forward to help block our escape.

We quick-walked back to the Brunch Club where the private room was waiting for us.

Gibson gathered me in his arms, crushing me against his chest. "Honey, I'm so proud of you."

Closing my eyes, I melted into him. I'd taken the final step and told the world who I was. A potent sense of relief washed over me. I could finally be me again.

"I never could have done that without you," I said quietly.

"I don't know about y'all, but I feel like a wrung-out washrag," Scarlett said, plopping into a chair. "How're you holding up, Callie?"

Gibson's arms loosened enough for me to turn toward her. "I'm okay, actually. I think it went well."

"It was perfect," Cassidy said.

"Any word on the Kendalls?" Gibson asked.

"Not that I know of," Cassidy said. "Dad was up half the night talking to the FBI. They're taking it seriously, that's the good news. But they're not exactly texting him the play-by-play. I don't think we'll hear anything until they make an arrest."

A low growl rumbled in Gibson's throat.

"I think it's working," Leah Mae said, looking up from her phone. "Bits of your statement are already being reported at some of the smaller news sites. It's only a matter of time before the big ones pick up the story."

"You know what we need now?" Scarlett asked. "A platter of bad-for-you food and a couple pitchers of mimosas."

That sounded perfect to me.

AN HOUR AND A HALF LATER, we'd all soothed our rough nerves with a good meal. Jayme declared the situation stable and left. I wondered if the Bodines were going to need a family lawyer anymore. The civil suit the Kendalls had filed would be dropped. Jonah Bodine Sr. was no longer a person of interest in a missing-persons case.

The truth was in the open now.

Jameson, Leah Mae, Jonah, and Shelby went out on a quick walk through town to see what was happening—if anything. They returned to report the crowd at Gin Rickey park had dispersed. Shelby saw the local news crew packing up their van. It looked like most of the reporters and bloggers had left, probably back to their offices or laptops in a race to be among the first to break the news.

They said the town seemed its usual self. A little quieter than summer. But they'd spotted Gert—Cassidy and June's

Gram-Gram—having a heated argument with her frenemy, Myrt, on the corner outside Yee Haw Yarn and Coffee. Wade Zirkel's fancy new four-by-four had broken down in the middle of Lake Drive and he'd been walking laps around it, scratching his head like he had no idea what to do. Mona Lisa McNugget had somehow gotten stuck on the roof of her coop and Bex and Fanny Sue had been busy trying to coax her down.

Just a typical Bootleg Springs afternoon.

Gibson leaned back, his arm slung over the back of my chair. He absently ran his fingers through my hair while we listened to Bowie spin a tall-tale style story about great-grandaddy Jedediah Bodine and his famous bootlegging shenanigans.

With our meal wrapped up and the press conference over, it was time to go home and wait. Gibson seemed reluctant to put more than two inches of space between us, even standing guard outside the ladies' room while I went in. His family wandered out onto the sidewalk, still chatting. He led me outside with an arm around my shoulders.

I couldn't wait to get back to Gibson's house. To the space and solitude. I wanted to get in bed and hunker down with him beneath the covers. Close my eyes and lose myself in him. Shut out the world and pretend it didn't exist for a little while.

Angry voices across the street made me turn. There was a commotion outside Moonshine. At first I wondered if Gram-Gram and Myrt's little spat had spun out of control. But then I saw the beige Lexus with Virginia plates parked down the street.

"It's them," I said. "They're here."

Gibson's arm shot around my waist, like he was about to

pick me up and carry me to his truck. The chatter around me faded, a ripple running through our little group.

And then I saw them.

Judge Kendall stood outside Moonshine, dressed in a crisp button-down shirt. He looked so much older than I remembered. His hair was thinning, and he wore wire-rimmed glasses. When I was young, he'd only worn glasses for reading.

And her. She'd aged as well. The lines around her eyes were deeper. Not smile lines. Imogen Kendall hadn't smiled enough to earn the pleasant-looking marks of a life well lived. Hers angled downward, both from her eyes and the corners of her mouth.

They were both well-dressed. Impossibly tidy without a wrinkle or a hair out of place. And in the moment that our eyes met—when they saw me for the first time in thirteen years—neither of them smiled. Not in that half-second of recognition. Not until the shock appeared to wear off and they seemed to recall they had an audience.

My mother gasped, clutching her chest. My father stepped close and held her shoulders, as if she needed him to keep her upright.

The world seemed to go silent. Conversations among neighbors on the street ceased. The people who'd started to gather around my parents halted, their eyes darting around, as if they weren't sure what to do. Even the air felt still, like Bootleg Springs itself held its breath, waiting to see what would happen.

"Oh my god," my mother said, her dead eyes locked on me. "Callie? Is it true? Is it really my daughter?"

Blinking a few times, I stared at her, momentarily dumb-struck. Nothing about this should have surprised me. Of course they were going to play the part of the heartbroken parents. Maybe they didn't know how close they were to having their lives upended. Or maybe they were arrogant enough to think they'd walk away from this.

"Imogen, it's her," my father said. His voice had considerably less emotion than my mother's. "She's come back to us."

As a unit, they took slow steps toward me. Down off the sidewalk and into the street. Their performance was good, I had to give them that. Bystanders who'd seemed ready to grab them and haul them to the police station—or serve up some Bootleg Justice—watched with wide eyes and open mouths.

I pushed Gibson's arm off me, disentangling myself from his grasp. I gazed at the two people walking slowly closer. Two people who'd done terrible things to me. So terrible, I'd left my whole life behind and started a new one with a new identity to protect myself from them. And I realized something.

They didn't have power over me anymore.

"My daughter," Imogen said, opening her arms. I couldn't think of her as my mother anymore. She'd given up that privilege a long time ago. "The nightmare is finally over."

"No," I said, my voice ringing clear and true. "No, for you, the nightmare is only about to begin."

They stopped in their tracks and a flash of anger crossed Imogen's face. A slight tic in her jaw and a twitch of her eye that would have once had me cowering in fear.

Not anymore.

I stepped off the sidewalk. "You did unspeakable things to me. You tortured your own child, trying to break my spirit so I wouldn't betray your awful secrets. I'm here to tell you something. You failed. You never broke me."

Her dead eyes narrowed, and her mouth pinched in a thin line.

I turned my gaze to the judge. He wasn't my father any more than she was my mother. "And you. I know what you're going to say. When people ask, you'll claim you never touched me. You never laid a finger on your daughter. And it's true. You never get your hands dirty. But your hands, and your soul, are mired in filth. You let her do it. You stood by while she hurt me, and you covered it up. Cleaned up her messes.

"I hope that was horrible for you. I hope it took time from your precious career and you've secretly harbored searing regret for marrying that monster. I hope it cost you a good chunk of your fortune to hide what she's done. Not just to me, but to Connie Bodine, too. What did it cost you to cover that up?"

For the first time in my life, I saw fear in Judge Kendall's eyes.

"You're finished," I said. "You tried to find me because you were afraid I'd come back and cause problems for you. You were right. I'm never going to stop until you get everything you deserve. So drop the act. You don't have to pretend you're happy to see me, or shocked that I'm not dead. You tried to ruin my life and you failed. But I'm sure as hell about to ruin yours."

The color drained from the judge's face. I was vaguely aware of applause on the street, my friends and neighbors cheering for me. But it seemed muffled and far away. I was laser-focused on the people in front of me. I watched with a grim sense of satisfaction as the judge's fear turned into something much more permanent.

Defeat.

He knew he was done. I'd seen that look in someone's

eyes once before—the only artist I'd ever worked with who had been too damaged for me to help. The judge's jaw went slack and his shoulders sagged. He was an intelligent man. He knew the kingdom he'd built was already crumbling and there was nothing he could do to save it.

Imogen, however, continued to stare at me with those cold, dead eyes. No emotion crossed her features. But I didn't think she was capable of feeling anything.

Cassidy stepped past me, and the rest of the street came back into focus. Fanny Sue Tomaschek, deputy sheriff, and Sheriff Tucker were closing in on the Kendalls, one on either side. Whether to keep the rumbling crowd away from them or to take them into custody, I wasn't sure.

"I'm gonna need y'all to clear out," Sheriff Tucker said. He approached them warily, one hand twitching like he was ready to pull his sidearm on them if necessary. Cassidy's body language matched her father's. "Go on home and stay there. Don't think about leaving town. We'll be needing the both of you shortly."

Gibson stepped in between me and the Kendalls. "Did you say everything you needed to?"

I looked up at his face. At those beautiful blue eyes beneath his furrowed brow. And I smiled. "Yes. I did."

"Good." He grabbed my arm and hustled me up the street. "Let's get out of here."

I barely noticed Gibson helping me into his truck. The roar of his engine while he drove us out of town. I was in a daze when he hit the brakes in front of his house and ushered me inside.

Cash greeted us, all barks and licks and excited tail-wagging. I giggled, crouching down to love on the silly one-eyed dog. And then I grabbed Gibson's hand and dragged him to his bedroom. Slid into his bed and pulled him in with me.

He wrapped me in his strong embrace. I felt safe. Whole. And loved. So loved I felt like I could do anything. I'd faced my demons and won. If Gibson asked me to, I was pretty sure I could fly.

42

GIBSON

The sound of my phone ringing woke me with a start. Callie stirred, making a sweet little sleepy noise when I pulled my arm out from under her. I hadn't meant to fall asleep. But my poor girl had been exhausted, and the feel of her slow breathing while I held her had made me drift right off.

I found my phone on the floor and answered, my voice hoarse. "Yeah?"

"You two all right?" Bowie asked.

"Fine, yeah. What's goin' on?"

"I have good news and bad news," he said, and didn't wait for me to pick which one I wanted to hear first. "The good news is, FBI rolled into town and took the judge into custody."

"Thank fuck. What's the bad news?"

"Mrs. Kendall is missing."

I sat bolt upright. "What?"

"Sheriff had two people watching their house so they

wouldn't leave. FBI showed up and the judge surrendered without a fuss. But his wife wasn't there. Not only that, the judge had a big bruise on his forehead. Looks like she knocked him out and got away, but we don't know how she got past the deputies."

"How long has she been missing?"

"Not sure," he said. "Cass just found out and called to tell me. The sheriff escorted them to their house himself. She went inside with the judge and that was the last anyone saw her. But that was hours ago."

Callie lifted herself onto her elbow, the sheet pulled up over her chest. She watched me with concern on her face.

I glanced at the window. The curtain was closed, but no light peeked in around the edges. It was dark.

"Fuck," I said.

"Sheriff's gonna send a deputy out to your place shortly. Just sit tight. And maybe stay inside."

"Yeah, no shit."

"Be careful, Gibs," he said. "I'm serious, man, I don't feel good about this."

"We will."

"I'll call you if I hear anything."

I hung up and tossed my phone on the bed. "Fuck."

"What's wrong?" Callie asked.

Cash woke up from his nap at the end of the bed, his ears twitching.

"The judge was taken in by the FBI, but his wife wasn't there. No one knows where she is."

Callie's face went white and she swallowed hard. "What do we do?"

I paused for a second, thinking it through. We could wait here. It was possible Mrs. Kendall had gone somewhere else.

Skipped town to avoid the authorities. But if she was coming after Callie...

"Did your parents keep a gun in the house?"

"Yes. They did. Said it was for home defense. The summer I was fifteen, Imogen took it out and left it sitting on the dining table for two days to scare me."

That did it. We were getting out of here. "Bowie said to stay here and wait it out. Sheriff's sending someone. But I don't want to sit around while an insane woman who wants you dead is on the loose. Let's toss some stuff in the truck and get out of town. We'll call my family when we're safe and let them know we'll be back when that psycho is behind bars."

"Okay," she said with a definitive nod.

We got up and started packing. Threw some things in a couple of bags, for us and for Cash. My mind was busy concocting a plan. Where we'd go. How we'd get out of town without being seen. I wished I had my Charger back from the shop. It guzzled gas like a beast, but it was fucking fast and cornered better than my truck.

Callie's rental car was an option. Although we'd long since returned her motel key from the little place she'd rented in Hayridge, she'd wanted to keep the car for a while so she had transportation, and she'd insisted the expense wasn't a problem. But I knew my truck like the back of my hand. And I could take it off-road if it came to that.

I dropped the bags by the front door. Callie was in the kitchen stuffing a paper grocery bag with dog food and treats. I went to the front window and pushed the curtain over a few inches to peek outside.

It was dark. Quiet. My truck was parked out front, Callie's rental car next to it. I did a double-take. There was another truck out there, parked in front of my workshop.

Lights were off, and in the darkness, I couldn't see if anyone was inside. From here it looked like Rocky Tobias's big pickup.

"Shit."

"What's wrong?" Callie asked. "Do you see something?"

"Either Rocky Tobias decided to pay us a very unexpected visit, or..."

"Or she's here," Callie finished for me.

"Could have stolen his truck." I let the curtain drop. My eyes went to the scar on Callie's face. At the evidence of the depth of Imogen Kendall's crazy.

I'd never seen true evil before today. But when I'd looked at that woman in the street, it had been like staring into the eyes of the devil himself.

Damn it all to hell, I'd been sleeping. A truck had pulled up and I hadn't heard it. I had no idea how long she'd been here.

"Call the sheriff," she said. "Didn't Bowie say a deputy is coming? We'll wait inside and they'll find—"

A crash of breaking glass filled the air and the front curtains billowed backward. Cash barked and I jumped in front of Callie. Grabbing her, I turned my back on the window, shielding her with my body.

Glass tinkled as shards broke free and fell. I glanced over my shoulder, still keeping Callie tucked safely beneath me. The curtains shifted, the breeze coming in through the broken window. I had to act, and I had to act fast.

"When I say go, we run for the truck. Don't stop. Don't look back. Get in and get down on the floor."

She nodded against me. Her body was tense, but she wasn't shivering with fear. I could feel her strength. Her resolve. Her survivor's spirit shining through.

"Call for Cash to come," she said.

"I will. Ready?" I loosened my hold on her. "Go."

I sprang into motion and shouted for Cash to come. Callie was already on her feet. I spun her in front of me and we rushed for the door.

She threw the lock and jerked it open. The truck was right there, my keys already in my hands. I just had to get it open and get her inside.

"Callie Dawn."

That voice sent a chill down my spine, but I didn't falter. Kept myself between Callie and danger while I slid my key in the lock, my hand steady as anything.

"Callie Dawn, you've been a very bad girl," Imogen said, her voice flat. "You always were. I told you what would happen if I didn't punish you, and now look."

I turned the key and the lock popped up. Cash growled and I unlatched the door. Didn't risk looking back.

"You betrayed us. That Bodine woman was going to betray us, too. She thought she was doing me a favor. Isn't that sweet? Bringing the news that you were alive to your poor, sad mother. So she had to die, just like you do now."

I shoved Callie inside and Cash jumped in after her. Slammed the door shut. "Get down."

With my heart beating so hard I thought it might burst, I ran around to the driver's side. Callie had already unlocked the door. I threw it open, jumped in, shoved the key in the ignition, and started the engine.

A shot rang out and I heard the bullet pierce metal. Callie hunkered down on the floor, covering her head. I hunched as low as I could, threw the truck into first, and hit the gas. Goddamn, I'd never been shot at before.

This was fucked up.

The tires skidded through the gravel as I whipped around in a circle. I flinched at another gunshot, glass shattering everywhere. Same fucking window Misty Lynn broke.

"Damn it. Not again."

I pressed on the gas, and we raced down my half-mile dive toward the road. Headlights flashed behind us.

"Stay down."

I whipped around the turn onto the road and gunned it to go faster, my foot lead on the gas pedal. Taking the corners as fast as I dared, I headed down. Up the mountain didn't lead anywhere. We'd wind up stuck on some dead-end dirt road in the middle of nowhere with a fucking psycho killer. Not smart.

So I raced toward town, the wind whipping through the cab, but the nutjob behind us matched my speed. She pulled up on a straight stretch, close enough to nudge my bumper. I held the steering wheel in a tight grip, keeping control. My eyes darted between the dark road and my rear-view mirror. I couldn't outrun her. My truck was sturdy and reliable, but not fast. Rocky's truck had me on speed, and Imogen drove with the limitless aggression of an evil psychopath.

"Brace yourself."

Cash yipped and Callie held on as best she could. Instead of leading this chase through town, I downshifted and yanked on the steering wheel, whipping us around in an almost U-turn onto the highway.

My foot slammed the gas pedal down, the force pushing me back in the seat. For a second, I thought we'd gotten away. She hadn't made the turn.

Then headlights appeared in my rear-view, closing in on us fast. The road curved and started climbing again. Maybe I could outrun her on the corners. Put enough space between us that I could turn off the highway onto a dirt road. Get into the trees, hit the lights, and she'd drive right by.

My jaw clenched with resolve, I kept my hands tight on the wheel and raced down the highway. Took the first corner so fast that the tires squealed.

We gained a little ground on the next turn, but she caught up when the highway straightened. I adjusted my grip on the steering wheel. Another corner was coming up fast. There were two more right after, a series of hairpin turns before the highway sloped down. This was our chance. I just had to keep us on the road.

I took the first corner, tires screaming. She matched my speed, her bumper right on mine. Leaning hard, I kept my foot on the gas and flew around the second turn, coming close to the guardrail.

Jerking forward, I almost hit my face on the steering wheel. She'd hit us from behind. The tires spun, the truck circling wildly. I fought the force of the impact, wrestling the wheel for control, feeling us spin. If we went over the side, we were dead. Callie was on the floor; she wasn't even buckled in.

I strained against the steering wheel, against the force of the truck spinning toward the cliff. Gritted my teeth and held on for dear life. For my life and my girl's.

Especially hers. I wasn't going to lose her now.

The tires caught traction and we jerked hard in the other direction. I heard a sickening crunch of metal and for half a second, I thought we'd hit the guardrail and were about to go over the side. Everything was dark and spinning, head-lights flashing across the trees.

Finally, we stopped. My heart raced, pumping massive amounts of adrenaline through my veins. We hadn't hit the rail. We were in the middle of the road, facing the way we'd come.

Imogen Kendall's stolen truck was nowhere to be seen. The guardrail on the cliff-side of the highway was torn open, the metal bent and twisted.

Callie looked up at me from her spot on the floor, her eyes big and wide. She had her body wrapped around Cash, her arms out to brace herself against the cab.

Everything was eerily silent. I looked around in every direction. No sign of the truck. It was like it had been a ghost, or a figment of our imagination, vanishing without a trace.

"Are you okay?" I grabbed for Callie, helping her into the seat. Touched her face, her arms, looking for damage. "Let me look at you. Are you hurt?"

"I don't think so." She looked out the windows, shifting in the seat to see out the back. "Bruises, maybe. Where is she?"

Cash jumped up in the seat and licked her face. She hugged him against her.

"I don't know. Stay here."

I opened the door, straining to hear... anything. An engine. A voice. Some sign of where she'd gone. I was pretty sure I knew, but I didn't want to take any chances.

Stepping out, I grabbed a flashlight I kept under the seat. Turned it on and swung the beam of light around. The other truck was gone.

There was a gaping hole in the guardrail on the side of the highway. I'd seen it look like this once before. We weren't far from where my mother had crashed—where Imogen Kendall had driven her off the road.

Taking slow steps, my body tense, I approached the guardrail. The land sloped down dramatically, almost a sheer cliff. I swung the narrow beam from my flashlight down.

Rocky's truck lay at the bottom, wrapped sideways around a thick tree. The driver's side was completely caved in, the top smashed like it had rolled several times on the way down.

There was no way anyone could have survived that crash, but I searched the area anyway. A woman like that could have very well made a deal with the devil. I wasn't taking any chances when it came to Callie.

Nothing. No sign that she'd gotten out of the truck. Besides, the cab was crushed.

I turned back and shook my head at Callie.

She got out and looked around warily.

"Truck went over the side," I said.

"Is she..."

"I can't see much, but I don't think anyone could have survived."

Cash jumped out and ran to the edge, barking a few times. Callie joined me on the side of the road and looked down at the wrecked truck.

We didn't say anything for a long moment. I slipped her hand in mine, wanting her to know I was here. Lending her what strength I could. Hoping she knew she didn't have to go through this alone.

She never needed to be alone again.

"It's over," she said, her voice almost breathless. Turning, she met my gaze. "Gibs, it's really over."

I brushed the hair back from her face. "Yeah, honey. It's over."

Tears broke free from the corners of her eyes. I pulled her against me and held her tight. Held her while she cried.

While her body shuddered with relief, releasing some of the fear and anxiety she'd held onto for so long.

"Thank you," she said into my chest. "Thank you for saving me."

"Beautiful girl." I kissed her head. "Thank you for coming home. You're the one who saved me."

43

GIBSON

*F*or the last thirteen years, Bootleg Springs had been famous for two things: Bootlegging and the disappearance of Callie Kendall.

To those of us who lived here, it was known for a lot more. For gossip that traveled as quick as the leaves changed in fall. For nosy, meddling neighbors who were always getting in each other's business. For resisting change, and not letting go of the past. For people who knew your name and your history.

And for people who stood up, and showed up, for each other. No matter what.

After Judge Kendall's arrest, and Imogen Kendall's not-so-tragic end, Bootleg Springs showed up.

They gave us a full day, which was more than I'd expected. We'd gone home that night, after the authorities had arrived on the scene—checked us for injuries and taken our statements. Callie was a bit banged up, but for the most part we were fine. All Callie had wanted was to climb back in bed with me and shut out the world. I'd been more than happy to oblige.

We'd both needed time to recover. To process what had happened. And the next day had dawned bright and beautiful. Or maybe that had just been my girl, smiling at me.

Food showed up on our doorstep, but family and friends had left us alone—mostly. They had assurances that we were fine and seemed to understand that we needed this. Scarlett hadn't been able to help herself. She'd stopped by once, only for a few minutes, saying she just needed to see us for herself.

In the peace and quiet of my acres of sweet solitude—now shared by the love of my life and our one-eyed dog—we'd rested.

Today, we'd reemerged. And Bootleg was ready.

Because what did good West Virginia folk do when one of their own had been through a crisis? They fed them. And in this case, it wasn't just me and Callie who'd been through the shit. Granted, we'd probably seen the worst of it. But all us Bodines had been through the ringer this last year or so. The whole town had.

So Bootleg Springs showed up.

Gin Rickey Park was once again buzzing with people. But this time, it looked more like a hoe-down or a town-wide picnic. Lines of tables held enough food to feed at least twice the population of Bootleg. Someone had made FOUND posters with Callie's old photo on them. Papered them all over the park, along with multicolored balloons.

Kids darted around the grown-ups' legs and a few old-timers engaged in a friendly—if a little wheezy—debate about the best way to trap a possum. Granny Louisa and Estelle had Devlin cornered by the food tables, fussing over him like... well, like grandmas. A group of women, including Leah Mae and Shelby, clustered together beneath a tree. Callie said they were talking about some new book they'd all been reading.

We sat on a red and white checkered blanket my sister had spread out on the grass. Callie and I shared a big plate of baked macaroni and cheese while Cash sat next to Callie's feet, gnawing on a bone.

Sheriff Tucker walked by and tipped his hat to me. I nodded. A good man, the sheriff. He and I'd had our run-ins when I was young, but even then, he'd been fair and helped my family out as much as he could. Now, I owed that man a lot. I was glad he was in charge of protecting our town.

He'd let Darren the lab tech return to his home in New York. Now that the FBI had taken over, Darren's fate was in their hands. It'd be up to them to determine the price he'd pay for taking that bribe. With the way he'd cooperated, I had a feeling they'd go easy on him. Seemed fair enough to me.

The lab he worked for had determined the real identity of the remains. A young woman who'd gone missing about a hundred miles from where her body was found, a year and a half before Callie. It wasn't the news that her family had been hoping for, but at least they had closure.

Scarlett and Cassidy were across from us, picking at the food on their plates, chatting about Scarlett and Devlin's house. Jenny walked by with Jimmy Bob. Caught my eye and gave me a warm smile, which I returned.

Bowie sat down next to Cassidy, leaning in to give her a kiss on the cheek. She proceeded to grab a brownie off his plate.

"Hey." He picked up a second one. "That's why I grabbed two."

"Where's Jameson? And Jonah?" Scarlett asked.

Bowie looked around. "Jonah's over there with his happy-hour class members. They're trying to get him to take his shirt off and do push-ups. And Jameson's up there." He pointed.

My brother was lounging on a thick tree branch, just above Leah Mae and Shelby's circle. He has his hat pulled down over his eyes and one leg dangled.

My family was all here. And none of us were alone anymore. The Bodines—and the Tucker girls, for that matter—were settling down. Who would have thought? Wasn't too long ago, it seemed like none of us knew how.

"This is amazing," Callie said, taking a bite of the baked mac and cheese. She shifted her position and groaned a little. "I also need to join one of Jonah's workout classes or I'm going to gain a million pounds. Everything around here involves food."

"She's not wrong," George said. He had a plate piled high and a half-eaten piece of cornbread in his hand.

Bowie gave George's stack of food the side-eye.

"What?" George asked, his mouth full of cornbread. "It's my cheat day."

June looked up from her book. "There is data that suggests temporary increases in caloric intake can be beneficial."

"See?" George grinned at June. "Thanks, June Bug."

"I love fall," Scarlett said, taking a deep breath. "It always feels like a fresh start. Seems especially appropriate now, doesn't it?"

"It does," Callie said. "The air gets cooler, the leaves change. The world gets ready to go to sleep for a little while. Feels like a time of renewal."

"Mom always liked fall," I said.

Scarlett smiled at me. "She sure did."

"What's going on over there?" Callie asked.

On the outskirts of the park, Misty Lynn's two bleached-out clones stood next to her car, both sobbing hysterically. Misty Lynn hugged one, then the other, making a dramatic show of wiping the mascara that ran down her cheeks. She'd caked thick makeup over the black and blue bruising Callie had given her. The makeup made it look worse, like she'd contracted a disease that made her skin flake off.

"Oh, Misty Lynn's making noise about moving out of Bootleg," Scarlett said. "Said she's gonna follow her mama and become an actress. Jimmy Bob tried to talk sense into her. Even Jenny had a go. I'm sure you can guess how that went."

"Good riddance," I said. "This place'll be a hell of a lot nicer without her around."

"I couldn't agree with you more," Scarlett said. "But I doubt she'll stay gone. She'll realize her mama's a waitress, not an actress, and following that hot mess of a woman ain't gonna get her anywhere."

Cassidy shook her head. "She's just trying to save face after Callie delivered some Bootleg Justice."

"Not nearly enough, if you ask me," Scarlett said.

I grunted my agreement.

"I don't know." Callie tilted her head, watching Misty Lynn attempting—and failing, since no one was paying much attention to her—to make a scene. "Even if she moves away, she'll be back sometimes to see her dad. I think her having to see Gibson live a happy life with another woman is the best Bootleg Justice of all."

Scarlett grinned. "Does this mean you're staying?"

Slipping my arm around her, I pulled her closer. "Damn straight she's staying."

She smiled at me, laughing softly. "Of course I'm staying. I'm home."

Scarlett sniffed loudly and suddenly burst into tears. I flinched backward, wincing. What in the hell was she doing?

"Oh, Scar, what's wrong?" Cassidy asked.

"I'm just so happy for my brother," she said through her sobs. "For all of us. Look at us, Cass. You're married to Bowie and Jameson's wedding isn't far off. I still can't marry Devlin till I'm thirty, but after that, he best be putting a ring on my finger. And my newest older brother is with an awesome girl, and someday they'll be raising babies right here in Bootleg. Only they won't fight all the time and Jonah won't be drunk. And now Gibson is with Callie and I swear to god, Cass, it's just too much."

Cassidy wrapped her arms around Scarlett and patted her back. "There, there, Scarlett Rose." She glanced at Callie. "Scarlett can hold her liquor like none other, but sometimes her feelings get a bit too big for her little body to contain."

Bowie laughed and stood. "I'll go get Devlin in case you need backup."

She beamed at him. "Thanks, my sexy husband."

"You're quite welcome, my beautiful wife."

"Y'all are so cute," Scarlett wailed.

I shook my head at my sister, but I kinda knew how she felt.

Cash was tuckered out from half the town playing with him. He scooted over and put his head in Callie's lap. Little guy looked like he was in dog heaven. Not that I blamed him. If my head had been in Callie's lap, with her fingers running through my hair, I'd have looked that happy too.

I leaned over and whispered a few kisses across her cheek. "Hey, honey."

She turned and met my lips with hers. "Hey."

"Do you mind waiting here for a bit? There's something I need to go do."

"Of course not. But is everything all right?"

I kissed her again. "Yeah. Everything's fine."

"Okay," she said with a smile. "We'll be here waiting for you."

"I know you will."

$\sim$

THE BOOTLEG SPRINGS Cemetery was on the outskirts of town behind a rickety old fence that had once been white. Generations of Bootleg residents had been laid to rest here. Some had grand headstones marking their resting places. Others had simple grave markers made of concrete or stone.

I walked up the path that I hadn't set foot on since we'd buried my dad. Before he'd died, I'd come out here once in a while to lay a flower on my mom's grave. But since Dad's casket had been added to the family plot, I hadn't been back.

Today I didn't have flowers for my mama. I had a more important reason for coming.

Shoving my hands in my pockets, I stopped and stared at the names on the grave markers. Jonah Daniel Bodine. Constance Faith Bodine. Small rectangles of concrete in the grass with names and dates. That was it. That was what was left.

"I know you thought I ruined your life," I said aloud. "Having me changed everything for you, in ways you never wanted. And I gotta say, taking it out on me, on a kid, was a shitty way to handle it. I didn't ask to be born, and I sure as shit didn't ask for y'all as teenage parents."

Taking a deep breath, I paused. "I can't stand here and say you did the best you could, because you didn't. But I'm done being angry about it. Maybe Scarlett's had it right all this time. Maybe it's better to keep the good stuff in here." I tapped my chest. "And let the bad stuff go.

"I ain't perfect, not by a long stretch. And there's probably a fair bit I don't know about y'all that made you who you are. There's a lot of both of you in me, whether I like it or not. But I'm not going to get anywhere if I stay chained to the past.

"Y'all let one turning point in your life, having me, halt everything. Full stop. Y'all never got past it. That resentment you carried colored everything you did from there on out. But hell if I haven't been doing the same damn thing. I let the yelling and the fighting and the anger stop me in my tracks. I've been living there, wallowing in it, my whole life. But no more. I ain't standing here fixin' to forgive you for you. I'm forgiving you for me."

I paused again, rubbing my chin, my chest blooming with emotion. I sniffed it back and cleared my throat.

"Tucked in there, among all the bullshit you put us through, was some good stuff. I can admit that now. That's what I'm going to take with me. As for the rest, I gotta let it go. Me wishing things had been different for all of us won't change the past. All I can do is make a better life for myself and the people around me. For my family. I'm my own man and I get to choose who I am.

"Dad, thank you for saving Callie that night. Mom, thank you for helping him. Thank you for risking yourselves to protect an innocent girl. I wish it hadn't led to more loss and pain. But I know if you were here now, you'd be proud of her.

"You were right to hide it from me. I might have done something stupid and gone to prison for it. So Dad, you did two good things for your son. You protected me from myself. And when you saved Callie, it meant she'd be around to come home and save me. She's the reason I'm standing here —the reason I have it in me to make peace with y'all.

"Not sure what else I have to say, except despite yourself, y'all made a bunch of damn good kids." I chuckled, shaking my head. "Bowie is a good man, all the way down to his bones. He's the guy I'm gonna look to when I wonder about how to be a good husband and father someday. He sets the standard.

"Jameson's got so much hidden under that quiet demeanor. All that artistic shit ain't just creativity. It's goddamn love and it's fucking beautiful to see.

"You never really knew your son, Jonah. He has your name and I'd like to think he's a bit like the man you could have been, had things been different. He cares deep. No matter the circumstances of his birth, I'm glad he's in the world.

"And your baby girl, Scarlett Rose. Shit, she's a force of nature, but hell if that girl doesn't know how to live. She's a big splash of color and light in our lives and her loyalty is unshakable. Mama, you'd be so proud of her. Honestly, I think you'd be proud of all of us. And maybe you are, I don't know.

"I wish you could see what your life together really accomplished. Maybe it wasn't a career in music, traveling the world. But I think it was something a lot bigger and more important than that. You created a family. A dysfunctional, sometimes fucked-up family, but a good one anyway. Full of the best people I know and a hell of a lot of love. If that's the legacy I get to leave when I'm gone, I'll have had a life worth living."

Looking down at the grass, I took another deep breath. I didn't know what I believed about death and the afterlife. So I wasn't sure if me speaking up now made a lick of difference. I doubted they could hear me.

But I wasn't really here for them anyway.

Satisfied, I left. Took my truck back to the park where my girl and my faithful one-eyed dog were waiting for me. Kinda like an old country song, only without the sad ending.

Maybe I'd just have to write one of my own.

44

CALLIE

*T*he air was getting cooler, but the town-wide party was still going strong. Someone started stringing up lights between the trees. Music played from the big speakers we'd used for my press conference and an impromptu square dance competition was in full swing.

Gibson strolled back across the grass. He was still ruggedly handsome, with those sharp cheekbones, square bearded jaw, and broad shoulders. But there was something different. The nearly-perpetual furrow in his brow was smooth and his icy blue eyes were clear—almost sparkling.

Cash woke from his nap, his tail already wagging, and jumped up to greet his daddy.

"Hey, buddy." He crouched down to rough him up a little. Cash rolled onto his back so Gibson could rub his tummy.

"Hey, you," I said, smiling at him.

"Hey, yourself." He leaned over and kissed me.

Cash jumped between us, trying to lick both our mouths at once.

Gibson laughed, sputtering. "Down, boy."

"You look happy," I said.

He sat down next to me, and Cash settled in his lap. "Happiest guy in the world."

I was, too. I'd never—not once in my life—felt so peaceful. So calm and assured. I could be myself, without fear. The people who'd hurt me would never hurt another person again.

I'd run away from this very town, seeking freedom. Returning here, I'd finally found it. Freedom, and so much more.

I'd found community and family. These were my people. Every last one of these moonshine-drinking, hooting, hollering, gossiping, food-delivering people. They'd always included and accepted me. And since I'd come back, they'd taken that to a whole new level. They'd shown me the kind of love you only read about in stories—the ones with nice, happy endings.

The kind of love that could overpower even the worst sort of evil.

And I'd found Gibson Bodine. A man who'd always had a little piece of my heart. Who'd been kind and decent to me. Made me feel safe and happy at a time when I'd desperately needed it. Who'd loved and protected me. Fought for me with everything he had.

I wasn't sure if I deserved all that, but I was going to spend the rest of my life loving him. Hoping it was enough.

An old Volkswagen van pulled up on the street on the edge of the park—where Misty Lynn had been before she'd left. That was odd. It seemed like the whole town was here already. And that looked a lot like...

Grabbing Gibson's arm, I gasped, sitting up straight. "Oh my god. Is that—?"

The door opened and a woman with a crocheted shawl over a long, loose-fitting dress stepped out. Her dark silver-streaked hair was in a bun and she wore a wide tie-dyed headband. She had bangles on both wrists and a crystal on a chain around her neck. She looked around with a pleasant, almost dreamy smile. Henna Holly, the woman who'd become my mom.

Quincy came around the front of the van, still looking like he'd stepped right out of the nineteen-sixties. Long hair, gone gray, with a thin headband around his temples. His shirt had an apple on it and said *Pierce Acres*. Like Henna, he wore a crystal around his neck, along with wide-legged jeans and a pair of brown Birkenstocks.

"Oh my god, they're here," I breathed. "How?"

Gibson spoke quietly. "I called them. Hope you don't mind."

"No," I said, tears already stinging my eyes. "Thank you."

Gibson stood and helped me up. I waved to them and Henna noticed me first. She grabbed Quincy's arm and pointed at me excitedly.

I ran toward them, Cash barking at my heels.

Henna's open arms caught me. "Sunflower. Oh, my sweet girl."

I hugged her, sniffing with happy tears. "I can't believe you're here."

"There's our girl," Quincy said.

Henna let go and I hugged him. "Quincy. You're speaking again. Is your vow of silence over?"

He squeezed me tight. "Sure is. Just in time, too."

Gibson stood behind me, one hand in his pocket, the

other holding Cash's leash. He watched us with a little smile on his lips.

"You must be Gibson," Henna said, her smile wide. She grabbed his face in both hands and planted a loud, smacking kiss right on his lips. She stepped back and he blinked in surprise. "Aren't you just wonderful. Look at his aura, Quincy. So strong and balanced."

"I'm sure it is, my blossom," Quincy said, his eyes crinkling with his smile.

"Sir," Gibson said, holding out a hand toward Quincy.

Quincy seemed amused and shook his hand.

Gibson turned to Henna, hesitating like he was afraid she might kiss him again. "Ma'am."

"No need for all that *sir* and *ma'am* stuff," Henna said. She flicked her hands around, like she was getting rid of the bad energy of formal titles. "Henna and Quincy are just fine. What a beautiful town this is."

Quincy parked himself right on the ground and Cash rushed over to lick his face.

"Gibson called you?" I asked.

Henna beamed at Gibson. "He sure did. Such a good man. He told us the whole story. Sunflower, I'm still not sure what to think. I'm so happy you're all right. As soon as we heard, we knew we had to come down here. After all those terrible events, I thought you could use my help cleansing your energy. But look at you. Your aura's so bright and lively. I've never seen you look so good."

"Thanks," I said. "I've never felt this good."

She looked past me to the still-partying Bootleggers. "This looks fun."

"Yeah, this is... well, that's pretty much everybody."

She clasped her hands at her chest, her wrist bangles dangling. "Oh, good. I can't wait to meet everyone."

Gibson and I took Quincy and Henna into the thick of the party. I introduced them to all the people I knew and loved here. The people from my past and my future. They spread hugs and their own brand of love all around. Henna gave out hugs and kisses like they were candy. She gushed about people's auras and the beautiful divine energy the town emitted into the universe.

Quincy zeroed in on the moonshine, happily drinking and playing with Cash while his wife socialized.

"So that's them," Gibson said. He put his arm around my shoulders while we watched Jimmy Bob Prosser trying to teach Henna to square dance.

"That's them," I said.

More lights twinkled as the sun went down. Bootleggers clapped to the lively music and people still ate and drank. Talked and laughed. Hugged and had good-natured arguments. I even saw Gram-Gram give Myrt a big hug over by the impromptu game of horseshoes someone had set up.

This day, this place. It all felt like a miracle. It reminded me that good people—truly good people—still existed in this world. In fact, most people were. But in this place—in this funny little town tucked in the mountains of West Virginia—amazing things had happened. The good guys had won. Love had overpowered darkness.

And my future stretched, bright and beautiful, before me. A future with family and friends. With holidays spent around a crowded dinner table. Weddings and baby showers and new babies being born. A new generation of little Bootleg kids who'd grow up here, among these wonderful people. With sunshine summers and snowy winters. With a family that loved them so much, they'd never have reason to doubt it.

As if he could feel the love trying to burst right out of

me, Gibson gathered me in his arms. He took a deep breath, smelling my hair.

"I love you, Callie," he said quietly. "I'm real glad you're home."

"Me too, Gibs. I'm so glad I get to stay."

The deep roar of an engine rumbled behind us. Gibson looked toward the street and his mouth dropped open.

"Holy shit."

A black Charger—nineteen sixty-eight, if I wasn't mistaken—pulled up next to the park.

"Is that your baby?" I asked.

"Darlin', it sure is."

The smile on his face made me giddy. He grabbed my hand and led me toward the car.

An older man with a long gray beard stepped out. He had a barrel chest and mechanic's hands, the kind that were perpetually stained with engine oil.

"Gibson," he said and stuck his hand out.

"Otis." Gibson took his hand and they exchanged a hearty shake. "I didn't know you were bringing her back today."

"Figured I'd surprise you. How does she look?"

I waited on the grass while Gibson inspected his car. He ran his hands along the fenders. Checked the doors, the little grin never leaving his face.

"She looks perfect. Better than new." He shook hands with Otis again. "Thanks, man. You need a ride somewhere?"

"No, my wife's a few minutes behind. She'll be along to fetch me. We'll settle up later. I can see you're busy." He nodded toward the park.

"Thanks. Feel free to stay for a drink," Gibson said. "Best moonshine in West Virginia."

Otis grinned beneath his long beard and patted his ample belly. "I just might do that."

I slipped my arms around Gibson's waist and looked up at him. "Happy to have your car back?"

"Yeah. But it's still not as good as having you back. Not even close."

"Still, I can't wait to ride in it."

"We'll drive it home," he said. "Whenever you're ready."

I knew Gibson was anxious to get behind the wheel of his Charger again, so we started the long process of saying our goodbyes. Scarlett had already set up Quincy and Henna with a cabin for the next few days. They were especially excited about the hot springs. I heard Henna say something about skinny dipping—she was firmly of the mind that clothing was always optional—and I made a mental note to let them in on the location of the secret hot springs. And the sign-up sheet. It was for everyone's benefit.

Once we'd hugged everyone goodnight, we walked back to Gibson's car. Cash wanted to sniff it out first, walking around with his tail wagging, sniffing everything. He peed on the tire, but Gibson just laughed. He let him in first so he could smell the inside. Then he swung open the heavy passenger's side door and ushered me in.

The smooth leather seat was comfortable and the interior was beautiful. It looked like it had been fully restored. I buckled my seat belt and Cash sat on the back seat, like he already knew that was his spot.

Gibson slid in slowly, clearly enjoying himself. He shut the door and ran his hands along the steering wheel.

"Damn, it's good to have her back."

With a grin at me, he turned the ignition. The throaty engine roared to life. He closed his eyes for a second, nodding his head. 'That's the stuff."

I rolled down the window and rested my arm on the door. "Okay, sexy. You wanna take your girl home?"

He smiled again—slow and sexy and heart-melting. "Yeah, honey. Let's go home."

EPILOGUE

GIBSON

*T*he Lookout was packed to the gills, everyone rushing in from the snowy cold night. Winter had its grip on the mountains of West Virginia. Puddles collected on the floor from bits of snow falling off people's boots. They hunkered down with whiskey and moonshine, letting the liquor burn off some of the cold.

My family was here, and none of them had a single clue about what was going down tonight. They took up tables—a lot of tables these days—laughing and talking together. Drinking and eating greasy fries. My brothers—all three of them—happy as could be with the women in their lives. My spitfire of a sister with her man. A good man.

Jenny and Jimmy Bob Prosser, who'd tied the knot just a few weeks ago. George and June, who, as far as I was concerned, had beaten out Scarlett and Devlin for unlikeliest couple in town. George and Shelby's parents, who'd settled here in Bootleg. Harlan and Nadine Tucker, enjoying a shared jar of moonshine.

I stood by the stage—I'd made us a slightly bigger one a few months ago—and pulled out my guitar. Glanced over at the tables filled with people I cared about.

This was going to be a real good time.

Scarlett was chatting up Oliver, Callie's boss from Attalon Records. He and his wife, Nat, had come out to Bootleg to visit. Almost gotten themselves stuck on the road up to my place. Californians didn't know how to drive in the snow. We'd set them up with a nice lakefront cabin for their stay and so far, they seemed to be enjoying themselves.

Callie had been glad to see him again. She hadn't been back to L.A. I'd been sitting with her when she'd called Oliver to tell him the full story last fall. About who she really was and what had happened to her.

She hadn't been sure what the future held for her as far as her career in music. But the answer had come from an unexpected place: that little song journal she carried around.

I remembered her writing down song lyrics when we were younger, but when she returned to Bootleg, I hadn't seen her writing. After the judge had been taken into custody—he was charged with a multitude of crimes that ought to keep him in prison for life—and his psychotic wife had left this world, she'd pulled out a journal one day and her pen had practically lit the pages on fire.

She'd started writing songs, all right. She couldn't seem to stop. And then Attalon Records had started buying the rights to the ones she didn't mind selling. Some were too personal—she saved those for herself, or for the two of us to sing together. But the rest, she happily sold to other artists. It allowed her to keep doing what she loved without having to live on the road.

Once in a while, a tangled-up musician would call her,

begging for help. She'd do that thing she did, talking to them in that sweet, calm voice. Getting serious when she had to. She'd remind them they could do it. Help them find the strength or calm or creativity they needed. Then she'd bark at them to get the fuck back to work.

Sexy as hell, my girl.

She delivered a couple of mason jars of moonshine to Quincy and Henna. They stuck out like sore thumbs in our little country bar, with their tie-dyed clothes, beads, and crystals. But they'd become regular visitors to Bootleg. And true to form in this town, Bootleg had folded them right on in.

I liked Callie's Blue Moon family. They'd taken care of her when she'd desperately needed it. Helped her heal and grow into the amazing woman she was now. I could have done without Henna's smacking mouth kisses whenever she saw me. But I was getting used to them. And, to be fair, she did it to my brothers too.

Callie kissed them both on the cheek and came over to join me by the stage.

"Are we about ready?" she asked.

"All set."

Hung and Corbin took their places. I sat on my stool and put my foot up on a rung. Settled my guitar in my lap. Callie took the stool next to me and adjusted the microphone in front of her.

"Hey, y'all," I said. I didn't usually open with a greeting or an introduction. But I'd invited everyone I knew to be here tonight, so it seemed fitting. "Glad to have everyone in out of the cold. Time to get going with a little music. What do y'all say?"

Clapping, whistling, hoots and hollers. Everyone in the Lookout cheered.

"All right, then."

I glanced at my girl and she smiled. Her hair was all blond now. No more funny colors. She'd dyed it recently, saying she thought it was time for a change. I thought she looked beautiful either way.

She nodded that she was ready, and I strummed the first chord.

It was a song she'd written. I'd helped her put music to the words. We'd never performed it for an audience before —not unless you counted Cash. He loved it, but we also fed him and gave him peanut butter smeared on dog toys, so he tended to love just about everything we did.

She sang the first lines, her sultry voice carrying through the room. The crowd was quiet, gazing at her. My fingers strummed the chords and I felt the music deep inside. The crowd felt it too, and their energy pinged off me. It was heartfelt and electric, feeding my soul. Making me smile.

I came in when it was my turn, my deep voice mingling with hers. Our eyes locked as we sang together. A song that told our story. About afternoons spent on the woods, a lonely girl and a bad boy with a guitar. About friends turned lovers, the slow dance of time not enough to keep them apart.

And about happy endings and coming home.

My heart was full as I strummed the final notes. Callie smiled at me so big and so bright, I thought she just might light up the whole place. Distantly, I was aware of the crowd cheering. More clapping and whistling. Hooting and hollering.

I waited, a sudden kick of adrenaline running through my veins. Smiled at my girl and tried not to let my nerves get the better of me.

The noise finally died down and I leaned closer to the

mic. "Thanks, y'all. And thanks for coming out tonight. I think most of y'all know, Callie and I were friends back in the day because of a guitar and a song. She wandered over to a log I was sittin' on while I strummed my guitar and she sat herself down like she knew she belonged there."

I adjusted the guitar in my lap while the crowed oohed and ahhed.

"And it was a song that brought her back home," I said. "So I thought it fitting that I do this here, tonight, after singing our song."

The bar went silent while I stood and lifted the guitar strap from my shoulders. Callie watched me hand my guitar to Hung, her eyes wide and hopeful. My heart beat so hard I was surprised the mic didn't pick up the sound.

But I looked into her beautiful eyes and I knew this was right. I'd known it almost from the moment she'd walked back into my life.

"Callie, my mama made me promise I'd never get married, except for one reason. Only if I was stupid in love."

She laughed softly.

"I'm happy to say, I'm stupid in love with you. And if being stupid in love means I get to spend the rest of my life with you, I reckon it's the smartest thing I'll ever do."

I lowered myself to one knee and she clapped her hands over her mouth. The crowded bar probably reacted, but I wasn't paying attention to them anymore. Just her. Just us.

I pulled the ring out of my pocket. A simple solitaire, just like I already knew she wanted.

"Callie, will you marry me?"

"Yes," she said, her answer muffled by her hand. She nodded, her hair falling into her face. Her eyes welled with tears. "Yes, Gibson."

With the biggest smile of my life, I took her hand, and slid my ring on her pretty finger.

Standing, I scooped her into my arms and held her tight. Rocked back and forth with her while everyone in the Lookout—our neighbors, friends, and family—all cheered for us.

It was funny how life had a way of coming full circle. Callie's disappearance had been like dropping a rock into still water. The ripples had started small, but widened as they went. Her life and her story had touched a lot of people. Even changed some lives.

Mine was sure one of them.

A guitar and a song. That was why we'd become friends. And a guitar and a song had brought her home. Now she was here, in my arms, where she was always going to stay. Here, in my hometown, surrounded by our family and friends. It was a fresh start. A new life. One we were going to live together, and live good.

For us—for all of us—Bootleg Springs was our happily ever after.

NEED MORE Bootleg Springs in your life? How about a special bonus epilogue, plus where are they now updates, and a look behind the scenes into the making of Bootleg Springs!

THE BOOTLEG SPRINGS Bonus Material is available exclusively as a free ebook. Visit www.BookHip.com/FHQNJB.

AFTERWORD

Dear reader,

Here we are, at the end of the journey. The Bodines have found their happily ever afters. Callie Kendall is home.

I've never experienced anything in my career quite like the anticipation, expectations, and reader theories surrounding this book. Don't get me wrong, those things were fun and amazing. But they did make writing this book uniquely challenging.

From the very beginning, Lucy and I knew Callie Kendall would be Gibson's heroine. Early in our brain-storming, we came up with the idea to have a town mystery. And once we decided it would be a missing girl, we knew we'd bring her back in the last book. It's where the series was leading the whole time.

For those of you on #teamcallie from the beginning - yay! I hope you made it through the first *Maya* chapter. I suppose if you're reading this note, you did.

If you weren't so sure about Callie as the heroine before

reading, I hope she won you over. All I can say is, it had to be her. There was no one else for our Gibs.

Grumpy heroes with a hidden heart of gold are one of my favorite types of character to write. When Lucy and I were brainstorming characters, I'm pretty sure I said, "I want him, and he's going to be an asshole."

There's something wonderfully satisfying about the broody guy who doesn't think he's cut out for love. They have such a fantastic character arc as they learn how to open themselves up to love.

Poor Gibson doesn't think love is worth it. He figures being alone is better. At least he won't get hurt.

But he does hurt. A lot. And it takes someone special to help him through those hurts. To help him find it within himself to forgive. And to decide he's going to move on from his past and embrace the love in his life.

And once he does, Gibson loves big.

Callie is a name you hear from the beginning of the series. For some in Bootleg, she's a curiosity. A story. The girl who disappeared.

For the Bodines, she becomes much more once they find her sweater among their parents' belongings. Callie's disappearance is pivotal in each of the first five books. In Whiskey Chaser, the scandal poses a threat to Scarlett and Devlin's brand new relationship. In Sidecar Crush, we find out it was the reason Leah Mae stopped spending her summers in Bootleg Springs, and lost touch with Jameson. And the reopening of the case puts a very unwanted spotlight on quiet Jameson.

The investigation comes between Bowie and Cassidy in a big way in Moonshine Kiss. In Bourbon Bliss, the case captures June's attention. The town's response to the media coverage brings Shelby to Bootleg Springs, which is how

George hears about the town. And in Gin Fling, Jonah and Shelby are swept up in the mystery, as well as caught in the crosshairs of the Kendalls.

But Callie herself is a woman, not a story. Not a mystery. She's a woman who took on a new identity. Who, after a childhood of abuse, refused to live her life as a victim. She grew into a confident, badass record producer who isn't afraid to put broody rock stars in their place.

I knew that in order for her to be a match for Gibson, Callie couldn't be timid or weak. She had to already have found her power and owned it. That doesn't mean she doesn't have her struggles, nor that she's immune to fear. But by the time we meet her, she's been standing on her own two feet for years. And while her life isn't complete (after all, she didn't have Gibson), she's more than capable of handling him.

They're everything the other person needed. She can roll with his moods and stand up for herself when it's necessary. He can protect her without smothering or demanding she change who she is to fit his whims. They not only love each other, they respect and care for each other deeply.

I hope this book was everything you wanted it to be. It's so bittersweet to say goodbye to this town and these characters. Writing this series with Lucy has been one of the biggest highlights of my career. I love this series with all my heart (almost as much as I love Lucy) and I'm both so happy to bring it to its final conclusion, and so sad to see it go.

Thanks for reading,

CK

ACKNOWLEDGMENTS

To all our readers who've come along on this journey. Thank you for your theories and your boundless enthusiasm. You made this FUN.

To Lucy Score, for being an awesome writer and an even awesomer human being. My life is better for having you and Mr. Lucy in it. Thank you again, and again, and again for this experience.

Thank you to my beta readers, Nikki and Jessica, for your time and feedback. And for saving my bacon by reading it on short notice.

To Elayne for your flexibility and for another great editing job.

To Cassy for all the beautiful Bootleg covers.

And thank you to my husband and kids for remembering my name and still loving me after I spent weeks in the writing cave and you barely saw my face.

ALSO BY CLAIRE KINGSLEY

For a full and up-to-date listing of Claire Kingsley books visit
www.clairekingsleybooks.com/books/

For comprehensive reading order, visit www.
clairekingsleybooks.com/reading-order/

∼

The Haven Brothers

Small-town romantic suspense with CK's signature endearing
characters and heartwarming happily ever afters. Can be read as
stand-alones.

Obsession Falls (Josiah and Audrey)

Storms and Secrets (Zachary and Marigold)

The rest of the Haven brothers will be getting their own happily
ever afters!

∼

How the Grump Saved Christmas (Elias and Isabelle)

A stand-alone, small-town Christmas romance.

∼

The Bailey Brothers

Steamy, small-town family series with a dash of suspense. Five
unruly brothers. Epic pranks. A quirky, feuding town. Big HEAs.
Best read in order.

Protecting You (Asher and Grace part 1)

Fighting for Us (Asher and Grace part 2)

Unraveling Him (Evan and Fiona)

Rushing In (Gavin and Skylar)

Chasing Her Fire (Logan and Cara)

Rewriting the Stars (Levi and Annika)

The Miles Family

Sexy, sweet, funny, and heartfelt family series with a dash of suspense. Messy family. Epic bromance. Super romantic. Best read in order.

Broken Miles (Roland and Zoe)

Forbidden Miles (Brynn and Chase)

Reckless Miles (Cooper and Amelia)

Hidden Miles (Leo and Hannah)

Gaining Miles: A Miles Family Novella (Ben and Shannon)

Dirty Martini Running Club

Sexy, fun, feel-good romantic comedies with huge... hearts. Can be read as stand-alones.

Everly Dalton's Dating Disasters (Prequel with Everly, Hazel, and Nora)

Faking Ms. Right (Everly and Shepherd)

Falling for My Enemy (Hazel and Corban)

Marrying Mr. Wrong (Sophie and Cox)

Flirting with Forever (Nora and Dex)

~

Bluewater Billionaires

Hot romantic comedies. Lady billionaire BFFs and the badass heroes who love them. Can be read as stand-alones.

The Mogul and the Muscle (Cameron and Jude)

The Price of Scandal, Wild Open Hearts, and Crazy for Loving You

More Bluewater Billionaire shared-world romantic comedies by Lucy Score, Kathryn Nolan, and Pippa Grant

~

Bootleg Springs

by Claire Kingsley and Lucy Score

Hot and hilarious small-town romcom series with a dash of mystery and suspense. Best read in order.

Whiskey Chaser (Scarlett and Devlin)

Sidecar Crush (Jameson and Leah Mae)

Moonshine Kiss (Bowie and Cassidy)

Bourbon Bliss (June and George)

Gin Fling (Jonah and Shelby)

Highball Rush (Gibson and I can't tell you)

~

Book Boyfriends

Hot romcoms that will make you laugh and make you swoon. Can be read as stand-alones.

Book Boyfriend (Alex and Mia)

Cocky Roommate (Weston and Kendra)

Hot Single Dad (Caleb and Linnea)

Finding Ivy (William and Ivy)

A unique contemporary romance with a hint of mystery. Stand-alone.

His Heart (Sebastian and Brooke)

A poignant and emotionally intense story about grief, loss, and the transcendent power of love. Stand-alone.

The Always Series

Smoking hot, dirty talking bad boys with some angsty intensity. Can be read as stand-alones.

Always Have (Braxton and Kylie)

Always Will (Selene and Ronan)

Always Ever After (Braxton and Kylie)

The Jetty Beach Series

Sexy small-town romance series with swoony heroes, romantic HEAs, and lots of big feels. Can be read as stand-alones.

Behind His Eyes (Ryan and Nicole)

One Crazy Week (Melissa and Jackson)

Messy Perfect Love (Cody and Clover)

ABOUT THE AUTHOR

Claire Kingsley is a #1 Amazon bestselling author of sexy, heartfelt contemporary romance and romantic comedies. She writes sassy, quirky heroines, swoony heroes who love their women hard, panty-melting sexytimes, romantic happily ever afters, and all the big feels.

She can't imagine life without coffee, her Kindle, and the sexy heroes who inhabit her imagination. She lives in the inland Pacific Northwest with her three kids.

www.clairekingsleybooks.com

Made in United States
North Haven, CT
15 April 2024

51337355R00278